What People Are Saying
about Sharlene MacLaren and *Livvie's Song*

Forever on my favorites list, Sharlene MacLaren is one of those rare authors who write "real" historical romance that quickens the pulse and nourishes the soul! Her books are page-turners that keep you up long into the night, and *Livvie's Song* is no exception—sleep deprivation at its very best! You won't want to miss this first book in MacLaren's newest series.

—*Julie Lessman*
Author, the Daughters of Boston series

In *Livvie's Song*, Sharlene MacLaren once again weaves words in her own special way, drawing her readers into life in 1926 Wabash, Indiana. From the first page, you'll walk off the street and straight into Livvie's Kitchen, where you'll feel right at home with the regulars. Sharlene brings Livvie, Will, and all the rest of her well-depicted characters to life in a way that pulls you into the story and holds you captive.

—*Janet Lee Barton*
Author of 16 novels, including her latest,
I'd Sooner Have Love

A historically accurate setting, relatable characters, and a storyline guaranteed to grab your heart can be found in every Sharlene MacLaren novel. For an enjoyable read, treat yourself to one of her stories today.

—*Kim Vogel Sawyer*
Best-selling author, *My Heart Remembers*

Romantically inspiring and uplifting, *Livvie's Song* gave me a new sense of nostalgia for Wabash, the town I call home. Heartwarming to my soul, this book was a true joy to read!

—*Heather L. Allen*
Archivist, Wabash County Historical Museum
Wabash, Indiana

Charming, fresh, and entertaining, *Livvie's Song* will not disappoint. Sharlene MacLaren has penned another winner with a new set of compelling characters in book one of the River of Hope series!

—Miralee Ferrell
Author, *Love Finds You in Tombstone, Arizona,*
and *Finding Jeena*

Livvie's Song

SHARLENE MACLAREN

WHITAKER
HOUSE

LIVVIE'S SONG
River of Hope ~ Book One

Sharlene MacLaren
www.sharlenemaclaren.com

ISBN: 978-1-60374-212-2
Printed in the United States of America
© 2011 by Sharlene MacLaren

Whitaker House
1030 Hunt Valley Circle
New Kensington, PA 15068
www.whitakerhouse.com

Library of Congress Cataloging-in-Publication Data

MacLaren, Sharlene, 1948–
  Livvie's song / by Sharlene MacLaren.
    p. cm. — (River of hope ; bk. 1)
  Summary: "In Wabash, Indiana, circa 1926, widowed restaurateur Livvie Beckman and Christian ex-convict Will Taylor discover a recipe for romance when God works in their hearts" —Provided by publisher.
  ISBN 978-1-60374-212-2 (trade pbk. : alk. paper) 1. Widows—Fiction. 2. Restaurateurs—Fiction. 3. Ex-convicts—Fiction. 4. Wabash (Ind.)—Fiction. I. Title.
  PS3613.A27356L58 2011
  813'.6—dc22
                      2011013298

1 2 3 4 5 6 7 8 9 10   WH   17 16 15 14 13 12 11

Dedication

To the fabulous "Baker Beauties," composed of
Charity, my beloved sister-in-law,
and her three gorgeous daughters,
Jamie, Jill, and Wendy;
my marvelous "adopted" niece, Shelly;
and, of course, my lovely daughters,
Kendra and Krista.
Y'all are so much fun to "play" with.
I love you more than you know!

Acknowledgments

I first rode through the picturesque town of Wabash, Indiana, while on a road trip with my husband. Its tree-lined streets, attractive old homes, and charming, well-preserved historic buildings caught my attention and compelled me to ask my hubby to slow down so I could take it all in. It was the river running through town, though, that truly cinched it. No question, I had to write a series about 1920s Wabash and include colorful, exciting, God-fearing, upstanding characters (and some not-so-upstanding characters). Story ideas started flowing almost immediately, and not long after that initial ride through Wabash, I drew up three somewhat sketchy outlines for the books that would comprise my River of Hope series.

Writing any type of fictional series, particularly one of a historical nature, always requires research, so, sometime later, my husband and I set off on another road trip, this time with Wabash, Indiana, as our destination. There, I met some very lovely, cordial, and generous people who were more than willing to answer my myriad questions and provide useful information regarding Wabash history. While this series is entirely fictional, many of the streets, locations, businesses, stores, and other sites are real. Therefore, I would like to thank the following people for their helpful insights and resources:

Ware Wimberly III, director, Wabash Carnegie Public Library;

7

Ruth Lord, technical services manager, Wabash Carnegie Public Library;

Tracy Stewart, executive director, Wabash County Historical Museum;

Heather Allen, archivist, Wabash County Historical Museum;

Pete Jones, columnist for the *Wabash Daily Plain Dealer* and Wabash historian;

Bill and Tracy Wimberly and Susie Jones, for their historical input;

Tom Kelch of the Reading Room Bookstore; and

Mary Beth Dolmanet, for her tireless assistance in putting me in contact with all the right people.

A great big thank-you to all of you!

Chapter One

May 1926
Wabash, Indiana

"Praise ye the LORD.
Sing unto the LORD a new song."
—Psalm 149:1

Smoke rings rose and circled the heads of Charley Arnold and Roy Scott as they sat in Livvie's Kitchen and partook of steaming coffee, savory roast beef and gravy, and conversation, guffawing every so often at each other's blather. Neither seemed to care much who heard them, since the whole place buzzed with boisterous midday talk. Folks came to her restaurant to fill their stomachs, Livvie Beckman knew, but, for many, getting an earful of gossip was just as satisfying.

Behind the counter in the kitchen, utensils banged against metal, and pots and pans sizzled and boiled with smoke and steam. "Order's up!" hollered the cook, Joe Stewart. On cue, Livvie carried the two hamburger platters to Pete and Susie Jones's table and set them down with a hasty smile. Her knee-length, floral cotton skirt flared as she turned. Mopping her brow and blowing several strawberry blonde strands of damp hair off her face, she hustled to the counter. "You boys put out those disgusting nicotine sticks," she scolded Charley and Roy on the run. "How many times do I have to tell you, I don't allow smoking in this establishment? We don't even have ashtrays."

"Aw, Livvie, how you expect us t' enjoy a proper cup o' coffee without a cigarette?" Charley whined to her back. "'Sides, our saucers work fine for ashtrays."

"Saucers are not ashtrays," stated old Evelyn Garner from the booth behind the two men. She craned her long, skinny neck and trained her owl eyes on them, her lips pinched together in a tight frown. Her husband, Ira Garner, had nothing to say, of course. He rarely did, preferring to let his wife do the talking. Instead, he slurped wordlessly on his tomato soup.

Livvie snatched up the next order slip from the counter and gave it a glance. Then, she lifted two more plates, one of macaroni and cheese, the other of a chicken drumstick and mashed potatoes, and whirled back around, eyeing both men sternly. "I expect you to follow my rules, boys"—she marched past them—"or go next door to Isaac's, where the smoke's as thick as cow dung."

Her saucy remark gave rise to riotous hoots. "You tell 'em, Liv," someone said—Harv Brewster, perhaps? With the racket of babies crying, patrons chattering, the cash register clinking as Cora Mae Livingston tallied somebody's order, the screen door flapping open and shut, and car horns honking outside, Livvie couldn't discern who said what. Oh, how she wished she had the funds to hire a few more waitresses. Some days, business didn't call for it, but, today, it screamed, "Help!"

"You best listen, fellas. When Livvie Beckman speaks, she means every word," said another. She turned at the husky male voice but couldn't identify its source.

"Lady, you oughtta go to preachin' school," said yet another unknown speaker.

"She's somethin', ain't she?" There was no mistaking Coot Hermanson's croaky pipes. Her most loyal customer, also the oldest by far, gave her one of his famous, toothy grins over his coffee cup, which he held with trembling hands. No one really knew Coot's age, and most people suspected he didn't know it, himself, but Livvie thought he looked to be a hundred; ninety-nine, at the very least. But that didn't keep him from showing up at her diner on Market Street every day, huffing from the two-block walk, his faithful black mongrel, Reggie, parked on his haunches under the red and white awning out front, waiting for his usual handout of leftover bacon or the heels of a fresh-baked loaf of bread.

She stooped to tap him with her elbow. "I'll be right back to fill that coffee cup, Coot," she whispered into his good ear.

He lifted an ancient white eyebrow and winked. "You take your time, missy," he wheezed back before she straightened and hurried along.

Of all her regulars, Coot probably knew her best—knew about the tough façade she put on, day in and day out; recognized the rawness of her heart, the ache she still carried from the loss of her beloved Frank. More than a year had come and gone since her husband's passing, but it still hurt to the heavens to think about him. More painful still were her desperate attempts to keep his memory alive for her sons, Alex and Nathan. She'd often rehash how she'd met their father at a church picnic when the two were only teenagers; how he'd enjoyed fishing, hunting, and building things with his bare hands; and how, as he'd gotten older, his love of the culinary arts had planted within him a seed of desire to one day open his own restaurant. She'd tell them how they'd worked so hard to scrimp and save, even while raising a family, and how thrilled Frank had been when that dream had finally come to fruition.

What she didn't tell her boys was how much she struggled to keep her passion for the restaurant alive in their daddy's absence. Oh, she had Joe, of course, but he'd dropped the news last week that he'd picked up a new kitchen job in a Chicago diner—some well-known establishment, he'd said—and he could hardly have turned it down, especially with his daughter and grandchildren begging him to move closer to them. Wabash had been home to Joe Stewart since childhood, but his wife had died some five years ago, and he had little to keep him here. It made sense, Livvie supposed, but it didn't make her life any easier having to find a replacement.

She set down two plates for a couple she'd never seen before today, a middle-aged man and his wife. Strangers were always passing through Wabash on their ways north or south, so it wasn't unusual for her not to know them. "You folks enjoy your lunch," she said with a smile.

"Thank you kindly," the man said, licking his lips and loosening his tie. "This meal looks mighty fine."

Livvie nodded, then made for the coffeepot behind the counter, sensing it was time for a round of refills.

A cloud of smoke still surrounded Charley and Roy's table, though their cigarettes looked to be nearing their ends. She decided not to mention anything further about their annoying behavior unless they lit up again. Those fools had little compunction and even less consideration for the feelings of others. She would have liked to ban them from her restaurant, if it weren't for the revenue they brought in with their almost daily visits. Gracious, it cost an awful lot to keep a restaurant going. She would sell it tomorrow if she had a backup plan, but she didn't. Besides, Frank would bust out of his casket if she hung a "For Sale" sign on the front door. The diner had been his dream, one she'd adopted with gusto because she'd loved him so much, but she hadn't envisioned his leaving her in the thick of it before they'd paid off their mortgage on the three-story building and turned a good profit on the restaurant.

Oh, why had God taken Frank at such a young age? He'd been thirty-one, married for ten years and a restaurant owner for five. Couldn't God have intervened and sent an angel just in time to keep Frank from stepping in front of that horse-drawn wagon hauling furniture? And why, for mercy's sake, did the accident have to occur right in front of the restaurant, drawing a huge crowd and forever etching in her mind's eye the sight of her beloved lying in the middle of the street, blood oozing from his nose and mouth, his eyes open but not seeing? Coot often told her that God had her best interests in mind and that she needed to trust Him with her whole heart, but how could she, when it seemed like few things ever went right for her, and she had to work so hard to stay afloat? Goodness, she barely had a minute to spare for her own children.

Swallowing a sigh, she hefted up the coffeepot, which had finished percolating, and started the round of refills, beginning with Coot Hermanson.

❦

Will Taylor ground out his last cigarette with the sole of his worn shoe as he leaned against the wall of the train car, his head pounding with every jolt, the whir and buzz of metal against metal ripping through his head. He stared down at his empty pack of Luckies and turned up his mouth in the corner, giving a little huff of self-disgust. He didn't really smoke—not anymore. But, when he'd left Welfare Island State Penitentiary in New York City in the wee hours of the morning, one of the guards had handed him a fresh pack, along with the few belongings he had to his name, and he'd smoked the entire thing to help pass the time.

Sharing the mostly empty freight car with him were a dozen or so other men, the majority of whom wore unkempt beards, ragged clothing, and long faces. They also stank to the heavens. He figured he fit right in with the lot of them. Frankly, they all looked like a bunch of bums—and probably were, for that matter. Why else would they have jumped aboard the freight car at various stations while the yardmen had their backs turned instead of purchasing a ticket for a passenger car? Will had intended to pay his fare, and he'd even found himself standing in the queue outside the ticket booth, but when he'd counted his meager stash of cash, he'd fallen out of line. Thankfully, the dense morning fog had made his train-jumping maneuver a cinch. If only it could have had the same effect on his conscience. He'd just been released from prison. Couldn't he get through his first day of freedom without breaking the law?

"Where you headed, mister?" the man closest to him asked.

He could count on one hand the number of minutes anybody on that dark, dingy car had spent engaged in conversation in the hours they'd been riding, and he didn't much feel like talking now. Yet he turned to the fellow, anyway. "Wabash, Indiana," he answered. "Heard it's a nice place."

Actually, he knew nothing about it, save for the state song, "On the Banks of the Wabash, Far Away," which spoke about the river running through it. He'd determined his destination just that morning while poring over a map in the train station, thinking that any other place in the country would beat where he'd spent the last ten years. When he'd overheard someone mention Wabash, he'd found it on the map and, knowing it had its own song, set his mind on going there.

He didn't know a soul in Wabash, which made the place all the more appealing. Best to make a fresh start anonymously. Of course, he had no idea what he'd do to make a living, and it might be that he'd have to move on to the next town if jobs there were scarce. But he'd cross that bridge when he came to it.

His stomach growled, so he opened his knapsack and took out an apple, just one of the few items he'd lifted from the jail kitchen the previous night—with the approval of Harry Wilkinson, the kitchen supervisor. The friends he'd made at Welfare Island were few, as he couldn't trust most folks any farther than he could pitch them, but he did consider Harry a friend, having worked alongside him for the past four years. Harry had told him about the love of God and convinced him not six months ago to give his heart over to Him, saying he'd need a good friend when he left the island and could do no better than the Creator of the universe. Will had agreed, of course, but he sure was green in the faith department, even though he'd taken to reading the Bible Harry had given him—his first and only—almost every night before laying his head on his flat, frayed pillow.

"Wabash, eh?" the man said, breaking into his musings. "I heard of it. Ain't that the first electrically lighted city in the world? I do believe that's their claim to fame."

"That right? I wouldn't know."

"What takes you to Wabash?" he persisted, pulling on his straggly beard.

Will pulled on his own thick beard, mostly brown with some flecks of blond, briefly wondering if he ought to shave it off before he went in search of a job. He'd seen his reflection in a mirror that morning for the first time in a week and had nearly fallen over. In fact, he'd had to do some mental calculations to convince himself that he was actually thirty-four years old, not forty-three. Prison had not been kind to his appearance; he'd slaved under the hot summer sun, digging trenches and hoeing the prison garden, and spent the winters hauling coal and chopping logs. While the work had put him in excellent shape physically, the sun and wind had wreaked havoc on his skin, freckling his nose and arms and wrinkling his forehead. When he hadn't been outside, he'd worked in a scorching-hot kitchen, stirring kettles of soup, peeling potatoes, cutting slabs of beef, filleting fish, and plucking chickens' feathers.

"Wabash seemed as good a place as any," he replied after some thought, determined to keep his answers short and vague.

The fellow peered at him with arched eyebrows. "Where you come from, anyway?"

"Around."

A chuckle floated through the air but quickly drowned in the train's blaring whistle. The man dug into his side pocket and brought out a cigar, stuck it in his mouth, and lit the end, then took a deep drag before blowing out a long stream of smoke. He gave a thoughtful nod and gazed off. "Yeah, I know. Me, too." Across the dark space, the others shifted or slept, legs crossed at the ankles, heads bobbing, not seeming to care about the conversation, if they even heard it.

Will might have inquired after his traveling companion, but his years behind bars had taught him plenty—most important, not to trust his fellow man, and certainly never to divulge his personal history. And posing questions to others would only invite inquiries about himself.

He chomped down his final bite of apple, then tossed the chiseled core onto the floor, figuring a rodent would appreciate it later. Then, he wiped his hands on his pant legs, reached inside his hip pocket, and pulled out his trusty harmonica. Moistening his lips, he brought the instrument to his mouth and started breathing into it, cupping it like he might a beautiful woman's face. Music had always soothed whatever ailed him, and, ever since he'd picked up the skill as a youngster under his grandfather's tutelage, he'd often whiled away the hours playing this humble instrument.

He must have played half a dozen songs—"Oh, Dem Golden Slippers," "Oh My Darling, Clementine," "Over There," "Amazing Grace," "The Sidewalks of New York," and even "On the Banks of the Wabash, Far Away"—before the shrill train whistle sounded again. They must be arriving in Wabash. Another stowaway pulled the car door open a crack to peek out and establish their whereabouts.

Quickly, Will stuffed his mouth organ inside his pocket, then stretched his back, the taut muscles tingling from being stationary for so long. At least his pounding headache had relented, replaced now by a mess of tangled nerves. "Reserved excitement" is how he would have described his emotion.

"Nice playin'," said a man whose face was hidden by the shadow of his low-lying hat. He tipped the brim at Will and gave a slow nod. "You've got a way with that thing. Almost put me in a lonesome-type mood."

"Thanks. For the compliment, I mean. Sorry 'bout your gloomy mood. Didn't mean to bring that on."

"Ain't nothin'. I been jumpin' trains fer as long as I can remember. Gettin' the lonelies every now and again is somethin' to be 'spected, I s'pose."

"That's for sure," mumbled another man, sitting in a corner with his legs stretched out. Will glanced at the sole of his boot and noticed his sock pushing through a gaping hole. Something like a rock turned over in his gut. These guys made a habit of hopping on trains, living off handouts, and roaming the countryside. Vagabonds, they were. He hoped never to see the inside of another freight car, and, by gum, he'd make sure he didn't—with the Lord's help, of course. He had enough money to last a couple of weeks, so long as he holed up someplace dirt cheap and watched what he spent on food. He prayed he'd land a job—any job—in that time. He wouldn't be choosy in the beginning; he couldn't afford to be. If he had to haul garbage, well, so be it. He couldn't expect to do much more than that, not with a criminal record. His hope was that no one would inquire. After all, who but somebody downright desperate would hire an ex-con? Not that he planned to volunteer that bit of information, but he supposed anybody could go digging if they really wanted to know.

He hadn't changed his name, against Harry's advice. "I'm not going to run for the rest of my life, Harry," he'd argued. "Heck, I served my time. It's not that I plan to broadcast it, mind you, but I'm not going to carry the weight of it forever, either. I wasn't the only one involved in that stupid burglary." Though he had shouldered most of the responsibility for committing it. The others had left him to do most of the dirty work, and they'd run off when the law had shown up.

Harry had nodded in silence, then reached up to lay a bony hand on Will's hulking shoulder. Few people ever laid a hand on him and got away with it, so, naturally, he'd started to pull away, but Harry had held firm, forcing Will to loosen up. "You got a good point there, Will. You're a good man, you know that?" He hadn't known that, and he'd appreciated Harry's vote of confidence. "You just got to go out there and be yourself. Folks will believe in you if you take the first step, start seeing your own worth. The Lord sees it, and you need to look at yourself through His eyes. Before you know it, your past will no longer matter—not to you or to anyone else."

The train brakes screeched for all of a minute, with smoke rising up from the tracks and seeping in through the cracks of the dirty floor. Will choked back the burning residue and stood up, then gazed down at his strange companions, feeling a certain kinship he'd never expected. "You men be safe, now," he said, passing his gaze over each one. Several of them acknowledged him with a nod, but most just gave him a vacant stare. The fellow at the back of the car who'd spent the entire day sleeping in the shadows finally lifted his face a notch and looked at him—vigilantly, Will thought. Yet he shook off any uneasiness.

The one who'd first struck up a conversation with him, short-lived as it had been, raised his bearded chin. The two made eye contact. "You watch yourself out there, fella. You got to move fast once your feet hit that dirt. Anybody sees you jumpin' off is sure to report you, and if it's one of the yardmen, well, you may as well kiss your hiney good-bye. They got weapons on them, and they don't look kindly on us spongers."

"Thanks. I'll be on guard." Little did the man know how adept he was at handling himself. The years he'd served in the state pen had taught him survival skills he hoped never to have to use in the outside world.

When the train finally stopped, he reached inside his shirt pocket and peeked at his watch, which was missing its chain. Ten minutes after seven. He pulled the sliding door open just enough to fit his bulky body through, then poked his head out and looked around. Finding the coast clear, thanks to a long freight train parked on neighboring tracks, he gave the fellows one last nod, then leaped from the car and slunk off into the gathering dusk, his sack of meager possessions slung over his shoulder.

First item on his short agenda: look for a restaurant where he could silence his grumbling stomach.

Chapter Two

"If we believe not, yet he abideth faithful."
—2 Timothy 2:13

After shooing away her last customer, Livvie flipped the sign on the front door to "Closed" and wiped her damp brow. Mother Nature certainly had presented them with several unseasonably hot, sunny days this week, and today had been no exception. Lately, it had felt more like midsummer than late May. Even with the sun setting, unusual warmth still hovered in the air.

In the kitchen, Cora Mae and Joe made conversation as they cleaned up, Joe stacking the kettles and fry pans on the long shelf above the stove, Cora tossing clean silverware into the wooden storage box on the stainless steel counter. Livvie didn't have to peek around the corner to know their movements. She'd memorized them over the past year, during which the three of them had established a routine of sorts. Those two would scour the kitchen while she set things to rights in the dining room, a task that included sanitizing the bar, tables, and chairs with a pungent mix of hydrogen peroxide and vinegar water. Obsessed with cleanliness, she had read a good deal about stopping the spread of germs and bacteria. She didn't want her restaurant to be responsible for anyone's untimely death, after all!

21

The same concern prompted her utter dislike of cigarettes. Why, if God wanted folks to fill up their lungs with smoke, he would have fitted them with smokestacks. Thankfully, Frank had shared her sentiments, and they had never permitted smoking in their establishment, even though almost every other restaurant and speakeasy in town did.

Blowing several strands of reddish-blonde hair out of her eyes, she set to pushing chairs into their proper places, sweeping crumbs off the tabletops, replacing the lids of the sugar bowls, picking up stray pieces of litter, and then sanitizing the surfaces and chairs. Next, she walked to the back of the restaurant to fetch her broom and dustpan.

No sooner had she begun sweeping than she heard, "Mom, Nate won't share his puzzle with me!"

She spun around at the voice of her eight-year-old son, Alex, his head poked through the opening in the door to the back room, his freckled nose scrunched in frustration. Her other son, Nathan, eighteen months younger, slightly rounder in the face but otherwise a spitting image of his brother, wriggled into view, peeking his head out right under Alex's. "I was, too. Alex is bein' bossy. 'Sides, it's my puzzle."

"So what? You're still s'posed to share everything. Mom even said."

"You don't share your truck very good!"

"Do, too!"

"Boys." Livvie stood the broom on its bristly end, grasping the handle with both hands, gathered a deep breath, and tamped down a smile. Her sons could be impish, but they were still her pride and joy—the products of unblemished love, and everything she lived for. "You know the rules. Share your toys, play quietly, and wait for Mommy to come and get you so we can go upstairs. I'm just about done here. Then, it's baths for both of you, off to bed, and one more day of school before the weekend."

"I don't want a bath," Nathan whined. "I already had one this week."

She bit back another smile at her younger son's protest. "You played hard at Aunt Margie and Uncle Howie's farm today," she replied, looking from him to Alex. "I can tell by those smudged faces. Sometimes, a body's just got to have more than one bath a week."

On most days, her boys walked the four or five blocks to and from Miami Grade School. In the afternoon, when they arrived home, they had a snack, answered her questions about their day at school, did their homework, completed a few chores, and played until it was time to go downstairs for the suppertime rush in the restaurant. They knew better than to get underfoot in Joe's kitchen or to pester Cora Mae or her when they were busy waiting tables, so they entertained themselves in the back room, which she had stocked with games, books, puzzles, crayons, and drawing paper. Every so often, she or Cora Mae would check on them and, if necessary, referee an argument.

On occasion, though, Livvie's older sister, Margaret, graciously offered to pick up the boys from school and take them to her house for a few hours. Today had been one of those times. Margie, fourteen years her senior and the one most responsible for having raised her, had two grown sons serving in the U.S. Navy —one in Japan, the other in the Philippines—so she jumped at every chance to watch Alex and Nathan. She said it soothed her soul to hear the squeals of children's laughter in her house again. Of course, she also knew the hardships Livvie had suffered since losing Frank, and, since his death, she'd been more than willing to step in and help whenever possible. She and her husband, Howard, ran a successful dairy farm three miles outside of town, and Howard claimed to love letting the boys tag along to the barn with him at milking time. While he and his hired hands worked, Alex and Nathan played with the barn cats, romped with the dog, checked out the newborn foals and calves, or picked wildflowers for their aunt. Occasionally, their uncle assigned them a small task to keep them busy and make them feel important.

"Can I go first?" Alex asked. "Nate always gets the water dirty 'fore I get in."

"Yes, it's your turn to bathe first," Livvie said, smiling as she took up her broom again. "Why don't you boys go put your things away? We'll head upstairs in about ten minutes."

There were two apartments above the restaurant, the larger of which housed their little family. The smaller one had been vacant for a couple of months, the elderly gentleman who'd lived there having moved when he could no longer navigate the stairs. Livvie had posted a "For Rent" sign in the front window several weeks ago. So far, however, there had been no inquiries.

Her sons disappeared, thankfully without further argument, and closed the door behind them. Seconds later, Joe emerged from the kitchen, sweat rolling down his pudgy face and dampening his white hair, which reached his shirt collar. "Heard you talkin' to your boys. You may as well go on upstairs with 'em. Cora Mae 'n' me are almost done here. We'll shut down the lights 'n' stuff. Been a long day, hasn't it? Good for business, though, I'll say that."

Livvie sighed, ignoring his suggestion that she take her leave. "I'm going to miss you, Joe," she said, pausing to rest on the broomstick. She gazed across the room at the older man, whose round, Santa Claus belly called for suspenders to hold up his trousers. "What am I going to do without you?"

Joe had been with them since Frank's death. Before that, he'd been a loyal customer who would step behind the counter with Frank on busy days to lend a hand. It had taken him little time to learn how things operated, and he'd graciously offered to take over after the tragic accident. But it had always been a temporary arrangement, meant to last only until Livvie could find a good replacement or he could sell his house in town, whichever came first. He'd sold his house a few weeks ago, and now, with his job in Chicago imminent, it was just a matter of days before he'd be leaving Wabash. With times being the way they were, Livvie had thought the "Cook Needed" sign on the front door would garner lots of hopefuls, but, to date, no one had expressed interest.

"Don't look so downcast, girlie. Things'll work out—you'll see. Got to trust the Lord, is all."

"Now you sound like Margie. She's always preaching at me."

"I'm not preachin'. I'm tellin' you the truth. I been sayin' lots of prayers for you lately. I know the money don't stretch quite as far as you'd like it to every month, but the Lord has a way of makin' things come out even—or haven't you noticed?"

"I've noticed, but I've also noticed that no one's come around asking to rent that upstairs apartment or to inquire after the job opening."

"That's 'cause everybody knows they can't fill Joe Stewart's shoes," Cora Mae called out, turning away from the stove, dishrag in hand. Her graying hair was falling out of her bun, and age lines were etched deeply into her forehead and around her eyes and mouth. Her otherwise pale skin bore small, brown patches—liver spots, folks called them.

"That's true enough," Livvie said, directing her gaze at the smatters of crumbs on the floor beneath the bar stools and chairs. She would have blamed them on untended children, if it weren't for the fact that she often saw adults drop bits of food and make no effort to retrieve them.

"When do you expect you'll be leaving for good, Joe?"

"Too soon, if you ask me," Cora Mae put in. "Our work's cut out for us if we have to train somebody new plus wait tables." She began to wipe off the counter that Livvie had just sanitized, her eyebrows set in a stubborn line. Livvie loved the dear lady, but why did she always have to be so blunt about everything?

"My new boss said he'd hold my job for up to two more weeks," Joe said, slinging a towel over his shoulder. "If you can hire somebody in the next week or so, I can have 'im trained."

"Or her," Cora Mae corrected him. "Nothin' wrong with hirin' a woman."

Joe angled her an imposing stare. "Why don't *you* take the job, then?"

"Me? I'm not slavin' over a hot grill. 'Sides, I don't have the knack for flippin' pancakes in the air."

Joe chuckled. "I wouldn't call that a requirement."

"Well, it's entertainin'. Who's going to keep me entertained after you leave?" This she said with a hint of orneriness, making Livvie suspect that Cora Mae felt just as she did about Joe's departure—sad, anxious, and a trifle betrayed. How could he leave them in the lurch like this, desperate and alone, while he went off and made a name for himself?

While Joe and Cora Mae kept up their banter, Livvie continued working on the floor, sweeping everything toward the front of the restaurant, where she gathered it all into a sizeable mound. Head down, she threw herself into her task, caught up in thought, mainly thinking about getting her boys to bed so that she could steal a few precious moments to unwind.

A rap on the front door put a sudden halt to her musings, and she looked straight into the eyes of a bearded stranger—piercing, absorbing eyes that studied her intently through the smeared windowpane. He was no small man, either, looking almost too tall to fit through the door, should she decide to open it. She would not.

"Come back in the morning, mister. We're closed." She didn't know why she couldn't rustle up a pleasanter tone, but that was the way of it. When he didn't move but mouthed the word "Please," she bristled. "We open at seven. The sign's right there on the door. Didn't you read it?"

"Yeah, I read it," he said, his tone muffled and hoarse. She tried to go back to her sweeping, but then he rapped again. "I sure could use a plate of food. Don't matter if it's cold." She kept her eyes to the floor. "I'll pay you double for your trouble."

Normally, she had a softer heart toward folks. Tonight, however, exhaustion prevailed.

"He looks like a bum. I never have trusted a man with a matted beard," Cora Mae said from behind the counter, voicing Livvie's very thoughts. "Not only that, he's as big as a grizzly. Whatever you do, don't open that door."

She turned and cast a glance at Joe. "He did say he'd pay us double."

He shrugged. "I got plenty of leftovers in the icebox."

"Don't do it," Cora Mae warned. "I'll have no part in it. I'm tired, and I'm goin' home. Ralph's waitin' on his supper." Ralph was Cora Mae's dog and her only family, really; she'd never married, had no siblings, and had lost her parents some years back. She lived in a little house on West Hill Street, just a few blocks away, and walked everywhere she went, no matter the weather.

"You go on, then," Joe said. "And, Livvie, you take your boys upstairs. I'll feed this drifter and send 'im on his way."

But something kept her feet fastened to the floor. Curiosity, maybe, or a sense of obligation to stick by Joe. Besides, she had a mound of dirt to pick up with the dustpan. "What if he has a gun and plans to rob us?"

"I'm leavin'," Cora Mae announced, scooting around the corner and heading to the back door. "I hope to see you both in the mornin'. Don't let your boys come out of that room."

"'Night, Cora," Joe said, his voice almost coarse. Then, to Livvie, he said, "I'll take that chance. I'm a pretty good judge of folks. He looks harmless enough." He advanced on the door and opened it a crack. The man didn't force his way inside. "You don't have a gun, do you?" Joe asked him. "This is a peaceable town."

The drifter raised both hands as if Joe were arresting him, and Livvie saw that he held some sort of bag—a pillowcase, maybe—in one hand. "Check me over, if you like. The knapsack holds everything I own, except for a harmonica, which is in my pocket. You'll find the rest of me clean."

"Clean? Hardly," Livvie murmured, mostly to herself, except the man must have heard her.

"Sorry for my shabby looks. I've been riding at the tail end of a freight train all day. If you'll just give me something to eat, I'll be out of your hair in five minutes."

"You can put your hands down," Joe said. "Come on in." He stepped aside to make way.

Livvie found herself craning her neck to take in the fellow's full height. So, he'd been too poor to pay his fare. The word *grizzly* didn't do justice to his physique. She'd always viewed Joe as large, but this man towered over him.

"Where'd you come from, that you been on a freight train all day, and where you headed?" Joe asked him.

The fellow's gaze traveled from Joe to Livvie, and he seemed hesitant to answer, as if he mistrusted them as much as they did him. "I've been out East. As for where I'm headed, I'm not sure yet."

"You visitin' somebody here in Wabash?" Joe persisted.

Sighing, the man raised an eyebrow at him. "Now, if I were, I'd be eatin' there, wouldn't I?"

Joe chuckled in his usual way, low and relaxed. "You got me on that one, mister."

The guy tugged at his thick, brown beard with hands that looked surprisingly clean. Even his fingernails looked dirt free. "Like I said, I'll pay you double for a plate of food. I know you're closed and all, so I won't take up more than a few minutes of your time."

He looked at Livvie again. "Ma'am, you just finish up what you were doing there."

Clearly, he didn't plan to divulge any personal details. This put her slightly on edge, but not so much that she feared he planned to do anything besides fill his stomach.

"No need to pay extra," Joe said, turning and walking toward the kitchen. "You just take a seat"—he pointed a finger over his shoulder—"while I rustle you up somethin' in a jiffy. I got roast beef 'n' gravy and some mashed potatoes left over from supper. That suit you?"

The huge man removed his hat, revealing a thick head of wavy, chestnut-brown hair. Another surprise surfaced when Livvie noticed how it shone, and not from the latest goop men put in their hair to make it lie flat and look wet. It was a bit too long for her liking, the way it covered his collar, and was rather unruly, but at least it looked clean, as if he'd showered that morning before setting off on his long train ride from who knows where. "That sounds mighty fine, sir, and I thank you."

Well, at least he's polite, Livvie thought, taking up her broom yet again. As she swept the floor, she watched him out of the corner of her eye, glad that he'd seated himself at a table under which she'd already swept. She had the uncanny sense that he kept a wary eye on her, as well, perhaps worried she might pick up where Joe had left off with the questions.

"Mommy, when're we goin' upstairs?" asked Nathan, bounding out of the back room.

"In a minute, honey. Go back—"

"Who's that?" he blurted out. Never one to shy away from strangers, probably because he'd grown up seeing them on a regular basis, he boldly approached the bearded man. "Hi, mister. You got a long beard. I haven't never saw you in here before. My name's Nathan. Well, usually, it's Nate, unless my mommy's trying to make a point. What's yours?"

"Nathan, please don't pester," Livvie admonished him.

"He's no bother, ma'am."

Livvie glanced at the man long enough to see that his eyes were the color of a flawless summer sky, and she wondered if he was aware of their penetrating brilliance, even when viewed from a distance. To keep from staring into them, she focused on her son. "Is the back room all picked up? We'll be going upstairs in a few minutes."

"Yep," he told her, then turned back to the man. "We live upstairs."

"Is that so?" The man raised one eyebrow.

"Yeah, and there's another 'partment next t' us, but it's empty, 'cause ol' Mr. Fletcher couldn't walk up them stairs anymore."

"Nathan James, don't talk so much," Livvie chided him.

"On the third floor, there's a dance hall. Mommy hates that, though, 'cause on Saturday nights, the bands come in t' play their music, and the poundin' keeps us all awake. But I don't care. Sometimes, Mommy pokes the ceilin' with a broomstick t' see if she can keep the folks from makin' so much noise, but Alex always says that's oilly, 'cause they can't hear a little broomstick whilst they're dancin' up a storm."

"Nathan, what did I tell you?" Both her boys had a tremendous bent for talking. Of course, they came by it naturally; their daddy had been the friendliest man one could ever hope to meet. Still, there were times when she'd like to stick Popsicles in their mouths to stop their yapping.

As expected, Alex emerged to investigate Nathan's new "friend" and joined the conversation almost seamlessly.

Rolling her eyes, Livvie lifted the broom, her chore complete, and started for the back of the store. Joe passed her with a hot plate of food and cast her an amused wink. "Come on, boys," she called over her shoulder. "I'm done down here."

"Mommy, this here man's name is Mr. Taylor," said Nathan. "He just got off the train. Isn't that somethin'? When're we ever gonna take a train ride?"

"You've been on the train plenty of times," she said, setting the broom and dustpan in the corner.

"Only to go to Manchester or Peru, and that one time we went to Marion to visit some old lady."

"That was my great-aunt," she clarified. "Come along, now. You've got school tomorrow."

"You boys best mind your mother," said Mr. Taylor. She looked at him and could have sworn she detected the slightest glimmer of a smirk.

Groaning in protest, the boys started to turn, but then, Alex looked back at Mr. Taylor. "You plannin' to come back again, mister?"

"Well, I don't know, young man. The food here's mighty good."

"Yeah, but Mr. Stewart has to go to Chicago, and then the food won't be so good anymore."

"You don't know that," challenged Nathan. "Mommy says there's lots o' good cooks 'round Wabash."

"But nobody cooks like Mr. Stewart. Anyways, that what Mr. Hermanson always says, and he ought to know, 'cause he comes in here lots."

Mr. Taylor's eyes twinkled as he chewed, his long beard quivering with the up-and-down motion of his jaw. "You boys sleep tight, now," he said between bites. Then, to Livvie, he said, "Good night, ma'am, and I do thank you for the food. As I said, I'll be sure to pay double."

"You've got Joe to thank for the food, and he's already told you, there's no need to pay extra." She paused and put an arm around each of her boys, who had come to stand on either side of her. "Good night."

He gave a slow nod and looked down at his plate, his cobalt eyes trained on his fork as he scraped up what remained of his meal. Livvie thought of the spare apartment upstairs and almost asked where he planned to bunk up for the night, but she quickly decided against it. Offering some dispossessed, scruffy-looking man a place to stay had the earmarks of trouble with a capital T.

Chapter Three

*"And we know that all things work together
for good to them that love God, to them who
are the called according to his purpose."*
—Romans 8:28

The next day dawned with only a partial view of the sun and a thick band of clouds threatening rain. Also, the temperature had dropped a good thirty degrees since yesterday, which would make Will's job-hunting jaunt downright brisk, especially with no jacket to his name. Drat! He should have taken the one Harry had offered him, but he never had been one for charity and had even refused the extra cash Harry'd wanted him to take. Now, he questioned his good sense. After counting in his head the cash stuffed deep in his pocket, he calculated how many nights he could stay here at the Dixie Hotel, one of the cheaper lodgings in town, before declaring himself completely broke. Two weeks, tops, he figured; maybe three, if he starved himself.

He knew he ought to shave his beard, but that would require preliminary cutting with a good, sharp pair of scissors. What he needed was a professional haircut, but he could hardly spare the money for a barber. Thankfully, he was able to at least take a warm bath. Cleanliness had to count for something.

After his bath, he dressed himself in his second pair of trousers and shirt, only to find the garments wrinkled beyond help. He went down to the front desk to ask about borrowing an iron and an ironing board, but he was informed by the middle-aged receptionist that they had none to lend.

"You sure?" he asked her.

"About the iron, yes. You can use the ironin' board, if you've a mind to," she responded drily.

When he didn't laugh, she looked down her hook nose at him and scowled. "I can see you need an iron, mister, but the only one we had got stole last week by one of our guests when he took off for Iowa. Mrs. Dillard plans to buy another on Monday, after she gets the books put to rights. You plannin' on stayin' here again tonight? Maybe she can borrow one for you."

"I guess I will," he said. "I'd appreciate that."

She made note of it on a piece of paper, then raised her head to give him an up-and-down perusal, tapping her pencil on the marred wooden countertop. "You got some sort of business dealings here in Wabash?" He supposed it was her polite way of saying, "What's a hobo like you doing hanging around here?"

"I...not exactly. I'm lookin' for a job."

She raised a sparse eyebrow. "That so? You could try the foundry or the baking powder factory. There's also the railroad yard. Good chance they need an extra hand."

"I'll do that. Thanks."

He walked out of the Dixie Hotel with an empty stomach, then trekked down to Factory Street at the south end of town, close to the river, where several factories, foundries, and other manufacturing companies operated. At every stop, though, he was met with rejection, either from the hiring boss himself or the first person to greet him from behind a cluttered desk or counter. Whether his disheveled appearance was to blame or they truly had no openings remained unclear. He knew only that his hunt for a job had not been a success.

But it was only the first day.

Don't let the ol' enemy discourage you right off the bat. Harry's parting words played in his mind. *Sometimes, the good Lord waits till the last minute to answer our prayers. One thing I'll tell you, though: He's always right on time.* Will ruminated that thought as he trudged along, searching shop windows and doors for "Help Wanted" signs.

By one o'clock, his stomach literally burned from hunger. Finding himself on Market Street again after having traipsed all over Wabash, he decided to return to Livvie's Kitchen in pursuit of a good, hot meal—forget the expense! Besides, he wouldn't mind getting another glimpse of that pretty woman's shapely calves. Women's fashions sure had changed during the ten years he'd spent behind bars, particularly when it came to dress length. At the train station yesterday morning, he'd found his neck craning more than once as one woman after another passed, toting youngsters, walking next to their men, or even sashaying along with an air of independence he didn't recall seeing years back. He thought of his mother—dead and buried, bless her soul—who had always worked in a long-sleeved dress with a hem that reached her ankles. Nowadays, it seemed women had no qualms about showing their arms clear up to their shoulders. *Well, good for them,* he thought. He never could figure out how they managed all that housework, not to mention barnyard chores, with layers of skirts and big, puffy sleeves always getting in the way.

He hadn't caught the name of the lady at the restaurant, but, since she lived upstairs with her boys—
and her husband, for all he knew—he could only
assume that she owned the place, and that her name
was Livvie, unless the restaurant's namesake was a
former proprietress. He paused to let a parade of cars,
noisy trucks, and horse-drawn buggies go by before
he jogged across the street. For a small town by New
York City standards, Wabash was a constant flurry of
activity—women going in and out of stores carrying
armloads of merchandise, men dressed in business
suits toting satchels and scurrying around or engaged in conversations on the street corners. It made
him wonder about their private lives—their families,
their homes, and their faith, if they professed any. The
town sure had its share of churches. He'd have to try
a number of them to figure out where he fit in best.
Granted, he might not fit in anywhere; was there any
church where an ex-con could feel at home? He supposed he'd add that concern to his long list of things to
pray about. At the top of that list was a job.

At the little diner, he twisted the knob and gave
the wooden door a slight shove, taking note of the restaurant's schedule, which was posted there: "OPEN
MONDAY THRU SATURDAY, 7 AM–2 PM & 5 PM–7 PM.
CLOSED SUNDAYS." Below the schedule hung a sign
that read, "Cook Needed." He'd had plenty of experience in the prison kitchen, had even learned a good
deal about food preparation, but he wouldn't think of
applying for a job in a restaurant—not if it would mean
divulging where he'd picked up his culinary skills.

As he entered Livvie's Kitchen, a bell jingled overhead to announce his arrival. Grateful for the rush
of warm air coming from a nearby radiator, he stood
there and glanced around, noticing several open tables.

The midday rush was apparently over, and only a few folks remained, some sipping mugs of coffee and poring over their copies of the *Wabash Daily Plain Dealer*, while others enjoyed a late lunch. A few people glanced up at his entrance, but none wasted any time gawking. He advanced straight ahead to the lunch counter and sat on the stool closest to the kitchen, where delectable aromas wafted from the oven—cookies and cake, if his nose wasn't failing him, and perhaps some cinnamon buns. The cook, whose name he remembered as Joe, stood at a counter with his back to him, holding a large bowl and stirring vigorously. He must not have heard the bell or the scrape of the bar stool legs. A further perusal of the place showed no sign of a waitress, so Will cleared his throat.

Joe spun around. "Well, hello again," he said with a friendly grin. He reminded Will a little of Harry, ever genial. "You come back for some o' them mashed potatoes, did you? Sorry to have to tell you, I fried up the last of 'em in potato pies for breakfast."

The mere mention of food made his stomach grumble. "Anything sounds good about now. What do you recommend?" He couldn't help it; he took another quick look around in search of one slim strawberry blonde with shapely calves when Joe wasn't looking.

"Got some fresh-caught bass today, straight out of the Wabash River, and mighty tasty, to boot. How's that sound?"

"Expensive."

"Nah!" Joe flicked a thick wrist. "Won't cost you any more than the meat loaf."

His mouth watered. "They both sound good."

"A little of each, then," Joe said. At the counter, which was slightly lower than the bar but still in view, he sliced the heels off a loaf of bread, tossed them aside, and cut the rest of the loaf into thin, even-sized pieces. He stuck two slices on a plate, and then, with a dinner knife, spread a slab of butter on each one before setting the plate in front of Will. "This should tide you over while I fix your meal. Fresh outta the oven."

The aroma of the buttered bread made him groan with pleasure. If he'd been alone in the place, he would have finished off each piece in a single bite, but he exercised self-control, not wanting to let on that he hadn't eaten since the night before.

"So, how'd you spend your morning?" Joe asked.

"Oh, walking from one place to another, looking for work. I'm afraid I don't look too appealing, though."

The cook angled him a pensive gaze. "You needin' some clothes? There's a store for the...um, needy... up the way. Believe it's on Main Street, somewheres between Wabash and Carroll streets. Salvation Army runs the place, far as I know. Bet you could find some extra clothes 'n' things in there."

"I might try that." Strange how Joe's suggestion hadn't put him off. Truth was, he was on the desperate side, and, apparently, it showed plenty.

"Here's today's copy of the *Plain Dealer*," Joe said, sliding a newspaper toward him. "You should check the classified ads."

"Thanks." Will took the paper and started scanning the "Help Wanted" column. When he heard Joe fire up the gas stove, though, he glanced up and watched him drop a big dollop of butter into a cast-iron pan, where it sizzled. Then, he opened the icebox and leaned inside, emerging seconds later with two eggs, two fish fillets, and a jug of milk.

"I saw that the Service Motor Truck Company had some openings in the production line." Will turned to the speaker, a casually dressed man who looked to be forty or so, sitting at a table against the wall behind him. "I read a sign that was nailed to a lamppost up on Canal Street last week. 'Course, they're probably filled by now, but you could give it a try."

Will nodded. "I thank you for that."

The fellow gulped down the rest of his coffee, gathered up his belongings, and pushed back his chair, the legs scraping against the wood planks. "Good luck there, mister," he said as he headed toward the door.

"See you later, George," Joe sang out.

Will turned and saw the man wave before exiting the restaurant.

"That there's George McNarney," Joe said, nodding toward the door. "Good man, George is. He and his brother, Ralph, run the meat market where Olivia gets her supply."

"Olivia?"

"Yeah, that nice-lookin' lady you saw in here last night, with them whippersnapper boys. Quite the handful, them two. She owns this place, buildin' 'n' all, in case you didn't already figure that out. She rents the apartment upstairs. It's empty now, as you probably heard. And she rents out the third floor to various clubs and such. It's mostly just a big hall—like a ballroom, I guess you'd say." Joe adjusted one of the burners on the stove, then turned back to face Will. "In the spring and summer, the Ladies' Garden Club gathers up there for their weekly meetings. They hold some sort o' community garden show up there, too. Then, there's the Kiwanis Club and the Boy Scouts comin' in for their weekly get-togethers. In the summer, there's always somebody fundin' some kind o' charity ball or 'nother. Oh, and on Saturday nights, there're dances up there, sponsored by the Wabash Rifle Club. They bring in country bands and a lot of local yokels. You got your fiddlers and guitarists and drummers. There's a piano up there, too. Most nights, you can hear that music clear down to LaFontaine."

"Hm. How about mouth harps? You ever hear someone playing one of those?"

"Can't say I have," Joe said, crinkling his brow. "But I recall your sayin' you carried one on you. Maybe you could jump up onstage some Saturday night."

"Oh, I don't know about that. I'll probably go up there some night just to listen."

Joe's forehead wrinkled again. "Livvie don't much care for them dances, but it's revenue, I tell 'er, and she ought to be happy for every spare nickel comin' in to put toward 'er mortgage. She and Frank got this buildin' from some rich guy over in Chicago. Truth be told, she'd've preferred to rent the restaurant space from that feller, but he got plain tired of comin' up here to check on matters, so he sold it to Frank for a steal. 'Course, it still ain't cheap ownin' a big piece of property, with all the maintenance and upkeep and whatnot."

"Is Frank Livvie's husband?" Will asked. He finished off his second piece of bread, wishing for one more slice.

Joe cracked a couple of eggs in a bowl and whisked them together with a smidgeon of milk. "Yep. He got hisself killed, though, back in early spring o' last year. Happened right here in front of the restaurant as he was gettin' ready to cross the street. A big ol' workhorse pullin' a wagonload of furniture spooked when a dog barked and ran in 'is path. He reared and came straight down on Frank, crushin' 'is chest. Sure was a tragic thing." Shaking his head, Joe dipped the fish fillets in the egg mixture, dredged them with flour, and placed them in the pan. The melted butter crackled, and a plume of steam rose. He adjusted the flame and let the fillets sizzle.

At that news, though, Will's appetite had drastically waned.

"I been helpin' her out for the past year," Joe went on, flipping the fillets, "but I'm headin' for Chicago real soon here. I got a daughter and some grandkids there—and a job in a mighty snazzy restaurant downtown. 'Course, Livvie's not too keen on me goin', but she'll make do. She's been scurryin' around, tryin' to find a replacement for me, but, so far, nobody's asked 'bout the position. Pay's not the best, you see. But she can't afford more. The account books don't look too good. Unfortunately, Frank went a little overboard with bank loans. Livvie didn't know too much about the financial end of things before he died. Now, she's learnin', slowly but surely."

"I used to do a lot of cooking and kitchen work when I lived in New York City," Will said. Man, he should have bit off his tongue before opening his big yapper, but his doggone sympathy for the woman's state of affairs had robbed him of all common sense.

Joe made an about-turn, his thick, white eyebrows spiked with interest. "You don't say! Where'd you work? What sort of experience d'you have?"

"Uh, not the sort you're lookin' for, I'm afraid. I was more or less an assistant to the chef—cook, rather." "Chef" sounded too hoity-toity. "It wasn't a highfalutin place, by any means." No way would he divulge any more than that. If he ever wanted a decent job in this town, he had to keep a tight lock on his colorful past.

"Sort of like Livvie's Kitchen, then?"

"Um...well, not exactly. It was some bigger."

"Bigger!" Joe turned and flipped the fillets again, sprinkled them with some salt and pepper, and lowered the heat. He walked back to the icebox and removed a pan. Yesterday's meat loaf, perhaps? Sadly, Will found that his immediate need for nutrition had been replaced by a nervous stomach. "What sorts of things did you do—as the assistant?"

"Anything and everything, I suppose."

"Such as?"

"Oh, I peeled potatoes and carrots, prepared the meat, sliced vegetables, did some canning, washed dishes, baked bread...you name it, I did it."

"What about the cookin' itself?"

"Sure, if Harry—er, my boss needed me to fry up something, I did it. I even baked a few cakes and pies for special occasions. But that wasn't often. Christmas, mostly."

"Did you like it? I mean, are you comfortable in the kitchen?"

"Yeah, sure. It's like...well...therapy, I s'pose you could say."

"Well, I'll be," said Joe, removing the lid from the pan and slicing off a good chunk of cold meat loaf. "That's somethin'."

"What is?"

"Your comin' into town like this, just showin' up at the restaurant twice in two days, and now announcin' that you used to help run a restaurant."

"Well, I didn't say that *exactly*."

"No, but it sure sounds like you got the capability for handlin' yourself in a cookhouse. Can you work under pressure? Are you used to cookin' for large groups?"

"What? Well, yeah, we served a good lot of people at once."

"No foolin'! New York's got some big restaurants. I wonder if I ever heard of your former establishment."

"I told you, it wasn't anything fancy."

Joe angled him a calculating gaze. "You think you might be interested in my job?"

Will's heart thumped so hard, it skipped a whole beat. "Your—here? Oh, no, I wouldn't—couldn't—do what you do. No way. I'd never do it justice. I mean, you got quite a reputation. No way could I fill your shoes."

"Well, you wouldn't be fillin' my shoes, young man, no more'n I filled Frank's. You'd be puttin' on your very own shoes and impressin' folks with your own skills. Everybody's different, so folks wouldn't be 'spectin' you to cook up meals the same as me. Maybe you'd even have some ideas for spicin' up the menu."

The very notion of being responsible for cooking the meals at a little diner, especially one that needed rescuing, revved his inner engine. He'd spent ten years doing time for a worthless crime. What he wouldn't give to help someone in need! And it did sound as if this Olivia had found herself in a financial bind. Was it possible that Harry's years of mentoring him in the prison kitchen had been a part of some divine purpose? Harry had often quoted a verse in the book of Romans that read something like, "All things work together for good if you trust the Lord." Will had a terrible memory when it came to the Scriptures, but the gist of the verse was simple and unforgettable. God works in the details of life, and He can take even the bad circumstances folks encounter and make them turn out for good.

"'Course, I'd need to convince Olivia," Joe added. "She's a stickler about certain matters when it comes to runnin' her business."

The assurance of things working together for good flew out the window when Will remembered the attractive little lady who actually ran the place. Joe could probably suggest that she hire him, but she would make the final decision. And something told him their first meeting hadn't impressed her one jot.

"Like I said before, I don't think I'm your man," Will said. "Surely, there's somebody else out there a lot more qualified."

"If there is, he ain't expressin' interest. I won't lie to you, young man; this is not an easy job. First, you got Cora Mae to contend with." Joe followed this remark with a chortle. "She gets put off pretty easy, but she's a good, hard worker, loyal as the day is long."

"You mentioned the lady's having some financial struggles. I don't see how I could help turn that around."

Joe turned back to the fillets, sprinkled a little more salt on them, and poked their centers with a fork. Will's appetite had started to revive, and his mouth was watering at the aroma.

"It wouldn't take much," Joe said. "Maybe you could look at the books, yourself. Are you good with numbers?"

Was he! The fellow had no idea. In his former way of life, he would have looked at the numbers, figured out how to triple them, and then, when the time was right, run off with all the profits. Thankfully, ten years in prison had given him a new attitude, not to mention faith in God, albeit faltering and babyish, and the assurance that he'd been forgiven his sins and granted a new chance at life. Still, a job as head cook in a local diner sounded too good to be true. He thought about all that Joe had said. "You know, I think it's best if I just run on over to that Service Motor Truck Company and see if they're still hiring."

The bell above the door jangled, and both men turned to see the newcomer. It was Olivia, hefting a big box brimming with supplies. Instinctively, Will leaped off his stool and went to relieve her of her load, but she promptly set the box on a table and looked from him to Joe and then back to him. "It's you again," she said with a scowl.

Man, he sure hoped the Service Motor Truck Company had a spot for him. He'd even offer to sweep their floors. No way would a proper little lady like her hire a no-good bum like him.

※

"What do you mean, you offered him a job?" Livvie demanded of Joe, trying to keep her voice to a whisper. She put her hands on her hips. "We don't know anything about him."

Joe wiped the counter where the "mystery man" had been sitting. "Settle down, Olivia. I didn't exactly offer him the job. That would be your responsibility."

"Well, he's going to have to wait a long while, because I'm not hiring him. He's a hobo, Joe. Did you get a good look at him?"

"'Course I did. I been talkin' to him, and, for your information, he didn't have any odors comin' off o' him. I wouldn't call 'im a hobo. Hobos tend to live off folks' handouts and sleep in alleys or under bridges. If you'll recall, he offered to pay double for his meal last night, and he paid in full today, as well, even told me before leavin' that he's been stayin' at the Dixie Hotel. Me? I think the guy's just down-and-out."

She felt the edges of her heart soften just a hint, but not her resolve. "Well, just the same, he doesn't look half capable of cooking an egg, let alone frying up a steak. You said he worked as a cook's assistant. That's a lot different from running a kitchen."

"In a much larger restaurant," he added. "The fella told me they served a lot of people at one time."

"How many?"

"I don't know. He didn't give an actual count."

"What's the name of the restaurant? We could write to them and ask for a reference, inquire about his credentials."

"You don't have time to wait for a reply, Liv. Time's runnin' out. Besides, he didn't give me the name, said I wouldn't know it, 'cause it wasn't a fancy place."

"So, he's being deliberately vague. Why'd he quit working there? Did he get fired? And why didn't he look for another job in New York, assuming he truly came from there? For all we know, he could be lying through his pearly whites. Does he even have teeth?"

Joe let out a long sigh and gave his head a shake. "Livvie, Livvie, Livvie. Yes, he's got teeth. Nice ones, I recollect. As for your questions, I guess you'd have to ask him yourself. He's headin' down to the Service Motor Truck Company to inquire about a job. George McNarney told him he saw a sign sayin' they were lookin' for workers. Good chance he'll land somethin' there today, and then you'll be out of luck."

Livvie let that notion settle in her mind for the briefest moment.

Joe laid a hand to her arm and lightly squeezed. "I got a feelin' about this guy, Liv."

"Yeah, so do I. And it isn't good."

"It seems to me he's your best bet for now," he said, dismissing her concerns. "If he doesn't work out, you can put the 'Cook Needed' sign back in the window. I'll be here for at least the next week to train 'im and see what skills he's got. I'll know in short order if the job's too much for 'im. In fact, I'll even fire 'im myself if it don't look like he's cut out for it."

"And then you'll be gone," Livvie said, well aware that her lower lip had shot out and her shoulders drooped.

He chuckled and gave her chin a light pinch. "You ever gonna forgive me for that?"

She fixed her gaze just above his white head of hair and crossed her arms in front of her belted, floral shirtwaist. "I don't know."

"You're very good at poutin', you know that?"

"Apparently not good enough," she said, whirling around to hide the moisture gathering in the corners of her eyes. She was ever determined not to let her emotions show, even to Joe. Just then, Quinn Baxter and Sam Campbell strolled in, and Joe waved them from behind the bar.

"I'm going upstairs," Livvie declared. "I have some laundry and a few other chores I need to tend to. You best lock that front door at two, or more folks'll come trickling in."

"Hey, Sam? Go back and turn the lock on that door, would you?" Joe asked, and the fellow complied. When Livvie started to walk away, he said, "Give some serious thought to what we talked about, would you, girl?"

She nodded silently, then headed for the stairs leading to her apartment, her chest heavy with a mixture of doubt and a strange sense that Joe was right. Time was running out, and she had to find a cook. Soon.

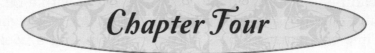

Chapter Four

*"I will hear what God the L*ORD *will speak:*
for he will speak peace unto his people,
and to his saints."
—Psalm 85:8

All day Saturday, Livvie kept an eye out for Mr. Taylor, half expecting him to show up at noon or, at the very least, suppertime. But he never came. Maybe he had started working at the Service Motor Truck Company and was taking his meals somewhere in that locale. She doubted the company operated on Saturdays, but what did she know? Many factories remained in operation six days a week.

Even Alex inquired about "that big man with the beard," asking if they'd ever see him again.

"I have no idea," she told him. "I suppose it depends on whether he liked Joe's cooking well enough." She tried to make light of his question, but, deep down, she wondered the same thing.

"Everybody likes Mr. Stewart's cooking," Alex said, bouncing a rubber ball on the wood floor. "Too bad he's leavin', huh, Mom? Who's gonna take his place?"

"If you're going to bounce that thing, young man, go outside," Livvie said, ignoring his query. Rather than walk out, though, he ceased with the bouncing.

In the kitchen, Joe stood with his back to them and flipped a hamburger patty on the grill. "Maybe Mr. Taylor don't feel 'specially welcome here."

"What do you mean by that?" Livvie asked, moving to the long counter and out of earshot of the handful of customers who still lingered after the supper hour. Alex followed behind, giving the ball a few more bounces. Livvie turned a disapproving gaze on him.

"You did give him your meanest stare when you walked through the door yesterday. He offered to carry that box for you, and all you could say was, 'It's you again!' like he was from the wrong side of the tracks and had no business takin' up space in your restaurant."

"Mom, did you do that?" Her older son's scolding tone made her face warm with the flush of embarrassment. In fact, the heat moved down her neck, and she broke into a sweat. How often she'd gotten after her boys for looking down on folks who were less fortunate. As if they had anything to brag about! Goodness, they could barely scrape two pennies together, but at least they had each other. Had she really been so crass as to turn her nose up at the man simply because she hadn't known him, hadn't liked his appearance, and, for reasons she couldn't identify, hadn't trusted him?

"Well, I might have been a little rude," she finally admitted.

"That's not nice, Mom. He didn't seem like a bad sort to me." Fortunately, Nathan occupied himself in the back room with his trucks and puzzles, or he surely would have added to the lecture. Oh, she hated it when her own children pointed out the error of her ways!

"Feller knows how to cook, too," Joe pointed out.

"You don't know that," Livvie said to his back, somewhat annoyed. "He was a cook's assistant, remember? And that presumes he was telling the truth."

"Still, might not hurt to pay the guy a visit over at the Dixie Hotel to judge for yourself. You can ask him if he got himself a job at Service Motors." Joe glanced around, one of his eyebrows arching smartly.

"You want me to walk over to the Dixie Hotel?"

"It's just a few doors down, Liv."

"I'm not worried about the distance, Joe Stewart."

He gave the hamburger another flip and pressed down on it with his long-handled metal spatula. "You could ask him about his former job, why he left it, how he landed himself in Wabash, how much kitchen experience he's got, and whether he's interested in workin' for you—on a trial basis, mind you."

"You want me to go with you, Mom?"

"No! I don't need anybody's help or suggestions." Annoyance tripped down her spine. "I am not going to any hotel looking for that man. Gracious, what would people think if they found out?"

"Oh, I'm sure they'd think the worst right off," Joe said with quiet laughter. "Probably be somethin' about it on the front page of the *Daily Plain Dealer* on Monday." He paused in his kitchen chore, looked skyward, and raised his right arm, making a wide arc with his hand as he said, "I can see it now: 'Respectable Restaurant Owner Olivia Beckman Seen Chasing after Bearded Drifter.'"

She failed to see the humor. "Oh, for goodness' sake."

A young couple stood up from their table at the front of the restaurant and walked to the cash register. Livvie forced a smile and left Joe to finish frying up his burger. Alex gave his rubber ball a few more bounces, and she paused and cast him a stern glance. "All right, all right. I'll go tomorrow," she called back to Joe.

That night, lying in bed, Livvie pulled a pillow over her head to drown out the loud music, intermittent spurts of laughter, and feet pounding out dance steps on the floor above her. What went on at these Saturday night dances, and how did folks muster enough energy to stay there well into the wee hours of the morning?

She thought about old Mr. Fletcher, the tenant who'd lived in the small apartment next to hers, and wondered if the dances were one of the reasons he'd decided to move elsewhere. But she somehow doubted it. Along with finding it more difficult to navigate the stairs, he'd also started going deaf. She missed the old soul. He'd furnished her with rent money and never caused a single problem. If only she could find someone to replace him—and a cook, for goodness' sake. She needed a cook!

Her thoughts drifted to the scruffy Mr. Taylor. It was difficult to picture him slaving over the stove, flipping pancakes or frying burgers, and even harder to imagine working alongside him. What did anyone know about him or his work ethic? If she hired him, perchance, what if he quit on her after Joe left? Cooking and waiting tables would then be left to Cora Mae and herself, and how would they ever manage? Maybe Margie would agree to lend a hand, but she was busy enough on the farm. She couldn't very well be expected to drop everything and come to her little sister's aid again, especially when she'd gone the extra mile for her too many times already.

While pondering all these thoughts, Livvie couldn't help but think again of the drifter with the long, thick beard and piercing blue eyes. She uttered a laborious sigh and rotated to her other side, dragging her blanket with her and again pressing her pillow to her ear. Oh, Lord, what to do? If Frank were here, he'd tell her to pray about it. Shoot, if Frank were here, they wouldn't even be in this predicament.

As much as it went against her wishes, it appeared she had no choice. She would pay Mr. Taylor a visit tomorrow afternoon.

※

Will threw a blanket over the single bed in his little square room on the second floor of the Dixie Hotel with a window that overlooked Market Street. No sooner had he sat in the chair beside the bed, propped his feet on the mattress, and started blowing a tune through his harmonica than a knock sounded on the door.

"Mr. Taylor?" came a woman's voice. "You got a visitor downstairs."

A visitor? Who even knew of his whereabouts? He went to the door and opened it wide. The clerk, whose name he'd learned was Myrtle Moore, stood in the dark hallway, resting the bulk of her weight on one foot. The front of her shirtwaist was soiled, probably from leaning against the hotel counter. She blew a wisp of grayish-brown hair off her forehead.

"Do you happen to know his name?" he asked.

"*Her* name is Olivia Beckman," she replied curtly. "She runs Livvie's Kitchen just up the block. I told her she could come up here of her own accord, but she declined. I guess she thought it wouldn't look right, her being a lady and all. Can't say I blame her. Shall I tell her you'll be right down?"

He lifted his arms and ran his fingers through his hair. Mrs. Moore shook her head at him and scowled. "Didn't help," she muttered.

He ignored the jab. "Uh, yes. Just tell her I'll be down in a moment. Thanks."

She arched her gray eyebrows at him and sniffed. "You'd do well to shave that awful hair off your face, young man. You aren't going to impress any lady looking like that. Not even those freshly pressed clothes you got on will do the trick."

He sniffed right back and shot her an impassive smile. "Thanks for the advice, ma'am, but I'm not hunting for a woman."

She gave a half nod, clearly skeptical. "I see. Well, I'll tell Mrs. Beckman you're on your way down, then."

He nodded, closed the door after her, and ran to his bag, rifling through it in search of a comb.

❧

She couldn't believe she'd actually swallowed her pride and come to visit Mr. Taylor. Why, it'd been downright embarrassing just to inquire after him. What must that starchy clerk, Myrtle Moore, have thought? Not that it mattered much. She barely knew the woman. Casting a glance around, she noted a marred-looking front desk, a bare coat rack by the front door, a wilted plant on a stand in front of one window, and a couple of side chairs with soiled-looking cushions in a far corner. On the wall above the chairs hung several paintings with mismatched frames.

She folded her hands in front of her and waited. The first footsteps she heard were those of Myrtle Moore. "He said he'd be right down," the woman said as she descended the staircase. "You can go sit over there, if you'd like," she added, pointing at the two chairs as she walked past Livvie.

"Thank you, but I prefer to stand." Shifting her weight from one leg to the other, Livvie looked at the oval braided rug beneath her feet, studying its pretty pattern and wondering at the patience it must have taken to create such a masterpiece. More steps overhead made her rein in her thoughts and turn toward the carpeted stairway.

When Mr. Taylor appeared, their gazes caught and held, and he hesitated briefly on the landing. Again, his arresting eyes caught her unawares, but for only a moment. Then, he lowered his heavily whiskered chin and lumbered down the stairs. He wore a white long-sleeved dress shirt and trousers that looked as if they'd been freshly pressed. My, he was a big man, so broad and muscular. She wondered what sort of face hid behind that shaggy beard. Was his jaw square or round? Were his cheekbones pronounced or ill defined? She couldn't even get a good glimpse at his mouth, the way his mustache draped over his upper lip.

She did see the grin that peeked through, revealing a nice set of teeth, which confirmed Joe's earlier observation. Well, that was something, at least. How many folks could boast a full set of straight teeth? Most couldn't, herself included. Every time she smiled at herself in the mirror—which wasn't often—she couldn't ignore the top tooth that turned in, overlapping the one beside it just slightly. Frank had always said it added to her charm. She disagreed completely. He'd always liked her flyaway, strawberry blonde hair, too, another source of contention for her. She never could get it to stay in one place, and the fine, wispy strands were always tangled because of her natural waves. Even now, she was compelled to tuck a shock of hair behind her ear. She wished she could have adjusted her side combs before the man appeared at the bottom of the stairs, or even that she had gathered it into a ponytail before leaving the apartment. She'd been toying with the idea of having her hair cut in one of those short bobs, which were all the rage now, but she hadn't mustered the courage yet.

"What can I do for you, ma'am?" Mr. Taylor asked.

She cleared her throat and longed for a drink of cold water to settle her nerves. His soaring stature did not help matters. Frank had been of a medium height and build, perfect in her eyes. "I—I've come to discuss something with you."

"Oh?"

Out of the corner of her eye, she detected Myrtle Moore's ears perking up like a bat's.

"Shall we...step outside?"

"If you've a mind to, sure."

She followed him to the door, which he opened for her. *A gentleman. Humph*, she thought as she stepped over the threshold. This particular hotel had no front porch, just a cement landing and stairs with wrought-iron railings. Fortunately, the sun had decided to show itself today, warming the air to a comfortable temperature that she suspected was in the mid-seventies. Even so, Livvie felt a sudden chill, and she folded her arms across her chest.

Mr. Taylor joined her on the stoop, his body taking up almost every square inch of remaining space.

"Well, I'm sure you're wondering what I could possibly want to discuss—or maybe you're not. I'm aware that Joe spoke to you about the position of cook, which will soon be available at my restaurant."

He rolled on his heels and gazed past her. "He mentioned something about it, yes."

Swallowing suddenly became a difficult task, but she managed it, then continued. "He told me you'd gone seeking a job at the Service Motor Truck Company. Were you successful in procuring a position there?"

"I may have been. They asked me to come back tomorrow morning and talk to the hiring manager. Said they have a few openings, and I would probably work out fine."

Strangely, her spirits took a dive. "Well, that's good, right? You must be quite relieved."

"Soon's I start making some money, I can get my own place, so, yes, from that perspective, you might say I'm relieved."

She pondered her vacant apartment. "Well, then, I suppose my coming here was quite in vain."

"I don't know. What'd you want to discuss?" He ran a hand through his thick, wavy hair—a nervous habit?—and focused his deep-set eyes on her face.

She dropped her chin to look at her pointy-toed beige pumps. A sudden updraft snagged hold of her yellow calico shirtwaist, and she quickly grabbed her skirt to hold it in place. "Well, I wanted to talk to you about your experience as a cook. Joe told me that you worked in a restaurant in New York before coming here. A large one, he said. I just thought...I don't know...that, perhaps, you might want to consider the possibility of...well...working for me."

"Working for you," he said. It wasn't a question. "You serious?" He started to laugh.

Despite the pleasant sound, she huffed in irritation. "Just what is so funny?"

"I've never worked for a woman before. I'm trying to envision it."

She blinked twice, as she refused to crack a smile, and pulled back her shoulders as far as they would go. "I don't intend to beg, Mr. Taylor. You can just give me an honest answer, yes or no. Are you interested or not?"

"Well, I don't know. You've caught me off guard. There is the matter of that job at Service Motors. I imagine the pay's pretty good."

Her spirits dipped further. "Yes, I'm sure you're right. I certainly would not be able to pay you what you'd make there."

"You can't get Joe to stay on, huh?"

She shook her head. "His daughter and grandchildren live in Chicago. They've been after him to move there, so I knew it was just a matter of time before he'd leave. He stepped in to help me out when my—well, that's beside the point."

"I already know your husband died, ma'am. Sorry for your loss."

"Oh." She gave a short sniff. "Thank you. One learns how to go on in matters such as these." She could come off with vim and vigor when she had a mind to. "So, are you going to give me a straight answer or not?"

"Are you going to tell me what you'd pay me?"

"I...I'm afraid it wouldn't be much. But there are benefits."

The faint twinkle in the depths of his eyes as they made a quick sweep of her body unnerved her. "Mind telling me what those might be?"

She scavenged her brain for a response. "Well, I assume you'd be doing something you enjoy. That's one benefit."

"What about that pay?" he asked, skipping right over her remark.

She tilted her head back to look up at him, ire building in her blood, and dared to stare into his mesmerizing eyes. "So help me, Mr. Taylor, if I hire you and find you to be an unscrupulous goon, I'll hit you over the head with my heaviest frying pan."

He tossed his head back and laughed. Back rigid, she stared at him, unsmiling, as the jovial sound rippled through the air. "I didn't intend that as a joke."

He put his hands behind him. "I can see that. I don't think I'm a goon. To my knowledge, no one's ever called me that." His whiskers twitched at the corners of his mouth.

"What about unscrupulous?"

"Doubt anyone would call me that, either—anymore, that is."

"Anymore?"

He shrugged. "Forget it."

She shook her head in dismay. "Just how *would* folks describe you, Mr. Taylor? I'm not going to hire you without a single clue as to your work ethic or your history, for goodness' sake. You'd best tell me something good."

"Something good? Hmm.... I went to church this morning. Does that count? Matter of fact, I haven't missed a Sunday for the past six months or so."

"You went—?" She couldn't believe it. No one looked less like the churchgoing type. Instant shame overtook her at her quickness to judge, as well as the reminder of her own sporadic attendance. For years, she and Frank had gone to church faithfully, until—

"You can close your mouth anytime now, ma'am." He gave her a knowing smile.

"Oh." She clamped her lips.

"So, what makes you think I'd want this cook job?"

"Well, Joe seems to have some sort of feeling about you. He has an innate ability to discern good character from bad, and, for reasons I have yet to figure out, he thinks I ought to give you a chance."

His left eyebrow rose a fraction as he stretched to his full height. "Well, you sure know how to make a guy want to work for you. Are you always this cheerful? I might consider taking the job just to get the occasional rise out of you. You're downright cute when you're mad, you know that?"

"Aargh!" She pushed a wayward lock of hair out of her face, but the breeze drove it back again. "I can see I'm wasting my time." She turned, intending to take her leave, but he caught her by the elbow.

"All right, all right. Listen. Let's see if we can strike up some sort of a deal, here."

She swallowed and gazed out at the street, watching a farmer maneuver his horse and wagon through the heavy automobile traffic. These days, more cars and trucks than horses occupied the roadways. Times were changing faster than the weather. "What sort of deal?"

"I understand you have some living quarters above your restaurant."

"A small apartment, yes."

"Well, what say you pay me just enough for a few monthly necessities, let me take my meals at the restaurant, and give me the space upstairs to stay in?"

She stared up at him. "You want free room and board, in other words."

"In exchange for working full-time, I'd say that's a pretty good deal. Joe tells me the business is struggling."

"He shouldn't have told you that."

"So, it's true, then. Well, if we put our heads together, maybe we could come up with some ways to turn a better profit."

She couldn't imagine putting her head anywhere near his. "I don't abide smoking," she blurted out.

"Well, I suppose that'll help keep me on the straight and narrow. I quit the nasty habit, in case you were wondering. Until a couple of days ago, that is. But, don't you worry. I've quit again."

His blue eyes flashed with unmasked humor, and, suddenly, her thick wall of wariness started to crumble.

Chapter Five

*"The L*ORD *preserveth the simple:*
I was brought low, and he helped me."
—Psalm 116:6

On Monday morning, rather than trekking down
to the Service Motor Truck Company, Will gathered
up his meager belongings, paid a curious-eyed Myrtle Moore the balance of his bill, and whistled on his
way out the door. Just before he left, he turned and
invited her to visit Livvie's Kitchen someday soon and
partake of one of his many secret recipes.

She stared at him, gape-mouthed. "That woman
actually hired you?"

He grinned back at her, then let the screen door
shut with a bang behind him. Soon, he was on his way
up Market Street, heading for his new job and his first
paycheck.

Joe Stewart had already fired up the stove and
oven when Will arrived at seven o'clock, and the smells
of coffee, fresh-baked bread, fried bacon, eggs, and potatoes soon began to permeate the little café. A few
men sat at the bar and bantered with Joe while they
sipped their mugs of coffee. Several other men, looking
like bankers in their business suits, were engrossed in
conversation at a table near the front window.

At another table in the center of the room, Olivia Beckman glanced up from her task—refilling the salt and pepper shakers, from the looks of it—and granted him a smile that seemed genuine. Her greeting of "Good morning, Mr. Taylor" passed for halfway pleasant. Dressed in the same knee-length yellow dress she'd had on yesterday, but now with an apron secured around her slender middle, she was about the prettiest female he'd ever laid eyes on. Not that he intended to dwell on that notion. He didn't know which would require more effort—slaving over a hot stove in an effort to please the customers, or catching the occasional smile from his lovely boss. Probably the latter.

The waitress named Cora Mae had her back to him as she waited on a couple of customers.

"Mornin', ma'am," he said to Olivia as he passed, noticing her faint floral scent.

Joe turned, revealing his slightly sagging belly, and sent him a wide grin, his eyes crinkling at the corners. "Hey there, young man. I got some pancake batter here for you. How good are you at flippin'?"

"Probably nowhere near as good as you, sir. The griddle ready?"

"Water's dancin' on it."

"Good sign," he said, walking behind the counter. The mere notion that this kitchen would one day be his ushered in a round of nervous jitters.

"Ain't many who can flip a pancake like ol' Joe, here," said one of the cook's cronies.

"I'm of the opinion it's not so much the flipping that makes a good pancake but the secret ingredients," Will replied. "Shoot, I can flip a rock, but would you care to eat one?"

Joe laughed. "He got you there, Quinn. You ain't dealin' with any pushover, I tell ya. This here feller's gonna give y'all a good run for your money. You watch."

Will appreciated the vote of confidence, but, right now, he felt about as bold as a tortoise crossing Market Street. He would be testing his memory to the limit to recall Harry's recipe for pancakes. In fact, when he sat down tonight to write him a letter and share the news about his new job, he just might ask him to send the recipe. And, while he was at it, he'd ask for a bunch of his other recipes—as many as he was willing to share. Thanks to Harry, meals in the prison dining hall hadn't been half bad. Heck, mealtimes were what the inmates at Welfare Island State Pen most looked forward to each day.

Harry wasn't the only cook there, of course, but he was everyone's favorite. The warden used to get after him for feeding the jailbirds such tasty food, but Harry refused to change his ways. He called the pen his "mission field," a place where he fed the mouths of hungry convicts, and then, as God led him, fed their hungry souls with the truth of His love. It'd worked on Will and a number of others, and they'd started a Bible study some months prior to his release. Whenever the Lord brought that group of men to his mind, he prayed they'd have the strength and stamina to continue meeting together. Living a Christian life behind bars meant enduring ridicule, even though most of the other inmates had never thought to mess with Will Taylor, what with his size and reputation.

"Just so long as he can fry me up a good hamburger, nice 'n' pink in the middle, he'll be fine in my book," said an old codger, who looked fit for the grave but had somehow managed to perch himself on a bar stool between two others.

Joe laughed and looked at Will, who then poured several spoonfuls of batter onto the griddle. Grease sparks popped in all directions. He kept his eyes trained on the pancakes, watching for the sides to brown to perfection before he flipped them over.

"You'll find Coot here is pretty particular about 'is hamburgers," Joe said, nudging Will playfully with his elbow.

"I'll keep that in mind."

The banter at the bar continued, and customers came and went, as Joe showed him around the kitchen, telling him where he'd find every utensil and tool he might need, then introduced him to everybody and his cousin. Will was amazed how Joe kept his cool amid each rush of orders. He himself sweat bullets, wishing to the high heavens he'd worn a short-sleeved shirt instead of this long-sleeved affair he'd bought at the Salvation Army secondhand store. Joe wore only a T-shirt and a worn pair of dungarees. *Live and learn.* The last time Will had worked in a kitchen, he'd had no choice but to sport black-and-white stripes.

Around ten o'clock, there was a lull, enabling them to take a break from cooking like fiends and start cleaning up. "The lunch crowd'll start filterin' in 'round eleven thirty, so now's when we start gatherin' stuff together for that," Joe explained. "Usually, Livvie 'n' Cora Mae help out, dependin' on what's on the menu. I normally do a daily special and have a kettle o' soup on hand, but you and Livvie can discuss that goin' forward. You did real good in that breakfast rush. I kept an eye on you, and you really got a knack for stayin' calm and handlin' yourself under pressure."

Will laughed. "I was just thinking the opposite. I guess you didn't see the sweat rolling off my brow."

"And into that forest on your face, I suppose," Livvie muttered as she came around the corner, carrying a stack of dirty dishes. It was the first time she'd spoken to him all morning, not counting her initial greeting. "I hope you didn't shed whiskers on anybody's breakfast." She set down the plates and topped them with a collection of silverware she pulled from her apron pocket. Then, she wiped her hands on her apron and turned to face him. "You didn't, did you?"

Man, she could be a killjoy. "Not that I know of, ma'am. I suspect they'd blend in pretty well, though." Those pursed, plump lips produced a shallow dimple in each cheek. Rather cute, actually. If he ever managed to get a good smile out of her, he might even see them at their peak.

The front door opened, and Will and Livvie both looked over to see a lone customer walk in. Cora Mae greeted the man and got him situated at a small table, where she stood and chatted with him. Hardly missing a beat, Joe went to the icebox and started shuffling things around, while Livvie stood over the trash bin and began scraping off what remained on the dirty dishes.

Will stepped closer to her and lowered his face within inches of her petite ear. "Do I detect some disgust at my facial hair?"

She scoured the plate in her hand even harder. "It doesn't do anything for me, if that's what you mean."

"Well, I'm not out to impress you, madam."

"Humph. I gathered that. Besides, I don't impress easily."

"You're just itching to see what I look like, aren't you? Admit it."

She paused and glared up at him. "I should say not. I don't care if you have the face of a toad. At this establishment, we uphold the highest standard of sanitation, and the idea of your—your whiskers falling into somebody's soup makes me shudder. That, Mr. Taylor, is the only reason I'd like you to shave. Or, at the very least, give some shape to that carpet."

He tugged on his beard, which had grown well below the second button of his dress shirt. "Shaggy" probably didn't come close to describing it. Heck, he couldn't recall the last time he'd seen his clean-shaven face. He probably wouldn't recognize himself. And he would have been lying to say he wasn't curious to see how much he'd visibly aged in the past ten years.

But this woman's telling him what to do ignited a spark of rebellion, never mind that she was his boss. "Now, see, that would require me to visit a barber, and, since I haven't received my first paycheck, well, I'm rather strapped for cash." Of course, he had more than enough money for a shave and a haircut, now that he could expect some pay soon, but he preferred to make her think otherwise. "If you'll recall, we did agree on a small stipend."

"Which you will receive in two weeks, provided you prove yourself a capable cook."

"Ah. Well then, I guess you'll have to put up with my shaggy appearance for a while longer."

"Livvie cuts her boys' hair," offered Joe, who had finally emerged from the icebox with a couple of defeathered chickens in hand. "Bet she could make quick work o' that beard o' yours."

Will folded his arms. "I bet you're right, Joe." He looked at Livvie and arched his eyebrows. "I'm just not sure I'd trust her with a razor."

"Well, that's good, because I wouldn't come any-where near that bird's nest," Livvie retorted, then turned on her heel, marched out of the kitchen, and resumed clearing tables.

Cora Mae approached the counter and plopped down a piece of paper, directing her gaze at Will. "Got an order for steak 'n' eggs. He wants the steak done medium and the eggs sunny-side up. Think you can handle that?"

What was it with these two women? Were they conspiring to make him miserable? Determined not to let her condescending tone test his patience, he gave her an overdone smile and snatched up the order. "Coming right up, Miss Cora Mae." When she started to turn, he said, "By the way, that's a mighty nice dress you're wearing. The color suits you."

Her eyes made a quick downward sweep of her blue gingham garb, and he detected the slightest hint of a blush as she swept a few strands of gray hair off her plain, round face. In truth, the dress had a couple of stains in front and looked to be about as worn as an old saddle. "Why—thank you." She picked up a damp cloth from the bar and set to wiping empty tables. Within a minute, she'd started humming a little tune.

Will went to the icebox for a meat patty and the prepared potatoes. At the sink, Joe chuckled while he rinsed a chicken under the faucet. "You're gonna do just fine 'round here, young man," he said with a grin. "Just fine."

❧

Despite what little information she had on Mr. Taylor's experience, Livvie found him to exhibit an air of confidence and know-how in the kitchen. She'd watched him fry up a batch of pancakes, crack and separate eggs, slice slabs of bacon and ham, and peel and dice potatoes, as if he'd done each task a thousand times before. And, little though she liked to admit it, it seemed that he would be a fair fill-in for Joe. He'd even started mingling more with the customers, winning them over with his charm, wit, and relaxed demeanor. Yet this made her suspicious. Plenty of people used their charm to gain folks' trust, only to take off with their money the next minute.

She prayed that would not be the case with Mr. Taylor. Hoped it wouldn't, rather. She hadn't been much of a praying woman since Frank's passing. How could she count on God to give her clear guidance if she didn't ask for it? There had been a time when she would have prayed good and hard for the right replacement for Joe. Instead, she'd relied on others to find him for her. Yet it struck her as almost providential, the way Mr. Taylor had wandered into her restaurant when her need for a new cook had reached a state of desperation.

At two o'clock, they locked the front door, same as every day, not to reopen till five for supper. Of course, Joe and Mr. Taylor would return earlier than that to get ready for the evening customers. Few people dined there on weeknights, even though Livvie had long tried to lure more patrons into her establishment for dinner Monday through Thursday. She figured most people were too tired after a long day of work to go out again. Of course, the regulars never failed to show, but their orders often consisted of nothing more than a cup of coffee and an occasional bowl of soup. Some days, it hardly seemed worth the extra money and effort to keep the kitchen open from five to seven.

With her tasks completed, Cora Mae scooted out the door at two on the dot. On her heels was Joe, who waved at Mr. Taylor before exiting.

Livvie pulled down the shade on the front door, where the sign that read "Cook Needed" was still taped securely to the pane. In haste, she reached behind the shade and peeled it away, crumpling it into a ball.

"That mean I passed muster, ma'am?"

She pivoted, unaware that Mr. Taylor had been watching. His blue eyes sparked with amusement. "I suppose you handle yourself as if you know your way around a kitchen," she conceded.

He tugged on that awful beard, as if trying to make it longer. "I'll take that as a compliment."

"Go ahead, but don't go getting all cocky and confident, Mr. Taylor. The true test will come once Joe leaves and you're on your own."

"Ah. I trust you won't throw me out on my ear."

"And I trust that you won't leave us high and dry," she muttered under her breath.

"What's that?"

"Never mind. Would you like to see the apartment upstairs?"

"I thought you'd never ask."

"Don't get your hopes up. It's nothing much to look at."

"Does it have a bed?" he asked, untying the strings of the apron Joe had insisted he wear. My, he was a giant of a man!

"Well, of course!"

"Then, I'll be happier than a dog with the biggest bone in the world." He chuckled softly.

And she couldn't help but return the faintest smile.

᪥

The stairway to the second and third floors was located just outside the back door of the restaurant. Olivia explained that he could access it either through

the back door or from outside, through the narrow al-
leyway on the side of the building. This was how the
partygoers accessed the third floor on Saturday nights.
Will had heard that those events gathered good-sized
crowds, and Joe had recommended he check them
out. He just might.

As they climbed the stairs, Olivia reached inside
her pocket and pulled out two sets of keys, each dangling from a short chain, and handed him one. When
they reached the second-floor landing, she held up the
largest key of her own set. "Use this one to unlock
the outside door." To demonstrate, she pushed on the
door, which squeaked and creaked as it opened, and
led him into a dimly lit hallway. "The only ones with
keys besides you are my boys and me." To his left was
a door, which he figured led to her apartment, since
it was adorned with two colorful drawings that had
the signatures "Alex" and "Nate" scribbled in the lower
left-hand corners. To his right was another door, and
at the end of the hall was yet another.

Olivia opened the unlocked door to his immediate right. "This is just a small storage room," she explained in a matter-of-fact tone.

He peeked inside. A window on the far wall revealed a two-story building next door, and another
window overlooking the alley ushered in enough light
for him to see a mishmash of chairs, a couple of rickety
tables, precarious-looking stacks of crates and boxes,
a cluster of fishing poles propped in a dark corner, and
a few baskets overflowing with assorted Christmas
decorations—strings of lights, tinsel, and some gaudy
ornaments. A lightbulb with a long, dangling chain
was affixed to the ceiling in the middle of the room.

Without further explanation, Olivia closed the
door and nodded in the direction of the end of the hall.

"That's your apartment. Your other key opens the door. I'll show you around, if you'd like."

"That'd be nice," he said, meaning it, as it would give him a whiff of her flowery scent now and again. Mrs. Olivia Beckman might be testy and tough, but she was feminine to the core.

Just like he'd done at the Dixie Hotel, Will rubbed his thumb along the rough metal edge of the key, feeling almost giddy. He'd gone more than ten years without unlocking a door. Now, he had a job, a place to live, and a key of his own. What more could a man possibly need?

The key worked like a charm. Will pushed open the door and stepped aside to allow Olivia to enter first. Then, he followed her inside and saw the tiny kitchen and the cramped living area beyond it. She'd said that the apartment was "nothing much to look at," but to someone who'd spent the past ten years sleeping on a narrow cot in a cell behind locked bars, this place looked like a castle. Sure, it had some peeling plaster and a stain on the ceiling, probably caused by a leak, and could probably use a fresh paint job and a little sprucing up, but what did he care? This was home, and all he wanted to do was slump into the ancient-looking sofa with the popped spring, prop his feet up on the dilapidated footstool, and read a good book while breathing in the blissful air of freedom. He knew that he'd probably have little time for reading, but the mere thought of it was enough for now.

Of course, his all-business boss took no note of his inner gladness and just began pointing things out to him. "This first door is your washroom. It isn't much, as you can see, but at least it has a tub, sink, and commode. I know it's old, but I did the best I could to clean it up after old Mr. Fletcher left. You'll soon learn the hot water takes a while to get up here, and it won't last that long if you plan to fill the tub more than halfway."

"I'll be sure not to. Thanks."

She craned her neck and fixed her emerald eyes on his beard. "Please, feel free to use up all the hot water tonight, if that's what it takes. You may also borrow my barber shears."

He lowered his chin and gazed at her, a teasing smile on his lips. "Well, that's downright generous of you, ma'am, but I have no need of them."

Rather than comment, she shook her head and heaved a sigh that sounded like it went clear to her toes. Why this bent to frazzle her intentionally? He supposed it had something to do with the way that spark ignited her hazel eyes—green one day, blue the next. The way those slender shoulders tightened. The way she pursed her pretty mouth, which, in turn, made her dimples deepen irresistibly. He would shave his beard at some point, had always planned to. Admittedly, the thing did resemble a dense timberland, and it bothered even him. But why shave it now when, by putting it off, he could enjoy Olivia Beckman's fiery spirit a little longer?

"Here's your kitchen, such as it is," she said, gesturing to their left. "The stove doesn't work that well, but, since you'll be eating your meals downstairs, you shouldn't need to use it often. Everything else is in working condition but old, as you can see."

Next, she swiveled to the right and opened another door, which led to a small bedroom consisting of a three quarter bed with a stained, lumpy mattress and a stack of folded bedding atop it. If he lay down and stretched out, his feet would surely extend over the end by at least six inches, but that had been the case since he'd reached adolescence. As in the storage room, a single lightbulb with a chain hung from the ceiling.

"The sheets and blankets have been laundered," Olivia said in her no-nonsense voice. "If you want to turn that mattress over, it might look a little better on the other side, but I make no promises." She nodded at the armoire in the corner, its doors hanging open, and the straight-back spindle chair, the only other pieces of furniture in the room. On the floor in front of the armoire was a braided rug that looked like it'd seen better days.

The wall beside the armoire featured a rectangular mirror and some curved hooks, where he figured he could drape his coat and hang some belts and maybe a shirt or two. He'd have to pick up some hangers at a five-and-dime, as there was none to be found in the armoire. Of course, he'd also need to return to the Salvation Army store for some more clothes to put on those hangers.

"You'll have to buy your own lamp and clock, as the ones that used to be in here belonged to Mr. Fletcher. As I'm sure you've noticed, the whole place is sparsely furnished and could use a little work." Olivia turned and gestured to the rest of the living area. "Of course, there's your living room. Mr. Fletcher had a Victor Victrola, and I'm glad he took it with him. His hearing was going, so he always played it louder than a train rumbles up the tracks."

Will thought of his harmonica, which he often brought out to play before going to bed. He'd have to ask her sometime if it kept her awake. Anything to stay in her good graces.

"And, speaking of trains," she continued, "you'll hear lots of them coming and going, what with the station being at the end of Market Street. I expect you'll get used to it, though, just as everybody else in town has done."

"Hm, yes, I've heard the trains, and I must say I enjoy the sound of them. I also understand there's music above us every Saturday night?"

"Aargh," she growled. "And dancing, loud banter, rowdy laughter, and, I suspect, Morris isn't the best at controlling the illicit stills in Wabash County, not to mention the under-the-table sale of spirits." She paused and looked at him, perhaps to assess whether he shared her disapproval of those who flouted the law, then went on. "The sheriff is well-known for keeping order, mind you, but he often looks the other way when it comes to issues he considers less important. Not that I agree with him, but that's the way of it. You'll meet him soon enough, I'm sure. Word will spread that Joe has been replaced, and he'll want to check you out, especially since you're new to Wabash. That's what he does, after all. The fellow has an eye for trouble."

Will didn't miss the warning in her last sentence. But who could blame her for being hesitant to trust him? He'd come to town on the late train just a few nights ago, a bum, essentially. For all she knew, he could be a mass murderer, and yet she'd hired him, anyway, out of sheer desperation—and confidence in Joe's intuition. He had to give her credit for going out on a limb for him. When the time presented itself, he'd be sure to thank her for that. But, first, he had to prove himself.

Thinking about the sheriff's inevitable visit made his nerves as agitated as a swarm of bees ousted from their nest. Yet he had nothing to be concerned about, really. He'd committed a senseless crime, yes, but no one had been injured, thank God, and he'd paid the price. The problem was, he knew he would never fully recover his former innocence. Once other people found out his history, they would forever label him a criminal, no matter how "good" he appeared or how faithfully he attended church. Well, if they forced him out of town, he wouldn't fight them. He would simply pull up stakes and head west.

Before leaving Welfare Island, he'd determined not to give in to worry, if he could help it. Only God knew his future, according to Harry—He even had a plan for him—and he should trust the Lord, no matter what. "You're a Christian now, son," Harry had said. "That makes you God's child. You can go to your heavenly Father and know beyond a doubt that He will never leave or forsake you. The Word of God tells you that very truth." Next, he'd rattled off a bunch of Scriptures to prove his point, but Will couldn't recall any of them right now.

"Well, I guess that's about it, Mr. Taylor," Olivia said, jumping headlong into his reminiscences. "I'll leave you to do as you please now. I expect Joe told you to return to the kitchen around four thirty to get ready for the supper hour."

"That he did, but I'll probably go down earlier so I can get started with the preparations."

The sudden arch of her blonde eyebrows indicated surprise and, he hoped, a hint of approval. She looked at him for a few seconds, seeming to weigh whether she should say what was on her mind.

"What is it?" he asked.

"Well, I...I was just thinking that since we'll be working together, we may as well call each other by our given names. Yours is Will, if I'm not mistaken, short for William, I presume?"

He nodded.

"Mine's Olivia, but you can tell by the restaurant's name that I mostly go by Livvie. That's what Frank—" She silenced herself.

"Your husband."

"Yes," she said with great reverence. "He's the one who started calling me that way back in...well, way back. Anyway, it stuck. He also gave the restaurant its name, even though I'd have preferred something like Wabash Café or Market Street Restaurant."

He briefly considered her former husband and wondered how he had managed to capture the affections of the enchanting Olivia. He must have been something, this Frank Beckman. "I like the sound of Livvie's Kitchen, myself," Will said offhandedly. "Bears a more personal ring." Then, he remembered what they'd been talking about. "Oh, yes—well, if it's all right with you, I'll address you as Livvie, and you can certainly call me Will."

She gave a slight nod, accompanied by an even slighter smile. It seemed she was determined to keep up an air of detachment, which was fine by him. He had no intention whatsoever of being on more intimate terms.

Proving himself in the kitchen would be enough of a challenge.

Chapter Six

"Fear thou not; for I am with thee:
be not dismayed; for I am thy God:
I will strengthen thee...with the right
hand of my righteousness."
—Isaiah 41:10

Clem Dodd, Rudy Haskins, and Hank Swain sat around Clem's kitchen table, smoking cigarettes and sipping whiskey he had brewed in his own still. "You sure he's still in Wabash?" Clem asked, licking his lips.

"Yeah, I'm sure," Hank said. "I seen 'im jump off the car at the Wabash train depot with my own eyes. Heard 'im say he was goin' there to look for a job."

Clem's wife, Florence, stood at the sink, washing dishes. Her dull, brown hair was pulled back in a knot at the nape of her neck, revealing a collar soiled from sweat. She always pretended not to be interested in their conversations, but Clem knew she listened with owl ears, the fat biddy. It didn't matter how many whuppings he'd given her; she still wanted to know his business. One of these days, he'd boot her out on her ear for good. Fool woman gave him too much trouble.

"You sure he didn't reco'nize you?" Rudy asked.

"I told you, I stayed deep in the shadows. And even if he done saw me, I had my hat pulled low 'n' my face painted with mud. I never would've recognized

79

'im, either, if I hadn't been watchin' outside the jail, waitin' for his release, and heard the guard call 'im by 'is full name. He's a big bruiser, let me tell ya. I swear, Will's a foot taller 'n' broader than last we seen 'im. Sportin' a long, thick beard, too. Anyways, I had my head down, smokin' my cig. Him and them fellas with 'im—a guard and some other old guy—never even seen me across the road, leanin' up against that lamppost. The one guy hugged 'im like as if they was long-lost buddies. Fairies, more'n likely."

"Get on with it," Clem said, irritated. He wanted to know exactly what they were up against.

"All right, all right. I followed 'im onto the commuter boat, keepin' my distance, mind you, then to the subway station, an' finally to the train depot. He took his sweet time studyin' maps 'n' stuff, and then he got in line to buy a ticket. Next thing I know, though, he's off searchin' for a freight car to jump. *Sheee-ooot*, I thought t' myself, *I ain't never jumped a freight train.* Good thing there weren't no yardmen around. It turned out easy as takin' a candy stick from a kid."

"What happened after that?"

"Nothin' much. Dull as dry toast. Here and there, bums jumped off, and others got on. Nobody said much, 'cept for one guy who talked some. That's how I found out Will was headin' for Wabash. Most o' them boozers stunk like the devil hisself. When he jumped, I decided to get off at the next station and buy me a ticket back to New York."

"You should've followed 'im around Wabash, you numskull," Clem said.

"For what?" Hank asked. "I did what you told me to do—figgered out where he was headin'. No doubt he'll be stickin' 'round Wabash, lookin' for a job."

"Yeah, and if he don't find one, he'll be movin' on to the next town," Rudy put in. "Then what?"

"Then, we'll find 'im," Clem said, trying to keep calm. "He's got those jewels we stole, and he ain't about to keep 'em for hisself."

"What makes you so sure? It's been almost eleven years since that robbery, Clem. Those jewels could be long gone. Prob'ly are, in fact."

"Shut up, Rudy, and quit bein' so negative."

"I ain't bein' negative. I'm speakin' the truth."

Clem ignored him. "We're going to have to go to Wabash to keep a close eye on 'im, watch his comin's and goin's for a while, and see if he leads us to the stash. We risked our fool heads for them jewels, and we deserve our share."

"He's the one who done paid for the crime. You think he's gonna spare us so much as a penny?" Hank asked.

"He better," Clem snarled. "Ain't our fault he got caught. Just shows we was smarter than 'im by escapin'."

"What if he got hisself an accomplice in prison?" Rudy asked. "It's more'n possible somebody else is involved by now. Might be the whole reason he chose to settle in Wabash. It's as unlikely a spot as any to hide a treasure."

Clem rubbed his three-day-old beard, took another swig of whiskey, and felt the burn of it clear to his toes. "We can't think about that now," he said with a hard swallow. "We got to come up with some sort o' plan for goin' to Wabash."

Florence spun around, skirts flaring. "You're serious about goin' clear to Indiana? What about the shoe factory? You can't just quit your job in hopes of recoverin' some long-lost treasure. And what are little Eddie 'n' me supposed to do while you're wanderin' all over the countryside?"

"Shut up, woman. This ain't your concern." Clem felt his gut tighten with fierce anger for the way his old lady always butted in to his affairs. All she ever thought about was herself and that kid—and Clem wasn't his father. "I ain't responsible for Eddie, and you know it. Why don't you go look up his daddy if you need money?"

She stuck out a pouty lip and turned back to the sink.

"She has a point, Clem," Rudy put in. "Hank 'n' me got jobs, too. What are we s'posed to tell our bosses? 'Uh, we need to take off a few days so we can recover some stolen property'?"

"I don't know. Make up somethin'. Tell 'em you got an aunt in Timbuktu who's dyin', and you got to go see her one last time," Clem spat. He threw a sneering glance at Florence. "Shoot, maybe I'll just go to Wabash on a permanent basis."

"You do that, and I'll divorce you, Clem," Florence said, hissing like a rattlesnake, her wet hands doubled into tight fists. "I'm sick and tired of your lawbreakin' ways." If Rudy and Hank weren't there, she probably would've hauled off and slugged him in the jaw. It wouldn't have been the first time.

"You go right ahead. I won't miss you or that redheaded brat o' yours one bit. You'll have to come up with the divorce money, though, since you're the one filin'. And your lawyer will be hard put to find me." He cackled louder than usual, his nerves raw and jumping. Nobody made him go crazier in the head than Florence. He'd give just about anything to be rid of her and find himself a woman who appreciated him and treated him the way he deserved.

"Oh, he'll find you, all right. I'll tell him right where to look."

That did it. He pushed back his chair, leaped up, took a giant step toward her, and put his hands around her neck, squeezing till her beady eyes bulged and she stopped making noise. Her fingers pulled at his wrists, her nails digging in to the skin. "You mutter one stinkin' word of what you heard us talkin' 'bout, and you're dead," he growled in her ear. "You got that, woman?"

Eyes wild, she managed a hasty nod of the head. He probably would have killed her on the spot if Hank and Rudy hadn't each taken an arm and dragged him away from her. She sagged onto the floor, gasping and coughing and clutching her throat.

When the kid started crying in the other room, she got to her feet and stumbled out, leaving the three of them in peace.

❧

Just after she'd come to believe that Joe was really leaving, but well before she felt ready for him to go, Livvie and her boys bid him good-bye at the train station. It was the Sunday following his final week as cook at Livvie's Kitchen. Cora Mae and a few others had come to the station to bid him farewell, then had gone, leaving Livvie and her boys alone with Joe and his luggage. She held her emotions at bay until the train whistle blew and the conductor bellowed, "All aboard!"

"Do you really have to go?" she asked for at least the dozenth time that day. "I know, I know, your daughter and grandchildren want you to come, and I don't blame them one bit, I really don't, but—"

He pulled her to him, wrapping her in a big bear hug. "I'll write soon."

"No, you won't," she sobbed into his shoulder. "You didn't even write your own daughter."

He laughed. "All right, then. I'll ring you on the telephone."

"That's better than an old letter, anyway." She stepped back and brushed the tears from her eyes.

"Are you ever gonna come back to visit us?" Nathan asked, squinting into the bright sunshine that streamed through the clouds as he looked up at Joe.

Joe squatted down next to him. "Well, now, what kind o' friend would I be if I didn't, huh? O' course, I'm gonna visit you. In fact, you can bank on it. In the meantime, though, you got to make Mr. Taylor feel at home in the restaurant, you hear?"

"I already am," Alex announced. "We played a game of cards yesterday. He learned me how to play Go Fish. He tol' me he mostly used to just play poker, so he's not very good at Go Fish. Mom won't let me play poker."

"Of course, I won't let you play that detestable game!" Livvie exclaimed. "I don't like you playing any game with those evil cards. They lead to gambling." Joe looked up at her. "I'm afraid that man is going to be a bad influence on my boys, Joe," she whispered.

"What's poker?" Nathan asked, tapping on Joe's bent knee.

"Oh, it's just a silly game, too complicated to explain right now."

"What's 'compilcated'?"

"It means it's hard, stupid," Alex answered in Joe's place. He kicked a small stick off of the platform.

"Alex, don't call your brother names. You know better." Fresh tears, these ones of frustration, trickled out of the corners of her eyes and made paths down her cheeks. She wiped them away, not wanting her boys to notice. So far, so good.

Joe stood and lifted her chin with his forefinger. "Everything's gonna be fine. You'll see," he said, his voice soothing. "I think Will's a decent man. Might be a little rough around the edges, but I've had some good chats with 'im."

"About what?" she asked.

"Oh, nothin' too deep, but I got a feelin' from the little he did tell me that he's been around the block a time or two and learned some worthwhile lessons along the way. He didn't go into detail, but I think he's had some hard knocks. That aside, the fella can cook. He's a real natural. Do your best to give him a chance, Livvie-girl."

She gave a long sigh and straightened her shoulders. "I'll try."

❧

At the sound of the train whistle, Will closed the book he'd been reading, *Streams in the Desert*. Harry had given it to him before he'd left Welfare Island, and he'd been lapping up the wisdom in its pages like a thirsty mongrel ever since his arrival in Wabash. Each day, he discovered something new and fresh about God's love and goodness.

It'd been a busy day thus far. Will had attended church, where he'd met Dan and Clara Gillen and been invited to their home for lunch. Dan owned and operated a poultry farm outside of town, so it had seemed only natural to have baked chicken. Will had complimented Clara so profusely on the meal that she'd given him the recipe for the batter. It had been passed down to her by her grandmother, and she'd never shared it with anyone else. He'd accepted it gratefully and promised that he'd feature it as a week-night special at Livvie's Kitchen—and that he'd keep the recipe a secret, too. The woman had glowed with pride. "You let us know when, and we'll be the first customers through the door that night. Isn't that right, Daniel?" she'd said, beaming.

"Only if you intend to pay my way, Clara," her husband had chortled with a teasing twinkle in his eye.

"Can we come, too?" one of their young sons had chimed in. "We don't hardly ever get to go to a rest'rant."

"I'll tell you what," Will had said to the boy. "The night I use your great-grandmother's recipe, your family's dinner will be on us." He knew he'd gone out on a limb, and he could almost hear Livvie's reaction: "You did *what*? Offered to let an entire family eat for free?" Since making the offer, he'd been trying to come up with ways to still the rough waters once they rolled in.

In fact, he'd been thinking a lot about Livvie— her restaurant, rather—tossing around possible ways to bring in more weeknight customers. One idea that struck a positive chord in his noggin was to use home cooks' tried-and-true secret recipes—the more confidential, the better. First, though, he'd have to get Livvie on board somehow.

He stood up from the springy sofa, walked to the window, and looked down at the quiet street, where only a few pedestrians meandered, and the occasional car zoomed past. The train whistle blew again, and he pictured Joe situating himself in a seat by a window, through which he'd wave at Livvie and her boys, feeling both excited to live near his daughter and grandchildren and regretful to leave his longtime cronies in Wabash. The night before, they'd thrown a pancake supper in his honor and stayed open late to allow folks plenty of time to say good-bye and wish him well. The band that played on the third floor had even come downstairs to play a few numbers. More than once, Will had been tempted to haul out his harmonica, but he'd been too busy flipping pancakes and frying up sausages.

A gentle, cooling breeze blew through the window, ruffling the white curtains. The street was empty now, and long shadows lay sprawled across the pavement, lengthening in the afternoon sun. He decided to take advantage of the weather and set off on a walk to the river. Turning to leave, he felt in his side pocket for his harmonica. Sure enough, it was there. He rarely went anywhere without it, never knowing when it might prove useful to pass the time or simply soothe his nerves.

He went to his bedroom and grabbed his jacket from a hook on the wall, then caught a glimpse of his reflection in the mirror. Man, he looked rough. Maybe it was time to do something about his craggy appearance. Tomorrow afternoon would be a good time to pay the barber a visit. Maybe that would put him in a better position with his pretty boss, which would come in handy when he approached her with his ideas for generating more business at the restaurant.

Once outside, he ambled up the alley, then turned onto Market Street, heading east. He hadn't taken more than a few steps when he ran headlong into Livvie and her boys. The first things he noticed were the sad looks on all their faces and Livvie's red, swollen eyes.

✼

Well, forevermore! With all the crying she'd been doing, Livvie had hoped not to meet anyone on the walk back from the train station. Her boys, loyal, protective little men that they were, had walked on either side of her, trying to cheer her with rote platitudes. All she wanted to do was go home and wallow in self-pity—after washing her face.

"Mr. Taylor! Our mom's real sad," Nathan spouted. He grabbed Livvie's arm and drew her to a snappy halt, as if he wanted Will to look her good in the face, maybe even take over the responsibility of comforting her. Livvie lifted her gaze to the sky and sniffed as mortification crept slowly up her spine.

"I can see that," Will said, his voice low and mellow. She imagined his blue eyes scanning her face. "Good-byes to old friends are always hard. Your mother's feeling bad right now and probably needs some time to think about things. I'm heading down to the river. Would you boys like to come with me? If it's all right with you, of course," he added to Livvie.

"Are you goin' fishin'?" Alex asked.

"Nope. Don't have any fishing gear. Just thought I'd go check out the river view. Maybe you boys could lead the way."

"Can we go?" Alex asked.

"Yeah, can we?" Nathan begged, jumping up and down.

"That...would be nice. Thank you, Mr. Tay—Will." It still felt unnatural to address him by his first name, but that had been their agreement. She could hardly believe it—she was about to have some time to herself, time to nurse her aching heart.

In her apartment, she shrugged out of her spring coat and hung it on a hanger in the little closet by the entry. Then, she moved down the hall, passed the kitchen and dining room on her left and the boys' bedroom on her right, and went straight into the bathroom. She flipped the light switch, then started the faucet, waiting for the hot water to reach the upstairs. When it did, she plugged the drain with the stopper and waited for the sink to fill. Meanwhile, she inspected her face in the mirror over the sink and gasped, horrified that Will had witnessed her in this state.

"Aargh!" she muttered to her reflection. "What difference does it make what he thinks? Gracious, am I off my rocker?"

When the sink was full enough, she stopped the water, then took a washcloth from the towel rack, rubbed it with a bar of Pears soap, and set to fixing her puffy face.

Chapter Seven

"When I was a child, I spake as a child,
I understood as a child, I thought
as a child: but when I became a man,
I put away childish things. For now
we see through a glass, darkly;
but then face to face: now I know in part;
but then shall I know even
as also I am known."
—1 Corinthians 13:11–12

They found the river at the end of a winding, wooded path past the train station. In the clearing was a little park with several picnic tables and a fire pit surrounded by some makeshift benches made from long boards resting on cement blocks. Traces of debris were scattered on the ground, including scores of cigarette butts and some old canning jars, which Will could only assume had held home-brewed liquor. He figured this was a popular hangout for young adults on Friday and Saturday nights.

The river stretched northeast, parallel to the railroad tracks, until it veered further east and out of sight. Reflecting the afternoon sunshine and clear-blue sky, the water appeared as rippling blue glass dancing prettily over and around fallen branches and protruding rocks. Looking west, Will spotted a canoe with two boaters paddling upstream—an easy task today, considering the calm conditions. He imagined that, after a heavy rainstorm, the river could turn quite fierce, and he'd even heard stories of severe flooding as far north as Canal Street, which was only a block south of Market. The boatmen looked to be having a grand time, and, for a second, he pictured himself maneuvering the river with Livvie, enjoying quiet conversation and allowing the boat to take them where it chose. *Downright harebrained notion.*

"You boys know how to skip stones?" Will asked, bending over in search of the perfect pebble.

"Nuh-uh," said Nathan.

"My dad showed me once, but I never got the hang of it," said Alex.

"Ah. Well, maybe I can take up the lesson where your dad left off. See, you were younger then. Now might be the perfect age to learn."

"What about me?" asked Nathan. "Ain't I the perfect age?"

Will chuckled and ruffled the younger lad's sandy-colored hair. It was close to the shade of his mother's hair but leaned more toward blond than auburn. "I guess one can never be too young or two old to learn stone-skipping. It takes a lot of practice, though. I know a guy who was able to get seventeen skips out of one stone. I never could beat his record. It's been a long time since I hurled a good stone across a lake or a calm river. Hope I haven't forgotten how."

"Naw, I bet you can still do it," Alex insisted.

"The trick is to find the perfect stone," Will told the boys. "Not too big, but big enough to go far when you give it a good toss. Shape and feel are important, too."

"What's a perfect rock look like?" Nathan asked, getting down on his knees to dig in the dirt.

"Well, let's see, here." Will seized a rock and studied it carefully. "It's got to fit real nice in the palm of your hand. Like this one, see?" He held it out for the two pairs of blue-green eyes to peruse. My, they took after their mother in looks. Made him wonder about their father. "This one's not the right shape, though." He tossed it back down. Nathan's shoulders slumped with disappointment.

"Don't worry; we'll find one. Searching for the right rock is actually a big part of the fun. Come on, help me."

"What shape does it got to be?" Alex asked.

"Sort of flat," Will said, "but not as flat as a pancake. It's got to have some roundness to it."

They kept up their quiet search, spreading out a bit, bent at the waist with their eyes trained on the ground.

"How's this one?" Nathan asked a few minutes later. He held up what looked like an ideal specimen.

"Hey, fella! You may have found it."

"Can you make it skip?" Nathan asked, his voice high with excitement.

"Hm. Let's see, here." Will took the rock in hand and tested it for size, shape, and smoothness. Then, he glanced out over the river. "Water's pretty calm. Won't work if it's too choppy. And those guys in the canoe are still a ways off. You don't ever want to try this if there's folks fishing or swimming, unless you want to get chased right off the riverbank.

"Okay, step one." He squatted down at their level, and they gathered in close. "Grasp the rock firmly between your thumb and forefinger, gently curling your other fingers under the stone like this, see?" He couldn't remember the last time he'd had an audience

with such rapt attention, unless he counted that prison fight he'd gotten into with Fat Lester, one of Welfare
Island's fiercest inmates, some two years ago.

The guy had had it in for him since their first
meeting, wanting to make it clear who was boss inside the prison walls. Will had mostly avoided him,
not wanting to fight him but knowing he could easily
defend himself if it came to that. And it did on the day
Lester had started ribbing him about his past, though
he'd known zip about it. He'd attached names to Will's
deceased mother that even the most shameless floozy
didn't deserve and accused his father of doing unfor-
givable things to him as a boy. That had been the final
straw before the brawl had broken out. Inmates had
placed bets and cheered loudly; guards had scurried
in from everywhere to stop the fight before it spiraled
out of control. It had ended when Lester had thrown a
punch at Will, who'd ducked, then hurled himself into
Lester's gut, knocking him to the ground. On his way
down, Lester's head had clunked against the cement,
rendering him unconscious. Of course, the episode had
been answered with a week's worth of solitary confine-
ment for both of them. Will would have lost his mind
if it hadn't been for Harry's daily encouragement when
he delivered his meals. He'd whispered short passages
of Scripture through the tiny opening in the door until the guard had ushered him away. After that, Will
had kept his nose clean, a feat made easier when Fat
Lester had unexpectedly received transfer papers to
another prison. Harry had called it an act of God; Will,
a blessed relief.

"What's step two?" asked Nathan, his impatient
tone bringing Will back to the present. He shook off
the nagging memory of Fat Lester and the prison fight

and stood to his feet. Gazing down at the two lightly freckled, innocent faces, he prayed that, despite his colorful past, he would somehow make a positive impact on the lives of these boys.

"Well, it's a lot in how you stand," he said, turning with one side to the water and crouching slightly, legs relaxed.

The boys watched intently and even mimicked his stance, even though neither one held a stone.

"Good, that's it," he encouraged them. "Now, see, I curl my wrist like so, and then I do this little snap and release." He let the stone fly through the air, and all three of them watched it glide over the water, hopping once, twice, thrice, all the way up to eight good skips. "Ah, see? I can do better, though. Didn't have quite enough spin on it when I snapped and released, and it's quite possible I wasn't low enough to the water," he explained, using the same tone he would in a serious conversation with another adult. "Lots of factors to consider. That's where the practice comes in handy."

Nathan started jumping up and down. "I want to try! I want to try!" he squealed.

"Well, all right, that's the spirit."

"Me, too!" said Alex.

And off they went in search of more perfect pebbles.

※

When an hour had passed and her newest employee had yet to return her boys, Livvie started to worry. What had she been thinking when she'd allowed Will Taylor to take her sons down to the river, and why hadn't she stipulated how long they could be gone? She barely knew him, had spoken only briefly to him during his week of training with Joe, and still knew nothing of his past. And yet she'd agreed to let her boys run down to the river with him, this man who'd introduced her son to a deck of cards and taught him Go Fish without her permission. What kind of a mother was she?

She glanced at the clock on the wall and tried to remember exactly what time she'd gotten home. Joe's train had left at three o'clock on the dot, she recalled, which meant she must have walked through her door around quarter after three. What in the world could they be doing? When 4:45 rolled around, she decided to march down to the river herself to see if she could find them.

She hurried down the street and made her way as quick as she could along the narrow path to the water. Suddenly, a sweet-sounding melody brought her steps to a halt. She listened for a moment, inching forward as she did to stay out of sight. At the first break in the trees, she hunkered down a bit and pulled back a leafy branch to steal a glance though a gap in the foliage. There in the clearing were her boys, seated on a wooden bench on either side of Mr. Taylor, legs dangling, admiring eyes staring up at him, as he played a tune on a mouth organ. She recalled his mentioning that one of his few possessions was a harmonica— not exactly the instrument she would have expected a man of his stature to play.

But then, she heard his rendition of "Rock of Ages." Oh, how the tender tone floated on the breeze, whispery and almost haunting. From note to note, measure to measure, he embellished the tune with tiny trills. Without forethought, Livvie clutched a hand to her heart and fisted the fabric of her coat. This was a side to Will Taylor she'd never seen—tuneful, soft, and vulnerable. Why had she worried about trusting him with her boys?

When the song ended, Nathan spoke first. "How'd you learn that thing?"

"My granddaddy taught me when I was just about this high." Will held out his hand parallel to the ground.

"That's how high I am," Nathan said.

"Then, I expect I was about your age. Once he taught me the basics, I just took off with it."

"Maybe you can learn me 'n' Alex how to play it."

"Well, maybe I can. You got to have a passion for it, though."

"What's passion?"

"Passion is...well, it's like a great love for something that just won't let go of you."

"Then, I gots a passion for Coca-Cola," Nathan declared.

Will laughed out loud and patted the youngster's tawny head.

"I got a passion for rock-skipping," Alex chimed in. "Can we do that again?"

"Another time, maybe. Right now, we'd best get you boys on back to your place before your mother comes looking for us."

At that, Livvie made a hasty about-turn, tiptoed away from the stand of bushes—and, she hoped, out of earshot—and set off at a run up the path, lungs burning, hair flying behind her.

❧

Will and the boys crossed to the other side of the street at the corner of Huntington and Market. Half a block from the restaurant, he spotted Livvie, sitting in a chair in the shade of the awning. She fanned her face—a strange sight, since today was not unbearably hot.

"You think our mom's done crying?" Alex asked.

"I wouldn't ask her, if I were you. You never can tell what might set off a woman's faucet," Will answered. He was hardly an expert on females, but it did seem that they had an inexhaustible supply of tears, and that the dam could break at any given moment, allowing them to spill forth.

"What faucet?" asked Nathan.

"Her tears, dummy," said Alex.

"Your brother's not dumb, just curious," Will said, his eyes trained on the feminine creature just yards away now. "I'd play things cool, if I were you boys; act like nothing even happened. And, whatever you do, don't remind her about Joe's leaving."

"Yeah, we don't want t' make her more sadder," Nathan agreed.

"Watch this," Alex said. "Hey, Mom!" He ran ahead of them toward the building. "Guess what we did?"

Livvie looked up and granted them a pleasant smile. It was the only genuine one he'd seen—pointed directly at him, anyway. Her dimples deepened, and, for the first time, he noticed her two top front teeth, one perfectly straight, the other turned in just so. Only one word came to mind when he laid eyes on her. Well, two, actually: *sweet* and *charming*.

In the restaurant kitchen, he began to fix them a light supper of roast beef sandwiches and leftover vegetable soup, even though Livvie had insisted at first that he need not go to any fuss. It was his day off, after all, she'd reminded him.

"Gotta eat, anyway," he'd said. "I might as well make enough for everybody."

Now, she said, "Well, at least tell me what I can do to help."

"You can get the dishes and tableware ready, if you want."

"Can I have a Coke?" Alex asked.

"Ooh, I want one, too!" Nathan shouted.

"Water will do just fine," Livvie said. "The soda pop is reserved for customers."

"But we *never* get t' have it," Alex whined. "Ain't ever'thing in this place ours?"

Will kept his eyes down and sliced each sandwich in half, while Livvie set four plates in front of him and reached for the glasses. "No, everything is not ours. It...well, it mostly belongs to the bank."

"But the bank don't work here," Alex argued.

Will fought to keep his mouth shut tight and his lips in a straight line.

"Oh, I guess you can have a small glass of cola, but just this once," she said.

Both boys cheered, and the subject of the bank was quickly dropped.

When they were seated together at a rectangular table, Will noticed right away how they resembled a little family. He and Livvie sat side by side, their shoulders bumping from time to time, and her boys, seated across from them, devoured their suppers and talked nonstop about their lesson in stone-throwing. They included every detail—how Will had broken his own record by getting ten skips in one throw, and how neither of them had been able to get so much as one, but they weren't discouraged, because Mr. Taylor had told them it took a lot of practice.

Livvie laughed at their enthusiasm and, every so often, reminded them not to talk with their mouths full. They'd swallow, take a swig of cola, and then continue, spouting about his harmonica and calling him the "best player in the world."

"So, where did you learn to skip rocks and play the harmonica, Will Taylor?" Livvie asked. She turned to face him, and he noticed that her olive green shirtwaist made her luminous eyes look more green than blue.

"I grew up a mile or so from a little lake in upstate New York. A bunch of my boyhood chums and I used to walk down there, and we'd practice by the hour. 'Course, we fished, swam, hunted turtles, and looked for crayfish, too. You know, the usual kid stuff." He snuck a grin at Nathan and Alex, then looked back at Livvie. "As far as the harmonica goes, well, my grandfather was a pretty musical guy. We used to sit out on the front stoop of his house, where he'd play while I listened and watched. Then, one day, he just handed it off to me and said, 'Here, you try it.' It just sort of started coming to me, real natural-like." He instantly regretted having divulged so much with hardly a pause to catch his breath. He should have taken a second to think before letting it all roll off his tongue. The goal had been to remain an enigma, and yet, here he was, relating details from his childhood to a woman he barely knew, and to her boys, who kept their eyes fixed on him like he was some kind of hero.

"And your parents...were they musical, as well?" Livvie asked, oblivious to his sudden wariness.

He supposed it couldn't hurt to answer a few more questions, as long as she didn't dig too deep. "Not especially. My mother could at least hum a tune, but my pa...well, he was pretty much tone-deaf."

"So, your grandfather who played the harmonica, he was your mother's father, I presume?"

"Yes."

She lifted her glass to her pretty mouth and took a few small sips. Will watched that hollow place at her throat go in and out with each swallow. Purely mesmerizing.

"Do you sing, too, Mr. Taylor?"

He met her gaze. "I can do a fair job."

She set the glass back down and looked at her sons. "He'll have to serenade us sometime, won't he, boys?"

"What's 'serenade'?" Nathan asked.

"Sing and play, dodo bird," Alex blurted out.

"Alex," Livvie said, lowering her chin in a disapproving manner.

"Sorry," the boy murmured, nudging his brother in the side. He picked up his sandwich and took another big bite.

Livvie picked up her own sandwich, turning it slightly in her hands. "Your family, do they all still live upstate?"

"No, they don't."

"Do you have any siblings?"

"Had a sister. She died."

"Oh, I'm sorry. Did she pass recently?"

His heart caught as the memory took him back twenty-one years. "She drowned. I was thirteen at the time, and Joella was seven." He cleared his throat. "I was supposed to be watching her."

Livvie gasped and held her sandwich in midair. Even her boys ceased eating. They seemed to recognize the moment as brutally serious.

"Your parents must have been devastated. Did they ever recover?"

"Nope," he said, shaking his head. "Whole thing was my fault. That's when matters between my folks and me took a drastic turn. Looking back, I'm sure my pa's anger influenced my mother's, as I used to hear them talking in another room about how they never should have entrusted Joella to my care that day, how irresponsible it was of me to have taken her to the lake, and on and on. Don't get me wrong; I know they loved me—no doubt there. They just failed to show it after that fateful day. It seemed like every time I walked into a room, about all I read in their eyes was shame and blame. And, of course, my mother never stopped crying."

That was when he'd taken up with the wrong crowd—a bunch of fellows all seeking approval, acceptance, and a place to fit in. To manufacture their own fun, they'd started smoking, drinking, and committing petty crimes—vandalizing vacant buildings and such—which had soon escalated into more serious offenses. He often wondered what had happened to that gang of troublemakers, particularly the ones who'd joined him in the jewelry store theft. Had any of them reformed over the past decade?

"...shouldn't have blamed you," Livvie was saying. Her voice pulled him out of his reverie and back to the present. "You were only thirteen." Good thing he'd had enough sense to clamp his mouth shut before divulging anything else. She'd fire him for sure if she learned about his stint in jail. "It must have been awful for you. Surely, you know that your parents probably blamed themselves and merely misdirected that blame because it made them feel less guilty." She shook her head. "It's all so sad. Where are they now? Do you ever see them?"

"They're both gone. Passed on a few years ago."

"Oh, I'm sorry—again. You've had a rough go of it, haven't you."

He shrugged. "No worse than anyone else. Look at you, young lady. Your life hasn't exactly been a bowl of juicy red cherries. What we choose to do with our circumstances is what truly matters. I mean, yeah, for years afterward, the Lord's grace and mercy seemed far off. I kept asking how a good and decent God could allow a young girl's life to end so tragically, with me in the middle of it all. But then, there came a time when I had to lay it all down, just give it up, you know? That made all the difference for me."

He had Harry to thank for getting him to that point, too, but he'd keep that matter to himself, lest she or one of the boys start asking about how he played into the scheme of things. Harry had also reassured Will that his folks had no business placing blame on him unless they pointed the finger back at themselves, as well. He'd been a mere lad, after all. Will recalled Pa's stern instruction as he'd climbed to his perch on the buckboard, preparing to leave: "Take care of your sister while I run some errands in town. Your mother's in bed with that bad case of influenza, so don't go running off, you hear?"

"Yes, sir. I'll watch over things," he'd promised. But, of course, he hadn't. No sooner had his father disappeared around the first bend in the dusty road than he'd dragged a balking Joella away from her dolls so that he could go fishing down at the lake. He'd never dreamed that she'd slip and fall from a steep cliff, hit her head on a rock on the way down, and tumble into the deep waters below. Even though he'd scampered down the hill to get to her, screaming at the top of his lungs for someone to help him, not a soul had heard his cries. By the time he'd found his sister and pulled her out, she'd already turned a strange, milky-white color.

He raked a hand through his hair to keep from shuddering at the memory. He supposed none of it mattered now; it hadn't, ever since his mother had died of pneumonia and his pa had overdosed on liquor and aspirin while he'd sat in prison. In the end, a broken heart was probably what had really killed them. After all, they'd lost their only daughter in a senseless accident, their only son to a life of crime.

"I could use a glass of water," Will said when he realized how desperately he wanted to change the subject. "Any of you need anything?"

"We're fine, and you don't need to wait on us," Livvie said.

He wanted to ask her when the last time was that she'd been waited on; when she'd last let someone else shoulder a burden of hers. Instead, he glanced over her head at the clock on the wall. "Man, where'd the time go?" He pushed back his chair, making the legs scrape loudly against the wood floor. "I'm going to start cleaning up the kitchen, if you don't mind, and then I need to run upstairs and change my clothes for church."

"Church? For the second time today?" She gaped at him as if he'd suddenly grown a third eye. "Isn't once a Sunday enough?"

Her remark made him toss his head back and laugh. "It's not a chore to me, Livvie. Fact is, I enjoy it. I've been attending that Wesleyan Methodist church at the corner of Market and Thorne. It's a bit on the strict side, I suppose, but they're a loving, generous bunch, far as I can tell. This morning, they took up a collection for a missionary couple serving in Siam. Let me just say that when the offering plate passed by me, it sure did look full to brimming. The reverend's sermon did a number on my conscience, too—always a sign of good preaching, if you ask me."

"Ha! Then I best not go there," she said, pushing a few strands of golden hair out of her face. Her comment was worded like a jest, but her tone was dead serious.

"Mom don't ever take us to church anymore," Alex said glumly. "We used to go, but that was before our daddy—"

"Alex, hush," Livvie said. She stood up hurriedly, making quite a racket with her chair.

"No, please—sit. You aren't even done yet," Will said, nodding at her half-eaten plate of food.

"I should help."

He smiled beneath his forest of whiskers. "Relax, would you? I'll take care of things."

She gave a hesitant nod and lowered herself slowly into her chair.

As he washed dishes and tidied up the kitchen, Will tried to think of the best way to go about offering to take Alex and Nathan with him to church sometime.

Chapter Eight

"But thou, O LORD, art a God full
of compassion, and gracious, longsuffering,
and plenteous in mercy and truth."
—Psalm 86:15

Will didn't know if Monday mornings were always this busy, or if more folks than usual had come out just because they'd heard about Joe Stewart's replacement and wanted to see how he measured up. He'd been flipping pancakes and French toast, browning bacon and sausage, and frying up one egg after another for the past hour with nary a break—and loving every minute of it. As a matter of fact, he hadn't had so much fun since...well, he couldn't recall.

Coot Hermanson sat on a stool at the bar and kept Will informed of everyone's comings and goings, making introductions whenever someone joined him at the counter, and waving folks over when they rose from their seats to leave. He probably should have saved his breath, though, because Will forgot everyone's name immediately after being introduced.

Livvie and Cora Mae had been moving nonstop, too, picking up breakfast platters at the counter and dropping off new order slips faster than a blink. Somehow, though, Will managed to remain calm and cool.

No more than a couple of sentences had passed between Livvie and him, for all of her running back and forth, but he did catch several glimpses of her mopping her shiny brow with her apron, promising Coot she'd be right back with the coffeepot, and bending to coo at a newborn baby in his mother's arms. Despite her busyness, she still took the time to acknowledge folks. And Will admired her for that.

Around eleven o'clock, when the breakfast crowd had dwindled to a few retired oldsters, Will started cleaning up the kitchen and thinking about the lunch menu. There would be the usual Monday soup options—chicken noodle and tomato—and the sandwich choices, which Cora Mae had scribbled on the blackboard: ham, roast beef, or chicken. Below these, she had listed their pie offerings at five cents a slice: apple, cherry, peach, and strawberry. They had enough pies to tide them over for the next day or so, but soon, perhaps as early as tonight, Will would have to bake a new supply. He looked forward to it, especially since he'd received a stack of recipe cards from Harry in the mail on Friday.

Will had nearly finished scrubbing down the pancake griddle with steel wool when the screen door squeaked open, ushering in a bulky man in uniform—an officer of sorts—with a bulbous nose, a pudgy face, and a trim, gray mustache. He stood just inside the doorway with his thumbs hooked in his belt, shifting his weight from one leg to the other as he surveyed the place in a way that put Will in mind of some Hollywood actor who played a shifty character in one of those moving pictures. Seeing that uniform put Will on edge, even though he had no cause for worry. Shoot, he'd done his time. Would he ever live like that was true?

Long-ago memories flashed in his mind—the sounds of gunshots ringing through the air, voices shouting, and feet pounding the pavement as the police gained on him; the sensation of lungs burning and heart thundering; the sight of Clem and the others hightailing it out of there in the wagon as he chased after them, running for his life, still clutching the leather bag of loot.

"Hello, Sheriff," Livvie greeted the man from her seat beside Coot at a table near the window, where the two had been chatting for the past ten minutes or so. Coot was probably on his fifth cup of coffee by now. Outside, his faithful black mongrel, Reggie, kept a constant vigil by the door. Every so often, he pressed his snout against the screen, as if waiting for a handout. Will reminded himself to save a plate of leftovers for the pup.

The sheriff touched a finger to the brim of his hat and dipped his chin, granting her and Coot the minutest smile. "Miss Olivia. Coot."

"Hello there," Coot said. "Fine morning, ain't it, Sheriff?"

"Yes, sir. Fine, indeed."

Will turned his attention back to his kitchen chores. He set the clean griddle on the stove, then picked up a cloth to wipe down his work space, trying to look busy. He wondered why Coot hadn't jumped up to make an introduction. Maybe his ancient bones were tired from the morning's activity.

The sound of boot heels clicking on the floor and keys jingling signaled the sheriff's approach, yet Will continued wiping the counter, feigning obliviousness.

"Anything I can do for you, Sheriff?" he heard Livvie ask. Out of the corner of his eye, he saw her following the sheriff toward the kitchen.

With a lazy turn of the head, he acknowledged the rotund fellow, who gave a simple nod as he lowered himself into a bar stool with a breathy sigh.

"Just a cup of coffee would do me well, Olivia," he said, keeping his eyes on Will.

"I'll get it," Will said, reaching for the coffeepot and a clean mug from the stack beside the coffeemaker. He glanced up at Livvie and noticed that several strands of wavy hair had escaped the silver barrettes she'd used to pull it back behind her petite ears. It took no little effort to force his eyes away from her, but he had a customer to serve. He plunked the coffee cup on the counter in front of the sheriff and filled it with the steaming, black liquid.

Livvie cleared her throat. "Sheriff Morris, I'd like you to meet Will Taylor. He's come to replace Joe in the kitchen. Mr. Taylor, this is the sheriff of Wabash County, Buford Morris."

Will wiped his right hand on his apron front before extending it over the counter. "Mighty nice to meet you, sir."

A wary-looking smile appeared on the sheriff's thin lips as he likewise reached up, and the two shared a solid handshake. "Same here," he said in a croaky voice.

"Mr. Taylor hails from upstate New York," Livvie put in, "but, in more recent years, he lived in New York City. He got his kitchen experience working at a big restaurant there."

Will felt a knot form in his stomach.

"That right? A big restaurant, eh?" Sheriff Morris took a sip of coffee. "What brought you clear to Wabash? You got family here?"

"No, sir." He weighed his words carefully while the knot in his gut tightened. "Just thought it sounded like a decent place to hang my hat. I'd had enough of the big city. I like a quieter lifestyle."

"Well, Wabash is a quiet town," Sheriff Morris affirmed. "We pride ourselves on keeping it that way." This he said with a hint of warning. Already, Will had the sheriff keeping a close eye on him, and he'd done nothing to warrant it except show up.

The man removed his hat and slid four fat fingers through his thinning gray hair, scratched the nape of his neck, then plunked the cap back in place with a short sniff. "Yep, Wabash is a mighty fine place. Isn't that right, Miss Livvie?"

"It surely is, Sheriff," she said. "Could I interest you in a slice of pie?"

"Well, now, if you're talkin' Joe's pies, I'll take you up on that offer."

And if they were Will's pies? What then? He decided to let the remark pass. "I'd be glad to cut you a slice, Sheriff." He walked to the icebox and pulled open the door. "We've got apple, peach, cherry, strawberry, and...hm"—he bent to peruse the choices—"looks like that's about it. I'm baking some more tonight or tomorrow."

"You bake pies, eh?" Another sniff gave way to a frown. "You don't look like the pie-bakin' sort. Ain't that somethin'?"

"He's goin' to give ol' Joe some competition, Sheriff," Coot piped up from his table. "Be forewarned."

Sheriff Morris tipped his head to the side and pulled on his sagging double chin. He did not look convinced.

At two o'clock, the restaurant was finally empty. Livvie had stolen away to her apartment half an hour earlier, and Will flipped the cardboard sign on the door so that it read "Closed." Then, he stepped out into the warm sunshine and headed up the street toward Bill's Barbershop.

Time to improve his image so that he looked more like the "pie-bakin' sort."

※

Livvie snagged the last of the week's wash, Alex and Nathan's play shorts, off the line, which stretched from one end of her apartment to the other. She folded the shorts carefully and laid them on top of the stack of freshly laundered items that needed to be ironed. Then, she untied both ends of the line from the hooks on the wall and wrapped the rope in a circle around her hand. As she returned the rope and her basket of clothespins to the high shelf in the corner closet where she kept them, she heard footsteps approaching on the staircase. She waited, and, sure enough, there was a knock. She scurried to peek out the front window, then flung the door open wide. "Margie!" she squealed.

They hugged, and Livvie pulled her big sister into the apartment. "Were you running errands in town?" she asked, taking Margie's hat and hanging it on the coat tree.

"Just started," Margie said, setting her large purse on the floor. She fanned her face with her hand and blew upward at the gray hairs that had fallen into her face upon the removal of her hat. "I thought I'd stop by and see my favorite sister before heading over to McNarney Brothers for some groceries."

"Your *only* sister," Livvie muttered.

"I heard the first homegrown strawberries are starting to come in," Margie said. "Want me to pick you up some?"

Livvie's mouth watered at the thought of biting into a ripe strawberry. "That would be wonderful, but I can go get—"

"I thought I'd run over to that new candy shop that Mabel Simpson just opened on East Maple Street, too—what was it? Daydream Chocolates?" she droned. "Heaven knows I can make my own fudge, but Howard insisted I bring him home a couple of pounds, anyway—not that he needs it, mind you. I'll put some away for Alex and Nathan. I heard the little shop is doing quite well, and Howard wants to make sure we do our part to keep it that way. You know as well as anybody how hard it is to keep a new business afloat." Margie stopped for a breath and walked ahead of Livvie into the living room. "How is that new cook working out, by the way?" She plunked her rather plump frame into Livvie's sofa and mopped her damp brow. "My, oh my, it's hot!"

The month of June had ushered in another heat wave, making Livvie's upstairs apartment uncommonly warm, despite the cross breezes generated by all the open windows.

"I suppose he'll work out fine. Today was his first day alone, you know. I miss Joe terribly."

"Well, that's to be expected, honey, but I'm sure this new fellow will catch on quickly."

She wouldn't mention that he'd already made the kitchen his own by rearranging the pots, pans, and baking sheets and moving the utensils to a different drawer. Nor would she let on how efficient the restaurant had been through the breakfast and lunch rushes, even with an overabundance of customers and their potentially distracting introductions and greetings. The exception to the generally welcoming atmosphere, of course, had been Sheriff Morris. He wanted folks to view him as watchful and protective, so, naturally, every newcomer was met with suspicious glances and peppered with questions. She was actually surprised that the sheriff hadn't been more forthright with his interrogation. Even though Will had divulged a few details about his past to her, she sensed that he'd left much unsaid.

"What's he like, anyway?"

"What?"

"Your new cook. What's he like? How old is he?"

"I haven't—I don't exactly know. He has a big, bushy beard." *And disarming eyes and an extremely large, masculine frame.* "It's hard for me to guess his age."

"Is he married? Does he have children?"

"No, I don't believe so. He came here alone."

Margie arched an eyebrow. "He does have restaurant experience, right?"

"Yes, yes, of course. Apparently, he worked in some large establishment in New York."

"Apparently?" Margie's forehead wrinkled like a raisin. "You don't seem to know very much about this new employee, Liv."

It embarrassed her to admit the truth of her sister's statement. "Well, Joe talked to him, and I went on his recommendation. He seems to believe Will—er, Mr. Taylor will do a fine job."

"Ah. So, the two of you are on a first-name basis already?"

"It seemed appropriate, since we work together."

"Of course." Margie gave a slow sigh. "Well, I suppose I trust Joe's judgment."

Livvie perched on the edge of the chair across from Margie. "He plays the harmonica, not that it has anything to do with…anything, I guess. He took Alex and Nathan down to the river yesterday, and I went to check up on them—he didn't know it, of course—and I overheard him playing for the boys. The music he made with that little instrument struck me as quite melodic and, well, just plain lovely."

"Really. The harmonica." Margie cast a glance at the window, where the sheer white curtains had caught an updraft and danced in the breeze. "Didn't old Mr. Foxworthy, Papa's friend, play a mouth organ?"

"I have no idea, Margie. You remember much more about Mama and Papa than I do. The house burned when I was ten."

"Almost eleven. You really don't remember?"

Livvie gave her head a slow shake and thought again about the day in early spring some twenty-plus years ago. The haziest of memories flitted across her mind—memories of thick smoke, her eyes pinched shut to avoid the sting of it; of her papa's arms whisking her up from her bed, carrying her outside, and setting her on the ground, well away from the flaming house; of Papa's voice, instructing her firmly to stay put while he went back inside to fetch her mama. Little had she known, while watching his shadowy figure stumble back inside the two-story structure, that she'd never see him or her beloved mama again.

From that day forward, her sister and brother-in-law had been her adoptive parents. They'd raised her as their own, along with their two boys, Duane and Keith, who had always been more like younger brothers than nephews to her. "I wish I could remember more about my childhood, but my memories prior to the fire are just a lot of mush."

Margie gave a sullen nod and played with the folds of her cotton skirt. "I suppose a traumatic event such as a house fire will do that to a child—erase memories, whether good or bad."

"I sometimes wonder if that hasn't happened with my boys regarding Frank's accident. They seldom talk about him anymore, even though I try my best to keep his memory alive."

"I know, honey, but I'm sure they remember more than you think they do. Especially Alex. Maybe they just don't feel ready to talk about it. Sometimes, these things take months, even years."

Outside, a car horn honked, and another one answered. Impatient drivers! It was a wonder more folks weren't killed on the busy streets of Wabash, what with all the traffic coming and going and pedestrians crossing the street wherever they chose. The advent of automobiles in recent years had certainly done much to speed up society—as if folks weren't already scurrying about like ants at a picnic.

"I know you're right. And I appreciate all that Howard does for the boys. They need that male influence in their lives, and he's always so good with them."

"Yes, well, it's no trouble. I just wish we had more time to give. They truly are fine little men. You have the Lord to thank for that, you know."

She did know, but she couldn't bring herself to validate Margie's claim. It seemed that she'd wandered away from God's everlasting arms, and that getting back to them would take great effort. She nodded briefly.

Margie made a little sniff and smoothed out her skirt. "Well, I should probably be on my way. It was good seeing you. I'll stop by again soon and take you and the boys out to the farm."

Livvie rose with her sister and tried to smile, although her spirits had dipped low during the talk of her parents and the perilous fire and then Frank's accident. "That sounds nice. What do you hear from those boys of yours?"

Margie started making her way to the door, and Livvie followed. "Oh, those crazy boys. I haven't heard from either of them in over a month. I guess the armed services keep them too busy to write. At least, that's what they'd like me to believe."

She stopped at the coat tree and grabbed her hat. At that precise moment, the familiar sound of feet racing up the back staircase alerted the women that the boys were home from school. They fumbled with the lock, and then their excited voices filled the hallway, getting louder and louder, until the apartment door burst open. "Mommy!" Nathan exclaimed, barely taking notice of Margie's presence. "You won't believe it!"

"I won't?"

He and Alex were both gasping for air, their faces red and damp with sweat.

"Tell me, tell me!" she urged them, expecting to hear about some exciting event from their final week of school. She could barely believe that in the fall, Alex would be starting third grade, Nathan second grade.

Instead, they announced in unison, "Mr. Taylor shaved his beard!"

Chapter Nine

"For thou art not a God that hath pleasure
in wickedness: neither shall evil
dwell with thee."
—Psalm 5:4

Will ran a hand down his face, still trying to get accustomed to the smooth feel of his clean-shaven cheeks and chin. Man, if he'd known how much cooler he'd be minus all those whiskers, he would have shaved them off long ago.

He found himself whistling a tune as he scooped a spoonful of flour out of the canister and sprinkled it on the wooden block. He also floured his hands, then took the metal bowl of dough out of the refrigerator and scooped up the stiff, round glob. Whistling still, he laid the dough gingerly on the block, then pulled apart a section of dough and, with a rolling pin he'd rubbed with flour, started pressing it into a smooth, flat circle. Why, he could almost smell the piecrusts baking in the oven now.

The aroma would always remind him of the day when Harry had first demonstrated how to make a fruit pie. He'd sung hymn after hymn as he'd rolled the dough, Will working right alongside him, and they'd baked pies by the dozen in the big oven. Thanks to Harry's patient instruction, he'd learned a good deal about food preparation—and even more about the

Lord. Strange how the two had somehow ended up going hand in hand.

He wiped his brow with his forearm, then glanced at the clock on the far wall. Suppertime started in half an hour. Anytime now, customers would start milling about outside, waiting for Livvie or Cora Mae to unlock the door and flip the sign to "Open." He stopped whistling and grinned to himself as he wondered how folks would react to his clean-shaven face. Chuckling, he recalled the stunned expressions on Alex and Nathan's faces when they'd bounded through the back door about an hour ago and found him sweeping the floor.

"Who're you?" a wide-eyed Nathan had asked, halting his steps to stare at Will.

"Is that any way to greet the fellow who taught you how to skip rocks?" he'd asked, pausing to lean on his broom.

At that, both boys had dropped their chins, narrowed their eyes to mere slits, and slowly advanced, staring good and hard. "Is that you, Mr. Taylor?" Alex had asked, scratching the tip of his freckled nose.

"It looks like his body."

"It sounds like his voice."

"It's me, all right," he'd said, smiling broadly. "Got rid of that fur on my face. So, what do you think?"

Neither had stopped staring. "Your nose looks littler," Nathan had observed.

"My—my nose?"

"No it don't, silly," Alex had insisted, poking his brother. "It's the same nose. It's his mouth. You can see his mouth now—and his cheeks."

"Yeah," Nathan had said, his blue eyes flickering with awareness. "Yeah, I never seen his lips before—'cept when he played that little mouth piano. Then I seen a little bit of 'em."

"Organ, dummy. Mouth organ," Alex had corrected him.

Almost unconsciously, Will had touched his nose while they'd chattered on, and he wondered if it seemed unusually large to other people. He didn't care one way or the other, really; he was just curious. More than likely, the absence of his beard simply made everything about his face look different, including the size of his nose. He laughed now at their earnest observations.

Then, he wondered what their mother would say when she saw his new look. Since their first meeting, she'd made no bones about how much she disliked his facial hair. Would she think that he'd shaved it to make her happy? He certainly hoped not. The truth was, he wanted to keep Sheriff Morris off his back, and he'd figured a clean-shaven look would go far to accomplish that end.

On the stove, a kettle of vegetable beef soup and another of chicken noodle simmered, and, on the counter, fresh-baked loaves of bread cooled on metal racks. Tonight's supper would consist of the usual fare: soup, bread, and fried chicken with mashed potatoes or hamburgers with French fries. Will had not abandoned his hope of spicing up the menu with secret family recipes, especially since he feared that once folks' curiosity about the new cook had tapered off, so would the number of customers they saw on a nightly basis. Perhaps, he could talk to Livvie tonight, once she'd put her boys to bed. The sooner they made some changes, the sooner they could turn this little business around for the better. He hoped she'd agree.

❧

"Flo, bring us some more o' that moonshine!" Clem Dodd hollered to his wife in the kitchen. Across the room, Rudy and Hank lounged in run-down chairs, while the cigarettes that dangled from their mouths spewed rings of smoke that swirled over their heads. Truth be told, both fellows disgusted him, but a cord of crime kept them bound tight together. Since their first robbery—a jewelry store—they'd committed plenty of infractions and petty thefts, from late-night muggings in subway stations to midnight break-ins at various stores, taking whatever they could carry and exchanging it for cash at a pawn shop. Sure, they had daytime jobs, but not the kind that provided enough funds to feed their favorite habits: smoking, drinking, and gambling. Besides, they found enjoyment in the thrill of doing the crime but not the time. They were darned good at what they did, and getting better with age and experience. Even without experience, they'd gotten lucky in that jewelry store heist, except for the fact that Will Taylor had kept the loot. It was high time they caught up with him and found out where he'd stashed the goods.

Florence entered the living room, carrying a tray of drinks. Her hair fell forward over her cheeks, probably in an attempt to hide the bruise he'd put on her left one after she'd mouthed off to him the night before. Fool woman didn't know when to shut her trap. They'd had another knock-down-drag-out after she'd put her kid to bed. He wasn't about to admit to the boys that he had a good-sized bump on his own head, which he'd had to nurse with a bag of ice. They'd never let him live it down.

He was getting plain sick of Flo, especially since she'd gotten bold and started dishing back his blows.

Their fights almost always had to do with money—she'd complain that he gambled away all his earnings; he'd tell her to go out and get a job. They generally wound up reducing each other's characters to squat, too, using the worst kinds of names and getting some kind of sick pleasure from it.

Flo set the bottle of home-brewed liquor on the coffee table without speaking to Clem or meeting his eyes. Good. At least she'd heard him on that count. "Keep your fat mouth shut when the fellas come over," he'd told her this morning. "You poke your nose in where it don't belong, and I'll cut it off, you hear?"

Apparently, she had, for she'd holed up in the kitchen and worked on the evening meal, having sent Eddie to her mother's house for the night.

Clem watched her leave the room. When she was out of earshot, he said, "I came up with a plan."

"Yeah?" Hank flicked his cigarette and lifted an eyebrow. "I bet it's just brilliant."

He ignored the jab. "I'll head to Wabash on my own and see if I can figure out what Taylor's up to."

"I thought you wanted all three of us to go," Rudy said.

"You both whined about havin' to leave your pathetic jobs, remember? I been giving it some thought, and it prob'ly wouldn't make sense for all three of us to traipse off to Indiana till we know what's what. I'll go on ahead, figure out where Taylor's hangin' 'is hat, and see if he's carousin' with anybody in particular. If I see anythin' suspicious, I'll call you and tell you to get your behinds to Wabash. I won't confront 'im on my own."

Hank lifted a corner of his lip and snorted, his eyes gone dark. "And what if you don't learn a blessed thing? What if our old friend is mindin' 'is manners? Could be prison taught 'im a thing or two."

Clem reached over to the coffee table and refilled his glass. Then, he brought it to his lips and took a long swig of the liquid, which sizzled like fire all the way down. He nearly choked, but he breathed deeply and gathered his wits as he waited for the burn to subside. "Then, I s'pose I'll come on back here."

"Yeah, right." Hank emitted a nervous cluck. "You're just lookin' for a way to escape that biddy out in the kitchen, and Wabash is soundin' pretty good about now. Don't matter that you know nothin' 'bout the place. You just wanna disappear."

"Don't be stupid," Clem spat. But, even as he hissed the words, he knew Hank's statement rang true.

❀

Livvie couldn't help stealing hurried glances at Will Taylor throughout the supper hour. Since shaving that shaggy rug off his face, he was just about the handsomest man she'd ever laid eyes on—with the exception of her Frank, of course. Gracious! What business did she have noticing another man's good looks? She had sworn to love Frank and no other till she took her dying breath, and not even Will Taylor's square-set face, wavy brown hair, striking blue eyes, and generous mouth would stop her from keeping that promise.

Meanwhile, Cora Mae hadn't excused herself for swooning over his absent beard. She'd made an utter fool of herself, going so far as to make Will blush. "I had no idea there was a fine-looking face under all that bushiness, Mr. Taylor," she'd crooned. "Why, if I were twenty years younger—"

"Cora Mae Livingston, behave yourself!" Livvie had scolded her. The woman's lack of delicacy was embarrassing.

Will had thrown Livvie a fleeting smile, and she'd noticed a twinkle in his eyes. She'd figured he was waiting to see what she'd have to say about his beardless face.

Of course, she'd said nothing, not wanting him to think it mattered one whit. He must have known that it did, though, considering how adamantly she'd encouraged him to shave. She should have thanked him for obliging her, but her pride wouldn't allow it.

At six o'clock, Charley Arnold and Roy Scott strolled in, cigarettes hanging from their mouths. Ire and dread immediately rose in her chest. She hadn't seen them in a good week and had secretly hoped they'd chosen another café, where they could puff away till the cows came home.

"Hello, boys," she greeted them, struggling to put on a friendly façade. "I have an open table right here by the door. I'd appreciate it if you'd put out those smokes before you settle in, though. You know good and well I have a no-smoking policy. This is a family restaurant."

Scowling, Charley tilted his middle-aged face at her. "It ain't right, Liv, you bein' th' only restaurant in town that don't allow it. I can't hardly enjoy a cup o' coffee without my smokes. You know that."

"Then, you may go elsewhere."

"But you got good eats here." His gaze filtered past the room of customers to the kitchen. At that moment, Will Taylor glanced up. "Well, I'll be hanged. He shaved off that beard. He sure looks diff'rent."

"Yes, he does," Livvie confirmed. "Now, would you please extinguish those disgusting things before they create a cloud in my restaurant?"

Neither man made a move to heed her request; they just ambled over to the table she'd pointed out and pulled out two chairs. She gave a loud sigh. "Don't sit down until you've stomped out those smokes on the sidewalk, please."

Cora Mae approached the table, pencil tucked behind her ear, pad of paper in hand. "Oh, leave 'em be, Liv. They're not botherin' anybody."

"They're bothering me," she maintained, "and they both know it." She appreciated Cora Mae's efforts to keep the peace, but this was one area where she refused to compromise. "Why do you two have to be so blamed stubborn?"

Roy chuckled and reached out to touch her bare arm.

She immediately wrenched it away and glared at him.

"Sorry, Livvie. We don't mean no harm. We just can't see the trouble in lightin' up."

"The trouble is, you're ill-mannered boors who can't abide one simple rule." Roy wasn't a bad-looking man, but his conduct was certainly lacking.

"What d'you fellas want for supper, anyway?" Cora Mae asked, snatching her pencil and preparing to write.

"Cora Mae, we're not serving them."

The men sat down in their chairs, which galled Livvie to her core, considering that she'd just told them not to sit. Was there anyone with a brain smaller than these two jellyheads'?

They narrowed their eyes to peruse the menu. "How's that new cook at fryin' burgers?" Charley asked.

"I'm doggone good," bellowed a voice that made the place fall silent. Clanging forks and knives quieted, and even the Pryors' four-month-old baby hushed her burbling. Livvie turned around and met Will's sterling eyes. He stepped between her and Cora Mae and extended a hand. "Will Taylor," he stated.

Roy pushed back his chair and rose, taking his hand. "Roy Scott's the name."

Charley remained in his seat but shook Will's hand when he thrust it under his nose. "Charley Arnold," he muttered coolly.

Neither man measured up to Will's stature. Surely, they'd noticed. Roy lowered himself into his seat again. "We been in here a time or two to sample your cookin'. It ain't bad," he said with a shrug.

"Yeah, I saw you last week," Will replied. "So, you want a hamburger, do you?" He stepped closer and rested his fists on the table.

Charley grinned. "Sure."

"With lettuce, tomato, and onion?"

"You bet. And a slab o' cheese, if you don't mind."

Will shook his head. "Don't mind at all. You want some thick fries to go with that? I make 'em extra greasy."

Charley relaxed and licked his lips. "Yeah, sure. That'd be great. And a tall, ice-cold Coke."

Will turned to Roy. "The same for you?"

Grinning with satisfaction, Roy nodded.

"There's only one problem, I'm afraid," Will said, stepping back and folding his arms across his chest.

"Yeah?" Roy said. "What's that?"

Will smiled, but not warmly. "These." As quick as a hawk swooping down on its prey, he seized the cigarettes from Charley and Roy's mouths, dropped them on the floor, and squished one under each of his boots. In the next move, he had both men by the fronts of their collars, so that their roundish guts were pressed against the edges of the table. The whole sequence happened in a flash, and, from the flurry of gasps and whispered remarks she heard from around the room, Livvie almost believed that she'd hired a magician instead of a cook.

His wry expression unwavering, Will said, just as cool as could be, "You won't mind not smoking while you eat, now, will you?"

Charley and Roy remained speechless for what seemed like a minute but actually amounted to about five seconds. Then, they quickly shook their heads, their faces flushed with embarrassment.

Cora Mae stood back and beamed like a harvest moon.

"Good. That's real good." Will relaxed his hold on them and brushed off their shirtfronts as they heaved loud breaths. "We sure do want your business, fellas, but I'm afraid we can't take it if you insist on smoking in the restaurant. A rule's a rule, after all. Agreed?"

In response, he got several hurried nods and two pairs of wide eyes staring back at him.

With that, Will turned and walked back toward the kitchen, his demeanor unflappable, even as hushed murmurings and bemused smiles circulated the room.

Fifteen minutes before closing time, Livvie starting helping Will with the cleanup process. She'd allowed Cora Mae to leave early, as she was expecting a cousin from Kansas. The restaurant was quiet, with only a smattering of patrons who lingered. Alex and Nathan had gone shopping with Margie that afternoon, and she'd offered to let them spend the night, assuring Livvie that she'd drive them to school in the morning. Tomorrow was the last day of classes—a half day, at that—so, they were wound tighter than drums. As much as Livvie enjoyed the peaceful silence, she looked forward to when they would come galloping home tomorrow afternoon in a flurry of excitement.

Will stood at the sink, scrubbing a soup kettle, and the sight of his muscles flexing where his short sleeves ended set off a strange, prickly sensation in Livvie's stomach. She tried to ignore it. "I want to thank you for what you did earlier," she said to Will's back.

He turned at the sound of her voice. "You mean with those two lugs? Pfff, they just needed a little reminding."

"I've been reminding them ever since Frank died. I guess, because I'm a single woman, they think they can push me around."

"Joe never did anything about it?"

"Joe was too easygoing to make much of a fuss about anything. I think he thought my no-smoking rule was a bit harsh. But I just can't abide the smell. Never could."

"It's your right to set the rules, Livvie." He wrung out the dishcloth and draped it over the side of the deep sink, then swiveled his body and leaned back against the counter. "All right, listen. Joe had his ways; I have mine. If you want to maintain this no-smoking rule, then I'll see that your customers comply."

A rush of gratitude skittered through her veins. "I appreciate that. Don't want you thinking you have to look after me, though. I've been taking care of myself for more than a year now."

For a moment, he regarded her with assessing eyes, then crossed his arms over his wide chest and arched a thick, dark eyebrow. "Managing just fine, are you?"

Shifting her weight, she looked him in the eye. "Most of the time, yes."

He rubbed his jaw, and, for a fleeting instant, she wondered at its smoothness. "I been thinking," he said. "You remember when you hired me, how I said that maybe you and I could work together on some ways to turn this little business around for you? Financially, I mean."

"Yes. What about it?"

"Well, I've come up with an idea or two. Wondered if I might bounce them off you tonight after we close up. I was thinking we could wait till you put your boys to bed, but, since you say they're spending the night at your sister's house, well, maybe we could just sit down here after closing time and bat some thoughts around."

"I...I guess we could do that."

Of course, she welcomed his wish to help her. How fortunate to have hired someone with genuine interest in seeing her little establishment succeed. Joe had been of the same mind, but he'd always made it clear that his employment at Livvie's Kitchen was only temporary. His primary goal had been to keep the restaurant afloat until she could find a replacement, not to invest time and effort for its future success.

The problem was, she didn't want Will Taylor going out of his way on her behalf. He owed her nothing, and vice versa. Still, it wouldn't hurt to hear him out, and having the boys gone for the night certainly afforded her the time.

"Great. I'll put on a fresh pot of coffee, then." He turned around and resumed washing dishes. "How 'bout a warm slice of pie while we're at it? You could stand to put a little meat on those bones."

So, he'd taken note of her figure, had he? Truth be told, she was as skinny as a fence post, no matter that she almost always had food at her fingertips. Ever since Frank's death, her appetite had been small, her passion for food diminished. "I'll try a piece, yes."

"Strawberry, blueberry, or peach?"

"Oh, my! So many choices." She considered them. "Strawberry, please."

He turned and smiled at her, his eyes crinkling at the corners. Mercy, but her stomach should not have tumbled at the sight!

Chapter Ten

*"These things I have spoken unto you,
that in me ye might have peace. In the world
ye shall have tribulation: but be of good
cheer; I have overcome the world."*
—John 16:33

"So, I was thinking we could provide a complimentary meal to the family the night we use their secret recipe," Will said to conclude his spiel about how they could attract more customers by cooking up long-cherished family recipes. He sat with Livvie at a table along the wall across from the bar area, where they'd been since closing the restaurant half an hour ago.

Livvie didn't answer immediately, and Will figured she needed time to process his idea. With his fork, he sectioned off another morsel of strawberry pie and let it melt in his mouth, then washed it down with a swig of hot coffee. Outside, a couple of dogs barked, a car horn honked, and a whistle announced an arriving train.

Finally, Livvie set down her fork and furrowed her brow. "A free meal for an entire family? Are you kidding? Some of these folks have swarms of kids."

"It'll be good for business," he rushed to say. "How's the pie?"

"Giving away food is good for business?" She blinked. "Oh, the pie's excellent, thanks."

"It's a gimmick, don't you see? The minute people find out about what we're doing, they'll start submitting their family recipes. Of course, I'll have to weed through them, decide which ones are worth trying, cook them up, and then use you and the boys and Cora Mae, maybe even Coot, as taste testers. We'll put it to a vote, choose a weekly winner, maybe even two a week, and then start advertising."

"Advertising?"

"Yeah. Maybe we could get your boys to make some big, colorful signs for the windows, their being on summer vacation and all. Making this a family venture would add interest. We want diners coming out in droves to taste the featured recipe, so we'll need to drum up some excitement. We could even get some ads printed up in the *Daily Plain Dealer*."

Livvie pinched the bridge of her nose and pressed her lips tightly together, causing her dimples to sprout. His stomach took a strange tumble. "Ads cost money," she reminded him. "Something that doesn't flow all that freely around here."

"Sometimes, you have to invest a little capital before reaping the rewards. I realize it's a gamble, but you'll never know if you don't give it a shot."

She thrummed her fingers on the tabletop and stared at him.

He stared back, lapping up the look of her hazel eyes, which gleamed with a hint of eagerness. He held his breath while awaiting her answer.

"How do you propose getting started?" She stilled her fingers, picked up her fork, and speared a piece of strawberry pie.

He started breathing again. "Well, I've already selected the first winning recipe."

Her pretty lashes flew up. "You have? Whose?"

"Clara Gillen's baked chicken. Do you know her?"

"I do, but how...?"

He went on to tell her how the Gillens had invited
him to dine with them following the Sunday service
several weeks ago, how Clara Gillen had wound up
sharing her grandmother's recipe for baked chicken
with him, and how he'd promised to use it without
ever divulging the secret. Livvie started chewing with
purpose, then quickly swallowed and cut off another
portion of pie. She then raised her coffee cup to her
lips and gazed at him over the rim. A glimmer of interest sparked more noticeably in her eyes, and he
could sense her resolve caving in like the walls of
Jericho.

"I know Norm Maloney, who works at the newspaper. He's a good friend of my brother-in-law," she
offered. "I'm sure he'd help with the ad."

"That's the spirit!"

"And Alex and Nate would get a charge out of
making signs for the windows. As I do every summer,
I've hired a high school girl to look after them while I'm
working. I'm sure she'd be happy to help, too."

He enjoyed watching her enthusiasm grow. It lit
her cheeks with a rosy hue and made her speak faster.
"And, if we get an influx of customers, I suppose offering a free meal to the family whose recipe we're featur-
ing won't really hurt our budget. I'm starting to think
this could work."

"Now you're talking!"

Before he knew it, she'd polished off her pie and
set her empty cup back in its saucer. He nodded at her

plate. "You want another piece?" he asked. "How 'bout some more coffee?"

"No, no, I'm fine, but thank you," she said with a sweep of her hand. Then, she angled him an inquisitive look and opened her mouth, only to clamp it shut again.

"You were about to say something?"

"Oh! Well...." She wrinkled her nose and shook her head. "It was nothing, really."

He wrapped his hands around his coffee mug and dipped his chin. "Seriously, what did you want to say?"

She blushed. "I just wanted to say, you...um, I like your...you know." She waved a finger at his face.

He stroked his bare jaw and gave a shameless grin. "You like the new look, do you? Well, don't go thinking I did it for you just because you hinted—more like blatantly told me—that you hated my beard."

"I didn't say I hated it, exactly."

"Well, you may as well have. Anyway, I've had the shaggy thing for years. It was time, and you were right—we don't need people complaining about finding whiskers in their soup."

They shared a pleasant round of laughter, after which they both had trouble deciding where to point their gazes. Livvie looked out the window, and Will glanced down at his fraying sleeve. It was almost time to make another trip to the Salvation Army store.

After a few more seconds of silence, Livvie spoke. "I'm still a little surprised to hear you go to church every Sunday."

"Really? Why do you say that?"

She rested her chin in her clasped hands. "I don't know; I guess I just didn't figure you for the churchgoing type when I first met you. You looked like—"

"A bum?" he supplied.

A sheepish smile caused her dimples to emerge. "The thought crossed my mind."

He let her statement hang between them for a moment. Then, he said, "I started attending regularly some months ago, when I made a decision to turn my life around. I told you about that."

"Yes, you mentioned it."

"God's got a long ways to go with me before He'll be halfway satisfied, though, I'll tell you that."

She looked down and brushed a few crumbs off the table. He lowered his chin again, trying to meet her eyes. "You ought to be taking those boys to church, you know."

Livvie looked up sharply. "You sound like my sister, Margie. She's forever preaching at me. 'They'll grow up to be hoodlums,' she says. 'You best teach them the ways of the Lord, Olivia Beth.'" She sobered and fumbled with her napkin, which she had refolded on the table. "I may start up again. Who knows?"

"May I ask what's keeping you from attending?"

Her brow pulled into a firm frown, and she straightened her slender shoulders. "I have a hard time figuring out how a good God could snuff out the life of a man in his prime, especially when he has two young sons who need him."

Will arched his eyebrows and brushed away the strands of hair that hung across his forehead. "You're not the only one who's asked that sort of question. Shoot, I've asked it myself. All I can say is, it's a matter of trust...Olivia Beth." He couldn't resist saying her middle name, now that he knew it.

She shrugged. "It's hard to trust someone who's let you down."

He leaned back, sizing her up. "I used to think the same—that God had let me down. But I've since learned that His love is much bigger than all my doubts. I'd rather believe in His all-knowing ways and constant presence than be floundering around with no real purpose or sense of peace about tomorrow."

A mystified expression washed over her face, and she looked thoughtful for a moment. Her burnished hair, held back loosely on each side with a silver barrette, fell across her delicate shoulders, and Will had a strong urge to reach across the table and examine its texture. To ward off the foolish temptation, he dropped his hands to his knees.

"After my parents died, my sister mostly raised me, so she's the one who kept me on the straight and narrow. And then came Frank, the finest Christian man I know." Livvie paused. "You said that your relationship with your parents soured when you were young. So, who tutored you in the ways of the Lord?"

Her question was fair, to be certain, but how to answer it without divulging too much information gave him pause. "Well, like I said, I've been going to church the past several months." *Starting with the prison chapel.* "So, I suppose I learned a great deal from listening to the preacher." *And the chaplain at Welfare Island.* "That, and reading my Bible." *And allowing Harry's words to soak deep into my soul.* "How'd your parents die?" he decided to ask. Instantly, he wished he'd had more tact, but Livvie didn't seem to mind.

"In a house fire when I was ten," she stated matter-of-factly, as if reporting the daily weather forecast. "My papa woke me from a sound sleep and hauled me out of our burning house. When he ran back inside to get my mama, he never came back out."

A shiver skipped up his spine as he imagined the crippling fear she must have endured while she waited for a glimpse of her parents, followed by the overwhelming grief of realizing they weren't coming out. "That had to be terrible for you," he finally said.

She fumbled with her napkin and shrugged one shoulder. "I've had plenty of years to deal with it. My sister was an amazing second mother to me, stricter than my own mama, but only because she carried such a weight of responsibility on her shoulders. Losing my husband was probably worse than losing my parents. Is that an awful thing to say?"

"Not at all. One day, you're raising kids together, and the next, you're alone, trying to figure out how to be both Mommy and Daddy to your sons, not to mention struggling to run a business and bring in enough money to support the three of you. That's tough."

She sniffed and raised her napkin to dab her eyes, which brimmed with moisture. "Please, let's not talk about me anymore."

He grinned and couldn't resist reaching across the table to touch the tip of her nose. "Then, what shall we talk about?"

She gave a tentative smile. "You."

"Me? No, I'm boring."

"Tell me about the restaurant where you worked in New York."

She sure could be a persistent little thing. "There's not much to tell."

"Well, why did you leave it—and New York, for that matter?"

He gave a long, laborious sigh, fiddled with the edge of his cloth napkin, and tapped his boot under the table. "I got tired of the big city—the sights, the sounds, the smells, the massive crowds of people—so, I jumped a train and came to Wabash." He grinned. "Is that good enough?"

Her expression sobered. "Jumped? As in, didn't pay for your ticket?"

"Yep. No secrets there. Rode in a freight car with a bunch of bums."

A frown flitted across her features. "Oh, yes. I'd forgotten. But you had a job in a fine restaurant...."

"I never said it was fine. It was a job, and that's all. Nothing special about it."

"But I thought Joe—"

He sucked in a deep breath. "I got a lot of practice and honed my skills, but that's about it."

"What about the name of the restaurant?" Blamed if she wasn't a nosy little doe. But then, he could hardly fault her. It still rocked his boots off that she'd hired him at all, hobo that he'd been—and probably still was in her eyes.

"The name slips my mind," he fibbed. "You see, we mostly called it by a nickname, and there were lots of those."

"Really? That's strange. I still remember the name of the first place I got a job. The Lukens Lake Hotel. I was a senior in high school, trying to earn some money for college. Little did I know I'd meet Frank that summer at a church picnic, and he'd sweep me straight off my feet before I had the chance to entertain one more notion of college." A faint grin played around her pretty lips, just enough to tease her dimples out. "My, that was a long time ago. Anyway, that was my first job—and I remember the name of the place like it's imprinted on the back of my hand or something." She paused. "Well, what were the nicknames you used for the establishment?"

How quickly the tide changed! One minute, they were discussing how to attract new clientele to the restaurant, and the next minute, she was trying to elicit details about his past. To avoid further inquiries, he stood up and feigned a yawn. "I think I'll turn in, Olivia Beth. Cute name, by the way." He tried to steal one last glimpse at her dimples, but they had vanished. "I'm anxious to get this new venture off the ground. I'm glad you're on board with it."

She flicked an imaginary crumb off the table. "You do carry around your share of secrets, don't you, Will Taylor?"

"Does it bother you that you don't know everything there is to know about me?"

"Not in the least. I just want to be sure you aren't hiding something that might create problems later."

"I wouldn't want that, either." He reached inside his pocket and drew out his pocket watch. "It's getting late. You want me to walk you up the back stairs?"

"I've been walking myself up those stairs for well over a year now, Mr. Taylor. I think I can manage."

"So, we're back on formal terms, are we?"

She drummed her nails on the tabletop and cast him a brittle smile. "Good night."

He nodded and left her sitting there by the window, where dusky sunlight sifted in and cast long shadows around the room. It took all his willpower to keep from turning around to see if she watched him walk away. Ten to one, she had her gaze pinned on his back, probably with eyes narrowed, as she speculated about the secrets he kept. My, how Olivia Beckman intrigued him, tested him, amused him, attracted him, and scared him willy-nilly. She came from a completely different world from him, and they had next to nothing in common. Darned if she wasn't a captivating, refined, independent woman with two sweet sons, and he an ex-con!

What could she ever want to do with a man like him?

❧

The days that followed went by in the usual flurry of busyness. Livvie decided to lay off probing Will for secrets from his past, at least for now. Everybody seemed to take to him like a pup to its littermate, and Coot Hermanson, whose opinion she valued above most others, had nothing but glowing things to say about him. "He's a fine cook. Likable, too," he'd said one afternoon when she had stopped at his table to chat during a lull. "Looks to me like you picked a winner, Liv."

"I had very little to do with picking him. Joe's the one who talked me into it."

"You don't sound completely sold."

She'd leaned across his table and shoved a damp cloth over the surface, wanting to appear busy. "He's so tight-lipped about his past, Coot. Makes me wonder if he's hiding something important."

With a harrumph, he'd pulled at the sparse whiskers on his chin. "I wouldn't worry. From what I know of him, he's a fine Christian man."

"With secrets."

"Oh, most people have secrets. He's not obliged to tell you everything about himself, is he?"

She'd rubbed an aching spot at the base of her spine. "I guess you're right. As long as he keeps my customers coming back, it shouldn't matter."

And keep customers coming back he did, especially when his new plan was put in motion. As predicted, Alex and Nate had jumped at the chance to create signs to advertise the family recipe campaign, which they had decided to call Family Feast. With the help of Sally Morgan, the girl Livvie had hired to watch them during the day, they had made posters to fill the windows. Sally, a cheerful, chubby girl with a saucy sense of humor, was the perfect match for her sons' vibrant personalities and boundless energy. She did the lettering and most of the artwork on the posters, and Alex and Nate added color with every crayon in their box of Crayolas. Already, folks were talking about the Family Feast and whispering among themselves about certain recipes they felt confident would qualify.

After much discussion between Cora Mae, Coot, Will, and herself, plus some input from Sally and the boys, they'd come up with a slogan—"We'll Test It, You Taste It!"—and a start-up date of Tuesday, June 29. With Norm Maloney's help in phrasing, Livvie had placed an advertisement in the *Daily Plain Dealer* with a headline that read, "Family Feast: An Eating Extravaganza at Livvie's Kitchen Every Tuesday and Thursday Night." The ad explained the rules simply: folks could drop off a copy of a treasured family recipe in the decorated box by the door, and, every week, Olivia Beckman and Will Taylor, the new cook, would sift through them, select the front-runners, test them out, and then vote to determine the best one. Winners would receive a free meal for the entire family and some royal treatment, as well—a harmonica serenade by Mr. Taylor, provided he wasn't too busy at the stove. All were welcome to enjoy the featured meal on these special nights for a flat fee of $3.50 per family. The remaining weeknights would be business as usual.

Livvie only hoped that the event would live up to its name.

⚜

Clem could hardly believe he'd come all the way from New York City to this squirrelly place. Stupid town hardly qualified as a metropolis. It had a few main streets, a city hall, a library, a train station, and some grocery stores. "What a Podunk place," he grumbled to himself as he scuffed along Market Street past the Hotel Indiana on Friday evening. He'd been here exactly three days and, so far, hadn't run across one measly piece of evidence that Will Taylor was about. He'd wandered by service stations, hobby shops, and meat markets; he'd even lurked around a few factories and watched the workers come and go between shifts, but there'd been no sign of him. Shoot, Clem had begun to worry that, even if he saw the guy, he wouldn't recognize him. It'd been ten years, after all.

He reached up to feel the wound inflicted by Florence when she'd hurled that brass candlestick across the room at him during their last scrap. Blasted woman had been madder than a junkyard dog when he'd told her he was cutting out, which hadn't made a jot of sense to him. Considering how much they hated each other, he would have thought she'd be glad to see him go. Of course, it was his money she'd miss. "Who's gonna buy our groceries an' pay our rent?" the fat wench had wailed. Clem kicked a twig out of his path and sauntered on, grousing at the memory of her hitting him square alongside the face and leaving a gash so deep, he probably should have had the doc stitch it up. Then, he snickered, recalling how he'd charged at her and grabbed a wad of her straggly hair, thrown her to the floor, and kicked her in the gut.

Horses trotted and cars whizzed up and down the street, while other pedestrians crossed wherever they could find a gap in the traffic. Clem stopped at the corner of Market and Miami, crossed the street, and headed for a little diner called Fred's Place. It looked like a dive, which suited his budget fine. Man, he missed his own moonshine. He'd have to ask around to see where he could buy some fresh booze.

Fred Place's was dark and dreary inside—and mostly empty. He had a feeling Fred couldn't afford the electric bill. "Howdy," came a voice. A shrimpy-sized fellow emerged from the bar, behind which the wall was lined with empty shelves. Blamed Prohibition! The guy wore an apron that was stained red, probably from raw meat, and his thin, white mustache matched his balding head of hair. "Help ya?"

"Yeah, I could use some supper. You must be Fred, eh?"

"That's me. Take a seat anywhere ya please." The fellow gave him a closer glance. "Geez-oh-Pete, who'd ya meet up with, mister? That's a nasty-lookin' cut ya got there."

He was getting plenty sick of the remarks complete strangers made about his face. For the hundredth time, he touched his palm to the tender, swollen wound. "This? Oh, couple o' cans toppled off a shelf and fell on me."

Fred shook his head and gave him the sympathetic stare he'd grown accustomed to seeing. "That had to've smarted."

"Yeah." Clem noticed a couple of other diners seated toward the back of the room, and one in the middle, across from the kitchen, who glanced up from his newspaper. Clem averted his eyes and shuffled to a table against the wall, then pulled out a chair and sat down.

"I ain't got much of a menu selection," Fred said, ambling over to the table. He handed Clem a soiled sheet of paper with a few items listed on it. But Clem didn't need to see "Vegetable beef stew" to know it was an option; the aroma filled the restaurant, and his stomach let out a quiet growl. "You'll see a bunch o' stuff got scratched off. I'll be closin' down my place in the next month or so."

"That right? Business is bad, eh?"

"Competition's pretty stiff. Wabash has its fair share o' restaurants and diners. In its time, my place was thrivin' pretty good, back before the stinkin' gover'ment banned booze sales."

"I hear you. Most harebrained thing they could've done, passin' that eighteenth 'mendment." He glanced at the long, empty bar. "This used to be a saloon, did it?"

"Sure 'nough. Folks said I oughtta make the best o' things, step up my cookin' skills an' such, but I never took much interest. Well, now I'm payin' for it. Yep, we'll be closin' 'er down end o' July. The missus and me are movin' to Texas, where our three kids settled a few years ago. My son says he's got a job for me in some factory. S'pose that's where we'll live out the rest of our days."

The fellow liked to talk. "I'll take some of that stew."

"The stew, huh? Good choice."

He didn't have much of a choice, as far as he could see. As he handed the menu back to Fred, he leaned forward and whispered, "You wouldn't happen to know where I might get me some home-brewed booze, would you?"

Fred jerked back, and his shoulders went as straight as boards. "No way, mister. I keep my nose clean."

"Oh, 'course you do. I'm not questionin' that one bit. No, sir. I just thought you might know of someone who...you know...but never mind. Sorry I asked. I'll take a Coca-Cola, if you've got it."

Shaking his head, Fred walked away and disappeared into the kitchen. Several minutes later, he returned, carrying a tray. In front of Clem, he set a bowl of steaming stew, a few packets of crackers, and a tall glass of soda with a straw.

"Don't mean to keep botherin' you, but you ever hear of a Will Taylor?" Clem asked. "Moved here a few weeks ago, I believe."

Fred scratched his chin, which looked as if it hadn't seen a razor in a few days, and frowned. "Can't say I have. Sorry 'bout that. It's a big town, though."

"Yeah, big town," Clem muttered.

He nearly inhaled the stew and asked for several refills of Coca-Cola. When he was almost finished, Fred brought him a newspaper. "It's a day old. I nearly tossed it, but then, I got to thinkin' ya might like to read 'bout the local news. Where ya from, by the way? Ya never did say."

He wasn't about to tell the guy squat about himself. "Oh, around. I'm just passin' through, actually. Good stew, by the way. I like the seasonin' you put in it."

"Ya like that? It's a combination o' spices 'n' herbs, a recipe I perfected with lots o' practice. 'Bout the only thing I can make good, though. Umm...." He looked in either direction, then tossed a folded piece of paper onto the table. "That there's a place where you can go to get ya some booze," he muttered under his breath. "Ya never heard it from me, though, ya got that?"

Clem reached up and slid the paper off the table, stuffing it quickly inside his shirt pocket. "Much obliged," he murmured in return.

Just then, the door opened, and both men turned. An armed officer strolled slowly toward them.

Fred stiffened. "Howdy, Sheriff."

As he always did whenever he laid eyes on the law, Clem tried to make himself invisible. He lowered his head and used the newspaper as his shield.

Fred cleared his throat and gave Clem a sidelong glance. "Excuse me, mister, but I got to tend to the sheriff. He comes in here most every night for my stew."

Clem nodded. "You go right ahead." He patted his pocket. "Thanks for...the newspaper."

The sheriff passed by with nary a look in his direction, his boots thudding beneath his bulky frame.

Clem relaxed a little and let his eyes fall on the rumpled periodical. He digested the first headline, skimmed over the article about some recipe contest at a place called Livvie's Kitchen, and then nearly choked on his soda when the words started registering. "Well, I'll be a mule's hiney," he muttered to himself. "I found the slimy so-and-so."

Chapter Eleven

"Let thy mercies come also unto me, O LORD,
even thy salvation, according to thy word."
—Psalm 119:41

*B*usiness was slow on Saturday, but what had Livvie expected? It was a spotless, sunny day, and almost everyone was outside, picnicking by the river, chasing butterflies, fishing, boating, working in the garden, or otherwise enjoying the weather. The boys had gone to Margie's house for the day, unable to pass up their uncle's invitation to take a ride on his tractor.

When Margie had offered to keep them overnight and take them to church in the morning, Livvie had relented. She knew she ought to be the one taking them to Sunday school and church, but she was secretly glad to have her sister do it, instead. When Frank was alive, they hadn't missed a single Sunday, and he'd be having fits about now if he knew how lax she'd grown since then. Why, her Bible had even collected a layer of dust. Not for the first time, she shoved down the mound of guilt that pressed at her heart's door. Somehow, a seed of bitterness had sprouted within her toward all things spiritual, and she couldn't seem to uproot it.

After saying good night to Emmett Wilson, her final customer, Livvie closed the door behind him and locked it, then flipped the sign around. As she did so, she glanced out the window and noticed a fellow leaning against a lamppost not ten feet away, his legs crossed at the ankle, a cigarette hanging out of the corner of his mouth. Something about him caused a lump to form in the pit of her stomach, and her discomfort grew when he made eye contact with her, touched the brim of his hat, and tipped his chin. He wore a tattered shirt, baggy denim overalls, and big boots, but his most salient feature was the deep gash on his left cheek.

She tried to tell herself that she had nothing to fear, that he was just being friendly, but the fellow kept staring, as if he meant to have a word with her. It was hard to imagine what he'd say, though, as she had never seen him before. A tiny shiver started at the base of her neck and shimmied down her spine. She averted her gaze to a boy darting across the street with his dog. When she peeked again at the peculiar man, he hadn't shifted his stance, but he now wore a leering smirk. As quick as she could, she jerked the window shade down.

"Something wrong?"

Her body jolted at the sound of Will's voice. She'd thought he was still in the kitchen, cleaning up from supper.

He chuckled. "Didn't mean to startle you. Why'd you pull that shade down so fast?"

She frowned. "A stranger was gawking at me. It's probably nothing, but, still, it gave me a fright. He's standing out there still."

One of Will's thick eyebrows jutted upward. "A stranger? Gawking?" He advanced to the door in two long strides and lifted the shade. "Humph. I don't see anyone." He stepped aside to the front window and peeked out through the horizontal slats in the blinds. "Nope, no one out there."

She hastened to his side and looked through the dusty pane herself. Sure enough, the guy had vanished. "He was right there—big as a gorilla, I swear—leaning against that lamppost and staring at me like he knew some sort of secret. He had a cigarette in his mouth." Desperation to make him believe her gushed through her like a fast-moving stream. "And—and he had a big purple gash on his cheek. Right here." She pointed at the left side of her face and peered up into Will's crystalline eyes.

Will set his hands on her shoulders, giving her a steadying squeeze as he bent close. "Shh, it's all right, Livvie. You don't have to try to convince me. I believe you, okay? It's just that he's not there now."

"Oh." She hushed, finding herself wholly aware of his hands on her shoulders. She couldn't tear her eyes away from his soft, comforting gaze, and another shiver, albeit one of a pleasant nature, created a wave of goose pimples over her arms. *Lord, his hands feel so tingly and...pleasant.* She was shocked by her own silent admission. Even more shocking was that, when she should have stepped away from the man's touch, she stood cemented to the ground, almost statue-like, helpless to move an inch.

"What did he look like?" Will asked. His voice was so low, it seemed to come from a distant room.

"What?"

His breath touched her cheek, and another dizzying chill streaked through her.

"The man, did he look at all familiar?"

"No, I've never seen him before."

"Well, maybe he just wanted something to eat. He probably saw you lock the door and turn the sign over. Maybe he—"

"It wasn't like that," she insisted. "I saw a certain look in his eyes."

"A certain look."

"Yes. Very strange and mysterious."

His hands brushed down her bare arms and stopped at her elbows. Then, they traversed back up again, almost caressing. Try as she might, she couldn't budge, even though decorum dictated that she should take one giant step back. Gracious! Will Taylor was suddenly a lot of man to contend with—all six-plus feet of him, and every inch muscle and brawn. She gulped hard and, in her head, heard a loud plunk at the back of her throat.

"I wouldn't worry," he said, his voice soothing. "As you saw just a second ago, he's gone now."

"Yes, thank goodness."

With his hands still lightly skimming her arms and his eyes still holding her face captive, she managed to eke out one word: "Well." A wealth of meaning surrounded that single, shaky syllable, which could have segued effectively into, "Now would be a good time to excuse myself," or "My, but it's humid in here."

To her relief, she didn't have to make the first move, for he dropped his hands to his sides, as if he'd read her mind. He returned to the front door, checked the lock, and then flipped up the corner of the shade for one last peek outside. "Still gone," he said, turning to grin at her. "You okay?"

"I'm fine." She cleared her throat and wiped her suddenly damp palms on her skirt. "I'll be going upstairs now."

"I'll walk you up."

"No, you don't have to do that. Goodness, I've been walking up there—"

"By yourself for over a year. Yeah, yeah, I know," he teased. "Come on." He took her gently by the elbow and led her toward the back of the restaurant.

And she went without resistance, all the while hating herself for acting the part of a helpless ninny.

At the landing on the second floor, she reached inside her skirt pocket and pulled out her ring of keys. "Thank you, Will. I'll see you on Monday morning."

Two couples dressed in their Sunday best paused in their giggling and said a hurried greeting as they whisked past them up to the third floor, no doubt on their way to a dance. "Yeah, Monday, if not before," Will answered, glancing briefly at the couples as they mounted the stairs. Then, he gestured behind him with his thumb. "I'll go down and close everything up. You have a nice day tomorrow." He stepped backward, keeping his eyes on her.

"And you, as well." She turned and unlocked the door. When she pushed it open, a whoosh of hot, stagnant air wafted at her. "Phew! It's stuffy in here."

"You should open all your windows to get some cross ventilation going," Will suggested.

She looked back at him. "Yes, I think I'll do that."

He smiled and turned to leave, but then, she thought of something to add. "You've been working out real fine in the restaurant, Will."

He swiveled on his heel and beamed at her. Oh, forevermore! Such a nice smile minus that shaggy beard.

"So, you don't regret hiring me?"

"Not yet."

He gave a low chuckle. "That's reassuring—I think. Good night, again."

"Good night." She watched him scuttle down the stairs.

At the door to the restaurant, he stopped and peered up at her. "I think I'll check out that dance tonight. You wouldn't want to go up there with me, would you?"

She put a hand to her throat. Was he asking her on a date? "Good gracious, no. But you go ahead." As if he needed her permission! She wanted to bite her tongue for sounding so ridiculous.

"Your loss," he said, waving.

She nodded and watched him disappear through the back entrance. Inside her apartment, she closed the door behind her, then slumped against it, pressing a palm to her chest to quiet her quaking heart. "My stars in heaven," she muttered. "What's gotten into me?"

❧

What had possessed him to touch Olivia Beckman? Granted, all he'd done was reach out to steady her, but it still qualified as a touch, especially since he'd let his hands linger there and run up and down her arms. He didn't know what he'd been thinking. She was completely out of his league. Still, it had been nice while it had lasted—standing near to her, close enough to have bent right down and kissed her pretty lips. And wouldn't that have sent her into a regular tailspin! She'd looked alarmed enough as it was when he'd invited her to check out the dance upstairs. He could only imagine what she'd do or think if he were to give her a light peck. Why, she'd fire him, for sure! And, since he needed this job, he decided it was best to mind his manners. Besides, he hadn't kissed a woman in about a dozen years, and he couldn't be sure he still knew how to go about it.

He surveyed the restaurant, satisfied with how neat and tidy it looked. The floor had been swept, the dishes washed, dried, and put away, the pots and pans returned to their proper hooks above the stove, and the bar area scrubbed clean. At the front of the restaurant, a single lightbulb glowed. Livvie liked to keep it on all night—not a bad idea, even though the streetlights outside put off enough light that shafts of it slanted through the window blinds, casting long shadows across the room after dark.

On a table by the door sat the box Alex and Nathan had decorated for the Family Feast, and, already, women had been stuffing recipe cards through the slot in the lid, hoping theirs would be selected for a Tuesday or Thursday night meal. Will could hardly wait to start testing the tastiest-looking recipes.

The sound of dogs barking made him curious about what had set them off, so he sauntered to the front window to take one last look outside. He nearly jumped when he saw a stout fellow in scruffy clothes ogling Livvie's Kitchen from across the street—at least, that's how it appeared to him. Could this be the same man Livvie had seen? On impulse, he yanked open the door, but the guy moved from his spot and scurried down an alley. Will was tempted to chase him, but for what? He could hardly fault someone for standing on the sidewalk on a hot summer night. He closed the door again, taking extra care with the lock, and then headed for the third floor.

Will couldn't begin to count the number of people in the expansive ballroom, which buzzed with loud chatter and rowdy laughter. Every window had been propped open, but that accomplished little, other than to usher in a breeze that pushed around the hot air generated by the mass of sweaty bodies. Arranged near the walls were a few tables and chairs, but most of the space was open, with people milling about, evidently waiting for the music to start. At the far end of the room was a makeshift wooden stage on which a few men were tuning guitars, fiddles, banjos, and whatnot. Will wondered if they planned to sing, as well.

He hadn't come up here to make friends or even socialize. All he wanted was to hear a few tunes. Prison had put him way behind in his familiarity with popular songs, not that he'd really cared. On his harmonica, he would play his own mix of jazz, blues, and folk music, singing intermittently to fill in the measures, and his mournful, twangy tunes would always attract a crowd when he and his fellow inmates were sent outside for fresh air or exercise breaks.

"Hey, good-lookin'. Want to have some fun?" came a sultry female voice. Was she talking to him? He turned and found himself face-to-face with a tall, buxom woman with fake-looking blonde curls that fell at her shoulders. Her painted eyebrows, brightly rouged cheeks, and long, batting eyelashes put him in mind of a harlot. And then, there was the matter of her low-cut dress! "I'm Marva Dulane. What's your name? You want to have some fun?"

Unease zipped through his veins. He did not want to get caught up with the wrong crowd, and this woman reeked of trouble, her potent, cheap-smelling perfume a sure giveaway. *Been there, done that*, he thought to himself. The last thing he needed was some hussy messing up his life.

"Name's Will Taylor, and I'm just here to hear some music. Nothing else."

"Nothing else?" Her plump lower lip jutted out in a pout as she reached up and fingered one of his shirt buttons with long, red nails that looked like talons.

He felt his back stiffen like a fence post, and raspy laughter immediately spilled out of her. "I'm not scaring you, am I, Will? Not a big, rough-and-tumble fella like you. Where you from, sugar? I've never seen you up here before."

He wasn't about to tell her anything. In fact, the less she knew of him, the better. He'd learned first-hand that women like this could be venomous. "You'll excuse me?" he said, stepping back.

She took him by the forearm and gently pressed. "Mercy, I love a man with muscles."

His eyes landed on a couple of robust-looking guys across the room, standing in a circle and talking. "Maybe you ought to attach yourself to one of those farmers over there." He had no clue as to their true occupations, but, with their sun-washed faces and bib overalls, they looked like the type to sit on tractors by day.

Marva glanced behind her and exhaled noisily. "Now, Will, do I look like the husband-stealing type?"

Her perfume was so strong, it should have been illegal. "Do you want me to answer honestly?"

Her talons sank deeper into his arm as she whispered in his ear, "You're not married, are you? It'd be an awful waste if you were."

He peeled her fingers off and smiled. "Excuse me, ma'am. I think I'll move a little closer to the stage."

"How about favoring me with a dance tonight, Will Taylor? I promise not to step on your toes."

"Sorry, I'm not much of a dancer." He started to walk away, but she stayed on his heels.

"I bet I could teach you a few steps."

The sizzle in her voice told him she had more than dancing on her mind. He had to get away from her.

"Hey, Taylor!"

"New cook at Livvie's Kitchen!"

He glanced in the direction of the voices and discovered Quinn Baxter and Sam Campbell, a couple of Livvie's regulars, pushing their ways toward him through the masses. "Good to see you, Will," Quinn said. "You come up here to play your harmonica? The band should be starting anytime now."

"What? No, I just...."

Miss Hussy stuck out her hip and looked at him. "Well, I'll be a sweet pea in a pod! You work for Livvie, do you?" She fingered his lapel and licked her rose-red lips. "Livvie and I went to school together. She's such a...."

But her words were lost under Quinn's piercing announcement: "Hey, Berkeley! I got you a fine musician. From what I hear, he plays a mean mouth harp." Quinn raised a beefy arm and pointed at Will.

Good grief! This was not how Will had intended the evening to pan out. He wished for a trapdoor when the man slipping a guitar strap over his shoulder—Berkeley, presumably—skimmed the audience to locate his target. The crowd quieted.

"Well, come on up here, mister," Berkeley said. "We could use some good harmonica playin'. Isn't that right, boys?"

"Durn tootin'. I ain't heard a good mouth harp in years," said another man as he rosined up his bow.

Will had wanted only to hang around and hear a few tunes. Tomorrow was the Lord's Day, and he didn't feel like staying out late. But, in the seconds he had to decline, he heard verbal encouragement from complete strangers—the brazen Marva included—and felt them nudging him in the direction of the stage. He brought a hand to his front pocket. Sure enough, the rectangular mouthpiece was still there. This was the first

time he wished he'd mislaid it. Shoot! His last perfor-
mance had been in a prison yard, with an audience of
inmates who'd always cheered him on. But what did a
bunch of jailbirds know about good music? He wasn't
even sure he really knew how to play the thing, never
having made a formal appearance or taken lessons,
unless he counted the few pointers his granddaddy
had given him. Mostly, he'd just experimented with it
till he'd gotten the sound he'd wanted.

As if God would give a hoot, he uttered a silent
prayer for divine help. After all, he didn't want to make
a complete idiot of himself. He also thanked the Lord
for the one good thing about his being pushed to the
front: Marva the Hussy got lost in the shuffle. For good,
he hoped.

"Name's Lewis Berkeley, but you can call me
Berk," the guy said as soon as Will stepped up to the
stage. "This here's my band." He made introductions
all around. There was Bob on the fiddle, Pinky on bass
guitar, Rollie on the upright piano, Mel with a banjo,
and a fellow by the name of Willard on drums. They all
greeted him, smiled, and offered a quick handshake.

It seemed necessary to explain himself. He
couldn't imagine what they'd need with a harmonica
player! "Listen. I don't quite know how I got up here.
I'm not going to lie; I've never performed—I mean, really played for anybody."

Berk smiled. "Name a song you know."

Which one? He knew dozens, probably hundreds.
Off the top of his head, he said, "'Oh, Dem Golden
Slippers.'"

"Ah, good old song," Berk said, and the others
nodded and readied their instruments. Berk set the
rhythm with the toe of his boot and gave a sharp nod

of his head, at which point Rollie made the piano near-ly jump off its casters with his intro, Bob made his fiddle sing with chords Will had never heard before, the drummer held the beat, and the others dove in as if they'd practiced the song a hundred times before—and maybe they had.

For the first few measures, Will simply listened, enjoying the sound and wondering how and where to cut in. Soon, he decided just to go for it. Sucking in a breath, he put the harmonica to his mouth, then blew into the reeds, moving his lips up and down the ten-hole scale. He concentrated on blending in and keeping to the background. Yet it didn't take long for him to get caught up in the music with a fervor that made him dominate the melody, doing improvisational trills and feeling freer than he had in a while. He was having the time of his life, thumping his foot on the wooden stage and taking in the enthusiastic claps, hoots, and roars of the swaying crowd.

Will Taylor was in his element.

Chapter Twelve

"The thief cometh not, but for to steal,
and to kill, and to destroy: I am come
that they might have life, and that they
might have it more abundantly."
—John 10:10

*L*ivvie moved about her apartment, trying to ignore
the deafening noise overhead. Could that band be any
louder? Granted, the beat was catchy, but it pounded
like a thunderstorm.

She didn't know why she was such a fuddy-duddy
when it came to these Saturday night events. The folks
who attended obeyed the no-smoking rule, as far as
she knew, and, while she doubted their compliance
with the ban on liquor sales, she'd never had to file a
complaint with Sheriff Morris. Yet. Not that reporting
it would do much good, considering his reputation for
looking the other way when it came to bootlegging.

Still, the various groups that used the space, including the Wabash Rifle Club, who sponsored these
dances, paid their monthly rent on time, thereby taking a financial load off Livvie's shoulders. She could
hardly complain about a little noise. And countless
folks had told her they went for a good time, nothing more. Why, she could be up there herself this very

minute if she'd accepted Will's silly invitation. Thank heavens she hadn't. Talk about rumors! She could almost hear them now: "Olivia Beckman must be done mourning her husband. Look, there she is with that new cook she hired. It's about time that woman started living again."

Never, she told herself. She would never stop mourning her loss. Besides, what would Frank think of her taking up with a mysterious man such as Will Taylor, never mind that he was a faithful churchgoer? Attending church could be part of a charade designed to make him appear to be someone he wasn't. Scowling at her bizarre thoughts, she walked to her bedroom to disrobe and begin her nightly routine.

And that's when it struck her. Unless her ears failed her, someone upstairs was playing a harmonica. Could it be Will Taylor? The stage was directly overhead, and she was often able to make out specific tunes. Sometimes, she even hummed along if the song was familiar. With her head tilted back and eyes gazing upward, she slowly unbuttoned her blouse, then lowered herself to the edge of her bed and listened with rapt attention. From "'Oh, Dem Golden Slippers," the band moved into the mellow-sounding "Deep River," followed by "Oh! Susanna," and then straight into "Dixie." The ease with which Will Taylor moved from one tune to another—if he was, indeed, the harmonica player—astounded her.

With nary a second more of deliberation, she buttoned her shirt again, hurried to the door, where her shoes were waiting, slid her feet into them, and scampered out the door and up to the third-floor landing.

In the shadows of a big oak tree, Clem watched people come and go from the third floor of Livvie's Kitchen—large, boisterous groups, cozy couples arm in arm, and everyone in between. Each time the door opened, the music swelled in volume, and he could have sworn that a mouth harp took the lead. He knew only one person who could wail on a harp like that, and that was Will Taylor. From what he could tell, the place looked to be a popular Saturday night hangout. Folks had parked their cars and buggies in every available spot along the street. He wondered who owned the building. From his dimly lit hideout, he'd watched Will escort that pretty little dame upstairs to the second-floor landing, and he figured there were several apartments on that level. After that, when Will had skipped back downstairs and in through the rear entrance to the restaurant, Clem had circled back to the front to watch from across the street. Good thing he'd snuck off before Will had opened the front door, or he might have been spotted, and he couldn't have that. Well, not yet, anyway. Oh, he intended to confront the guy, but there was safety in numbers, so he'd wait till Hank and Rudy arrived, when they would put their plan in motion. He only hoped that Hank would do his part. Fool had gone all skeptical on him lately.

Clem took a drag on his smoke and smirked to himself as two lovebirds sauntered past, giggling and whispering to each other, completely oblivious to his lurking. For some reason, he thought about Florence and his total lack of affection for her. Oh, he supposed he'd felt something at some time, but that had been several years and even more adulterous affairs ago. Sweat beaded on his brow and under his armpits as bile welled up in his gut. He spat, just missing his boot. *Man, that woman packs a wallop!* Not for the first time today, he ran a rough hand over his torn cheek, still swollen from that wretched candlestick. Thing probably weighed ten pounds. He should have gone for his gun after she'd flung it at him, but he'd figured she'd go for hers, as well, and he hadn't been sure who was the faster shot. So, he'd stumbled out of the house instead, cursing at her even when he was out the door, holding his face as blood squirted out between his fingers.

Blamed brainless woman! That was the last he'd seen of her, save for a quick glance the next morning. And, with a little luck, he would never have to lay eyes on her again. He'd spent the night in the vacant building next to their apartment, nursing his wound as best he could with a couple of rags. In the morning, a noise outside had brought him to the window, and he'd watched her jump inside a cab, probably to go pick up her kid from her mother's house. When the cab had disappeared around the bend, he'd rushed next door, grabbed the belongings he needed to survive, and taken every dollar and cent he could find, even those hidden in jars and under cushions. Then, he'd hit the pavement running, all the way rejoicing that he was through with that nagging swine. *Let her get her blasted divorce*, he thought. *She'll hear no argument from me.* It was high time he found a woman who showed him a little respect, who doted on him and catered to his needs. Flo had never been able to acknowledge that men have needs. More bile had gathered in his throat, and he hurled a wad of it out into the night.

Across the street, the door off the second-floor landing opened, and he watched with interest as that pretty little vision of femininity from the restaurant stepped outside, locked her door, and then dashed up to the third floor, her shoulder-length, burnt golden hair flying haphazardly behind her. She wore the same knee-high dress as before, which showed off her shapely calves. Now, there was a woman who could soothe his hankering.

Clem sniffed, dropped the butt of his cigarette to the ground, and snuffed it out with his heel. Man, he could use a good stiff drink about now. Once the sun set entirely, he'd scope out the whereabouts of Orville Dotson, the man whose name and address Fred had scrawled on the folded piece of paper he'd passed to him. Apparently, this Dotson fellow operated a still outside of town, and he was anxious to try his product. With a little luck, he'd be drinking himself into a stupor tonight.

Tomorrow, he'd call Hank and Rudy and tell them to get their sorry backsides to Wabash—the sooner, the better. A treasure of jewels lay hidden somewhere, good chance nearby, and they had a right to their shares, no matter that Will had served time while they'd gotten off scot-free. That's what he got for being a numskull.

❧

Livvie put a fist to the center of her chest and held her breath. Goodness gracious! Hadn't she vowed never to set foot in this wretched dance hall? Other than to check for shattered windows, broken chairs, and the like, she never came up here.

The door was open just a crack, and Livvie peered inside, seeing nothing but the backsides of folks who swayed and clapped to the musical strains of "Dixie." Gazing over their heads, she looked at the stage and, sure enough, saw Will entertaining the crowd with his toe-tapping rendition of the popular tune. Mercy, but he could play that thing!

By now, folks had started singing, their bodies still moving with the music:

> I wish I was in the land of cotton,
> Old times there are not forgotten,
> Look away, look away, look away,
>   Dixie Land.

> In Dixie Land where I was born in,
> Early on a frosty mornin',
> Look away, look away, look away,
>   Dixie Land.

Why, I haven't sung that song since…I don't know when! she thought. She'd had no reason to sing. Now, though, her lips tingled, almost aching to mouth the words.

The energetic clapping and lively singing continued as Will's harmonica-playing soared with fervor. Before she knew it, Livvie found herself standing close to the stage and heard her less-than-stellar singing voice join in the chorus. Oh, but it felt good to sing at the peak of her lungs!

> Then I wish I was in Dixie, hooray!
>   hooray!
> In Dixie Land I'll take my stand
>   to live and die in Dixie,
> Away, away, away down South
>   in Dixie,
> Away, away, away down South
>   in Dixie.

Another verse commenced, followed by the chorus and then another verse. When the song finally concluded, Livvie clapped and cheered right along with everyone else—until reality hit her with a giant thud. What was she doing, smack in the middle of this crowd of exuberant partiers? And what would Frank say? Livvie had been raised to believe that dancing was a sin, and Frank had been adamantly opposed to it, as well. Initially, he'd refused to rent out the upstairs space to bands and such, but the need for extra money had eventually overruled his qualms. Still, he never would have dreamed of setting foot inside this dance hall on a Saturday night.

She wondered how Will Taylor, a churchgoing Christian, could do such a thing with no compunction. Overwhelmed with regret, she began slinking backward toward the door. And that's when she made eye contact with Will. A moment after their gazes locked, he started to step down from the stage, eyes still trained on her.

Someone called out, "Hey! You know 'Bill Bailey'?"

Will paused, turning in the direction of the voice. "Yeah, but I think I'm played out," he said.

"Aw, come on! You're just gettin' started," someone else lamented.

"You got some talent there, Mr. Taylor," said one of the band members.

"Is that what they call a 'C' harp?" Sam Campbell asked. "How long you been playin' it?"

Will held up the harmonica for the crowd to see. "Yep, she's a 'C' harp, but I play a number of other types. It's just that this ten-hole 'C' instrument is most compatible. And I've been playing since I was about this high." He pointed near his waist.

Livvie turned around and started walking toward the exit, hoping no one would recognize her. She made it to the door and was about to pull it open when she heard someone call out, "Well, look who's decided to grace us with her presence!" The voice belonged to Ted Barnes, who owned and operated the Eagles Theater. "Good to see you, Mrs. Beckman. You come up here t' dance, did you?"

She pinched the skin at her throat and turned. Why did the entire room have to get so quiet? One would have thought they'd all seen a ghost fly across the room! "No, I just heard the music and...grew curious, that's all." She looked straight at Will. "Very nice playing, Mr. Taylor. I had no idea you were so gifted."

"Well, thank you, ma'am," he said with a grin and a slight bow.

"He's gifted, all right," said a dolled-up woman as she stepped into the light of the stage and looped an arm through Will's, sending a wave of hushed whispers across the room.

Livvie recognized her as Marva Maxwell Dulane. The two of them were close in age, but they'd never been friends, as Marva had often badgered her in school and made fun of her "puritanical" ways. Her blatant dislike of Livvie had never faded, something Livvie didn't understand but had long since quit trying to figure out. Divorced and living on the outskirts of town, Marva had a reputation as the town trollop, and, truth be told, she made her plain uncomfortable.

"If he can cook half as good as he can play that mouth harp, I can see why you hired him to run your kitchen," Marva cooed, sidling up cozily to Will as if she'd known him a long while. Could she be any more brazen?

Livvie tamped down a lump of irritation with Marva and Will and pasted on a smile. "Hello, Marva," she said with a sweetness that almost sickened even her. "Good to see you." *Lord, help me resist the temptation to say something unseemly.* It was a pitiful prayer, she knew, but she was out of practice, after all.

"And you," Marva drawled coolly. "Although, I must say, you're the last person I would have expected to see up here." She looked around the room and snickered. "We'd better tame it down, folks. Livvie's a little too clean for the likes of us."

Yet no one else laughed.

"Actually, we all might be a little too clean for you, Marva Dulane," said Quinn Baxter, pushing his way forward through the masses as a round of good-natured chuckles arose. "I think it's great Livvie joined us. It's about time she let her hair down."

"Yes, indeed," someone else said.

"You're right, Quinn," said another.

"Um, thank you, everyone." Her cheeks burned. "If you'll excuse me, though, I think I'll go back downstairs. Good night."

There was a chorus of "Good nights," and Livvie smiled. But her face dropped when she saw Will wriggle his arm free of Marva's and step down from the stage, as if he intended to follow her.

"Mr. Taylor, you ain't leavin', too, are you?" asked the man everyone called Berk. "We're just gettin' started up here."

"'Fraid so. I didn't come here with the intention of performing. Like Mrs. Beckman, I was just curious. But you folks have given me a real nice Wabash welcome, so I thank you."

"You're mighty welcome, son. You stop on by any Saturday night, and we'll put you on this stage," Berk said.

"I might just do that, on one condition: that you all get yourselves to church the next morning. Me, I've been going to that Wesleyan Methodist church a few blocks over."

"I swear, when I even walk past a church, the building starts to tremble!" said a gravelly voice Livvie recognized as Orville Dotson's.

"Yeah, the Lord don't look so kindly on that business you run on the side, Orv," spouted someone she didn't know. She did, however, know that he was referring to the illegal still on Mr. Dotson's property. This prompted a wave of laughter and murmurs—the perfect opportunity to escape unnoticed.

Livvie slipped out the door and onto the landing, remarking to herself how brave Will had been to encourage folks to go to church. Dance halls were not exactly considered ideal sites for evangelism.

The air had cooled some, she noticed as she descended the stairs, and an orange glow of sunset still flirted with the horizon. Outside the door to the second floor, she reached inside her pocket for her keys, keeping her eyes on the alley below. A sudden chill chased up her back at the sight of that stranger she'd spotted earlier, still puffing on a detestable nicotine stick, his tall, chunky frame leaning against a thick tree trunk. His eyes looked as if they could burn her skin.

Was it mere coincidence that she'd seen him twice in the same evening, or did he have ill intentions toward her? If so, what were they? And, more important, what was the reason for them? She had never seen this man before and couldn't imagine what interest he might have in her.

Feeling a surge of rare boldness, she returned her key to her pocket, marched to the end of the landing, and leaned over the railing. "Is there something I can help you with, mister?"

He didn't acknowledge her but tossed his cigarette to the ground and snuffed it out with his shoe. Then, he gazed up at her for a lingering moment, his face expressionless, before turning and starting down the alley. Seconds later, he had vanished into the murky shadows.

∾

Blast! He'd wanted to walk Livvie down to her apartment, maybe even speak a few more words to her. Perhaps, a conversation wasn't out of the question, if he left now and knocked on her door. But, before he was able to make any headway, Marva Dulane snagged him by the arm again.

"You can't possibly leave yet, Will Taylor. We haven't even gotten acquainted."

"Uh, Miss Dulane, you should know—," he began, but Quinn Baxter and several others cut him off mid-sentence as they crowded around to talk about his fine playing and barraged him with all kinds of questions, from where he'd gotten his instrument to how he'd come to play it with such skill. He'd intended to tell Marva that he knew her type too well and had even dated women like her before the Lord had come into his life. It was just as well that he hadn't. Her type was not wont to be convicted by such a statement.

Several minutes later, the band members reconvened on the stage and picked up their instruments for another set. This distracted Marva, or appeared to, and Will tried to excuse himself.

"What about that dance, Will?" she asked, ignoring his attempt.

"Look, Miss Dulane." He raised his eyebrows at the pesky woman. "I think you have me wrongly pegged."

"It's actually Missus," she corrected him, "but that's all right. I'm divorced. Call me Marva."

He sighed. She was a determined thing; he'd give her that. "All right. Marva." Her long eyelashes made several up and down sweeps, slow and deliberate. She wasn't a bad-looking woman. Heck, at one time, he would have considered her a catch. But ten years in prison had changed his heart and altered his perspective on many things—his taste in women, for one. Nowadays, a woman like Olivia Beckman, not a minx like Marva Dulane, had the power to turn his head. Of course, he had no business looking at a woman of Livvie's caliber. Shucks, he wasn't even interested!

Marva's eyelashes kept fluttering up at him. If she played her cards right, she could probably find herself a good man, but he was pretty sure the way she played didn't attract the "staying" kind.

"Sorry, Marva. I'm not your type."

She set her hands on his shoulders and used her thumbs to play with his shirt collar. "You sure? I got the feeling you're not as innocent as you'd like us to think you are. You might be a church boy now, but you weren't always, were you? Fess up, Will. You can tell Marva."

He quickly stepped out of reach. "You're a crazy woman, you know that?"

A hysterical giggle spilled out of her. "A few have told me as much, but I don't mind. Shoot, maybe they're right."

He gave a soft chuckle to cover his irritation. "You ought to go to church yourself. You'd soon discover you're looking for happiness in all the wrong places."

"Pfff, all that church stuff doesn't interest me, Will. And, don't worry; I'm plenty happy."

"Well, good. Then, you don't need me."

He started to turn, but she seized his arm—a little too hard for his liking. "But that's where you're wrong, Will," she said, her voice husky. "I love a challenge, and that's what I see when I look into your baby blues."

Unbelievable. He shook his head several times. "Good night, Marva Dulane."

This time, she let him go.

Chapter Thirteen

"Treasures of wickedness profit nothing:
but righteousness delivereth from death."
—Proverbs 10:2

The Family Feast kickoff at Livvie's Kitchen was fast approaching, and preparations were under way. Cora Mae had had the brilliant idea of decking out the restaurant in red, white, and blue streamers to commemorate the upcoming Fourth of July holiday, and Livvie had purchased enough red and white gingham from the milliner at Beitman & Wolf Department Store to fashion a pretty tablecloth for each table. After the Fourth, the streamers would come down, but the new tablecloths could stay year-round.

Sally and the boys had busied themselves making more colorful posters to advertise the event, then traipsed all over town to tape them up in the windows of stores, banks, service stations, and the post office, and to nail them to lampposts. Nate had wanted to put a sign in the window of another diner, Sky Blue Restaurant over on Canal Street, but Sally had explained that the competition wouldn't look too kindly on that idea. His standard "Why?" followed by "What's 'competition'?" had obliged her to explain as best she could, in terms that a six-year-old would understand. "Well, if a girl likes a certain boy, and then along comes another girl who also likes him, well, that's competition. They're both competing for the same boy."

According to Sally's account of the episode, they'd trudged along in silence for half a block until Nate, having thought things over, blurted out, "You mean, there's boys and girls what like each other in Mommy's restaurant?"

"No, dodo bird," Alex had responded. "There's two girls what like the same boy!"

Livvie wasn't sure which of her sons had missed Sally's point by a wider margin, so she'd done nothing but smiled.

Will had prepared Clara Gillen's baked chicken for Sunday dinner last week, and the recipe had passed the taste test by a country mile, according to the judges: Cora Mae, Coot, Livvie, the boys, and Will. "Succulent" described it well, with its blend of five herbs and spices, a squeeze of lemon, and some other key ingredients.

Besides the chicken, Will had served cheddar mashed potatoes and gravy, steamed green beans, homemade applesauce, which had been canned the year before, and his own secret-recipe rolls, which were fast becoming a signature item at Livvie's Kitchen due to their irresistible texture and hint of sweetness. Many folks had joked that they could make a meal of the rolls alone.

Yes, Will Taylor had basically abolished the notion that men didn't belong in the kitchen, and yet he didn't possess one feminine trait about him. Whether tossing a baseball with Alex and Nate in the back alley, lifting heavy crates of produce and other restaurant supplies, or taking the boys fishing with the equipment she'd offered him—Frank's gear—he was the epitome of manhood. And it rankled Livvie plenty to realize she'd noticed.

The morning of June 29, Livvie dressed the boys in blue shorts, red-and-white-striped shirts, and navy Red Goose shoes, having splurged at J. C. Penney and Miller's Shoe Store. She'd had to empty her savings jar to make the purchases, but having her boys spiffed up for the opening night of Family Feast seemed worth it. Besides, she'd purchased the shoes one size too big, figuring that if the boys' feet didn't grow too fast, they could wear them clear through Christmas and maybe beyond.

Livvie didn't have a patriotic dress, but she did have a lightweight cotton one of blue fabric with tiny white flowers, a scooped neck, and cap sleeves. With some spare ribbon she'd found in her sewing drawer, she had fashioned a red bow to tie at the top of her ponytail.

A special table near the front of the restaurant had been reserved for the Gillen family, and Livvie had decorated it with a beautiful centerpiece—a Mason jar filled with fresh-cut flowers from Margie's garden—for Clara to take home. She'd also tied ribbons around four candy sticks and placed one at each setting.

By 4:45 p.m., a line had already formed outside the front door. Livvie tried soothing her jittery stomach but without success. "Oh, my gracious, I'm so excited—and nervous, too, I'm afraid," she confessed to Will, who was mashing a huge pot of steaming potatoes. With every depression of the metal tool, his arm muscles flexed, and she found the distraction a pleasant substitute for fear.

He paused and looked up long enough to cast a warm gaze at her. "This is your night to shine, young lady. Make the most of it." He returned his attention to the potatoes, sprinkling them with a pinch of salt and some ground pepper, pouring in a generous amount of thick cream, and then adding a hunk of butter and a mound of grated cheddar. One thing she'd learned from observing him over the past several weeks was that he didn't have much use for measuring cups and spoons. She'd also noticed other things: his perpetually jovial manner, his gentle way with her sons, his sense of humor, his calm efficiency, and, most intriguing, his deep interest in spiritual things.

Most every morning, in between cleaning up the breakfast mess and getting ready for lunch, he situated himself at some corner table to study his Bible for a few minutes. "Got to finish reading this passage I took up before coming down here this morning," he sometimes said. On occasion, Alex and Nate interrupted his solitary study with their antics, but he never let it bother him; he just smiled and, often, closed the Book and joined in their banter.

Mostly, though, the boys had learned that when Mr. Taylor sat down with his Bible and a cup of coffee, they ought to show respect. Sally did her best to keep them outside or, on rainy days, contained in their playroom at the back of the restaurant. Seeing Will's dedication had produced a good dose of guilt in Livvie's spirit for her lack of devotion to the Lord, so much that she'd dusted off her Bible last week and set to reading it each night after tucking her boys in bed. On every page, she sought reassurance that the Lord still loved her, despite her utter neglect of Him. She also searched for an explanation, even clues, as to why He would have swooped up her husband at such an early age. While she found a measure of comfort in the Good Book, those frantic searches for answers often resulted more in unrest than peace, and she wondered what was wrong with her, since it seemed to have the opposite effect on Will.

"You watch. It's going to be a good night, Livvie Beth," Will said as he set down the masher. Then, he plopped a lid on the heavy pot and slid it to a back burner. That he'd tacked on her middle name made her feel a mixture of panic and pleasure. On the one hand, she was glad they'd established a comfortable rapport; on the other hand, it rattled her to think he viewed her in so intimate a manner—and that she rather enjoyed it.

Sudden gratitude washed over her for the interest Will took in her restaurant. Of course, he wanted a job, so it was only natural for him to want her business to succeed. And what was she doing? Standing there, worrying! Wanting to make herself busy, she stepped up to the bar and began straightening the salt and pepper shakers.

That task didn't take long, though, and she next surveyed the restaurant to see what else needed to be done. Cora Mae had arranged and rearranged the table settings until they lined up perfectly. The boys and Sally walked around, making sure that nothing was out of place. Soon, they would take their posts by the door as "official greeters" and welcome each patron.

Coot, at her invitation, had come in through the back door ten minutes early and now sat, reading the *Daily Plain Dealer*, at a front table she had reserved for him and three friends. She hadn't wanted to make him stand in line in the relentless heat. How grateful she was that the ceiling fans were in working order!

She turned back to the kitchen, where Will stood over the stove. "I want to thank you for all you've done for me—for us," she said, mopping her damp brow with the back of her hand. She knew her cheeks were red from all of her scurrying about, for she'd checked her reflection in the mirror in the tiny washroom at the back of the restaurant just minutes ago.

Will swiveled and leaned back against the counter next to the stove. Beads of perspiration peppered his forehead, as well, but he appeared not to mind. Working in the kitchen was a hot job, even more so when the outside temperature still hovered in the high eighties and the humidity hung over them like a sodden blanket.

He folded his hulking arms across his chest and grinned. "If you want the truth, I'm having myself a barrel of fun."

"You are?" She was surprised—frightened, rather—by the way his remark sounded like something Frank would have said. The two could not have been more different in looks and personalities, but they shared the same fondness for all things culinary. Joe had been keen on cooking, too, but his heart hadn't been in it to the same extent, and he'd stepped into the role of cook after Frank's death more out of compassion than passion. He'd long been a loyal customer at Livvie's Kitchen and had enjoyed lively conversations with Frank. After he'd taken over in the kitchen, he'd perfected his culinary skills, albeit more out of necessity than genuine enthusiasm. Frank, on the other hand, had verged on obsessive when it came to the restaurant business, and Livvie sometimes wondered if Will didn't share the same zeal.

"It's been a pure pleasure watching everybody's excitement, especially your boys'. They're about as keyed up as two fleas in a dog pen. Even Sally's jumped in full tilt."

Livvie shot the threesome a quick glance. "They are having fun, aren't they? Sally's agreed to help me wait tables if it gets to be too much for Cora Mae and me. You should see the line forming outside. I think it stretches halfway up the block."

"I'm not surprised, what with all the advertising and talk around town."

"What if we can't seat everyone?"

Will winked at her. "Then, I expect folks will have to stand around and wait till a table clears."

"In this heat? What if they grow tired of waiting and leave?"

"After getting a whiff of that chicken? Uh-uh." He shook his head. "We'll put a sample on a plate and have Alex take it outside and run it under people's noses. That ought to give them incentive enough to hang around."

Not seeing the humor in his remark, she continued to fuss. "What if people linger too long at their tables? Should we give them a time limit at their tables?"

He frowned. "Now, that would be downright rude, ma'am."

"Yes, but what if—?"

He leaned forward. "What if the proprietress has a fainting spell?"

"Oh." She pressed a hand to her pounding chest, fretting that he could very well be right. Wouldn't that just take the cake? "I am a bit worked up, aren't I?" She fanned her hot cheeks.

"Here." Turning, he snatched a cup from a high shelf and filled it with water from the tap, then handed it over. "It's not very cold, but it's wet. Drink it and then take a few deep breaths. Try to relax. Everything's going to be fine."

"Thank you." She did as she was told, gulping down at least half of the liquid before seeing Will's eyes on her. My, he had lovely eyes, as warm as the day. She averted her gaze and pretended to study her fashionable, toeless shoes. Normally, she wore cotton roll-down socks and white sneakers, regardless of her attire, because she believed that practicality and comfort were more important than style. Tonight, though, she had deemed it necessary to look her absolute best. She'd even used a smidgeon of Helena Rubinstein's Cherry Red on her lips, a dab of blush on her cheeks, and a touch of mascara on her eyelashes. Gracious, if Margie and Howard suddenly decided to drop in for supper, she would earn a scathing look for adding color to her face. *Not to worry*, she told herself. *No one ever leaves the farm at milking time.*

"Can't a guy tell his boss she looks lovely?"

Goodness! If her cheeks hadn't been red already, they were now. "I suppose it couldn't hurt."

He grinned. "Well, then, consider it done. Matter of fact, you look downright fetching."

The giggle that tumbled out caught her unawares. "Fetching? I haven't heard that term since my grandpa used it to charm my grandma into bringing him his slippers, newspaper, and coffee."

"Are they still living?"

"What? No, no, they passed on several years ago, but my memories live on."

He nodded. "I know what you mean—about the memories."

She remembered his sister's tragic drowning and the awful sense of responsibility he'd carried afterward, all thanks to his parents. Had he called up that memory even now? Not wishing to cast a pall of sadness on the moment, she quickly downed the rest of her water, then set the glass on the counter with a thud. Taking a breath that started in the depths of her lungs, she looked at the clock on the wall and pulled back her shoulders, determined not to let her nerves get the best of her. "Mr. Taylor?" she said with resolve. "I do believe it's time to feed the masses."

"I think you're right, Mrs. Beckman."

"Is it time?" Alex squealed from his station at the front door.

Nate jumped up on the chair next to the window and peeked through the shutters. "There's a whole bunch of people out there, Mommy."

Coot lowered his paper and gazed over the tops of his wire-rimmed reading spectacles. "Smells mighty good, Will."

Cora Mae hustled to the door, putting one hand on the lock and the other on the sign. Livvie couldn't remember her ever being so eager to open the restaurant, and she'd been happy to grant her permission to do the honors. With eyes darting from Livvie to Will, she asked, "Are we ready?"

Mercy, it felt like the starting line of a horse race, the way everyone quieted, as if waiting for the signal.

Livvie bit down hard on her lower lip, then broke into an easy smile. "It's time," she announced.

Cora Mae flipped the sign from "Closed" to "Open" and made fast work of the lock. When she opened the door, folks began swarming in like a bunch of bees coming home to their nest.

⟋⟍

Clem, Hank, and Rudy took drags of their cigarettes and watched the commotion across the street as folks pushed and shoved their ways through the door of Livvie's Kitchen. "All I can say is, he's gettin' hisself quite a reputation around town. Feller can cook, is what I hear," said Clem. "They been advertisin' this twice-a-week supper event called Family Feast. There's signs posted all over the place 'bout it."

Hank ran a hand down his whiskery face and stared ahead. "Maybe one of us oughtta go in 'n' sample his eats. I can keep a low profile."

"Pfff," Rudy snapped. "You rode the train with 'im. He'd prob'ly reco'nize you."

"We never even made eye contact, but what does it matter? Ain't we gonna make our presence known tonight?" Hank guffawed. "What say we all march in there and ask for a table? I wanna watch 'im squirm when he first lays eyes on us."

Rudy grinned and threw down his smoke, grinding it into the sidewalk with his boot. "Yeah, same here."

"Just shut up, both of you. We ain't gonna go in there now and draw attention to ourselves. Sheesh! It's a good thing somebody 'round here's got some common sense."

"What're we gonna do, then?" Rudy asked.

Clem took a long, slow draw on his cig, narrowed his eyes at the diminishing crowd of diners, and then blew two perfect smoke rings. "We're gonna wait till closin' time, that's what we're gonna do. When everyone's cleared outta there, we'll walk in and make ourselves at home." He gave a slow nod, felt for his pistol, and grinned. "That sound like a plan?"

"Yeah, a measly one," Hank replied with a scowl. "What're we gonna do after that? You dragged us all the way to Wabash, Dodd. You better have some kind o' grand scheme cooked up."

Clem spat on the sidewalk. "I think better when I'm in the moment."

"In the moment?" Hank squawked. "In other words, you ain't got a plan."

"Just shut up, will you?" Clem cursed so loud that a horse standing just a few feet away turned its head and snorted. He cleared his throat and mentally counted to ten. If he didn't, he knew he'd reach up with both hands and strangle Hank. He had to get his bearings. "Okay, listen. We need to keep our cool, hear? The way I see it, we'll wait till the nanny and that old maid waitress leave the restaurant, and then Livvie, the woman who owns the place, takes them boys o' hers upstairs. That's when we'll go inside and have ourselves a nice little chat with Taylor."

"What if he don't let us in? Don't they lock up after closin' time?" Rudy asked.

"We'll get in, one way or 'nother. From what I've observed, the back door's always unlocked. Customers don't come and go from there, but Taylor and the rest o' them do all the time. There's two apartments on the second floor. Taylor lives in one, and that pretty little lady and her kids live in the other."

Hank smirked. "Wouldn't surprise me none if they shared one on occasion."

"Be quiet, you idiot! It ain't like that." The very notion made Clem's gut take a surprising tumble. "She's way too good for the likes o' him. I been watchin' 'er, and she's got some class to 'er."

"Whoa! Listen to you, Dodd," Hank said. "You don't have a crush on that filly already, do you? Cripes, you can't even handle the woman you've got, and that doozy you got on your mug proves it." Hank laughed so hard, he had to bend over and hold his stomach. "I'm tryin' to picture it. Man, Flo must've had the upper hand in that particular scrap, huh? How many rounds did you two go this time?" He had Rudy laughing now, which made Clem fume with inner rage.

He dropped his gaze to his pocket, from which the grip of his pistol protruded, and wrapped his hand around it. The men caught the maneuver and sobered.

"I could blow you both outta here right now, you know that?"

"Don't be stupid, Clem. Hank was just joshin' you," said Rudy, knocking Hank in the arm. "Tell 'im, Hank."

"You're plumb crazy in the head, Clem," Hank said instead. "You haven't been right for some time now. I wouldn't be surprised none if Flo's been throwin' some secret ingredient in your firewater."

"Put a lid on that trap, Hank. She ain't, neither." He narrowed his eyes at Hank and squeezed the pistol handle tighter. "I knew I shouldn't've sent for you two blockheads. You ain't said one smart word since you got off that train."

Shifting his weight, Rudy looked up at the dusky sky, then down at his shoes. "So, Clem, what're you gonna say to Will when we go in there?"

Clem took a couple of deep breaths to settle his jumping nerves but kept his eyes square on Hank. "We're gonna ask 'im where he stashed them jewels and then tell 'im we want our share."

"Just like that." Hank didn't look impressed.

"You got a better plan?"

"Nope. This is your party, Clem." Hank snickered. "Me and Rudy's just along for the ride, right, Rude?"

Rudy looked as scared as a mouse in a snake hole. Stupid fellow never did have any backbone.

Clem ran a hand down his wounded cheek and flinched. The thing still hurt like blazes, all because of that evil wench. "Once we got what's comin' to us, you guys can go and do whatever you please. Me? I'm hangin' 'round Wabash."

"Yeah, figured you might. Next time you go home, Flo might kill you, eh? I'd run, too, if I was you," said Hank.

Clem sniffed. "I ain't runnin'. I'm just done with that woman, that's all."

Across the road, the line of folks waiting outside Livvie's Kitchen grew shorter as more and more were allowed in. Every so often, a few people would exit the restaurant, satisfied expressions on their faces, which set off a round of excited chatter from those still waiting. It was as if they hadn't eaten in a month.

Automobiles and horse-drawn carriages sped up and down Market Street, while people exited offices, stores, and bank buildings and scurried past, returning to their nice little families in their tidy little houses. Clem sneered to himself, thinking how this was a textbook example of a small town, where trust ran as deep and as long as the Wabash River itself. It occurred to him that he could probably snatch a few bucks out of a cash drawer in any number of these businesses, and no one would be the wiser.

The way these two no-goods had been acting lately, the idea of working alone was downright appealing. Besides, it plain excited him to watch Olivia Beckman's comings and goings.

Yes, Wabash was looking better by the minute.

Chapter Fourteen

"Therefore if any man be in Christ, he is a
new creature: old things are passed away;
behold, all things are become new."
—2 Corinthians 5:17

Will couldn't believe the turnout they had for opening night. They'd filled the restaurant to its maximum capacity—sixty—and dirtied every single plate, so Livvie had kept up a constant cycle of washing and drying dishes, only to fill them again with food for the next round of hungry customers.

"How are we doing on food?" Livvie asked him during a brief lull.

"I think we'll have enough, provided nobody waits till the last minute to show up. Now that I have a better idea of numbers, I can plan accordingly for Thursday's meal."

"Helen Brent's scrumptious pineapple pork chops," Livvie said, smiling. She licked her lips, completely unaware of how the innocent move made him long to swoop down for a hurried kiss. Holy smokes! Who was he to even entertain such a notion?

He nodded. "Those should draw another good-sized crowd. Are you ready for that?"

Her smile grew, revealing more confidence than he'd ever seen in her; so wide, in fact, that her slightly crooked top tooth gleamed in the overhead light. *Charming. No other word for it.*

"I'm—I'm overflowing with readiness!"

He laughed. "That's good. I'm glad you've decided to enjoy yourself. Here, deliver these plates to your famished patrons." He passed off two more plates of hot food as Cora Mae arrived with six empty ones and Sally with three. Livvie shrugged and giggled. "Your turn to wash," she said to Cora Mae, brushing past her like she owned the place.

"Hey, Will! When you goin' to play that there harmonica? The posters did advertise entertainment."

Will looked up and saw Harv Brewster, one of Livvie's regulars, who stopped in for coffee most every morning on his way to work. He was seated at a table with his wife and another couple he didn't recognize.

"Yeah, time's a-wastin'," said another.

Will glanced at the wall clock. Ten after six.

"Go on," said Cora Mae. "I'll wash these up in a jiffy. Livvie will be right back, and she can help me." When he didn't move immediately, she gave him a gentle shove. "Go!"

Without further hesitation, he reached inside his pocket, then sauntered toward the center of the room. By the time he got there, the place had quieted, save for a few whiny kids. Will licked his lips, gathered a deep breath, put the instrument to his mouth, and broke into "Oh! Susanna." In seconds, he had the roomful of diners singing along, clapping their hands, clanking their silverware on the tables, or tapping their feet to the wild rhythm.

He played until he lost track of time. Evidently, he had prepared enough food to last the rest of the evening, for he was never called back to the kitchen. When the restaurant finally cleared of its last customer, Cora

Mae wiped the tables and straightened the chairs, Livvie swept the floor, and Will finished the dishes. Alex and Nate raced around, collecting sugar bowls and salt and pepper shakers, which they arranged in rows on the countertop to be refilled before breakfast tomorrow.

When the last pan had been toweled dry, Will hung the dishcloth on a bar over the sink, then surveyed the restaurant and reflected on the night. Overall, the event had proved a huge success. Of course, Livvie had yet to count the cash drawer, but he didn't doubt the number would be high, even after deducting what they'd spent on food, advertising, and wages. The confidence that Livvie's business would carry on gave him a great deal of satisfaction, especially since he'd played a part in it. At some point, if Livvie learned to really trust him, he'd ask to take a look at the books. Maybe he could find a way for her to hire another waitress or two without making too deep a cut in the budget. Livvie worked herself to the bone, and, with two active boys clamoring for her attention, she needed to take a day off now and then.

Alex and Nate each plunked one final sugar bowl on the counter, then zipped behind the bar and into the kitchen area in a game of chase. "Whoa," Will said, nabbing them by the arms and drawing them to his sides. "Stand still while I tell you what a great help you were to your mother." Out of breath, the sandy-haired boys stopped moving long enough to gaze up at him, their faces dotted with summer freckles. "You did a fine job of greeting everyone at the door tonight. I got nothing but good reports about you."

Nate stretched to his full height, which, in Will's estimation, measured four feet—pretty tall for his almost seven years. "Mrs. Conrad from our old church told me I grew so much, she hardly reco'nized me."

"Is that so?" Will put his hand on the boy's blond head and tousled his hair. "Your old church, eh?" He glanced up to see if Livvie had heard and saw her pause with her broom several feet away. "What church might that be?" he asked.

Both boys raised their shoulders in a shrug. "That one over there with the brown bricks," Alex said, pointing at the restaurant's east wall.

"The Wabash Holiness Life Church," Livvie clarified. "It's about five blocks away, corner of Miami and Sinclair."

"Ah, that one," Will said with a nod. "I passed it one Saturday afternoon on a walk around town. That where your brother-in-law and sister attend?"

"Yes, and I was raised in that church. I started attending with my parents as a little girl and just continued after moving in with Margie and Howard. It seemed only natural that Frank and I would go there after we married."

"What about Frank's family? They live around here?"

She resumed sweeping, her eyes trained on the floor, but she cast him an occasional glance while she talked. "No, most of them live in Canada. He came down here one summer in high school to visit his aunt and uncle over in North Manchester and wound up staying. They attended the same church as we did, so that's how I came to meet him. Since Frank's death, I...I haven't wanted to go back there. Too many memories."

Cora Mae walked up and wrung her damp rag over the sink. "I keep tellin' her to go somewhere else," she said, inviting herself into the conversation. "I know Margie and Howard wouldn't mind, as long as she was going somewhere—and takin' them boys, for goodness' sake. They need to be in Sunday school on Sunday mornings, not playing checkers in their pajamas."

"Stop your preaching, Cora Mae," Livvie said with a lighthearted tone. She tucked a few wisps of hair behind her ears, then bent over to sweep a pile of accumulated dirt into a dustpan. "You're not telling me anything I don't already know."

"Well, that's reassurin'."

Evidently bored with the adults' banter, Alex and Nate started taunting each other, trying to step on the other's toe. Soon, they darted off in the direction of their hideout at the back of the diner, but not before snagging a couple of cookies off a platter.

"You can come to church with me on Sunday," Will blurted out.

Livvie lifted her head to look at him, then stood up straight and brushed her skirts. "Oh, I don't think...I mean...."

"You could come on your own, of course," he quickly amended. "Or, I could just take the boys to Sunday school."

Her expression relaxed. Had he been too bold in inviting her? He certainly didn't want her getting the wrong idea. "They'd like that," she said with a nod.

"You can't just send your boys off to church without you, Livvie Beckman. What would Frank say to that?" Cora Mae spouted.

He couldn't help it. He plain liked Cora Mae Livingston and her forthright manner. When she had something to say, she didn't dawdle. "She does have a point," Will said. "Your boys would be better off if their own mother took them to church."

Livvie stood there for a moment, chewing her lower lip. Then, she straightened her shoulders and cleared her throat. "Well, I'll think on it."

"Humph," Cora Mae muttered, untying her apron and throwing it over her arm. "Don't know what there is to think on." She headed for the back of the restaurant. "You just get yourself up on Sunday mornin', haul them boys out of bed, and say, 'The Beckmans are going to church.' It's as simple as eatin' a slice of pie."

Chuckling, Will snatched another dishcloth off the counter, rinsed it under the faucet, wrung it out, and draped it over the edge of the sink.

"You know I love you, hon, and don't mean to fuss at you," Cora Mae was saying to Livvie as they hung up their aprons on hooks on the back wall. Out of the corner of his eye, Will saw the older woman gently brush several strands of hair from Livvie's eyes. "I just want what's best for you. Right now, I happen to think you gettin' back to church is the best thing for you and them boys."

"It's time to go home, Cora Mae!" Livvie crowed. "I think this heat is getting to you."

"I'm going, I'm going." Cora Mae looked at Will. "You made a fine meal tonight, Mr. Taylor. You pretty near impressed the whole town."

"Thanks, Cora Mae. Get some good rest tonight. Breakfast will be upon us before you know it."

She groaned. "Did you have to remind me?" Waving, she slipped out the back door, leaving Livvie and him alone, with the exception of her boys, whose exuberant voices could be heard coming from the back room.

Livvie sighed and shook her head, her mouth curved seemingly unconsciously into a smile. "Cora Mae gets a little carried away at times." When he thought she was about to corral the boys, she walked back toward him, instead. "She's worse than Margie and her hovering."

"Like she said, she only wants what's best for you."

She stopped a few feet short of him and tapped her fingers on a nearby tabletop, looking thoughtful. "I know I should get back to church. Perhaps, I will try that Wesleyan Methodist church, after all."

"Sunday school starts at ten. We can walk together...or not, your choice," he said with practiced nonchalance, even as he sang a silent melody in his head.

"I suppose it'd be silly not to walk together. I have some umbrellas, just in case it rains."

"We wouldn't want to melt."

Although it looked like she had something more to say, her mouth clamped shut when the boys emerged from the back room, Nate whining that Alex had taken his wooden truck away from him. "It's time to go upstairs," she announced, passing over Nate's complaint.

The younger boy suddenly leaned into Livvie's side and yawned. She put a loving arm around his shoulder and looked at Will. "Cora Mae was right. It was a good night. I should probably count the cash drawer right now, but I'm too tired."

"Did you lock it up good and tight?"

"Yes, I have the key right here." She patted her skirt pocket.

"Good. Tomorrow morning will be soon enough to count your earnings."

They bid each other good night, and he watched the threesome amble to the back door, Nate and Livvie arm in arm, Alex shuffling behind them, examining the toy car he'd allegedly snatched from his brother.

When the door closed behind them, Will gave the restaurant a fast scan, then headed to the front to check the lock and adjust the window shades. Before he reached the door, though, it burst open, and three men rushed inside.

"Well, hullo there, Will," said the heaviest-set fellow. He looked vaguely familiar, even with his hat brim low over his brow. As Will's eyes traversed to the other two, he seemed to hear alarms sounding in his head and had to scramble for his senses. What in the world had prompted these deadbeats to come to Wabash?

"You're still open, right?"

"Clem Dodd?" he asked, squinting in shock.

Clem removed his hat and dragged a scruffy hand through his thinning hair. "In the flesh. Come all the way from New York. You happy to see us?"

Will shivered with dread. "Not especially. Sorry, fellas, we close at seven. Normally, our 'Closed' sign is put out by now, but I guess it got overlooked tonight. You'll have to leave."

"Huh? Is that any way to treat your old friends?" Clem asked.

Will studied the overweight slob, noticing his tattered, smelly clothes and the crusty gash across his left cheek. A sickly realization dawned on him. "You're the one who's been hanging around here for the past several days. Livvie saw you the other night."

"Yep. We made eye contact. She's one fine-lookin' woman."

Bile began to collect at the back of Will's throat, along with a strong urge to pick up Clem by his collar and throw him out on the sidewalk. "You gave her a scare."

"Really? Didn't mean to." Clem took a gander around the restaurant. "She must be rakin' in some good dough, prob'ly turned a good profit tonight, what with that long line o' diners you had comin' and goin'. How'd you manage to land a job straight out o' prison? Or don't she know 'bout your past? You plannin' to rob her someday soon?"

Will's stomach clenched tight, and he uttered a silent prayer for clear direction. While he wanted to plow head-on into the lot of them and throw them clean across the street, he'd learned a thing or two about common sense over the years, and, right now, he figured staying calm was about the smartest thing he could do. That, and refusing to address Clem's stupid questions.

"How did you find me, and, more important, why?"

Hank spoke for the first time. "Guess you didn't reco'nize me on the train that day you came into town. I was there, hangin' back in the shadows. Followed you here."

He sifted through his memory. Shoot! He should have canvassed his fellow riders more closely that day, but freedom had given him a false sense of security. "I can't imagine what difference it would make to you where I went after serving ten years for a crime you participated in. Did you notice I never named any of you as coconspirators? You ought to be thanking me for that right about now."

Hank and Rudy slunk back a tad, but Clem kept that snide, sneering expression in place. "Sorry, that ain't why we came—to thank you for showin' us mercy. No, actually, we come to ask you what you did with the goods."

Will could take them all down, and he knew it, but he didn't want to break anything or make a scene. "What goods? I walked out of that prison with nothing but a change of clothes and a few personal items. That's it. And if you think I'm about to join up with you fellas again, well, you're dumber than a box of toys in the attic. I'm toeing the line from here on out."

Clem swept four filthy fingers through his greasy, brownish-gray hair. He'd lost a front tooth since the last time Will had seen him. That he'd ever run around with these creeps and even considered them friends made him want to retch. Another prayer shot up to heaven, this one for protection and the right words to use to get rid of them. Forever.

"By goods, I'm talkin' 'bout them jewels you lifted. Where are they? Newspapers reported a week or so after the robbery, they never recovered the loot. That means you done somethin' with that leather pouch I gave you. We was in this thing together, remember? And we think we deserve our fair share."

Will could hardly keep from laughing. "You're kidding, right?" Now he did chuckle as he scratched the back of his neck in disbelief. "Sorry to disappoint you, boys, but you're chasing a dream if you think I have anything to give you."

"Wasn't we all in agreement that we'd split the loot four ways?" Rudy's whiny voice chimed in for the first time. In Will's estimation, Rudy had always been the one with the smallest brain. Of course, back then, he'd run a tight race with him.

"Sorry to have to put it to you like this, but the treasure is long gone."

Clem jerked his head back. "What do you mean, it's long gone? You must've stashed it somewheres. We figure you befriended somebody whilst you was in that prison and struck a bargain with 'im. For a price, he'd go to your hidin' spot, snatch up that bag of jewels, take it someplace discreet—like Wabash, here—and run off with 'is share, and then you'd be set for life once you got out."

Will couldn't contain his sudden burst of laughter. "There are so many holes in that theory, I could sift flour with it. First of all, there are no jewels, and there wasn't a single friend in prison I'd have trusted with them, anyway. You don't go to jail to make friends, unless you have no hopes of getting out. A jailbird's number one job is to keep his nose clean. Nice try, though." He tried to sober himself but first had to let out some lingering chuckles. "Listen, boys. I didn't 'stash' that pouch anywhere. I threw it down a sewer drain when I was running from the cops. The police searched for days in the area where I said I made the drop but came up short. If somebody found it, he isn't telling. I didn't want to be caught with the loot because I thought it would save my skin, which was foolish, it turns out, because one of the cops spotted me from a block away, running out of the store with that bag in tow. So, in a sense, they caught me red-handed, even though there wasn't any evidence on me when they finally nabbed me." He looked from one of the three sorry men to the next. "You boys ought to have learned a lesson from me. Crime never pays. Get out of it before you all wind up in the Big House."

Clem narrowed his beady eyes at Will. "Don't think for a second I believe your tale about tossin' them diamonds 'n' such down a sewer drain, Taylor. You ain't that stupid."

"Yeah, I am, but thanks for your vote of confidence," he joked. "Unfortunately, back then, I had the smarts of a toadstool. Anyway, I don't care what you believe."

Clem stood cemented to the floor, his face so red, it looked as if letting out his breath would cause his head to explode. "Perplexed" best described Hank and Rudy's expressions.

Will scrambled to come up with a way to still the waters and then to get these goofs out of Livvie's Kitchen. He decided on telling the truth.

"Look, I feel bad you came all the way from New York thinking to get something you thought you deserved. I really do. But the truth is, even if I had stashed that bag of gems somewhere, I would have turned it in. I'm a Christian now, and my conscience would not have allowed me to walk through that prison gate without making everything as right as I could. I wrote a letter from my jail cell to Mr. Samson at Samson and Sons Jewelers and apologized for breaking down his door and stealing from his jewelry cases. Unfortunately, I can't pay him back, so the letter had to do. He never did reply, not that I blame him. He's probably still steaming with anger."

They all stood there for several seconds, their mouths gaping.

"You sayin' you found religion?" Rudy finally asked, keeping his head down. He ground his toe into a groove in the wood floor.

"Yeah, I did. The jail cook introduced me to Jesus, told me the Lord loved me, in spite of all I'd done."

"So, you—"

"Oh, for cryin' in a rowboat, this ain't no revival service!" Clem screeched.

Rudy recoiled. Hank just stood there stewing to himself, whatever thoughts he had on the subject staying tucked deep inside him.

"This Jesus junk is nothin' but a cover-up," Clem spat out. "You're just playin' the religion card to get us outta your hair."

"It's not religion I've found but a relationship with Jesus. You are right on one point, though: I'd like to get you out of my hair." *Especially before Livvie overhears Clem's raspy voice from her second-floor apartment and comes down to investigate.*

Chapter Fifteen

"Let not mercy and truth forsake thee:
bind them about thy neck; write them
upon the table of thine heart: so shalt
thou find favour and good understanding
in the sight of God and man."
—Proverbs 3:3–4

Livvie left the boys to their game of marbles in the living room and gathered the soiled clothes and linens for tomorrow's wash. In the small room off the kitchen, she separated them by color and fabric in two piles on top of the washing machine, all the while pondering the success of the very first Family Feast. As she worked, she hummed "It Had to Be You," one of the tunes Will had played for the clientele.

Grinning, she silently marveled at his talent for making that little instrument sing with precision and intensity. It seemed Will Taylor had endless abilities. A real showman, that's what he was—in the kitchen, on the stage, and even while mingling with strangers. The more she observed him with Joe's old cronies, the more it struck her how easily he blended in, conversing with young and old alike, relating with equal comfort to the aged Coot Hermanson and her young boys. Watching his interactions, especially with her sons, sounded a

196

chord of optimism in her heart. Why, she'd heard nothing but glowing remarks from patrons about the evening, from the unforgettable meal Will had prepared
to his gracious, welcoming ways, and how they could
listen to him warble on that harp for hours. She had to
admit, she'd been quite charmed, herself.

And her boys—my, how they'd been perfect gentlemen all night, ushering entire families inside, taking
them to their tables, and pulling out the ladies' chairs.
Many of the customers had been so impressed that
they'd promised to return weekly, making her wonder
how they would accommodate so many people on a regular basis. Frank would be so pleased to see how well
things had gone for Livvie's Kitchen ever since Joe had
left for Chicago. Or, would he? A part of her could see
him turning up his nose at the way Will Taylor had tak-
en over his kitchen, moving things around to suit his
preferences. And what would he think of her agreeing to
go to church with him this Sunday? Would he turn up
his nose at that, as well? Not that it mattered, of course.
He'd been gone well over a year. Surely, he didn't expect
her to wallow in self-pity forever. But what on earth was
she thinking? It wasn't as if Will had shown any romantic interest in her. Goodness gracious! An invitation to
church could hardly be confused with a proposal of
courtship, especially with her boys in tow.

She shook her head to free it of such fanciful no-
tions, then shuffled down the hall to her bedroom to
gather a few more items to launder. In the living room,
the boys had found something to squabble about, so
she called out a threat of early bedtime if they didn't
stop. Silence instantly followed. Considering how tired
they had to be after a long day of play and helping out
at the restaurant, they ought to have been eager to

go to bed, but that was almost never the case. Rather than inquire about their dispute, she decided to finish her chores.

Piano music echoed through the back alley; it came from Isaac's Restaurant, one block south on Canal Street. Most people referred to Isaac's as a speakeasy, and, while Isaac Winters didn't have liquor on the menu, plenty of people went into his establishment sober and came out quite the opposite. Livvie sometimes wondered how, in this time of Prohibition, he got away with selling alcohol. But then, she recalled the rumors about Sheriff Morris's fondness for the stuff. Considering that he had been elected for two consecutive terms, she figured most of Wabash's good citizens held the man in high regard, despite his weak enforcement of Prohibition laws.

The piano player at Isaac's switched from honky-tonk to a quieter tune, and Livvie found herself meandering to the open window that overlooked the alley between her building and the Gaylord & Bambauer Drug Store. The night was unusually warm, yet pleasant, and the curtains ruffled in the gentle evening breeze. Below, two cats faced off with each other, their backs hunched in readiness for combat. "Scat!" she scolded them, poking her head out the window. When they scampered away in opposite directions, she smiled with satisfaction. She ducked her head back inside and prepared to get back to her chores, but something quite different grabbed her attention: the sound of the screen door of the restaurant slamming shut, followed by a rowdy voice that overpowered the other night noises.

"He's a blame fool," said a cranky male voice. "I swear, them stolen jewels are hidden somewheres. Got to be."

"He said he tossed 'em in a sewer drain, Clem. It makes pretty logical sense to me," said another.

"You'd think a dancin' duck was logical," the first one spat back.

"He does seem different from ten years ago. Gettin' religion would explain that," said a third fellow.

The threesome started making their way down the alley in her direction, so Livvie stepped to the side of the window, then crouched down and peeked over the sill, keeping an ear to the open window and an eye on their sauntering figures. She couldn't make out their faces in the shadows, but she could tell they weren't familiar. What did they mean by stolen jewels, and just whom were they referring to when they said that "he tossed 'em in a sewer drain"? Surely, they weren't speaking of Will, even though she felt certain they'd just come from her restaurant. She would recognize that rusty squeak anywhere. The door had been making the sound for years, and, while she'd asked Frank countless times to fix it, she'd grown accustomed to hearing it. Her stomach twisted in a sickening knot, and she put a hand to her throat, gulping down a bitter taste. It would seem she still had much to learn about her cook. Just what had he been involved in before coming to Wabash?

"Religion? Really, Rudy. I'll eat my boots if he got religion. He made too good a crook. Fellas like him don't reform easy," said the one who'd spoken first.

A crook, did he say? A panicky sensation crowded her chest.

"He got caught, didn't he? That ain't bein' such a good crook."

The three men stopped directly under her window, and she heard the strike of a match. Were they lighting up? She stood up just high enough to see one man draw something shiny from his pocket. A gun?

"Put that thing away 'fore somebody sees it," said one fellow. "Sheesh, you're nuts. I'm gettin' back on that train tomorrow. I got no time to mess around this jerkwater town. New York's got a whole lot more opportunities for me. This plan o' yours stank from the beginnin'."

"I'm with Hank. I ain't hangin' 'round, neither."

"Suit yourselves, fools. Just don't expect no piece o' the pie if I discover he stashed them stolen goods 'round these parts."

"You're the fool, Dodd. Didn't you hear 'im? There ain't no pie, and I believe 'im. Will seems...I don't know. Different."

"Bosh. You two squirrels got leaks in your think tanks. Good riddance to both of you."

They set off again, their voices turning garbled as they moved further up the alley.

Livvie stood up fully and sucked in a cavernous breath, then slowly expelled it. "So help me, if that man's a thief, I'll show him the door faster than he can say tiddlywinks," she muttered under her breath, more angry than troubled by what she'd overheard. She needed to learn Will Taylor's true identity, and, suddenly, tonight seemed as good a time as any. Yes, indeed. No matter what he thought of the intrusion, just as soon as she was sure her boys were asleep, she would march across the hall and knock on his door.

And then, she'd demand answers.

❦

In the big, claw-foot tub, Will soaked the sweat off his body till his skin felt waterlogged. And then, he soaked some more. He couldn't believe the sudden appearance of the old gang. He could have sworn he'd seen the last of them years ago. Matter of fact, they should have been wise enough to stay away. How did they know he wouldn't wring their necks for leaving him stranded at that jewelry store and letting him take the rap for the crime? Lucky for them, he felt no bitterness, even though he would have preferred never to have laid eyes on them again. Talk about putting a damper on the events of the evening! And the claim that he'd stowed those jewels in some remote spot to retrieve once he was free? He'd never heard anything so asinine.

Clem Dodd hadn't changed a bit, not counting the wrinkles and caked-on dirt he and the others had accumulated over the years. Will hoped he'd convinced them that he had no idea as to the loot's whereabouts, and that he had, in fact, given his heart to God, so that he wouldn't have kept it, even if he had hidden it somewhere. After a quick prayer that Clem and his cohorts wouldn't do anything stupid, he dragged himself up, stepped out of the tub, and began toweling off. Next, he reached for his jeans and the T-shirt he'd laid out on the linoleum floor. Tonight would be a good time to search the Scriptures for a fresh dose of strength and encouragement. Maybe he'd even write a long letter to Harry. High time he brought his friend up-to-date on all the latest happenings. Too bad he didn't feel more optimistic at the moment, especially in light of the impressive turnout they'd had at the first Family Feast. Harry would be proud of the way he'd readjusted to the world outside prison, finding a good job and a fine church, making friends, and even taking a couple of fatherless boys under his wing.

A loud rap sounded at his door, ending his musings. His mind went on immediate alert, and his first thought was that Clem and his boys had broken into the building, or that he'd forgotten to lock the outside door, but wouldn't he have heard them in the hallway? Besides, he distinctly recalled turning the key in the lock and then hanging it on the hook by the door when he'd stepped inside his apartment. Having no gun in his possession, he went for the next best thing—an old broomstick. Holding it as he would a baseball bat, he prepared to strike the first thing that moved. But, when he opened the door just a crack, all he saw was a perturbed-looking strawberry blonde, arms folded across her heart, hazel eyes narrowed, and mouth set in a stubborn line.

He lowered the broom and lifted his eyebrows. "Livvie? Is everything all right?"

"Of course not. May I come in?"

"Um...." He stepped aside, opened the door, and gestured with an outstretched arm. "Sure, be my guest."

She marched right past him almost before he'd gotten the words out, then quickly swiveled and stared at him face-on, looking prettier than anything he'd ever seen with her hair mussed, her eyes shimmering like wet gold, and her expression fiery and unwavering. "All right, Will Taylor. It's time you told me who you really are."

✻

"What? Haven't I already told you?"

Was he kidding? "Not enough, you haven't. All I know is your name, and a few tidbits about your family."

"Ah, so you've been thinking you'd like to get to know me better. Is that it? Funny, I've been thinking the same about you," he said with a devilish grin. It took all of her resolve not to give in to that charming wit. "How 'bout you start?" he asked, winking.

"How 'bout not?" She smiled pertly. "I want to know the name of the restaurant where you worked in

New York, exactly why you left that job, and the name of your former employer, so I may call him."

His put-on smile faded as his shoulders dropped a notch. "All that, huh?"

Continuing the stare-down, she put her hands on her hips and waited. He remained silent, so, she added, "I heard some men talking under my window a while ago. They mentioned your name and something about some stolen jewels. I'm pretty sure they'd just left the restaurant, because I heard the screen door slam, which tells me one thing. They stopped in to see you."

His mouth formed an o before he bit down on his lower lip and gave a slow nod. "What exactly did you overhear?"

"Uh-uh. I'm not giving you a chance to come up with more lies. I want the truth, and I want it now, or I'll...." She chose to keep the alternative open-ended.

"Fire me?" he suggested.

"Maybe."

"I figured you might, so that's why I've been somewhat private. I don't think you really want to hear the whole truth, Liv. It's not a very pretty story."

Frank had called her Liv, and she'd always liked it, but she didn't know how she felt about hearing it from Will. Didn't he have to earn the right to use her nickname? Her stomach tied itself into a fast knot. "You might as well go back to the beginning. For starters, why did you have to jump a freight train to come to Wabash? If you left a decent job in New York, wouldn't you have saved enough money for the fare?"

He moved behind her and closed the door. "Hm. Did I ever say it was decent?"

He had her there. Clearly, she'd made too many assumptions about this man. "If you didn't like your job, why on earth did you jump into another restaurant position?"

"Because I love to cook."

"But you just said—"

"You want something to drink?" He gestured at his own tiny kitchen, where a vase of fresh-cut flowers adorned the little counter. "I have some lemonade in the fridge."

It did sound refreshing, but she shook her head. "What I want are answers, Will." No point in telling him how lovely the flowers looked, or how impressed she was by his wish to brighten up the otherwise drab little space. What kind of man did that?

He sighed, lowered his head, and rubbed his chin, as if feeling for his absent beard. "Are your boys sleeping?" His voice went suddenly hoarse, and she wondered if his nerves had started jangling.

"They are, and, considering how tired they were, they won't wake up till dawn."

"That's good." He gestured toward his living room, where the old sofa with the protruding spring rested against the dull blue wall. Above it, a lackluster painting she'd purchased at a secondhand store hung, slightly crooked. "Sit down?"

"Fine." She moved to the frayed chair next to the couch and settled into it. The sun had set and given way to dusk, and Will leaned over to pull the chain on the ancient lamp beside the sofa before lowering his muscular frame onto the seat cushion. Low light filtered through the sparsely furnished room, revealing a Bible with a well-worn black cover on the small corner table at one end of the sofa. The sight of it wove a web of tangled emotions in her heart. What would she do if she found out that keeping Will in the kitchen would put her boys and her in harm's way? She'd have to let him go, wouldn't she? The very notion set her heart to thumping, for as much as she didn't want to acknowledge it, she'd grown attached to him. Furthermore, as far as she could tell, he was a much better person than she, a man of faith and integrity. What part could he possibly have had in stealing jewels?

For the span of a minute, they sat in utter silence and stared at each other, she awaiting some sort of confession, he apparently trying to decide where to start. He lifted one of his big legs and crossed it over the other, then clamped hold of his bare foot around the ankle. The sight made her feel surprisingly vulnerable. To her best recollection, she'd seen only two men barefoot—her husband and Margie's—and something about seeing Will in such a primitive, untailored state sent her pulse spinning. Not only that, but a dim shaft of light from the glowing lamp struck his damp, chestnut hair and made it gleam in a way that caused a strange surge of affection to swirl inside her, even as she clenched her jaw and fought the ridiculous feeling.

"Well?" she said, peering at his chiseled face. She forced her shoulders back to preserve her sense of control and clasped her hands tightly together in her lap. "Are you going to start talking, or do you want to answer my questions one at a time?"

Sober as a stick, he blinked twice and cocked his head. A loose lock of hair fell across his forehead, so he brushed it away with one hand, then clasped his ankle again. He lowered his gaze, his eyes trained on something off to her side—a chair? A book? She couldn't be sure. Then, he cleared his throat. "Those fellas you heard tonight...I used to run with them several years ago, and one of them...well, you've seen him before." He let his eyes connect with hers again.

"I have? Where? When?"

206 ᴄᴏ Sʜᴀʀʟᴇɴᴇ MᴀᴄLᴀʀᴇɴ

"The guy with the gash on his face who spooked you the other night—he's been hanging around town, first to find my whereabouts, and then to watch what I've been up to and scope out the place."

She held her breath. "Who is he, and who are those other men?"

"You want the plain truth?"

She nodded slowly.

"They're crooks."

"Crooks? Then, that would make you—"

"The same thing, yeah, but in the past tense. Livvie, I served time in jail. Correction: a state prison. Welfare Island State Penitentiary, to be exact. It's in New York."

"And the restaurant...?" she asked, unable to control the sudden quivering in her voice or tamp down the deep sense of dread pounding in her head.

"...was not a restaurant at all but the prison kitchen."

She pressed her mouth shut, drew her brow into a deep frown, and breathed in several gulps of air before letting them back out, her hands leaving her lap and grabbing hold of the arms of the chair. "Prison?" she whispered. "For how long?"

"Ten years. Ten long years."

"So"—she could hardly speak the words—"you actually stole some jewelry?"

"Afraid so." With the back of his hand, he wiped his brow, which glistened with beads of sweat. "I went along with those goofs on a number of petty crimes. I had little to live for back then—no sense of purpose— and I found a sense of belonging with those guys. Fact is, I'd considered different ways of ending my life before I met that gang of no-goods. Once, I tried to jump off the roof of a five-story building, but, even then, I failed like a soaked match." He cut loose a hollow chuckle. "I didn't have the courage to go through with it."

Livvie's shock silenced her for a moment. "Well, of course you didn't," she finally managed. "And it's a good thing. Everyone has some reason or another to go on living. Life is never completely without purpose." Had she truly said that? She couldn't even count the times she'd tried to search for meaning, herself, after Frank had died. Yes, she had her precious boys, but the deep pain of her loss had sometimes gripped her so hard, she'd found it nearly impossible to drag her limp body out of bed, even for the sake of her sons. She'd never confessed this to Margie, but, for several weeks following Frank's accident, her boys had had to rouse her from sleep and plead with her to go downstairs to work. Thankfully, Joe, Cora Mae, and the other waitresses she'd employed then had always seen to it that the restaurant opened on time. As far as she knew, folks saw her as staunch, strong, and stable, never suspecting otherwise! She was struck with the realization that she'd had fewer and fewer bad days since Will's arrival. Why, he'd even handled that tiresome pair, Charley Arnold and Roy Scott. Granted, they hadn't been dining at her place nearly as often, but the new customers who came to check out the handsome new cook more than made up for their business.

"I learned the purpose of life in prison, of all places, thanks to Harry Wilkinson," Will continued. "He was the head cook there, and I wouldn't be a Christian today if he hadn't told me about God's love and forgiveness. The way he presented the gospel message made it seem so appealing. I mean, after my little sister drowned, I'd pretty much lost all sense of being loved and accepted, let alone forgiven. But with God, I had this chance at a clean slate. That sounded good to me. And surrendering my heart did something else: it took away my anger and resentment. For years, I'd blamed God for not preventing Joella's death, when, really, it wasn't His fault, or even mine, and it certainly wasn't my sister's. It was simply her appointed time to leave this earth. Once I started looking at it that way, my whole attitude changed, and my behavior took a turn for the better. Only God gets the credit for that."

Almost moved to tears, she chewed her lower lip, trying to decide how to respond. It was amazing how, in a few short minutes, his admission of his past sins had prompted her to think about her own shortcomings. In the course of Will's brief yet candid confession, she had recalled all the times she'd blamed God for Frank's accident, never once considering that she might be wallowing in self-pity and neglecting her own sons. Additionally, her once-strong faith had all but disappeared. *Lord, forgive me*, she prayed. *I've been a terrible example to my sons. When I should have been praising You in spite of my grief and looking for ways to honor and bless Your name, I let my trust in You wither and wane. Please, help me find my way back.*

"I can be gone tomorrow, if you want," Will went on. "I don't want to cause any problems for you. I'm pretty sure if I left town, Clem and his sidekicks wouldn't hang around. I misled you, Livvie, and I'm eternally sorry about that. Believe me, if I'd suspected for a second that they'd come looking for me, I never would have taken this job. I just hope you and your boys will forgive—"

"Will," she interrupted him.

"Yes?"

Her fingers fidgeted with a little tear in her apron hem as she scrambled to find the right words. "You're not going anywhere," she heard herself say.

"I'm not? I honestly think it'd be best for everybody if I did."

"At first, I thought the same," she admitted, "but I don't see what that would accomplish. I'd have no cook, and do you know how long we looked for someone to replace Joe? Weeks. If you left now, I might be forced to close down."

A thoughtful expression washed over his face, tanned bronze from the few afternoons he'd gone down to the river to fish with one of Frank's casting rods. "You do make a point. And what would become of the Family Feasts?"

"Exactly. I received nothing but glowing remarks about the meal, and I would hate for the plan to die overnight."

"I just hope Clem and his cronies don't come back seeking revenge. That's my only concern. It wouldn't be good if news got out about my prison term, either. I'm afraid there'd be plenty of talk, not that I'm worried about my reputation, but I don't want folks thinking ill of you for hiring me."

"I appreciate that, but I don't think you have to worry too much about those fellows. Two of them said they were going back to New York on the next train."

"That'd be Rudy and Hank."

"Yes, those were the names I heard. The other seemed determined to stay. Said he wouldn't be sharing the pie with the rest of them."

"The pie."

"He's certain you hid the stolen goods somewhere, and he wants his fair share." She paused, chewing her lip again. "And there's something else, Will. He flashed a gun."

"Guns always did give Clem a false sense of security. I'll stay on guard, but, chances are, he'll head out with those guys in the morning. One thing about Clem Dodd—he's a lot of talk, minus the gumption."

Livvie looked at her lap and pondered her next words. "There's something I have to ask you."

"Ask me anything now. It's all out on the table, Liv."

She raised her chin and examined his face. "Do you still have those jewels? I mean, I want to believe you, but...."

He sat forward in the sofa and let his eyes roam over her face, as if searching out every detail. "No, Liv, I don't have the jewels, but I don't fault you for doubting me. The truth is that I threw them down a sewer drain. I know, sounds stupid, but that's exactly what I did."

"Two of those men said the same thing, but the other fellow didn't sound convinced."

"Clem Dodd's determined to get what he thinks he deserves for the small part he and the rest of them played in the robbery. Fact is, I was the one who did the deed—broke the lock, smashed the glass case, scooped up a fistful of diamond rings, ruby necklaces, earrings, and the like, and ran off with them. Meanwhile, the store had an alarm at the police station, and, before we knew it, we heard sirens. Clem and the other fellows hightailed it out of there in the 'getaway wagon' before I knew what was happening." With creased brow, he gave his head several fast shakes. "You don't know how many times I've regretted that stupid act, and to throw away those precious gems was even dumber. The jeweler had replacement insurance, but I should have just handed the bag over to the cops when they caught up with me. Fool that I was, I thought they wouldn't be able to prosecute me if I came up empty-handed, but there was a witness who'd seen me run out of the store, bag in hand."

She pondered his words, a part of her wanting to sympathize, another part wishing she could wash her hands of him here and now, and still another part knowing she needed him in order to keep Livvie's Kitchen open. And then, there was the matter of that dread gun. Oh, Lord, what was she to do? She certainly couldn't ignore the lurking possibility of danger. Not with two young sons to protect.

As if he'd read her flurry of thoughts, Will brushed his hands together and inclined his head toward her. "Livvie." He spoke in a near whisper. "I meant what I said when I told you I'd leave. I don't want to put you or those dear boys of yours in any sort of danger. And, while I'm sure I can take care of myself with regard to Clem Dodd, I don't want to put your business or your clientele in jeopardy. If you are the least bit concerned about that, and you want me—"

"I've already told you, I want—need, rather—you to stay." She couldn't afford to let on that she'd grown accustomed to seeing him every day, that she enjoyed his company. Heavenly, merciful days! Whatever would Margie say if she discovered her little sister's attraction to an ex-convict, Christian or not? "You're staying, and that's that."

Chapter Sixteen

*"For I know the thoughts that I think toward you, saith the L*ORD*, thoughts of peace, and not of evil, to give you an expected end. Then shall ye call upon me, and ye shall go and pray unto me, and I will hearken unto you. And ye shall seek me, and find me, when ye shall search for me with all your heart."*
—Jeremiah 29:11–13

Will was amazed at the recent turn of events. First, Clem and his thugs had shown up at the restaurant with their loud talk and empty threats, and then, after overhearing their crass blabber outside her window, Livvie had come marching across the hall to confront him about it. He'd long known that the day would come when she'd discover his shocking past; he just hadn't pictured it happening quite this way, with Clem, Hank, and Rudy spilling the beans. Oh, but he'd seen lightning in those blue-green eyes when he'd opened the door, broom at the ready to clobber whoever had forced his way inside. And then, after she'd divulged what she'd heard, he'd fully expected her to give him the ax. Instead, here she was, insisting he stay on as cook, even though she knew about his past, as well as the potential for trouble in his future.

Granted, she had a point about needing a cook, but, surely, another Joe Stewart would come forward if she advertised her immediate crisis.

"Livvie, I could jump on the morning train tomorrow and remain an enigma for the rest of Wabash's days—no doubt to everyone's benefit," he heard himself saying.

She stood, so he followed suit, watching her brush the wrinkles out of her cotton skirt. In the sticky air, her coppery hair had coiled into tiny ringlets around her temples and fell in soft swirls over her proud shoulders. What he wouldn't give to reach up and test its texture! To stay on the safe side, he clasped his hands behind his back.

"It would not be to everyone's benefit, Will," she said. "In the short time you've been here, you've already impressed a good number of folks with your excellent cooking skills. If you suddenly disappear, you'll be more than an enigma; you'll be a source of suspicion and mistrust. Would you really want to leave the fine folks of Wabash in that kind of quandary, especially in light of your Christian testimony?"

He could now add "smart" and "sensitive" to the long list of Olivia Beckman's attributes. "You're right; I don't want people thinking I had to run to save my skin or protect my reputation. Maybe I should just come clean with folks, tell them about my sordid past."

"And what would be the point in that? Why deliberately give people a reason to doubt you or find fault, not to mention spread senseless gossip? If and when they discover the truth, you can let them make up their own minds about you. By then, most of them will have gotten to know the real Will Taylor, so your past won't matter."

Genuinely warmed by her words, he dared to inch forward. To his surprise, she didn't retreat. "You make several interesting points, Livvie Beckman." Some kind of citrus scent wafted off of her, whether from her skin or hair, he couldn't be sure, unless he leaned closer. "Does it matter to you?" he asked. "My past, that is."

"A bit, I suppose." Her answer drew him up short, yet not to the point of making him step back. "But everyone deserves a second chance. Goodness, how could anyone live to see twenty if he's never given a chance to redeem himself after making a mistake?"

"I've made some big mistakes in my lifetime," he confessed.

"And now you're different. You said yourself that God gave you a clean slate."

"He did, indeed. Thanks for reminding me of that."

Her gaze connected with his, and he couldn't help himself. With nerves jangling, he unlocked his hands from behind him and lifted one to her forehead. "These few strands here look like they need tending." He lightly fingered the loose tendril, looping it around his index finger as he toyed with the idea of kissing her, especially when she closed her eyes and expelled an airy, shaky breath. A quick calculation reminded him that it had been eleven years since he'd kissed a woman, and the last one had been some floozy whose name and looks he couldn't recollect.

As he'd studied the Bible in prison, the Lord had convicted him of many things, including the importance of treasuring a woman in the way God intended. Not that he didn't still possess those old longings that made him purely male, but he'd finally figured out how to curb his instincts and desires before they led to out-right sin. If she wanted to be kissed, she'd have to send him a clear message before he took the next giant step. So, he released the tiny curl and brushed his knuck-les gently against her cheek. For weeks, he'd marveled at that lightly freckled skin, and he delighted now in its warmth and utter softness. A muscle flicked at the corner of her mouth, making his throat go as dry as hot sand. *Lord, she's a beautiful woman—too beauti-ful for someone like me. What am I even thinking?* But, even as he questioned his sanity, he raised his other hand and cupped her cheeks, as he might a fine crys-tal vase. Blast, it sure would simplify matters if she'd jerk away from him about now. He could apologize all over the place, promise never to come so close to kiss-ing her again, and then see her to the door.

But she stayed firmly grounded, with her face tilt-ed upward, almost like an invitation. So, with pound-ing pulse, he leaned closer and, ever so gently, touched his mouth to hers. It wasn't an exploratory kiss, by any means; just a slow, tender, feathery one that made his heartbeat skitter out of control. He moved his hands to her shoulders and pressed gently, but she kept her arms at her sides, while her long eyelashes fluttered against his cheek. As their breaths tangled in the vel-vet warmth of their first kiss, only one word came to mind: *magnificent.*

❀

Heavens to Betsy! What was she doing? To say that her eager response to Will's kiss shocked her would be putting it lightly. Why, it flat-out flum-moxed her! She was still mourning Frank, for good-ness' sake, and kissing another man—an ex-convict, of all people—seemed to smack of betrayal. Yet, even as these thoughts tripped through her mind, she allowed the brush of his lips to continue. The rapturous sensation sent the pit of her stomach into a wild swirl, and she couldn't hold back the sigh that rushed out of her. Gracious! Any second now, she'd be wrapping her arms around his neck. If ever there was a kiss to melt her tired soul, this one fit the bill.

Time, place, and all that he'd confessed just moments ago fell away like broken shackles as Will's hands left her shoulders and slipped around the small of her back, drawing her closer. She gladly leaned into him, moving her hands behind his waist and looping her thumbs under his leather belt. It had been months and months since she'd been touched so tenderly. Oh, but she missed Frank, even as she lost herself in Will's warm kiss, and wished for just one more chance to hold her husband. They had shared a precious love, Frank and she, but busy lives and active boys had often interfered with intimacy. Quick embraces and pecks on the cheek would tide them over for days at a time. Sudden regret washed over her for not loving him deeper, longer—fuller. A tear ran down her cheek. "Frank," she whispered.

Will instantly pulled away, frowning, and dropped his hands to his sides, his beautifully shaped lips still wet from the intimate moment. "You called me Frank," he stated.

At a loss for words, she stood there, dazed, wondering if it was true. With all her might, she struggled to recall, but overwhelming emotion clouded her memory. At last, she whispered, "I didn't really, did I?"

"Yes, you really did." She detected no animosity in his voice, just a hint of hurt.

"I'm sorry. I—I don't know, I must have been—"

"Thinking about him," he finished.

How could she deny it? She stared up at him without speaking.

A smile, deliberate and somewhat pained, slowly eased onto his face. "It's all right," he said, using the pad of his thumb to wipe away the lone tear on her cheek. "It's fully understandable. He was your husband, Livvie, and you lost him suddenly and tragically. I'm the one who should be apologizing. Don't know what possessed me to kiss you. I told myself not to do it, that you weren't ready for it. Good grief!" He swept a hand over his furrowed brow. "He hasn't been gone all that long. I hope you won't despise me or let this silly kiss affect our working relationship."

"It's been more than a year," she murmured. *Silly kiss?* So, it had meant nothing to him? "Life goes on. Most days, I manage quite fine, if I do say so, myself. And, no, I don't despise you. Mercy, if this was anyone's fault, it was mine. I'm the one who knocked on your door. I could have easily waited to talk to you in the morning." A worrisome thought sprouted in her head that perhaps she'd secretly wanted to experience his touch, upset as she'd been by what she'd overheard outside her window. In her heart, she knew Will was a good man, and all she'd really needed was reassurance. Well, he'd reassured her, all right—and topped it off with a delicious, decidedly not silly kiss.

The trouble was, it had stirred up memories of Frank and even prompted her to speak his name.

Land sakes! Will would never want to kiss her again, and that realization somehow left her feeling dejected and alone.

At the restaurant the next day, not so much as a word was spoken about the kiss. In fact, Will treated her as if nothing had happened, so that she began to wonder if she'd merely imagined or dreamed the entire incident. Of course, she hadn't, for the experience of that mesmerizing moment played over and over in her head like a picture show. Moreover, she couldn't forget the conversation she'd overheard beneath her window or erase the troublesome suspicion that the man with the scarred face would show up again.

※

With their constant nagging, Cora Mae, Coot Hermanson, Alex, and Nate had managed to talk Livvie into going to church with Will the following Sunday. He'd invited her days ago, but, ever since that kiss, he'd been hesitant to even talk to her for fear of getting fired. He should have known better than to kiss a widow who still carried a hot torch for her husband, especially when that widow was his boss! When he'd awakened the morning after the kiss, he'd vowed to keep their conversations strictly professional and to work as efficiently as he could in the restaurant and then hurry upstairs to his apartment after work to minimize interaction. During the days, he fussed over the boys and Sally, since their presence at Livvie's Kitchen made the time go faster and lightened the atmosphere.

Thursday night's Family Feast was an even bigger success than Tuesday's, with a line of customers that stretched more than half a block. At the patrons' urging, Will once again took a break to entertain them with his harmonica, and everyone put down their utensils to clap their hands and sing along. When he went up to his apartment after work that night, he pondered the events of the past several days and realized that he'd never had more fun or felt more accepted.

On Saturday night, he found himself performing onstage in the dance hall again, this time with a different band that was no less welcoming of his participation than Berk's. Apparently, his harmonica fame preceded him, for as soon as he walked through the door, trying to blend in with the crowd, someone shouted, "Will Taylor to the stage! Will Taylor to the stage!" Soon, the entire room entreated him with one voice. To his dismay, the dolled-up Marva Dulane immediately rushed to his side with hungry eyes, as if she were ready to sink in her hooks. What would it take to convince her to find another fishing hole?

The stage was a welcome retreat. To his relief, folks crowded her out whenever he stepped off the stage between sets, all of them oohing and aahing over his talents and posing questions about his instrument. Some who recognized him from Livvie's Kitchen told him how much they enjoyed the Family Feast nights, and that they'd been telling friends and neighbors all about the event. Will thanked them for supporting the restaurant, and, if the Lord moved him, he made sure to give God the credit for his talents, whether culinary or musical.

He'd seen no sign of Clem Dodd or his cohorts since Tuesday night and held out hope that they'd all jumped on the train the next day. Still, every time he left the restaurant, he kept an eagle eye on his surroundings, half expecting Clem to step into his path. Not that the fellow scared him one iota, but his presence in this pleasant, peaceful town concerned him. He knew the damage Clem was capable of doing.

On Sunday morning, the sun showed up in all its golden perfection, warming Will's shoulders as he strolled up Market Street with Livvie and her boys;

Alex and Nate were abuzz with excitement as they chattered giddily about going to church—and with him, no less. Their constant volley of questions—"Is the Sunday school teacher nice?" "Do we get to draw a picture?" "Are we gonna hear a story?" "Do we gots to be quiet?"—kept him busy thinking of answers. He was not at all familiar with the Sunday school classes for children, so he simply told them to be good listeners and learn as much as they could about Jesus.

As they walked along, he cast Livvie an occasional glance or a smile over the boys' bobbing heads. She smiled in return, but he detected a wariness in her manner, which he credited to either her annoyance with him, her apprehension over returning to church, or both. So, he directed most of his attention to Alex and Nate so that Livvie could ponder her thoughts in peace. How did she feel about setting foot inside a church without Frank? Would resurrected memories stir up deep emotions, or would they bring her closer to healing? Was she worried that folks might jump to the wrong conclusions about her and him? Worse, would she wish she'd never come? He found himself praying for her as they clipped along the nearly deserted street. Traffic was almost nil, with every business closed up tight, and only a few dogs roaming about, sniffing at scraps. In front of them, a couple of squirrels scampered down a tree trunk, then ran right back up again, in what appeared to be a game of tag. Across the street, some birds settled on a telephone wire and set to warbling, their "talk" mingling with Alex and Nate's conversation. Will smiled and gazed past the boys at Livvie, but, this time, she kept her eyes trained straight ahead.

The worshippers at the Wesleyan Methodist church that morning couldn't have numbered more than sixty, but the warmth of the smiles, greetings, and handshakes at the door more than made up for sparse attendance. Something told Livvie that even if these folks were to learn about Will's past, they wouldn't think of shunning him.

First to greet her and the boys was Clara Gillen. "How nice to see you, Olivia!" she exclaimed, shaking Livvie's hand as if working a pump handle with vigor and purpose. "Welcome to our service!"

"Thank you. It's nice to be here. And, please, call me Livvie."

The woman beamed, her smile as bright as a shiny, new button. "Well then, you must call me Clara. Oh, and might I add how tickled I was that you featured my grandmother's recipe on the first night of Family Feast? I heard Thursday night was even busier. I'm sorry we couldn't make it, but we're planning to come again next week. What a wonderful idea you had for bringing new customers into your fine little diner!"

Livvie gave Will a hasty glance and found him engaged in conversation with several other male parishioners, among them Dan Gillen, Clara's husband. "You have to give Mr. Taylor the credit for that."

Clara leaned forward and lowered her voice. "He's a fine man, that Will Taylor. Mighty good cook, too, just like your Frank, may he rest in peace. We had Will join us for lunch a few weeks ago. Say, you two wouldn't want to be our guests today, would you? I made plenty of roast beef and potatoes. I always make extra, never knowing who might be joining us."

"Oh, I don't—"

"Can we, Mom?" Alex tugged on her sleeve. "We don't ever get to go to nobody's house for Sunday dinner! Well, 'cept Aunt Margie's, I guess."

"Do you got any kids?" Nate asked Clara.

She clasped her hands together and bent forward at the waist. "I certainly do. My boys are teenagers, but I bet they'd still enjoy your company. They could take you out to see all our chickens and livestock. Would you like that?"

"Sure! My uncle Howie has chickens on his farm. He gots one named Mildred that he says he can't eat, 'cause he's real attached to her. 'Sides, she gives good eggs. She only has one eye, though, 'cause a rooster poked out th' other one. He's a mean thing. The rooster, not Uncle Howie."

Clara tossed back her head and laughed. "Yes, yes, I knew who you meant. Too bad about Mildred's eye. Well then, it's settled. You'll come for dinner."

"Oh, but—," Livvie stammered.

"We'd love to, Mrs. Gillen," Will's voice interrupted her as he broke away from the group of men to join them. "You don't have any objections, do you, Livvie?"

Even if she did, she'd be hard put to argue right there in front of kind Clara Gillen. Sundays were generally her days to relax and gear up for the week ahead, but she heard herself reply, "No, I think it'd be lovely."

If ever she'd heard a sermon intended just for her, it was the three-point message Reverend Clarence White preached that day. It actually might have been four or even five points; she couldn't be sure. Yes, he wandered off topic more than once, but he still packed a mighty punch and managed to speak truths that resonated in the core of her soul.

"Some folks view life as having no real meaning or purpose," he said. "Perhaps, you've suffered a great loss or struggle with finances or a rebellious child. Maybe some of you believe that God has dealt you an unfair blow. Whatever your circumstances, the Lord brings hope and healing, and He clearly understands our difficulties, no matter how heartrending.

"You might be roaming around with a void in your heart that nothing and no one can fill. Did you know the Lord can fill that empty space and give new meaning to your life?

"If anyone had reason to be bitter and angry toward God, it was Job, and there were times when he questioned God's divine dealings. Yet, Job also held out hope for better days. He knew that his Redeemer lived, and that, in the end, he would again stand upon the earth and see God.

"My friends, your suffering can serve to make you better; as it does, the Lord equips you to help others through their sufferings."

At the close of the reverend's message, Livvie found herself wiping her eyes and wishing for a handkerchief.

As if reading her thoughts, Will produced one from his side pocket, then gently touched her arm.

"Thank you," she mouthed, appreciating the gesture, yet feeling mortified that he'd caught her in so vulnerable a state. Now, she supposed he'd want to talk about it afterward.

She shouldn't have worried, though. All the way to the Gillens' farm, as she rode with Will and her boys in a horse-drawn tram driven by David, the older

Gillen boy, Alex and Nate prattled nonstop about their Sunday school classes, and no one had a ghost of a chance of getting a single word in edgewise. It was one of the few times she was genuinely thankful her boys loved to babble.

The Gillens were a friendly lot. While David and his younger brother, Jonathan, took Alex and Nate outside to show them around, Dan Gillen took Will into the room where he kept his antique gun collection, and Livvie and Clara talked in the kitchen. Since Clara had everything under control—carrots simmering on the stove, potatoes baking in the oven with the roast, a Jell-O mold setting in the refrigerator, and fresh-baked rolls cooling in the pan—there was little for Livvie to do but stand at the sink and dry the clean dishes that were handed to her.

As she chatted with Clara and heard bits and pieces of the men's discussion in the other room, Livvie relaxed and began to enjoy herself. And that's when it struck her.

Life had started to feel normal again, and she had a strong hunch that Will Taylor played a big part in that.

Chapter Seventeen

"The LORD is King for ever and ever:
the heathen are perished out of his land."
—Psalm 10:16

On the last day of July, the month came rolling to an end, but the heat certainly did not. Livvie strolled up Market Street on her way to McNarney Brothers Meat Market under a blanket of thick, threatening clouds, and the air was so heavy, she worried she wouldn't make it back to the restaurant before the skies opened up. Perspiration trailed down from her hairline and dotted her forehead and cheeks in a most unladylike fashion. Every winter, she longed for summer and vowed never to complain about the heat, yet, here she was, protesting again. At least she wasn't alone in her discomfort. Everywhere she looked, folks were fanning themselves with newspapers and wiping their damp brows. Across the street, she noticed three men in conversation, one pointing up at the dreary clouds, the other two nodding dolefully. These days, as much as she hated using up the electricity, she sometimes opened her Frigidaire just to feel the blast of luxuriously cool air.

At the corner of Market and Wabash, Livvie paused, waiting for the streetlight to change. She watched a flock of birds enjoy a free bath in front of City Hall, where a small but steady stream of water from a leaky hydrant up on Hill Street had formed a convenient little pool for the feathered creatures. My, but she'd give just about anything to join them. If Alex and Nate were at her side, they'd surely beg to go jump in the puddle. As it turned out, they were spending the day at Margie and Howard's farm because Sally had left on a day trip with her parents.

Since Will's luscious kiss, not one mention of it had risen up between them, nor had he made a single move to repeat the act. She and her boys had been walking with him to the Wesleyan Methodist church every Sunday, looking almost like a family, but he always made sure to walk between her boys and converse mostly with them. He included her, of course, but avoided any in-depth dialogue. Even at the restaurant, he joked with everyone but her, which she found ironic, considering how he'd expressed hope that the kiss—the "silly kiss"—would not affect their working relationship. And now, he barely acknowledged her, making her wonder if regret weighed heavily on him.

She couldn't count how many times she'd recalled that tender moment, reliving every second and reflecting on the electrifying impact it had made on her soul. Why, his lips had been as soft as velvet. Would she ever get to experience them again? Probably not, considering that she'd spoken her dead husband's name! Why should Will even consider risking a repeat? She pursed her lips as she continued along the sidewalk, taking care to avoid the cracks in the cement. Would that childish superstition about breaking her mother's back ever cease to haunt her? Gracious, she felt like a ninny.

Attending church again had affected her on many levels, awakening emotions, stirring needs in her heart, and poking at her conscience, a result she hadn't anticipated. Although the Wesleyan Methodist church wasn't the one in which she'd been raised, the presence of God and the sense of His love and forgiveness bowled her over at every service, and the people were so warm and welcoming, including her in conversation and inviting her to various church functions. During the services, each hymn they sang seemed to have been selected especially for her, as if the choir director knew she needed those words to minister to her. And the pastor's messages, while they were never too profound, continued to feed a hunger in her soul.

As for Will's former friends, she'd seen nothing of Mr. Dodd or his sidekicks, and she hoped with everything in her that they'd gone back to New York for good. She would never forget the look in Clem's eyes or that awful-looking gash across his cheek. He must have gotten into a terrible fight with someone—or something.

"Afternoon, Mrs. Livvie!"

She whirled at the sound of the female voice and smiled. "Well, if it isn't Sofia Rogers and her handsome little brother, Andy." The siblings caught up to her, and together they crossed the side street, Livvie scooting to dodge a "present" that a passing horse had just left behind. On the corner, they stopped to talk.

"How are you two?" she asked, looking from Sofia to her brother. Sofia couldn't be a day over seventeen, and yet she'd been fully responsible for taking care of her brother for two years, ever since their parents had been killed in a train wreck. With sorrow in her heart, Livvie recalled how devastated the children had

been, especially little Andy, who had developed a no-
ticeable stutter following the accident and was teased
mercilessly by the other boys. She'd learned this from
Margie, who had taken the pair under her wing and
checked in on them as often as she could. Sofia was a
strong, stubborn thing, though—full of determination
and grit, and, as Margie had put it, not one to cotton
to pampering. After the accident, she'd agreed to stay
with Howard and Margie for a few weeks, but, before
long, she'd insisted that her brother and she would
manage fine on their own in their parents' home. It
was on the outskirts of town, a couple of miles from
Margie and Howard's farm. Sofia had refused to burden anyone and continually turned down Margie and
Howard's offers to have Andy and her move in permanently with them, at least until they could get their
feet back on solid ground.

Margie had pleaded with her, but Sofia would
have none of it. A wisp of a thing, she pulled back her
narrow shoulders and held her head high whenever
she came into town. She'd slipped into the role of par-
ent with determination, dutifully getting little Andy
ready for school every morning before she headed to
class, herself. She'd taken a double load of classes and
graduated early. Now, she worked nights for a cleaning service down on Factory Street, tidying business
offices and making just enough to get by, according to
Margie. From what her sister had said, Sofia worked
from 9:00 p.m. to 5:00 a.m. while her brother slept. After her shift, she went home, woke up her brother and
got him ready for school, and then slept for five or six
hours. The only time Livvie had ever seen the girl cry
had been at the cemetery at her parents' funeral, and,
even then, she'd kept her tears to a minimum. Such a
stalwart girl, and yet as pleasant as the morning sun.

Livvie bent at the waist and touched the tip of Andy's nose. "My goodness, you're growing tall, young man. How old are you now?"

"S-s-seven."

"Right between the ages of my sons, Alex and Nathan!" she said, ignoring his stutter. "You ought to come over and play with them sometime this summer. How would that be?" The boys didn't know each other, since hers attended Miami Grade School, while Andy had class in a one-room schoolhouse in the country. But she knew how easily her boys made new friends.

Talking was clearly painful for Andy, who merely nodded and gave a timid smile. Sofia laid a hand on her brother's shoulder. "That would be mighty nice sometime. Thank you for the offer, ma'am. We're heading over to the barbershop right now. Can you tell this little rascal needs a haircut?"

True enough, the boy's brown hair fell haphazardly across his forehead and covered his collar at the nape. Livvie reached out and gave his hair a tousle. "My boys could use a trim, as well. Their hair grows faster than butter melts on a hot skillet!"

After chatting with her a bit longer, the pair headed up the street hand in hand toward Bill's Barbershop. *Such an amazing young woman,* she mused. *And how quickly she's had to grow up.*

A bell jingled as Livvie pushed open the door to McNarney Brothers Meat Market. Behind the counter stood George and Ralph McNarney, both wearing long, white aprons, permanently stained with blood and who knows what else. They were helping customers, but they raised their heads and acknowledged her. "'Mornin', Miss Livvie," George said. His friendly demeanor was one reason Livvie gave his store her business. "You come in to place your weekly order?"

"I did, but please take your time. I'm in no particular hurry."

A woman Livvie recognized as Rosalind Leonard reached across the glass case and accepted two wrapped packages from George, then stepped aside to the cash register. While Ralph rang up her order, she turned to Livvie, who had moved to the back of the line.

"That new cook of yours sure has a knack for fixing fine food," Rosalind said. "I hear you've been doing a good business, especially since you started those Tuesday and Thursday night specials. Thomas and I plan to come next week. As a matter of fact, I've got a recipe to enter. Came from my great-aunt. Maybe you'll choose it!"

"It certainly can't hurt to enter, Mrs. Leonard," Livvie said with a smile. "I will warn you, our box is chock-full with everybody's best recipes. We'll look forward to seeing you, though. And, you're right; Mr. Taylor is talented in the kitchen." And talented at kissing, too, though she would keep that information carefully concealed.

"He plays that there mouth harp like nobody's business, too," said Steven Bronson, owner of Bronson Hardware on North Cass Street, who was several spots ahead of her in line.

Behind him, Alvin Hardy, the town's mortician, shifted the weight of his scrawny body to the other foot, obviously not caring one hoot about the discussion.

"I heard him play at the community dance above your restaurant a couple weeks back," Steven added. He took his package from George and moved toward the cash register as Alvin Hardy stepped up to the counter.

With a wave good-bye to Livvie, Rosalind Leonard headed out the door past the incoming customer, Minerva Washington, who was accompanied by her young son, Kenneth. My, but the McNarneys ran a busy store.

"Wished he would've hung around to play a few more tunes," Steven continued. "I saw you there, too, Mrs. Beckman. Don't think I've ever known you to go up there before."

"No, that was my first time, Mr. Bronson," she admitted.

Just then, an incoming train sounded its whistle, but that didn't muffle the sniff of indignation that came from the elderly Josephine Harper, who stood three spaces ahead of Livvie. "A den of iniquity, that place," she muttered. Livvie couldn't see her bony, weathered face, but she could imagine her pinched expression of disapproval, with those beady eyes narrowed behind her dark-rimmed glasses. Heat traveled up Livvie's neck and trickled out into her cheeks.

Steven turned around with a gleam in his eye. "Why, Mrs. Harper, are you calling me an iniquitous individual?" He then turned back around, extended his upturned palm to Ralph McNarney, and accepted his change. After dropping the coins into his hip pocket, he tucked his package of meat under his arm and looked at Mrs. Harper again. "All folks do up there is listen to music, enjoy good conversation, and dance a few jigs. It's pretty harmless, actually. You want me to pick you up next Saturday night?"

Quiet laughter could be heard around the room. "What? Well, I never!" Mrs. Harper exclaimed, obviously failing to see the humor.

Livvie stifled a giggle. She doubted Mrs. Harper had ever seen the inside of a dance hall. Ducking her head, she covered her grin with three fingers.

"I'm just joshing you, ma'am," Steven said with a wink. Then, tipping the bill of his cap at Livvie, he headed for the door. The train's screeching brakes and final whistle nearly drowned out the lingering chuckles.

❧

Shaded by its branches, Clem Dodd leaned against the thick trunk of an old elm tree and puffed on his cigarette, his eyes fixed across the street on the meat market Olivia Beckman had entered just moments ago. He'd followed her there, walking a distance behind her on the opposite side of the street. Little did she know how fond he'd grown of watching her jaunt about town when she wasn't busy waiting tables, her knee-high skirt flaring with every step, and that reddish-blonde hair of hers bouncing off those pretty shoulders. He finally admitted it: he'd become more interested in her whereabouts than in Will Taylor's comings and goings.

But he hadn't forgotten about Will. The more he mulled over the guy's claim that he'd thrown the jewels in a sewer drain, the more inclined he became to believe it, especially with the corroborating details Rudy and Hank had dug up in the city library when they'd gotten back to New York. It turned out that the *New York Times* had run an article some seven years ago about a young boy who'd discovered a leather draw-string bag bearing the initials C.B.D. and containing fine jewels. The boy had turned the bag in to the New York City Police Department, and the article was more of a human-interest story than an investigative piece, with a headline that read, "Young Boy Chooses Honesty over Jewels." Whether the police had ever matched those jewels with the burglary four years prior was not clear from the article. This made Clem wonder if Will even knew about the bag's recovery. Something told him he didn't.

One thing stood out above all else, though: Clem remembered that bag. It had belonged to his father, Charles Benton Dodd, who had passed it down to him. When he'd been planning the robbery, it'd seemed like the perfect place to stash the gems—lightweight, yet strong and sturdy. Of course, he hadn't counted on Will Taylor throwing it down a sewer drain and having the thing wind up in a ditch in a neighborhood some five miles outside the city.

Keeping his gaze locked on the meat market, he took another long drag off his cigarette and mentally counted the money he had left in his billfold. It was enough for a few more nights at the old hotel, the Western House, before he robbed another unsuspecting soul. The Western House wasn't Wabash's fine Hotel Indiana, by any means, but it sure beat his pad in New York, which was nothing but a filthy hole in the wall, thanks to Flo's lack of housekeeping abilities. If he'd learned one thing about the little town of Wabash, it was that folks were trusting—too trusting for their own good. Just last week, he'd managed to pull off a pickpocket's trick on three unsuspecting targets: first, a fellow sorting through his mail in the post office; second, a lady who'd left her purse wide open while she tended to her cranky child in the grocery store; and, third, a fellow dressed in a dapper suit and bowler hat, with whom Clem had "accidentally" collided on a busy sidewalk. A hastily muttered "pardon me" was all it had taken to walk away several dollars richer.

The lovely Olivia Beckman emerged from the market empty-handed, save for that long-strapped shoulder bag she never went anywhere without. Maybe he ought to rob her. Of course, if he did, he'd want more than just her money. Yessir, a fine specimen like her had much more to offer than mere cash. He'd watched her long enough to know her routine. Every Thursday, she went to McNarney Brothers Meat Market to place her order for the following week's meals, and then, like clockwork, a delivery boy pulling a wagon behind his three-wheeled bicycle left the market at five o'clock to deliver orders to her and to others. Some days, Clem had half a mind to rob the kid, but he figured most of his deliveries were prepaid, so he probably had little to no cash on hand. Besides, robbing a kid would draw too much attention. As it was, he had to watch his step and steal just enough to make people wonder where they'd spent their last dime. So far, his scheme appeared to be working fine, and he had yet to run out of money.

Olivia strolled along, every so often stopping to speak with passersby. He, in turn, paused to watch her reflection in store windows, enraptured by her every move. Outside J. C. Penney, she stopped for a moment to gaze at a blue floral dress on a skinny mannequin, and he pictured her wearing it. She leaned forward, evidently to check the price tag, which hung from the sleeve. Then, she shook her head and walked on.

Outside Oh Boy! Produce, she stopped beside a display of watermelons, over which hung a big sign indicating that they were fifty cents apiece. When a fellow in an apron stepped outside and began to chat with her, she pointed at the fruit stand, and he nodded, no doubt confirming an order.

On she went, past Bradley Drugstore and Kramer Cleaners, to the Crystal-Renee Beauty Shop, where she paused and studied the posters of women with short bobs and straight bangs. He surely hoped she wasn't considering cutting her beautiful mane.

A few drops of rain fell, and she stepped up her pace. Clem did, as well, yet still managed to keep his distance. The clock tower bell sounded three gongs, marking the hour. One of those newfangled European-looking cars called a Whippet sped by, just missing a dog that darted across the street. By now, the rain came down in sheets, so Livvie disappeared inside Woolworth's five-and-dime, just a block away from her restaurant, to wait out the storm, no doubt. Thunder clapped in the distance, so he made an about-turn and headed for the nearest cover: Ruby's Café. Might as well grab a cup of coffee and smoke another ciga-rette. Then, he could make his way across the street to J. C. Penney.

Man alive, wouldn't Olivia Beckman be surprised to open a package containing that blue dress she'd admired in the window?

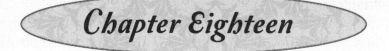

Chapter Eighteen

"The LORD is my light and my salvation;
whom shall I fear? the LORD is the strength
of my life; of whom shall I be afraid?"
—Psalm 27:1

*L*ivvie couldn't imagine what was contained in the package she received the next day, addressed in sloppy writing to:

Livvie's Kitchen
Attn: Olivia Beckman
Market Street

Wabash, Ind

"Surprised"—"flabbergasted," more like it—described her emotions upon opening the box and seeing the familiar cap-sleeved dress of robin's-egg-blue cotton flocked with ivory motes—dotted Swiss, the fabric was called. And then, she had to tack on "puzzled" and "slightly alarmed." She held it up to herself, gathering it at the waist, and twirled around, loving the way the full skirt flared and feeling certain it would be a near perfect fit. Who could have had so much as a clue that she'd been admiring this very dress in the window of J. C. Penney ever since it had appeared on the mannequin? Her sister, maybe, but she doubted even Margie knew her that well. And, if she did, would she have made such a spendthrift purchase? Hardly. Margie didn't abide wasting money on such frivolities as store-bought dresses. No, for her, such purchases as chocolates and fresh strawberries were the height of extravagance.

Plainly put, the whole thing was rather eerie. Still, the dress was lovely, and the anonymous note, scrawled in the same, sloppy handwriting as the address, seemed innocent enough:

> thought you'd look nice in this.
> Wear it soon.

How peculiar that the giver had decided to remain anonymous! Perhaps, someone had taken pity on her sorely lacking wardrobe and decided that, with the Family Feasts occurring twice a week, she ought to at least look the part of successful proprietress.

"What've we got here, missy?" asked Coot, seated at his usual table. All his cronies had left after a long, drawn-out breakfast, and he had started to stand, himself, albeit slowly. Outside, Reggie, his faithful canine, got to all fours and stretched, then gazed through the screen door, awaiting a snack of leftover bacon and eggs. "I saw the package Bud delivered to you. Looks like you got yourself a purty dress."

"Yes! Isn't it the loveliest thing you ever saw?"

"Mighty fine, indeed." He looked it up and down. "Where'd you order it from?"

"I didn't order it. That's the strange part."

"Oh?" He hobbled closer.

"Coot." For just an instant, she hoped it had come from him.

Apparently, he'd sensed her suspicion. "Don't go lookin' at me like that. You know I don't have the slightest inklin' 'bout women's stuff. Now, if you'd told me you wanted a fishin' pole, I could have accommodated you."

She giggled. "Oh, Coot, you know I don't fish."

"Fish? Who said that magic word?" Will said as the back door slammed shut behind him. "I'm going fishing this very afternoon. You want to tag along, Coot?" He set down the two large trashcans he'd emptied in the barrel out back to burn later. Then, brushing his hands on his pants' legs, he approached them, pausing by the counter to pick up the plate of leftovers he'd set there earlier.

"I ain't been fishin' in ten years," Coot said. "Reached the point in my life where I'd rather just eat 'em without havin' to catch 'em. Lookie here at what Bud just delivered to Miss Livvie."

Will gave the dress a hurried glance, and his eyes popped. "Mighty fine dress, Liv." He tacked on a low whistle before moving to the door, where a drooling Reggie waited. He pulled open the door, lowered the plate onto the pavement in front of the black dog, and patted his head before rejoining them. "Your sister send that to you?"

"This isn't her handwriting, so, no, it couldn't have been. The truth is, I don't have a clue who did."

Will eyed the note she clutched in her hand. "May I have a look?"

She handed it over, and Coot edged closer to get a glimpse of it, too. "That don't look like a lady's handwritin'," he asserted.

One of Will's thick eyebrows rose a fraction, and he passed the note back to her with nary a glance in her direction. "Humph. Guess you got yourself a secret admirer." In his tone, she detected the tiniest hint of something unusual. Surely, he wouldn't have been so bold as to buy her a dress and then feign ignorance! True, he'd kissed her, but, in the weeks since, he'd managed to keep it out of their conversations and had shown no interest in repeating the act. The few times that he'd walked her upstairs at the end of the workday, he hadn't lingered to chat; he'd simply tipped his chin at her and said a friendly good night. As for the dances on Saturday nights, he had not extended another invitation to her—not that she would have accepted, but the gesture would have been considerate. She knew he attended regularly, for she often overheard his harmonica serenades, followed by thundering rounds of applause and rousing whoops of appreciation from the audience. He'd certainly become popular on account of his bounteous talents, not to mention his good-humored personality. More than once, she'd recalled the way Marva Maxwell Dulane had hung on his every word, not to mention his arm! Had he taken a special interest in her? And, if he had, did he even know of her sordid past—the rumors of it, at least?

"You wouldn't happen to know who sent her that fine dress, now, would you, Will?" Coot asked with a devilish grin.

Prickles of heat crept up Livvie's neck and scuttled straight across her cheeks. To hide her embarrassment, she lowered her gaze to the dress and found that the hem stopped at the knee, an inch or so shorter than the drab, gray dress she now wore.

"Me?" Out of the corner of her eye, she saw Will shift his weight. "Sorry, I can't take the credit. Maybe one of her girlfriends bought it for her."

Girlfriends? Livvie nearly laughed. The few female friends she had were married and had mostly fallen by the wayside since Frank's death, either from not knowing how to act around her or from having less in common with her. All of them treated her kindly, no question there, but, one by one, they'd simply drifted away. Not that she blamed any of them. She was a hardworking widow with young children, and she couldn't think of another woman who could relate to her situation. There were other widows in town, of course, but none as young as she. No matter; she'd come to accept her circumstances and was beginning to learn and grow from them. If anything, she'd developed an entirely new understanding of the grieving process. And, thanks to the sermons she'd been hearing every Sunday, the Bible reading she'd been doing to sate her recent thirst for the Word of God, and even Will's Christian testimony, her bitterness and anger toward God had dissipated significantly.

"No, none of them knows I've been admiring this dress for some time."

"Well, it must have been somebody who knows you awfully well," Will said in a tone that she could have sworn held agitation. "Coot has a point. That looks like a man's handwriting."

Feeling irritated herself, she crumpled the note and stuffed it inside her apron pocket, then went about folding the dress and laying it back in its box. "Well, I can't express my gratitude until I figure out who sent it."

"How you plannin' to do that?" Coot asked.

"I don't know. Maybe I'll walk over to J. C. Penney and see if they can tell me who purchased it."

Coot frowned. "It's clear somebody admires you and wanted to give you a gift, an anonymous one. Why spoil the guy's fun?"

She paused. He did have a point. Even the Bible talked about giving gifts in secret, lest the benefactor receive recognition and think too highly of himself. When she looked at Will to see if he would add to Coot's advice, all she saw was a slight shrug of the shoulders. The oaf! She ought to invite herself along on his little fishing excursion just to spite him. She could wade in the river, make a racket, and scare off all the fish.

❧

For a host of reasons he couldn't sort out, the dress and its mystery sender put Will in a sour mood. He'd seen that poorly penned note and known without a doubt that it hadn't come from any woman. Besides, it'd had a few smudge marks on it, and he'd detected the faintest odor of nicotine. That some man assumed she'd finished mourning her husband and thought she might be ready to start dating again pulled at his innards. She wasn't ready. She'd proved that to him some weeks ago, when he'd planted that kiss on her soft lips and, in return, heard her husband's name whispered in his ear. He was half tempted to post a sign in the window that read, "Olivia Beckman is still mourning her late husband and is not available for dating. Please cease with the anonymous gifts!"

It was plain absurd to be jealous. He didn't have any claim on her just because he'd kissed her, which had been a dumb move on his part, anyway. She could do as she pleased, for Pete's sake! Still, he knew that

242 ⌒ SHARLENE MACLAREN

if and when she wore that dress, the question of who had sent it would nag him to no end.

At two thirty, alone in the restaurant after cleaning up from breakfast and lunch, he starting preparing for supper. When everything was ready, he headed to the back door to retrieve the tackle box and fishing pole Livvie had lent him some weeks ago. "It was Frank's, but he would want someone to use it," she'd said. He'd planned to invite the boys along, but Sally had taken them to her house after they'd spent the morning at the public library. Livvie usually minded them in the afternoon hours when the restaurant was closed, but today was an exception. Sally sure had developed a love for those boys, and it appeared that the feelings were mutual.

Will pushed open the screen door, then pulled the other door shut to close up the place. And that's when he noticed a second fishing pole, propped next to his against the building. He glanced around and discovered Livvie, leaning against the tree in the alley, dressed in a low-waisted, sleeveless yellow dress that looked like it'd seen better days. On her feet were toeless shoes, and a wide-brimmed, khaki-colored hat completed the outfit. Her hair hung in a long ponytail across one shoulder. If he'd ever seen a more fetching sight, he couldn't recall when, and his gut did a complete somersault. "Livvie!" *Lord, have mercy on my thumping heart.* "What are you doing out here?"

"Waiting for you." She unhurriedly stepped away from the tree and sauntered in his direction. Her skirt flared in the warm breeze, revealing those shapely calves behind her slender shins.

"Oh?"

"You said you were going fishing, and I thought I'd join you."

"I heard you tell Coot you don't fish."

"I don't."

He scratched his head and felt a grin tickle the corners of his mouth. "All right, then. Come on." He picked up both fishing poles and handed one to her, then hefted the tackle box and metal pail. "Hope my worms didn't shrivel up in this heat."

"Worms? Don't you use those shiny wooden lures? There are a bunch of them in that tackle box. Frank always—"

"I'm sure he did, but I prefer live bait. That's why I went looking for night crawlers at four this morning."

"What?"

"You heard me." He set off at a fast pace, and she matched it, her breath coming in huffs.

"You do that often? Get up to hunt for night crawlers?"

"If I plan to fish that day, sure. You and the boys can come look with me sometime, if you like."

"At four o'clock? No, thank you. Do we have to walk so fast?"

"Yep."

When they reached the river, he spotted a few fishermen upstream wearing waders. Afternoon was not the best time for fishing, particularly when the water moved at a good clip, but, with a little "divine luck," as he liked to call it, he might catch a few bluegills and maybe even a bass. He wouldn't mind a catfish, either. Some folks weren't wild about the flavor, but, in his opinion, fried up with the right batter, catfish made a tasty bedtime snack, even if he'd have to air out the odor from his small apartment.

He was still trying to get used to the fact that Livvie had decided to tag along with him. Surprisingly, she had talked a blue streak the entire way to the river. Granted, it hadn't been a long walk, but he began to wonder if she'd chattered the entire time on purpose. If she had, and if she kept it up, he'd be hard put to catch anything, and that didn't bode well for his hankering for some good, fried fish.

"I think the Family Feasts have been a great success so far. I saw Sandy Flood at the bank yesterday, and she told me she'd never tasted such excellent meat loaf as you made last Thursday. Oh, and when I ran into the Stingers at the market the other day, Paul said Joyce would never have to cook another Tuesday or Thursday night, as far as he was concerned. Isn't that wonderful? The money keeps pouring in, and I'm sure we'll exceed our budget by a fair piece this month."

"That's great, Livvie. Exactly what we were aiming for. Now, what you do is, take the excess and apply it to your mortgage and other outstanding loans."

"Oh, I will, I will. At this rate, I'll have those bills paid lightning quick."

He moseyed over to his favorite fishing spot, where he'd managed to catch a few bluegills and some small bass on other occasions. Propping his pole against a stump, he crouched down to open the tackle box and take out the canning jar he'd filled with moist soil and several fat night crawlers.

Out of the corner of his eye, he saw Livvie rest her pole next to his, kick off her summer shoes, throw her hat down beside them, and wander down to the water's edge. He had a hard time concentrating on that dumb jar of worms once she put her back to him and dipped her toes into the water, then quickly jumped back with a shriek.

"The river's freezing! I thought it'd be warmer." Slowly, she dipped her foot in again and proceeded to inch her way further into the water, picking up her skirt as she eased along.

Grinning, he started threading the sticky worm onto the hook at the end of the line, still distracted by the beguiling sight just a few yards away. "Watch where you step, Liv. The rocks can get pretty slippery."

No sooner had the words left his mouth than down she went with a splat, landing on her backside.

He threw down the fishhook, leaped to his feet, and ran to her, crouching at her side and helping her to a sitting position. "You all right?" he asked, putting an arm around her shoulder for support. "Did you hurt yourself? Man, you went down hard."

He expected her to shed a tear or wince, at least, from humiliation, if not from pain. Instead, she started to giggle, and her dimples appeared like two deep canyons. "Oh, gracious, look at me!" There she sat, sprawled in the water, her legs spread in a *V* and her skirt floating up around her knees, as her bare feet wiggled in the water. Her ponytail was entirely drenched and hung down her back like a long, drippy dishcloth. She continued to giggle, and the sound, which had begun as a gentle ripple, soon crescendoed into a loud, infectious wave. Soon, she was holding her stomach, as if to keep it from bursting wide open.

At first, he didn't know what to make of her— he'd never seen her engaged in such riotous laughter—and his mouth twitched at the corners, wanting to smile. He shook his head in disbelief and couldn't decide whether to laugh himself or settle her down. Either she'd knocked something loose in her noggin and gone a bit zany in the head, or she truly found humor in her predicament. "Are you...all right?" he asked once more.

"You goof." She pushed him smack in the center of the chest with both hands and knocked him off balance, so that he fell backward onto the riverbank. Next, she proceeded to scoop up two handfuls of water and splash his face and shirtfront.

"Hey! W-what'd you do that for?" he sputtered.

More giggles tumbled uncontrollably out of her, and he broke into a smile, which soon turned to full-out laughter. Righting himself, he leaned forward and dipped his hand into the water, giving her a dose of her own medicine as he splashed her face. She gasped, eyes and mouth as round as marbles, and then returned the act.

Soon, they were both splashing each other like a pair of giddy ducklings, until he managed to snag her by both hands and hold her firmly, despite her squirming. "Enough, you rascal," he laughed. Cold water dripped off the tips of his nose and chin, and his soggy hair hung in front of his face, partially blocking his vision. He dared not let go of her hands to brush it away, though, lest she start up her shenanigans again.

"All right, now, young lady. Answer me honestly. Can you stand up?"

"Of course I can, silly. The only thing I hurt was my pride."

"It doesn't seem to be suffering all that much," he said with a grin. "Come on, then. Up with you." He tugged gently on her arms and brought her to her feet. She, of course, was soaked from the top of her head to her bare toes, and he tried to resist feasting his eyes on the places where her dress clung to her body. Dropping his hands to his sides, he gazed down at her face, amazed she still wore a smile.

"I haven't laughed that hard since...since...I don't know when!" she confessed, clutching her chest.

A chuckle rumbled out of him. "I think it's safe to say we'd better hang up this whole fishing idea, don't you?"

"What do you mean? I'm off to a good start, don't you think?"

He couldn't stop his mouth from gaping and his eyebrows from arching. "Sure, if you call falling on your fanny a good start." He swept the wet hair out of his eyes.

"Well, you have to admit, it was funny."

The urge to touch her wet cheek nearly overtook him. "I do. And I'm glad you gave me permission to laugh."

"Did I do that?"

"Well, maybe not in so many words, but when you started splashing me, I figured that gave me the right. By the way, I don't think I deserved that kind of treatment. I'm about as wet as you now."

"You were taking the whole thing too seriously, Mr. Taylor."

Now he did touch the tip of her damp nose. "Only because I thought you might have hurt yourself, Mrs. Beckman."

She stood slightly uphill from him, which brought their faces dangerously close—close enough to kiss. But he didn't dare do that. Instead, he took a small step back and glanced behind him at his fishing pole, still lying on the ground, a night crawler dangling from the hook. "Do you want to at least go back to your apartment and change out of those wet clothes?" he asked.

"Why? It's hot today. Look over there." She pointed upriver. "Some folks are even swimming." Sure enough, a family of five was wading and splashing around near a sandbar. "We'll both dry if we stay in the sun."

He couldn't help but give her face a thorough assessment. If there were any flaws, he couldn't find them. Matter of fact, he couldn't name one woman he'd met whose looks matched hers. "If you're sure, then."

She put her hands on her hips and straightened her posture. "I'm stubbornly certain."

"You're stubborn, all right." He turned and walked back to where he'd left his fishing gear. "All right, then. Let's start with how to bait a hook."

"Wait. I don't want to actually touch anything but the fishing pole."

"How do you expect to learn the sport if you won't bait a hook?"

"I just want to hold the pole," she stated again, stepping up beside him. All traces of her smile had vanished.

He scratched the back of his neck. "All right, madam. I'll bait your hook, but you have to watch me do it."

"I might just do that." She crouched down beside him, and her hips brushed his side.

If she only knew what she did to him!

�֍

The two of them had been at this fishing business for almost two hours, and they'd talked almost non-stop, covering so many topics, she'd lost track of them all. The latest subject was the Saturday night dances and how Margie would be scandalized if she found out that her little sister had gone up there. "She thinks it's a place where sinners gather," Livvie told Will.

"Could be that it is," he replied. "But Jesus spent a lot of time mingling with sinners. How can we expect to reach people for Christ if we never rub shoulders with them? Wherever I go, I try to let my light shine, whether it's up on that stage playing my harmonica or just talking to people. I guess prison life kind of taught me how to do that. Now, if you want to see a den of iniquity, visit the state pen!"

He made a good point. Maybe she'd raise it with Margie—if she ever mustered the courage.

She had laid down her pole long ago, deciding she didn't need to fish in order to enjoy the warmth of the sun's rays while she sat on a stump by the water's edge. Besides, Will had caught five fish to her one, and what was the fun in that? Fishing required too much patience, something she didn't have in large reserve.

"Have you seen that Clem character since the night he and his friends paid you a visit?" Livvie decided to ask.

Will shook his head. "Not so much as a sign of him. I'm pretty sure they all went on their way."

"That's a relief. You must have done a good job convincing them of the truth."

"I'm praying that's the case. Don't want to see any of their faces ever again, unless it's a snapshot in some newspaper when they're sentenced to prison."

"Do you think they're still committing crimes?"

"Oh, no doubt—small ones, most likely."

"And they've never been caught?"

He shook his head and reeled in his line, then cast it in another direction. "It's just dumb luck that they haven't."

"The Lord has truly changed you, hasn't He?"

"He's working on me, I'll say that." He gave her a sideways glance. "Seems to me He's working on you, as well."

"I think you're right. Attending church again has helped a lot. The sermons always speak to me."

"Funny, I thought they were meant for me."

She smiled. "Thanks for inviting the boys and me. We needed to get back to church, and Alex and Nate really like their Sunday school teachers."

"And Mr. Constant does a fine job of teaching the adult class, don't you think?"

"Yes, he raises interesting questions for us to discuss," she agreed. Even this afternoon, she'd spent time mulling over their recent study of the book of Acts, specifically, the many miracles wrought by God and the formation of the early church. "At our last class, someone raised the question of whether God still performs miracles today. I didn't have anything to contribute to the discussion, but I've been thinking a lot about it."

He took his eyes off the floating bobber several yards out and looked at her. "And what were you thinking, Livvie?"

She folded her hands in her lap. "That He's working a miracle in me right now."

He nodded several times and grinned. "I like that."

They sat in silence for a few moments, until she picked up a good-sized stone and threw it in the water. As planned, it landed close to his bobber.

"Hey! Watch it, young lady," he admonished her with a mock glare. "You're scaring away my fish."

She crossed her bare feet at the ankles and smoothed out her skirt, which was finally dry, albeit wrinkled. Her cheeks stung with sunburn, and she regretted not having worn her hat for most of their earlier outing. "I'll confess, I tagged along with you today intending to make a pest of myself. Did I do a good job?"

The sound of his laughter was warm, rich, and deep. "I'd say you more than succeeded." When he turned and looked at her, she didn't miss the twinkle in his eye.

Chapter Nineteen

"The Lord is merciful and gracious,
slow to anger, and plenteous in mercy."
—Psalm 103:8

With the aid of his stolen binoculars, Clem had watched Will and Livvie all afternoon from behind an abandoned railroad car, and he'd quickly grown weary of their constant blather and intermittent laughter. Unfortunately, he couldn't make out a word they said, but he sure did see their mouths going at it. That they got on so well irked him to no end. Taylor didn't deserve the attentions of that kind of woman. She was much too refined for him. Did she even know that the stupid fool had spent ten years behind bars? Maybe Clem needed to send her another anonymous note to inform her about Taylor's past. And another thing: Why in the world wasn't she wearing her new dress? He'd thought she would've put it on the first chance she got. Instead, she wore that tattered yellow thing. Surely, she appreciated her gift. Man, what he wouldn't have given to watch her open it!

Around four o'clock, they started to gather their belongings and make ready to leave their fishing site, from the looks of it. Clem focused the binocular lenses and watched Will fetch Livvie's fishing pole from the ground. As he handed it off, Clem thought he detected some significance in the way he looked at her. Did Taylor honestly think he stood a chance?

Disgust curdled at the bottom of his gut. If anyone could make her truly happy, he could. He had the know-how to make a lot of money; he just needed to pull off one good heist—maybe right here in Wabash, where he had his choice of banks—and he'd be sitting pretty. He'd never robbed a bank by himself before, but he had enough confidence in his abilities to know it could be done.

He scratched the deep scab on his left cheek and thought about his loser of a wife, wondering if he oughtn't contact her to let her know he'd send her the money for a divorce. When he'd first laid eyes on Olivia Beckman, he'd known he'd found the woman of his dreams at long last, and he couldn't get out of his marriage to Flo fast enough.

※

Weeks passed, and, before anyone could figure out how it'd happened, the hot, humid days of August were upon them. The Family Feast nights were becoming almost more than three adults could handle on their own, and so, with fear and trembling, Livvie took Will's encouragement to heart and hired an assistant cook—a middle-aged, dark-skinned man named Gus Anderson, who had plenty of kitchen experience, having worked at various establishments around town for more than a decade. She also hired an additional waitress, Georgia McIntire, whom she'd employed before having to let her go in light of the hard times that followed Frank's death. As it turned out, the girl had just lost her job in a factory that had closed, and she'd been ecstatic when Livvie had asked her to return to the restaurant.

Will had assured Livvie that the extra help would make things flow easier and benefit everyone, as the improved service would stimulate business and thereby increase revenues. It would also allow Livvie, Cora Mae, and Georgia to take off one morning per week, and the news had nearly sent Cora Mae into a fainting spell.

The longer Will had worked at Livvie's Kitchen, the more he'd come to love it, and his passion for cooking and baking had grown ever stronger. Yet, while the boom in business was good news for the restaurant, it demanded more of his time and energy, and laboring day after day in a hot kitchen had started to take its toll. So, he was forever grateful to Livvie for agreeing to hire an assistant for him.

From his viewpoint, Wabash was fast becoming a city on the move. Even in the months since his arrival, new businesses had opened their doors, banks had been launched, the automobile industry had boomed, service stations and car dealerships had started popping up around town, and work had continued on the new Linlawn High School. Everywhere he looked, construction crews were digging new foundations and laying bricks. Of all the places he might have chosen to settle in after leaving Welfare Island, he didn't think he could have picked a better town than Wabash. And that was not counting a certain strawberry blonde, her two towheaded sons, and a thriving little restaurant where he happened to work.

On a typical Saturday morning, as he scoured the griddle after flipping pancakes and frying eggs for the breakfast crowd, Will thought about the day he'd spent with Livvie at the river back in July and wondered if he ought to invite her fishing again. Maybe it was better if he left it up to her to tell him if she wished to join him.

After all, she'd made no bones about inviting herself the first time. If she wanted to go again, she'd probably show up at the back door with her fishing pole, as before. The last thing he wanted was to make her think he had romantic feelings for her, even though there was no denying he did. Most nights, it took him forever to fall asleep, as his mind was filled with pictures of how she'd looked that day. Truth be told, his heart turned to mush every time she entered the room, and he often thought he'd reached the point of no return. But a simple reminder of the fateful name she'd whispered after the kiss they'd shared was all it took to defeat that notion. He knew better than to dwell on the far-fetched prospect of romancing Livvie. Frank Beckman would always live on in her heart, and Will doubted she'd ever find room there for anyone else.

Earlier that morning, after the breakfast rush had slowed, Livvie had taken her boys to a city park for some recreation. Cora Mae and Georgia were taking a Coke break at a table in the back, and Gus was busy cleaning out the refrigerator and organizing the kitchen shelves. At the front of the restaurant, a couple of customers enjoyed a leisurely breakfast and engaged in quiet conversation, giving the place an overall sense of peace and serenity—until the door opened and Sheriff Morris walked in, his gun holstered at his side, his belt sagging beneath his oversized belly.

The jumpy feeling fueled by years of living on the wrong side of the law poked at Will's nerves, just as it did whenever an officer in uniform sauntered in, whether it was the sheriff, one of his deputies, or a policeman.

Sheriff Morris set his eyes on Will and immediately crossed the room, sat himself down on one of the bar stools, and crossed his pudgy hands on the countertop. "Mr. Taylor," he muttered with what sounded like forced politeness. They had yet to become anything closer than acquaintances, and Will preferred to keep it that way.

"'Mornin', Sheriff. What can I do for you?"

"A cup o' coffee would be fine. Black."

"You got it." He whipped around, nabbed a cup from the shelf, and filled it to the brim with the strong, steaming liquid.

"Good to see you, Sheriff," said Gus, pulling his head out of the refrigerator. "How's business? You caught yo'self any bad guys lately?"

Will set the cup on a saucer under the sheriff's nose, stepped back, and folded his arms, glad for Gus's pleasant manner. Having lived in Wabash his whole life, the fellow got on well with folks and seemed to find it easy to converse with almost anybody.

Sheriff Morris sniffed, took a swig of the hot brew, and nearly choked. "Sheesh, this stuff is strong," he said, ignoring Gus's greeting.

"Sorry, it's been on the burner since early this morning," Will told him. "By ten thirty, it's apt to taste like tar. I'll make a fresh pot right away."

"Don't bother." The sheriff lifted the cup to his lips again, took another swallow, and set it back down with a look of disgust. He then glanced at Gus and gave a cursory nod. "To answer your question, Gus, business is pretty slow, with the exception of a few robberies reported. I actually came by to ask Livvie if she's come up short on any of her daily earnings."

"She's not here," Will spoke up, "but I can tell you that she hasn't mentioned anything about coming up short." He knew she would have told him if the cash drawer had failed to balance. "Who's been robbed?"

The sheriff turned his gaze on him, and Will was sure his eyes held suspicion. Having lived in Wabash a mere three months, he supposed he hadn't quite passed muster with the man.

"A few businesses 'round town...McNarney Brothers Meat Market, Red Goose Shoe Store, Garland's Flower Shop, and Kramer Cleaners, to name a few."

"You mean, there're more?" Will asked.

"That ain't good," Gus said, sticking his head back inside the refrigerator. The temperature was expected to reach ninety degrees this afternoon, which probably explained why Gus seemed to be taking his sweet time cleaning out the icebox.

"Yeah, there're more, all right. Folks are now sayin' they noticed a shortage in their cash drawers some time ago but figured they'd either given customers too much change or miscalculated the total and undercharged, so they didn't file a report. Now, with formal reports comin' in, others are surfacin'."

"That's too bad. I hope you get to the bottom of it." A nauseating sensation swirled around his stomach when he recalled the number of times he'd played a part in similar robberies. As much as he'd wanted to fit in with the gang of guys he'd called his friends, his conscience had never failed to tell him that what he was doing in the name of fun was just plain wrong. That hadn't stopped him back then, though, because crime was like gambling. It got a good, strong hold on you and wouldn't let go. You pulled off a successful heist, and the triumph of that event spurred you on to the next, and the next, and the next. To most thieves, there was always a better job around the bend, and half the fun was in the planning—who breaks the window? Who enters first to trip the alarm? Who grabs the goods? It was a game of sick thrills. By the grace of God, he would never return to a lifestyle of such destructive activities.

"Oh, we'll get to the bottom of it, all right," the sheriff was saying, his beady eyes drilling into Will's, as if probing them for a sign of guilt. "And, when we do, we'll make the crook—or crooks—pay back every last penny. If there's one thing I can't abide, it's a thief."

He shouldn't have let the sheriff's words get to him. But it was the way he'd said them, and his manner of staring at Will, that bothered him. It was as if he knew his secret, even though Will was sure no one could have told the sheriff about his past. Livvie knew better than to breathe a word about it to anybody. As for Clem Dodd, the guy stayed as far as he could from men in uniform. Good grief, Will remembered him saying that even army soldiers gave him the creeps.

"I'm prone to agree with you, Sheriff. Folks who steal are jus' plain cruel," Gus said, emerging from the refrigerator to set a carton of eggs on the counter.

"You got that right," the sheriff said, his steely eyes still trained on Will.

Keeping his arms crossed and his feet planted on the floor, Will stared right back, as if to bore holes through the sheriff's skull.

The sheriff broke eye contact when he picked up his cup for another swig of stale coffee. Swallowing loudly, he set it down again, huffed a loud breath, and splayed his hands on the counter to push himself up from the stool. "Well, I'll be on my way, then. Just wanted to check with Livvie on that money issue, but I guess you've answered my questions as best you could. I'm makin' the rounds at the businesses up and down this street to see if anybody else has come up short on cash." He sent Will one last look and tipped his cap at him. "I thank you for your time, Mr. Taylor."

"Not at all, Sheriff."

"Bye, Sheriff Morris," Gus called from inside the refrigerator.

Little more than a grunt was the sheriff's response.

Ignorant slob, Will thought, watching the guy's back till he pushed open the screen door and ambled outside into the sweltering heat.

"When's Aunt Margie pickin' us up?" Alex asked for at least the tenth time that afternoon.

Livvie looked at her watch. "It's only ten after two. She said she'd be here at closing time, so she'll be along soon."

"Why can't Will come, too?" Nate asked. Somewhere along the line, the boys had taken to calling him by his first name, at his urging.

"You already asked that, dummy. Mom said he's goin' fishin'."

The truth was, Margie hadn't invited Will, nor would it have occurred to her to do so. She knew very little about him, other than that he worked for Livvie and seemed a friendly sort whenever she happened inside the diner, which wasn't often. Livvie had yet to tell her how they'd shared a kiss, how she'd tagged along on one of his fishing excursions, how their friendship was growing, and how he'd served time in prison, the detail that would upset her the most. Gracious, if Margie ever got wind of his being an ex-convict, she would insist that Livvie terminate his employment at once, and then she'd probably encourage the man by way of a formal letter to leave Wabash altogether, lest he tarnish the town's fine reputation and corrupt its impressionable youth.

Livvie loved her sister to pieces, even owed her her very life, but Margie had a strict set of beliefs when it came to such things as church attendance, dress, hairstyle, and observance of the Sabbath, which she always spent quietly reading the Scriptures and praying. Why, when Livvie had been a young teen, her sister had refused to wash the Sunday dinner dishes until Monday morning. Thankfully, she'd eased up on many of her rituals, and her kitchen now shone spotlessly on every day of the week.

"I'd rather go fishin' with Will," Nate groused.

"Me, too," Alex put in.

"Don't be silly. You love going to Aunt Margie and Uncle Howie's house. Besides, Aunt Margie has a brand-spanking-new car, and she wants to take you for a ride. Won't that be fun?"

As the three of them sat on the bench in front of the restaurant beneath the shade of the awning, awaiting Margie's arrival, the boys swung their feet back and forth, Alex's touching the ground, Nate's merely skimming it. My, but they were growing up fast.

"Yeah, but Will's teachin' us all sorts of different stuff. Uncle Howie only teaches us farm stuff, but Will knows other important stuff," Nate said.

"What 'stuff' are we referring to?" she asked, looking up the street for any sign of a sparkling red Chevrolet Superior four-door sedan with the staunch, independent Margie behind the wheel. She might be a fuddy-duddy when it came to keeping her outward appearance plain and modest—why, she didn't even wear her wedding ring!—but, when it came to her automobiles, Margaret Grant demanded only the finest. And Howard knew better than to deny her.

"Like catchin' frogs 'n' turtles," Alex was saying.

"And throwin' rocks 'n' chasin' crabs," Nate added.

"Chasing crabs?" She was mildly intrigued.

"Yeah! You pick up a rock and find one under it, and then you try to catch it, but it gets away, and Will says that's best, 'cause those things'll pinch you," Nate explained, scrunching up his sunburned, freckled nose. His expressive eyes helped to tell the story.

"And he's learnin' us the harmonica, too, don't forget," said Alex.

"He's *teaching* you," Livvie corrected him.

"And he's also learnin' us the right way to hook on worms," Nate added.

She figured she may as well leave the grammar lessons to their teachers. "So, you like Will, do you?"

"Yeah, he's the best!" Nate said.

"Will's great!" Alex echoed.

"Did someone just use my name in vain?" Will appeared around the corner of the building, fishing gear in hand. As usual, her heart took a tumble at the sight of him.

"Will!" Alex and Nate shouted together.

"We wanna go fishin' with you instead of goin' to Aunt Margie's farm," Alex explained.

Will's thick eyebrows lifted, and his mouth turned down at the corners. "What? And disappoint your aunt and uncle with your absence? I'm sure that would make them very sad. Next time, okay, buddies?" They dropped their jaws to pout for a moment. "Hey, I'm putting something extra good on the menu tonight. Want to know what it is?"

"Yes!" came their suddenly cheery reply.

At that, he crouched down beside them, and Livvie couldn't help but notice the breadth of his thighs through his Levis, stretched taut over his muscular legs. Mercy, he would be the death of her yet!

He leaned closer to the boys, and Livvie found herself lowering her head to their level. She heard him clear his throat and whisper, "Chocolate cake with the best chocolate frosting you ever tasted."

"Haw!" The boys' mouths and eyes had gone as round as tart pans.

Lately, Will had fascinated Livvie even more with the way he handled her sons. One minute, they could be whining louder than a Model T's brakes, and, the next minute, they would be laughing uncontrollably at something Will had said. He had a talent for turning their focus off of themselves and onto something else. Come to think of it, he'd even used his inimitable technique on her a time or two.

A horn blew from somewhere up the road, turning all four heads to the west end of Market Street. Several pedestrians stopped to gawk as the shiny red vehicle pulled up to the curb. "Is that Aunt Margie's new car?" Nate asked.

"It sure is," Livvie said. For a moment, she remained seated on the bench, transfixed by the fresh look of the big, glossy red box on wheels, with four doors that would keep out the cold in winter and windows that opened to let in the breeze on a hot summer's day.

Will gave a low whistle. "Very nice."

"My sister's husband spares no expense when it comes to her desires," Livvie said as she finally stood up. By now, the boys had deserted the bench and run to see their aunt, still seated behind the wheel.

Livvie looked from Margie to Will, who turned and gave her an assessing gaze. "I wasn't talking about the car. I see you're wearing that fine new dress your secret admirer sent to you. You should know, I'm feeling a little jealous."

"What?" She jerked back her head and felt a fluttery sensation sail up her spine. "Oh, for goodness' sake, it doesn't even fit me that well. See? It's a little loose in places and too tight in others." As soon as she pointed that out, she felt a blush warm her cheeks.

"Humph." He fastened his gaze on hers. "I hadn't noticed."

Margie sounded her horn once more, which drew the attention of several more pedestrians. Will strolled up to the partially open front passenger window, leaned down, and tipped his fisherman's hat at Margie. "Mighty fine car you have here, ma'am."

Margie rolled down the window so that it was open all the way. "Why, thank you, Mr. Taylor! Howard insisted we needed a new car. Men! They always have to have the latest toys."

"Isn't that the way of it?" he replied with a chuckle. But Livvie knew better. This man owned little more than his harmonica, his Bible, and a few outfits from the Salvation Army store.

And Margie wasn't fooling anybody by blaming her husband. Howard liked his farm equipment, but cars? He'd be happy to drive his dilapidated truck to the ground.

"Well," Livvie said, stepping up beside Will and pointing to his fishing pole. "Catch some big ones."

"If I do, you want to help me eat them later tonight?"

"What? Me? I mean—"

He touched her cheek. "Got a smudge mark."

"Oh." She licked her finger, then rubbed the spot. "Is it gone?"

He nodded and grinned, a simple gesture that seemed to release a flock of butterflies in her stomach. "All gone. It wouldn't be a date. In fact, bring the boys."

"Well, that's…good. I mean, its not being a date and all. But what about the dance?"

"I thought I'd stay home tonight, maybe serenade myself—and you, if you'd like."

The very notion of Will serenading her—and the boys, of course—made her giddy. It would be the first time she'd been serenaded, unless she counted over-hearing Frank trying to sing in the bathtub.

"I'll think about it."

"Olivia Beth, are you coming?" Margie asked. The boys had jumped into the backseat and were bouncing around, checking out everything there was to see on the car's interior.

"How long do you think it'll take you to think about it?" Will asked in that gravelly voice.

"I…um, well, I guess it shouldn't take any time to think about, so, yes, we'll come."

He let out a long, slow breath. Relief?

"We'll be back in a few hours," she added.

Will nodded and stepped forward to open the door for her. Smiling, she slid onto the upholstered seat, which was hot against her skin. Without even looking, she knew Margie's eyes were drilling into her side.

Once Will shut her door with a wave, her sister put the car in gear, and they jounced up Market Street. They'd gone no farther than a block when Margie started with her questions. "Does that man have eyes for you, Olivia Beth Beckman? And where on earth did you get that dress? Gracious, it has no sleeves!"

Chapter Twenty

"Be sober, be vigilant;
because your adversary the devil,
as a roaring lion, walketh about,
seeking whom he may devour."
—1 Peter 5:8

*F*inally, she'd worn the dress! And he'd be darned if she didn't look fine. Clem swelled with pride to see it on her, knowing that he'd bought it—well, actually, he'd lifted it from its hanger and stuffed it under his shirt. He'd begun to think she'd thrown it away or given it to someone else. Or, worse, that she hated it.

In the horse and buggy he'd rented from the livery, he waited around the corner from the restaurant until he saw Will head off toward the river. Then, he maneuvered the rig onto Market Street and began to follow the red car at a distance. Trouble was, automobiles traveled at a much higher speed than this stupid four-legged animal, so he'd have to make the fellow clip along at a faster pace than usual. He used the whip a couple of times to get him moving, then hung back quite a way so as not to be spotted. Once they were outside of town, he followed the car a mile or so down a dusty road, then watched it turn into a long driveway leading to a farm, from the looks of it. There was a white, two-story house with a wraparound porch, a big barn, and a bunch of outbuildings. In the surrounding fields, herds of cattle and a few horses grazed on grass.

A good quarter mile back from the driveway, beside a cluster of tall oaks, he pulled on the reins. "Whoa!" he commanded the nag. Then, he hauled out his binoculars, leaned back in the springy seat, and made himself comfortable.

My, she looked grand in that blue dress. Those bratty little boys did nothing for him, but she could make a man mighty happy, and, well, he could show her a good time, too. He intended to do that, and soon. "Very soon," he said aloud.

The horse snorted, as if in agreement.

Through the binoculars, he watched the two boys disappear inside the house, while Olivia and her sister lagged behind, their lips moving in conversation. She was prettier than any picture he'd ever seen. He swallowed down a lump of desire and began scanning the wide expanse of land, focusing on the areas that looked unused and uninhabited. How much property did these people own, anyway? Hundreds of acres, if what he'd heard from Orville Dotson was correct. Far in the distance, he spotted what looked like a ramshackle building. Was it deserted? He'd have to investigate. Maybe it'd make a cozy little den for him to hide out in, a private place to take his woman. He was getting sick of wasting his cash on hotel rooms. Wouldn't it beat all if he found a place to call his own, right on Livvie's sister's property? Ha! Who would ever think to look there?

Of course, he'd have to be cautious in his comings and goings, as well as when moving around in the little shack, lest he draw attention. But he felt certain no one would detect a low-burning candle or two, given the distance.

As soon as dusk fell, he'd set out through the cornfields to check out the place. With a little luck, it'd be emptier than a sinner's heart, and a perfect spot to set up housekeeping.

⚜

Will had whistled and hummed the afternoon away, not caring that he'd snagged only a few bluegills, black crappies, and rock bass in the river. He'd tossed half of them back, and the other half were barely respectable enough to fry up as a snack. He doubted the boys would be too fond of his fare, anyway, and he hadn't thought to ask Livvie if she liked eating fish. He knew only that she didn't like catching them. To be safe, he'd be sure to have leftovers on hand, including a plate of cookies and a pie from the restaurant fridge. That ought to suffice.

It wouldn't be a long night, with tomorrow being Sunday, but the idea of spending time with Livvie and the boys, plus walking with them to and from church tomorrow, had his mind wandering into territory he knew he should avoid. Hadn't he convinced himself that Livvie needed more time to mourn, that her heart still belonged entirely to Frank? When she came downstairs to work every morning, she probably envisioned her late husband standing over that hot stove instead of him, an ex-con. What was he doing, standing here and daydreaming like a lovesick fool?

"Hey there, good lookin'! Catch anything?"

He whirled at the sound of the husky, female voice, and his soaring heart plummeted. "Well, if it isn't Marva Dulane," he said, forcing a cordial tone.

"What brings you to the river this afternoon?" He immediately began reeling in his line.

"Don't leave on my account."

He glanced at the used wristwatch he'd bought at the Salvation Army store. "I have to go, anyway. Time to start preparations for the supper crowd."

"You sure do put in a lot of hours at that place."

"It's my job." He crouched down, opened his tackle box, and started putting away his gear. Even with his eyes on his work, he could see her standing there, hands on her nicely rounded hips, skirt flared around her knees, blonde hair tossed to the side, and eyes intent on watching his every move. He'd glanced only briefly at her face, but it hadn't escaped his attention that she'd gotten all dolled up for this meeting. And that unnerved him. For all he knew, she'd seen him head toward the river a couple of hours ago, and this was no chance encounter. "You didn't answer my question," he said. "What brings you down here?"

"Oh, I'm just out walking." He glanced at her high heels. Likely story. "I saw you down here when I came through the thicket." She left his side and picked her way over the bumpy terrain to peek inside his bucket, still sitting by the water's edge. "Aw, you got a bunch of babies in there."

Her remark sparked a chortle. "Thanks. Don't tell anyone, okay?"

She maneuvered her way back and reached him as he snapped the box closed and stood. "Your secret's safe with me, Will Taylor."

"Good." He went to retrieve his bucket of pathetic-looking fish, and the lavender scent he caught as he walked past her nearly knocked him over. Gee whiz! Had she emptied an entire bottle of perfume over herself? Hefting the bucket, he started down the narrow path, arms full.

To his dismay, she followed him. "I thought you said you were taking a walk."

"I was. But I reached my destination, which was the riverbank, and now I'm heading back."

"Oh. Funny how we're both going back at the same time."

"Yes, isn't it?"

From the night he'd met her, he'd known she spelled trouble. Women like Marva Dulane didn't give up easily. Hadn't he made it clear she didn't interest him? A more drastic measure might get the message to her, but dumping a bucket of smelly fish on her head wouldn't sit well with the Lord. So, he decided to pray. Why was prayer so often a last resort? Perhaps because his situation seemed so trivial. Yet he remembered Harry telling him that the Lord cared about every aspect of his life. *Lord, I know I'm a grown man, and I should be able to take care of myself. But I need Your help. Please, protect me from this woman's possessive claws.*

Walking in silence, they came through a copse of trees, crossed an open lot, passed the railroad station, and emerged onto Market Street. As he headed in the direction of the diner, with Marva by his side, he hoped she'd gotten the hint that her company didn't thrill him.

"I thought I'd come to Livvie's Kitchen tonight. Got a special table where I could sit and watch the handsome cook at work?"

He stopped in the middle of the sidewalk and looked at her, blinked, and swallowed. "Marva, you are free to come to Livvie's, if you want. It's a public establishment. But don't come with the intention of watching me. You and I don't have a thing in common."

She drew back her shoulders, which were bare, as the rounded neckline of her cotton blouse had fallen down on both sides. "Oh, but I think we do, Will," she said, her voice gravelly and bold, her smile fiendish.

He set down the bucket of fish, which had suddenly grown heavy, and switched the tackle box to his other hand. "How's that?"

"You like to live dangerously. We've got that much in common."

"You're wrong on that count. I lead a private, quiet life."

Her laugh came off a bit frenzied. "Is that right? Well, I happen to know there's another side to Will Taylor. Oh, I know you call yourself a Christian and all, but"—her chortle deepened as she placed a flat palm to his chest—"don't think you can fool ol' Marva."

Alarm bells rang in his head, and he brushed her hand away. "What are you getting at?"

"Oh, Will, you silly man, I've known about your past for some time now—ever since I made the acquaintance of your friends Hank and Rudy. They told me all about you. We met out at Orville Dotson's farm, real late on the night before they went back to New York."

Like a pinpricked balloon, he felt the air go out of him. Cars whizzed past them; a train arrived at the station, its brakes whiffing as the gigantic locomotive slowed to a stop; horses galloped by; and wagons bumped along. But none of these sounds truly registered in his head. The names "Hank" and "Rudy" were all he could hear.

"Oh, don't look so worried, honey." Marva reached up and brushed something off his shoulder. This time, he tossed her hand off of him with a twist of his body, then stared down at her, almost nose-to-nose, breath-to-breath. She was up to something, and it wasn't good. "It's not like I plan to tell anybody about your past." She shrugged. "Not yet, anyway."

He gritted his teeth to the point where he felt pain shoot through his jaw. "What do you want from me, Marva?"

She threw back her head of dyed-blonde hair and laughed. "A little attention would be nice. I'm not such a bad sort. Like I told you a while back, you and I have more in common than you might think. We both like living on the edge."

"And I told you I'd changed. My life has been completely different since I asked God to take control."

"See, I just don't buy all that religious nonsense. Hank and Rudy told me you're a remarkable crook. I admire that. I can't explain it, but there's something so appealing about a man who breaks the law. It gets my blood to rushing, you know? And then, to think you're an ex-convict, on top of everything else. What the folks of Wabash wouldn't do to learn a little bit about your history! Mystery man comes to Wabash to escape his past and change his identity. Can't you see the headlines now?"

Run, Taylor, run. The Bible story of Potiphar's wife trying to seduce Joseph came to mind. Marva Dulane was nothing short of evil. He took a deep breath and held on to his senses. "I can't do a thing to stop you from going to the papers, but I wish you wouldn't."

She put her hand on his bare arm and applied pressure. "I could easily be talked out of it, Will. What say you and I—?"

A red sedan honked as it passed, drowning out the remainder of her sentence. He glanced up at the car, and his chest immediately collapsed when Livvie's eyes, full of confusion and hurt, connected with his.

❦

As soon as Margie pulled up to the curb in front of Livvie's Kitchen, the boys bolted out the back door. "Bye, Aunt Margie. Thanks for the ride!" Alex said.

"Thanks! Bye!" Nate shouted, then slammed the door, which made Margie wince.

The two raced up the alley between the restaurant and the drugstore, having spotted some friends playing there. Livvie was ashamed that they'd forgotten their manners completely. Unfortunately, she didn't have the gumption to call them back to apologize. At least they hadn't seen Will standing with Marva Dulane half a block back. The woman was a man magnet. Frank used to call her a "percolator with no filter," meaning she didn't care what she said or how she said it; when she wanted something bad enough, she went after it with gusto, no holds barred. She'd even tried to turn Frank's eye one time. One time. Until he'd given her what for, explaining that he was a married man in love with his wife, and she'd do herself a favor by never coming near him again. As far as Livvie knew, Marva hadn't graced her restaurant since.

Out came a loud and heavy sigh. She would not be one of Will Taylor's pawns. No, sir. She had gone beyond playing silly teenage games. Plainly put, if he wanted to associate with the likes of Marva Dulane, he could go and have his fun, but he could also stop inviting her and her sons to his place for dinner, because she would not be taken in by his charms. The way he was standing there in the middle of town for everyone to see, looking all comfy and cozy with

Marva Dulane, made her want to spit right on his shoe! And, if she could have kicked herself in her own behind for being so foolish, she surely would have. To think that she'd come so close to giving her heart away again! Goodness gracious, what would Frank think?

Oh, Lord, help me to stop asking that foolish question, "What would Frank think?" He's not here anymore, and it's time I accepted it. Instead, help me to start asking myself what You would think.

"Well, I see Marva has her feelers out for that cook of yours," Margie observed. "Doesn't surprise me at all, as good-looking a man as he is. But, Marva Dulane! You really ought to warn him about her."

Her sister's words barely registered. She stared ahead, arms crossed, chin and jaw set as firm as cement.

"Livvie, did you hear me?" Margie leaned across the seat and touched her arm. "Knock me over with a straw, you don't like that man, do you? In a romantic sense, I mean. I saw him give you a certain look today when I picked you up. He's your employee, Olivia."

That woke her up. "Of course, I don't like him in a romantic sense, Margaret. Don't be ridiculous! Even though he is a fine Christian man." Why did she feel the need to defend him, especially when she was madder at him than a trapped coon?

"Why would a 'fine Christian man' associate with the likes of Marva Dulane? And in public, no less!"

That got up her dander even more, and not because she wanted to protect Will's reputation. As much as she loved her sister, Margie could be terribly judgmental. "Even Jesus hung around with the dregs of society, Margie."

"Well, I suppose that's true, but I can't imagine the Lord looking too kindly on a Christian man seeking out someone of her caliber. I've heard that she's broken up many a happy marriage."

"Since when have you listened to gossip, Margie?"

"I don't actually listen; I just get bits and pieces while I'm waiting in line at the bank or the post office or the market. You know how it goes. Sometimes, you just...overhear things, and you can't help it. I realize it's all speculation—women talking just to hear themselves talk—but, still, you do learn things."

Livvie huffed a sigh, then relaxed a bit. "I know. In the restaurant, I hear all sorts of murmurs about this and that. But I don't repeat them."

"Nor do I."

"You just did!"

"To my sister. Oh, for pity's sake, never mind." Margie turned and looked behind her. "Where do you suppose he met her, anyway?"

"At the dance hall upstairs."

"Haw! He goes to those horrid dances? What kind of Christian example is that? I'd stay clear of Will Taylor, Olivia."

In spite of her inner turmoil, Livvie almost laughed. "He works for me, Margie."

"Well, perhaps you ought to think about looking for someone to replace him."

"What? Just because he goes to the dance hall some Saturday nights?"

"I can't imagine why any upstanding Christian would. Nothing but a bunch of boozing, smoking sinners attend those events, and the music, why, it's...it's so...worldly."

"I rather like it."

"Oh, my stars, you do not! You've said yourself it's loud and raucous."

"Mr. Taylor plays the harmonica, did I tell you that? And very well, I might add. He's been known to go up on the stage and perform with the band on Saturday nights."

Another gasp flew past Margie's lips.

"I even went up there one evening," she added, waiting for the explosion.

Margie's eyes bulged like two bowling balls. "What on earth possessed you to do that?" she hissed.

"The music. It was lively and appealing."

"Sin is appealing, Olivia Beth."

"For heaven's sake, I didn't sin by going up there. Besides, I stayed only a few minutes."

A long moment of silence passed while Margie brooded.

"I started going to church again," Livvie finally said. "I've been going to the Wesleyan Methodist church."

Margie turned and faced forward, her shoulders dropping, as if in surrender. "Well, that's certainly a good thing. Of course, you know I wish you'd come back to your roots at Wabash Holiness Life. I miss seeing you in the third pew from the front on the right side."

"That was our family pew when Frank was still alive. You should know, I don't plan to return. I needed a fresh start, and I've gotten one at the Wesleyan Methodist church."

"I see. Well, as long as they preach the Word—"

"Yes, I can assure you, they do." Her sister could be so brassbound. As if her salvation depended upon attending the same church she'd gone to as a child!

"How did you happen to pick that particular church?"

"Mr. Taylor invited the boys and me."

"Ah. I see." She turned to look behind her once more, the seat squeaking beneath her body. "I see he's still talking to Marva. Do you suppose he's inviting her to attend church with him, as well?"

Ignoring her sister's sarcasm, Livvie thanked her for the ride and got out, closing her door before Margie could say anything else.

Chapter Twenty-one

*"He that is slow to anger is better
than the mighty; and he that ruleth
his spirit than he that taketh a city."*
—Proverbs 16:32

Will's stomach ached, as if a hole the size of a golf ball had been bored into it. And, as a result, he had flubbed order after order: burned several steaks that were supposed to be rare, served someone a side of carrots instead of peas, topped an order of mashed potatoes with hot fudge instead of beef gravy, and dropped an entire plate of food when he collided with Gus. After burning yet another steak, Will had let Gus take over cooking and busied himself with other things.

"What's going on with you, Will?" Cora Mae asked only midway through the supper hour. She stood at the sink, rinsing soiled plates. "You're as jumpy as a flea."

Now, he looked past Cora Mae at Marva Dulane, who hadn't budged from her table since the restaurant had opened that evening. She sat there, eyeing him over the rim of her cup as she sipped her coffee. "Nothing," he lied. "I'm fine."

"Right. And cats bark at the moon. You and Livvie have a fallin'-out? She's not herself tonight, either."

He shook his head. "I don't have time to talk, Cora Mae. Sorry."

"Sure you do. The rush is over, and things have quieted down." She nudged him in the side. "Does it have anything to do with *her*?" she whispered with a backward nod toward Marva.

Before he could open his mouth, Livvie approached and laid an order slip on the counter, giving him a sharp, cursory glance. "Gus, one more," she said.

"Got it." The fellow turned and snatched up the paper from the counter. *Thank the Lord for Gus Anderson*, Will thought as Livvie turned and went to check on her customers.

"Well?" Cora Mae prodded him.

"Could be," he admitted. Cora Mae knew nothing of his past, and he wasn't about to enlighten her. It was enough that he'd told Livvie. Yet, now that Marva also knew, he worried the entire town would soon get wind of it, and he'd be put on the next train out of here.

Cora Mae shuddered. "She's nothin' but trouble, Will."

"Tell me about it."

"So, you know about her, then?"

"I've heard she's had a couple of husbands, and her hobby is collecting men."

"You heard right. Her other hobby is helpin' Orville Dotson distribute his goods. She makes a decent livin' workin' for him."

"His goods?"

"He operates a big still in his barn. Manufactures enough booze to supply all of Wabash County and beyond. 'Course, it's all a 'big secret.' Sheriff Morris pretty much turns his head. He's opposed to Prohibition, as you might've guessed."

"I'm not surprised."

"Don't get me wrong; he upholds the law in every area but that."

"So, it'd do no good to report your findings to him, is what you're saying."

She held up her hands. "They're not my findings. I'm just repeatin' what others refer to as 'common knowledge.'"

He nodded. "Interesting."

By six forty-five, the restaurant had emptied, save for a few stragglers. Gus began scrubbing down the stove, Livvie and Cora Mae cleared the tables, Georgia refilled the salt and pepper shakers, and Alex and Nate zipped around the place. Will wiped the countertops, trying to ignore Marva Dulane, who also remained at her table. A few minutes later, she rose from her seat and approached him, her hips swaying excessively.

"You make a fine chicken à la King, Will Taylor," she said.

"Sure took you long enough to eat it."

She tossed her head back and laughed. "I was too busy watching the cook, I suppose."

"It's time you left, Marva."

"Yes, I know. Besides, I have other commitments."

"I'm sure you do." He was thinking about what Cora Mae had said about her job with Orville Dotson and almost mentioned it. But he decided to save it for another time, after he did some digging.

She leaned over the bar area to play with a button on his shirt. "When can I see you again, Will?"

His smile was brief and cold. "How's never?"

She scowled. "We'll see. Don't forget about those little tidbits of information I picked up from your friends...."

"Are you trying to blackmail me?"

She stood up straight and flicked her blonde hair with the back of her hand, then stuck out a pouty lower lip. "'Blackmail' sounds so harsh, Will. But you can call it what you want."

An icy sensation traveled through his veins, and he had to concentrate on breathing. "You best get to your commitments, Marva."

Devilish laughter spilled out of her. "My, my, I do believe the good Christian boy is showing some righteous anger. Don't worry; I'm leaving. But I'll see you soon." She blew him a kiss and turned on her heel, making a point to promenade slowly past the three women working in the restaurant.

Livvie watched her strut out the door, then shot Will a stinging glare. He supposed he could forget about the plan for her and her boys to come to his apartment for dinner tonight. Well, if she wouldn't come to him, he would go to her. One way or another, he intended to get her alone and explain the whole situation concerning Marva Dulane.

And, if he had the courage, he'd tell her something else, as well.

᳇

If she weren't so irritated with him, Livvie might have felt a wee bit sorry for Will, considering all the orders he'd muddled. Thankfully, Georgia had been the one to wait on Marva all night, and she did mean all night. Livvie had begun to think the woman would never leave—another major source of irritation, since she had taken up an entire table that could have been filled with two more shifts of paying customers. At a quarter to seven, she'd finally stood up and ambled over to Will, clutched his shirtfront, and whispered something to him. And he'd returned an intimate comment of some sort.

Well, no matter. She did not intend to pine over Mr. Will Taylor another minute. He could have Marva Dulane with no interference on her part.

She'd managed to avoid any conversations with him that evening, except for a little while earlier, when he'd told her that they needed to talk. "I have nothing to say to you," she'd replied. "Well, I have something to say to you," he'd retorted. Cora Mae and Georgia had been working nearby, so he hadn't pressed the matter.

Now, it looked like everyone was gone but Cora Mae, who was tidying chairs. It was time for Livvie to round up her boys, who whooped like hyenas as they raced around the tables. "Come on, Alex, Nathan. We're going upstairs," she announced.

Just then, Will came around the bar and nabbed her by the arm. "We need to talk, Livvie. I'm serious."

She raised her chin and wriggled her arm free of his grasp. "I think it's clear where your interests lie, Will, and I don't want to talk about it."

"If you think I have eyes for Marva Dulane, you're completely off base."

"And you're completely loony if you think I'm going to stand here and listen to another word. Alex! Nathan! Upstairs, you two!" The tone she used was one her sons were not accustomed to hearing, and they immediately quieted down and made a beeline for the back door. She followed on their heels, leaving Will in the kitchen.

Back in their apartment, Livvie drew a bath for the boys. They put up the usual fuss but changed their tune when she told them they could bathe together. While they splashed around in the tub, she went to the kitchen for a drink of water. She had just filled her glass and was starting to sip when a knock came at her door, loud and demanding. "Livvie! Open up this instant."

She glanced at the clock. It was a quarter after eight, less than an hour since Will had tried to talk to her. She should have known he wouldn't let the matter rest. She poured the rest of the water down the drain and set her glass in the sink. Then, expelling a deep breath, she walked to the door. Shoulders pulled back for a show of courage, she unlocked the latch, turned the knob, and pulled the door open. Will stepped inside uninvited, determination carved into his expression. Taking hold of her arms just above her elbows, he drew her close for a long, relentless kiss. "Taken aback," "shocked," "nonplussed," and "dazed" were hardly sufficient to explain how she felt. "Enraptured" came close.

As quickly as the kiss had begun, it ended, but he didn't drop his hands; he just squeezed her upper arms and stared down at her with those intense blue eyes. "I love you."

"What?" Her heart had stopped beating; she was sure of it.

"You heard me. I love you. I can't help it. It just happened. And whether you ever return the feelings is beside the point."

"But, Marva—"

"Is nothing to me. You, on the other hand"—he gently tapped the tip of her nose—"are everything. I didn't mean for this to happen, Livvie. I know you still love your husband, and always will, but I was going to burst if I didn't get my feelings out in the open. I also realize I'm nowhere near good enough for you, and that it's plain foolish for me to be spilling my heart out to you like this.

"Now, if my continued employment at the restaurant makes you uncomfortable, I'll happily leave— well, maybe not happily—and look for another job in Wabash. But, if you don't mind my staying, then I'll make every effort to stay out of your way, and—"

She put two fingers to his lips. "Shush, would you?"

He complied, his breathing jagged and hurried, as if he'd just run a long way. She removed her fingers from his mouth, and he dropped his hands to his sides, knotting them into fists.

"I do still love my husband," she said. "And, you're right; I always will. But I do not want you to stop working in the kitchen." She bit her lip hard and dropped her chin. "I feel things for you, Will; I truly do. But—"

"It's fine, it's fine. I understand. You don't have to explain anything."

Tears suddenly stung her eyes, and a sob that had caught in her throat worked its way out. "I never imagined another man taking Frank's place."

He let out a heavy sigh. Then, with both hands, he cupped her cheeks in the gentlest way and raised her face so that her eyes met his. "Don't get all worked up, okay? This doesn't have to turn into something complicated. I told you how I feel, and that's that. Let's just leave it there, all right?"

Confusion fueled a fire in her chest as she silently asked God for peace and discernment. Suddenly, she had to know. "What were you doing talking to Marva on the sidewalk today when Margie drove us back into town? You two looked so...intimate."

"Intimate?" His brow crinkled.

"And then, she sat at that table all night, watching you like some kind of famished hawk—in my restaurant, no less."

"I'll admit, she's got this thing for me."

"I'll say."

"It's more like a sick infatuation. May I come in, Liv?" He reached behind him and quietly closed the door. "I need to tell you some things that happened today regarding Marva Dulane. Can we sit down and talk?"

"Mommy!" Nate yelled from the bathroom. "Alex keeps throwing water in my face."

She pressed her fingers to her temples and closed her eyes, imagining what the bathroom floor must look like. So many emotions swirled in her head.

"Want me to go tend to them?" he asked. "We can talk after they go to bed. Or, I can come back later, if you'd rather."

"No, you can stay. The boys will be excited to see you. We might have a hard time getting them to bed, though, once they learn you're here."

His warm hand grazed her cheek, and he gave her a lazy smile. "Makes no matter to me."

As he tiptoed down the hall toward the bathroom, she waited to hear the boys' shouts of elation at seeing him. She wasn't disappointed. And, while she could not yet bring herself to say those three important words, she was sure her sons would have no trouble.

❧

It couldn't be more perfect. The shack looked like it was a deserted church or schoolhouse with a step-up platform at the front, rough plank walls, and uneven wood floors. Clem shone his flashlight all around and discovered an ancient stove with a broken pipe standing in the center of the room, which probably measured about twenty-five feet on each side. Two of the walls had three windows each, only four of which had their glass panes intact.

It hadn't been easy wading through rows of corn and tall weeds to reach the tumbledown building, and finding the front door behind a thicket of brush had been an even bigger challenge, with only the moon and his torch to light the way. After all, he hadn't dared explore the place during the daylight hours. He'd hitched the horse and buggy behind some trees on a deserted trail about half a mile away and hoped no one would come upon them. He hadn't passed a single horse or automobile on his trek down the dirt road, though, so he had no real worries about that happening.

He dug into his cloth sack and drew out the candlestick he'd brought, along with the holder and a box of matches. He fit the candle in the holder, then set it on the rickety table beside the stove. It took him several strikes, but he finally lit a match and then touched it to the candlewick. All at once, everything came into view—a few broken chairs, a dilapidated bench that could have been a church pew, some empty crates stacked against the wall, and, of all things, an ancient piano at the front, which looked to have collected about an inch of dust. A crackling noise made him whirl around, flashlight pointed toward the sound. A couple of mice scuttled across the room and disappeared behind a box.

"Blamed varmints," he mumbled. "Y' best scoot out o' here, 'fore I bring my lady by. Don't think she'll appreciate sharin' this place with any four-legged critters."

Outside, an owl hooted, and the moon sent a slice of light through a cracked windowpane. Clem dragged a chair over to the table where the candle burned, plunked himself into it, crossed his legs at the ankles, and lit a cigarette. Tomorrow, he would call Flo and tell her he wanted that divorce. He'd rented a post office box, so her lawyer should have no trouble getting him the necessary paperwork. Shoot, he'd even send her cash to cover the lawyer fees, if need be. Of course, he'd have to steal it first.

He reached inside his sack once more and pulled out the bottle of whiskey he'd bought off Dotson. Carefully, almost reverently, he uncorked it, then took a long swallow, enjoying the burn as it went down. Settling back, he closed his eyes, ready to dream about his beautiful bride-to-be.

⚜

"So, now you know the whole story," Will said, having told Livvie all about the day's events concerning Marva Dulane. They'd been sitting together on her sofa for the past hour, ever since putting her boys to bed, after which Livvie had whispered that her sons had never agreed so readily to turn in for the night.

"I'm thinking about going to the sheriff in the next county to file a complaint against Orville Dotson," he went on. "There's no reason he should be allowed to keep up that illegal operation. If Buford Morris isn't man enough to put a stop to it, then somebody else has got to step up."

"I wouldn't do that, Will," Livvie cautioned him. "You'd be stirring up a wasps' nest. What if one or more of Dotson's customers gets word that you reported him and comes after you? A lot of people depend on him for their supply, and they wouldn't think too kindly of someone stepping in to put a stop to his business. Besides, I don't know what a sheriff from another county could do, since it's not in his jurisdiction."

"He could take it to the next level. I've been doing some checking, and the Bureau of Internal Revenue, a branch of the Treasury Department, has been tasked with enforcing the law, and they've developed some crack Prohibition agents. There's a commissioner and a director of Prohibition who share the power, and they don't have much mercy for these small-time operations. They usually shut them down within days of discovering them. Dotson's probably due for some jail time, and maybe Marva would go, too, for her part. I don't know the extent of her involvement, or if what Cora Mae told me is just hearsay, but it'd be worth it to hire a prosecutor to investigate."

He paused and reached for his coffee cup, which sat beside Livvie's on an end table. It took a heap of self-control to resist touching her shoulder. Not that he didn't long to pull her close and kiss her silly, but, now that he'd revealed his feelings to her, he had to be careful not to force the issue. If she was ever going to love him in return, he wanted her to do so unreservedly and without any pressure.

She folded her hands in her lap and briefly studied them. "I can understand all that, Will, but you have to remember, you're trying to protect your identity, and so you need to be careful about your involvement. At the very least, you should pray for guidance about the best way to proceed. As for Marva, if you tell her that you know what she's up to with Orville Dotson, it might be enough to make her back off."

"You make an excellent case, Mrs. Beckman. Especially the part about praying first."

"I'm a little slow, Mr. Taylor, but I'm beginning to get my spiritual legs back. And it feels good."

Chapter Twenty-two

"Let not your heart be troubled,
neither let it be afraid."
—John 14:27

On Wednesday morning, Livvie flipped the "Closed" sign to "Open," unlocked the front door, and opened it to usher in her first customer—Coot, of course. Although the morning temperature was mild, Reggie panted at Coot's side, as if the afternoon sun were already beating down on his shiny, black head. In his usual fashion, he waited for Livvie to pat his head, then turned several circles and settled himself on the cool sidewalk under the awning.

"Morning, Coot." Livvie leaned forward and kissed his weathered cheek.

Without a word, he handed her a Mason jar filled with an array of beautiful wildflowers.

"Are these for me?"

"I'm expectin' so," he said as he stepped inside. "Or, might be they're for Cora Mae or Georgia. There's a note tucked down inside, but I didn't look at it. Found 'em right here by the door, sittin' all pretty-like."

"Oh, drat! I thought they were from you," she lamented with a touch of sarcasm.

"I told you when you got that dress, I don't know nothin' about givin' women gifts."

289

"It's okay, Coot. I'll forgive you this time." She laughed, carrying the jar of flowers toward the kitchen. "Take your usual table. I'll get your coffee."

"I'll get it for him," Will said, lifting the coffeepot from the burner and winking at her. "Mmm, you smell good." She felt herself blush from the neck up and turned to look at him, but he'd already sailed past her to serve Coot.

Since uttering those three special words on Saturday night, he'd made no mention of them. That was not to say that he hadn't had plenty of opportunities to do so. He'd walked with her to church on Sunday, as usual, but kept quiet about it, and he hadn't even made a move to sit next to her in the pew; the boys had sat between them, as usual. After the service, while Alex and Nathan joined in a game of tag in the churchyard, folks had greeted them in the friendliest ways, discussing the fine weather, the brush fire out behind Zeke Barlow's barn on Friday night, and the new Silver Flag Service Station on the corner of Maple and Fall, where the prices already seemed cheaper than those at the Red Top. Helen Brent had approached the group clustered around Will and Livvie and asked them if they planned to attend the annual church picnic in a few weeks. Livvie hadn't known how to respond, so Will had answered on her behalf. "Well, it sounds like a grand time. Not sure I can speak for Livvie and her boys, but I'll make every effort to attend." Had that been his subtle way of dismissing any suspicions that they were a couple?

Since neither Cora Mae nor Georgia had arrived at the restaurant yet, Livvie took the liberty of reaching into the bouquet and pulling out the folded piece of paper tucked among the stems. Her heart thumped lightly against her chest to think that Will might have gone out early to pick the flowers. Eagerly, she unfolded the paper. To her dismay, the handwriting matched that of the scrawled note she'd received with the blue dress.

Livvie,
You looked perty in the dress. I wached you from afar. I emagined myself holding your hand and walking right down Market Street. But that will come. Enjoy these flowers picked jest for you.

Who was this person who'd been watching her? And why didn't he just come forward?

Uneasiness crawled across her skin as she refolded the note and jammed it inside her skirt pocket.

Will let out an exaggerated sigh on his way back to the kitchen. "Ah, you still smell nice. Pretty flowers. Whose are they?"

"Mine, I guess."

The back door opened, and Cora Mae and Georgia both entered. Distraction kept Livvie from fully acknowledging them.

"What do you mean, you guess? Who're they from?" He came to a standstill before her, coffeepot in hand.

She gave him a hard, sober stare. "You didn't send me that dress, did you? Be honest."

His forehead furrowed. "That blue dotted dress? No, sorry, I didn't. Why do you ask?"

"Well, someone sent it to me, and I want to know who!" she blurted out.

"Morning, everybody. What's going on?" Cora Mae snatched her apron from its hook by the door and tied it around her waist, secured her hairnet, and then turned and glanced at the bar. "Ooh, pretty flowers! Did you pick 'em, Liv?"

Gus came in through the front door, along with two customers, Walter and Minnie Ballard, giving her a moment to think up a response. This was no time to get worked up, not when she had customers coming in and Coot sitting there, listening to the exchange.

"No, I didn't. Somebody gave them to me." She forced a fresh smile. "Wasn't that nice?"

"Humph. I'll say," Cora Mae mumbled. "Can't remember the last time somebody gave me flowers. Let's see…in fourth grade, maybe. Herbert Jenkins picked me three droopy dandelions during recess." She shook her head in dismay. "Yep, that was the last time."

Everyone but Will and Livvie set off in various directions to tackle the day. Gus fired up the stove and oven, Georgia waited on Coot, and Cora Mae greeted the Ballards and led them to a corner table.

"Let me see the note, Liv," Will insisted. "I saw you tuck it in your pocket."

Without argument, she brought it out and handed it to him. He perused it in silence, perhaps reading it more than once. "He thinks he's going to be walking down Market Street with you? Hand in hand?" He frowned. "Who is this character? Did you keep the other note you got with the dress?"

"Yes, why?"

"Where is it?"

"In my dresser drawer."

He pressed the note into her palm and folded her fingers over it. "Put this one with it. We might need to pay a visit to the sheriff."

※

Later that afternoon, after the lunch hour had passed, Will stood outside J. C. Penney and studied the skinny mannequin wearing the infamous blue dotted dress in the window display. He decided that it looked much better on Livvie than on the plaster model, but he detested it just the same, all because of the notion that someone—a man, judging from the sloppy handwriting—had given it to her. Moments later, he pulled open the heavy door. If he'd ever stepped inside a department store, he couldn't recall it, but here he was, standing amid racks of dresses, skirts, and fancy blouses.

"May I help you, sir?"

He pivoted on his heel and faced a middle-aged clerk with graying hair and a pleasant smile. "Yes, I was wondering about that dress in your display window."

"Ah, the blue dotted Swiss. Shopping for your wife, are you?"

"What? Uh, no, just...shopping," came his feeble reply.

She frowned. "Your girlfriend, then?"

"No, I just have a question about the dress. That's all."

"Oh." Her darkish eyebrows rose with the single word. "What would you like to know?"

"Well, this will probably sound utterly strange, but, a few weeks ago, I'm not sure of the date, somebody, probably a man, came into your store to buy a dress identical to that one." Already, she gave her head an adamant shake. "And I was wondering if you might remember who bought it." Her head didn't stop moving from side to side, and her lips were tightly pursed.

"Or, if you can't recall, would you happen to know if another clerk—?"

"Sir, no one bought that dress," she interrupted him.

"I believe you're wrong. Someone I know received that very dress, and I'm—we're—trying to determine who—?"

"A dress like that was stolen from our rack. It was the only one we had in stock, besides the one you see on the mannequin. Can you tell me who has it now?"

᙭

On Thursday morning, after a breakfast he'd washed down with a few swigs of whiskey, Clem leaned against the cold brick wall of the train station and pressed the public phone to his ear, awaiting his wife's croaky voice. "Come on, come on, pick up the blasted phone," he mumbled, turning his back to the folks coming and going. He knew no more than a handful of people in Wabash and had given his own name to only one person, Marva Dulane, so he had no worries about being recognized. He just didn't like standing in a public building in broad daylight. He was used to skulking in the shadows by day and sneaking around in the glow of the moon by night. A train whistle sounded in the distance. He slammed down the receiver, hearing the nickel jingle in the metal coin return. Then, he yanked a tattered piece of paper from his pocket and smoothed it out as best he could to read the numbers. He detested his mother-in-law, but, since Flo basically lived at her house, he figured that was where he'd find her. So, he rattled off the phone number to the operator on the other end, reinserted the nickel, and waited.

On the fourth ring, he shifted his weight in irritation. Finally, a puny-sounding female voice answered. "Hello?"

"Flo?"

"This isn't Flo. Who's this?"

"Who's this?" He wasn't about to reveal himself to a complete stranger. "Where's Flo? I been trying to reach her. Is this Nettie O'Dell's house?"

"Yes. Clem? This is Pearl."

Pearl was Florence's sister from New Jersey. He could count on one hand the number of times he'd actually spoken to her, but he did recognize her voice, now that she'd said a few words. "Where's Flo?"

"She's...not here."

"Well, when'll she be back? I need to talk to her. She tol' me before I left she wanted a divorce, and I'm ready t' give it to her."

"Where are you, anyway? Ma tried to contact you. Flo never did tell her where you went, not that it makes much difference now. The authorities will find you when they want you. Some friends of yours, Hank Swain and Rudy something or other, got thrown in jail, but maybe you already knew that. They got caught red-handed breaking into a service station. Now, the police are holding them for questioning on several other crimes. Rumor has it they're naming you as an accomplice.

"Eddie's fine, in case you wanted to know, but then, you never did care much about that sweet little boy, did you? Probably 'cause he isn't yours. Ma's taking full custody of him. He'll be in good hands with her, mark my word."

His head felt like mush. "What are you—? Just hold it a second, okay?" He cursed. "Slow down and

296 ～ SHARLENE MACLAREN

stick to one subject. First, I got to know what's goin'
on with Flo. And that other stuff...tell it to me one at a
time, would you?"

"I'll give it to you straight, then. Clem, Florence is
dead. She ran out in front of a train in Harlem a week
ago. Some say it looked like she did it on purpose, but
I can hardly believe she'd do that to herself, with the
way she loved Eddie an' all. But Eddie's daddy, Florence's no-good lover? She started up with him again,
but he found himself another woman, which broke my
sister's heart, so I suppose it's possible she killed herself on purpose. I won't believe it, though. I think she
just got all distracted, what with Eddie's daddy running off on her.

"Anyway, the funeral was two days ago. Like I
said, we tried to locate you, but nobody knew where
you were. Of course, I'm sure those Hank and Rudy
fellows would've known, but Ma wouldn't even try to
find them. Then, we found out they were both in jail.
Won't be long, and you'll be joining them. Can't say it'll
make me sad, or anybody else, for that matter."

He'd heard enough. He slammed the receiver back
on the hook and slowly turned, fearing that if he moved
too fast, his breakfast and the whiskey would all spill
out in a smelly mess on the cement floor. Dazed and
dizzy, he pulled a dirty handkerchief out of his front
pocket and mopped his face, which was drenched with
sweat. Through clouded-over eyes, he made out the
figures of people passing by, then spotted the door. Air.
He needed air. On his way to the exit, he bumped into
several people. "Hey, watch it!" one fellow growled.

Flo's dead. Got to get my bearings. Flo's dead. He
staggered out of the station and stumbled blindly up
the street, his ears buzzing like two bumblebees in a

singing contest, as he tried to process the news. When he reached the corner, he turned left onto Huntington and headed south toward Fulton. If he remembered correctly, Fulton was a short, quiet street by the river. With a little luck, he'd be able to stay there while he sorted through his jumbled thoughts and figured out his next move. Hiding out was his first priority, especially in light of what he'd learned about Hank and Rudy. That, and having a warm body by his side to soothe his cares. He'd have to put his plan in motion even sooner than he'd thought.

✺

Livvie marched up Market Street at two o'clock sharp, her arm draped with the blue dress, which was freshly laundered and pressed. Coot's dog, Reggie, followed on her heels. He never left the restaurant while Coot was inside, and she liked to think that he felt it his duty to escort her to J. C. Penney and protect her as she returned the merchandise.

Mercy, how humiliating to think she'd worn a stolen dress! When Will had reported his findings to her last night, she'd hardly believed it. And now, she couldn't wait to get the thing off her hands.

Just outside the entrance to the store, she turned and pointed at the dog. "Wait here, Reggie," she ordered him. The mutt looked up, whined, and then sat back on his heels in what seemed to be a begrudging manner. She smiled down at him. "Don't worry; I'll be no more than a minute." With that, she pulled open the door and approached the first clerk she laid eyes on.

✺

Watching from a dark alley, Clem seethed with anger when he saw Livvie heading up the street carrying the blue dress. Hadn't she admired it in the window for days before he'd finally found the perfect opportunity to snatch it off the rack and then gone through the fuss of wrapping it up and mailing it to her? Typical woman, she didn't appreciate a gift when it was handed to her on a platter. Made him wonder what she'd done with the flowers he'd picked for her out in front of their new house.

"Soon, my dear, soon," he muttered under his breath, "I'll shower you with gifts you wouldn't dream o' givin' back."

It had taken him all morning to adjust to the idea of Flo's being gone, and, by now, he had come to think of her death as a sort of sign. No Flo meant no wife. No wife meant no divorce. It also meant he had the freedom to do as he pleased. In the back of his rented wagon, he'd stashed at least a month's worth of supplies from the general store, the hardware store, and the market: candles, matches, a hammer and nails, cigarettes, potatoes, bread, carrots, jerky and other dried meats, apples, raisins, jars of olives and pickles, baked beans, canned fruit, a can opener, mouse traps, and a mishmash of other items. He'd stolen only a portion of the goods, though, knowing he couldn't haul away so much stuff without being spotted. Back at the house, he already had a good stash of Dotson's whiskey, so he was set in terms of booze. From the Salvation Army store, he'd bought a lumpy mattress, two pillows, two blankets, a kerosene lamp, soap and towels, some plates and silverware, and some rope— plenty of rope. Unfortunately, until his lady grew accustomed to the way he ran things, he figured he'd have to tie her up. It wouldn't be long, though, till he had her eating out of his hand.

"Yes, siree. Soon, my dear—maybe as early as tomorrow, if me 'n' that crazy Marva lady play our cards right."

❋

"Where'd Livvie go?" Will asked. He'd just come in the back door after dumping a load of garbage in the barrel and standing there awhile to watch it burn, making sure no sparks ignited the nearby tree branches.

"I saw her head out the front door a few minutes ago," Georgia said. "Which is where I'm going now. I'll see you back here around five."

"Did Cora Mae go with her?" he asked, but the door closed before he finished his sentence.

"One of Cora Mae's friends stopped by in her car some time ago. Guess they went down to the river."

Will turned on his heel. "I didn't know you were still here, Coot."

"Waitin' for my dog," he said. "Dumb brute insisted on goin' with Livvie on her walk."

"I gave her strict orders not to go off by herself."

"Guess she don't like bein' told what to do. Always was an independent little thing, even when Frank was around. Anyway, she ain't alone. She's with Reg. That dog won't let a flea come near her. Best ol' hound dog in the State of Indiana, my Reggie. Great protector."

With the kitchen clean and everything in order for the evening meal, Will released a long breath and came to sit down at Coot's table. "I suspect she took that dress back to the store. Ever since I told her someone had stolen it, she couldn't wait to return it."

"Don't blame her none for that. Some sick fool thought he could impress her with it. Wonder if he'll ever come forward."

"He'd better not," Will stated. "I'll wring his ever-lovin' neck."

Coot chuckled. "I'd like to watch you do that." He quickly sobered. "You ain't seriously worried 'bout this mystery fella, are you?"

Will ran a hand down the back of his head and massaged his neck. "Don't know that I'd call it worried. Concerned, maybe, and annoyed. I know it's probably nothing. Shoot, it could be some rascally teenage boy. It's the fact that the dress was stolen that irks me, though. That's serious business."

"Have you tried goin' to the post office to see if you can figure out who mailed the thing?"

Will grinned. "You old sage. You sure know how to read a fellow's mind."

"It's one o' them skills that comes in mighty handy."

"You want to come with me?"

"To the post office? Naw, me 'n' Reggie got to get back to the apartment for our afternoon nap, soon's he 'n' Livvie get back here. Want to be all rested up for tonight's Family Feast. What're we havin', by the way?"

"Meat loaf and mashed potatoes. Fannie Parker's recipe."

"Mmm-mm. That's bound to be mighty fine. Haven't had meat loaf since...since...."

"Last week, when I served it up to you, Will Taylor style."

"Oh, yeah. I'm sure Fannie's version won't come close to competin' with yours."

A few minutes later, the door opened, and Livvie walked in, Reggie on her heels. Rather than lope over to his master like a loyal dog, though, he stayed by her side.

"I thought I told you not to go off by yourself," Will said, trying to sound calm.

"It's broad daylight, Will. What's going to happen to me? I wanted to take that dress back to the store. Everyone else had other things to do, so I set off on my own." Reggie whined. "Well, with Reggie at my side, that is." As if satisfied by the recognition, the dog lay down in the center of the room, beneath a whirring ceiling fan, which created a comfortable draft.

"Well, I'm headin' back home," Coot announced. "You comin', Reg?"

The dog didn't even lift his head; he just lay there, looking up at Coot with his big, brown eyes.

"Huh. Ain't that somethin'?"

"He can stay here and nap, if he wants," Livvie offered.

Coot scratched the top of his head and stared down at his companion. "All right, then. Guess I'll leave 'im here. See you folks later."

As soon as Coot was gone, Will walked to the front door and turned the lock. "Walk with me to the post office, Liv."

"The post office? Do you have something to mail?"

"Nope. I want to see if somebody there remembers who mailed that dress to you. I know it's a long shot, but it's worth a try. And I'd like your company."

"Well, seeing as the boys are at the park with Sally, I guess I could spare the time."

With a forefinger, he traced the outline of her jaw, and she didn't protest. It was the first time he'd touched her since last Saturday night, when he'd barged into her apartment, swept her weightless figure into his arms, and shocked her with his eager kiss and then his profession of love. He'd vowed not to press her to return the endearment until she was ready, but he hadn't promised not to woo her with tenderness. "Besides," he said, "a little walk would do us good."

She smiled. "I just returned from a walk."

"With Reggie. Did you two have a lively conversation?"

"Yes, we had quite a lengthy discussion about his views on Prohibition, dance halls, and harmonicas."

He threw back his head and gave a hearty chuckle. She, in turn, released a gentle ripple of laughter. Man, it felt good to share a moment of humor.

As they prepared to set out, Reggie got up from the floor, his tail wagging. Evidently, he'd decided to join them. When they reached the post office, Reggie sat outside at attention, opting not to lie down. Will couldn't figure him out. "Has that dog ever acted so protective of you before?"

"Never," Livvie replied. "I don't understand why he refuses to leave my side all of a sudden."

"Maybe he's got a sixth sense about something," Will said, holding the door open for Livvie. "I've heard that dogs can often detect when trouble is brewing long before it shows up. My granddaddy once had a dog who pranced nervously and howled like a banshee before a storm, even when the skies were still blue and cloudless."

"Hm. Well, I hope you're wrong about the possibility of trouble brewing," she said as she stepped past him.

A woman who looked haggard and spent but had warm, friendly eyes approached the counter. "What can I do for you?"

Will pressed his palms onto the countertop. "Got a question for you, ma'am."

The door opened, and he glanced behind him. Two more customers breezed inside, one with a stack of envelopes, the other with a package. He would have to be brief.

"A few weeks ago, someone came in here and mailed a good-sized package, and we were wondering if you might be able to recall his name."

"Well, what did he look like?"

"I don't know. That's something I was hoping you could help us with."

"What kind of package was it?"

"A box about this big"—he demonstrated the package dimensions with his hands—"addressed to Livvie's Kitchen, attention Olivia Beckman, if that helps."

She gave him a blank stare. "Sorry, it doesn't ring a bell. I'll need a lot more than that to go on."

"Bud was the mail carrier who delivered the parcel," Livvie put in.

"That doesn't help. Bud never waits on folks at the counter. It's just me and Ruth, and sometimes Mr. Ewing, the postmaster. I can ask them later if they recall anything about it. I wouldn't get my hopes up, though. We got lots of customers coming in here all day long."

Just then, someone behind them cleared his throat.

"Well, I thank you for your time," Will said, fighting down a swell of disappointment. "If you do happen to recall anything, would you kindly ring up Livvie's Kitchen?"

"I will."

They thanked her and were heading toward the door when she called after them, "Oh, and I've been hearing a good deal about that Family Feast you've been holding at your restaurant. I mean to come by one of these nights."

"You do that," Will replied, holding the door for Livvie.

Outside, Reggie gave Livvie a good sniffing up and down. "Reggie, stop that," she ordered him.

"He's got some kind of love affair going on with you," Will teased.

"I'll say he does."

He leaned closer and whispered, "And I don't blame him one bit."

Livvie gave him a playful slap on the arm. He laughed and dared to take her hand for all of half a block, until the pedestrian traffic picked up. It was nice while it lasted.

Chapter Twenty-three

"The heart is deceitful above all things,
and desperately wicked: who can know it?"
—Jeremiah 17:9

*F*riday morning found Clem sipping fresh-brewed coffee spiked with whiskey as he surveyed his comfy little abode from a wooden straight-back chair in the corner. Outside, crickets and birds sang a summer chorus as the day's first rays of sun burst through the open window. He'd been extra careful yesterday in making sure no one followed him out here. Sure, he'd taken a chance by traveling in broad daylight, but he'd needed more than just candlelight to accomplish all that he'd wanted to do. To his relief, he'd located the well and an outhouse. Life couldn't get much better. Why, this place was a regular paradise!

A ways down the path, the horse nibbled on the grain Clem had bought and drank from the bucket of water he'd hauled out to him. The rig rental expired today, so he planned to return it tonight and then hitchhike his way back. By then, his woman would be well situated, probably tied to a chair, and they could hole up here for the next few weeks, at least, before he'd need to go back to town for more supplies. Of course, that would mean pulling off another heist in the meantime in order to afford them, but he had plenty of time. Beyond that, he had no plan; he'd simply take life as it came, which pretty much described the way he'd always lived.

Surveying the space once more, he decided it looked downright inviting, from the table and two chairs in this corner to the mattress propped on the six-inch-high platform at the front and topped with a neat pile of pillows and blankets to the crates of food and supplies stacked against one wall. Shoot, he'd even found some framed artwork—a dusty old painting of Jesus—and had hung it on the wall. The discovery pretty much confirmed his suspicion that this building had been a church at one time. That ought to afford his new bride a sense of comfort. All right, so this wasn't some luxury hotel. But it still beat his former apartment and the cost of rent. That had been expensive enough, and then Flo had almost always been tardy with the payments, which meant being charged more. *Flo.* For the briefest instant, he pictured her mangled body smeared across the railroad tracks and a bunch of folks gathered around to gawk at her. To blot out the image, he immediately dumped a few more drops of whiskey into his coffee and took a big gulp. Stupid woman, walking in front of a train. The idea made him eager to get on with his new life, to make his new wife his in every sense.

Wouldn't Taylor have a fit when she went missing? And, with Livvie out of the picture, the flamboyant Marva Dulane could have at him. Chortling to himself, he took out a cig and stuck it in his mouth. He struck a match, lit the end till it caught hold, inhaled the sweet smoke, and then blew it back out in two perfect rings.

❧

At a quarter past twelve, Livvie looked up from the table she was setting and saw Marva Dulane strut through the door, dressed like a flapper in a loose-fitting, sleeveless yellow dress with a low waistline and a plunging neckline. A strand of beads was wrapped three times around her neck, yet still hung down to her hips, and rayon stockings with beige high heels accentuated her shapely legs. Blonde curls cascaded out from under the edges of her bell-shaped felt hat, the same creamy yellow as her dress.

"Whew! Would you look what the cat dragged in," Cora Mae muttered with a shudder, then went back to clearing the table next to Livvie's.

To say that heads turned when she walked in would be quite the understatement, based on the rubbernecking that occurred. The only people who seemed to have missed her grand entrance were Will and Gus, who stood at their posts in the kitchen. But the whispers that circulated the room would bring them up-to-date in no time, she supposed.

Evidently, Cora Mae was not impressed. "Who does she think she is, waltzin' in here like that?" she hissed through clenched teeth. "This isn't a nightclub, for goodness' sake."

"Hush before someone hears you," Livvie said. The sight of Marva sashaying through her door had annoyed her plenty, but her whispered prayer for staying power kept her from expressing it. The Lord had done some serious housecleaning in her heart lately. Yes, it was awfully audacious of Marva to make such a show in her establishment, but she had to trust that God was in control and would grant her whatever it took to deal with this woman's presence. She quickly prayed the same for Will.

"You don't have to put up with her paradin', do you? Look how everyone's watchin' her."

Livvie stepped back from the table. "Yes, Cora, I see that."

"Well, are you going to do anything about it?"

"Yes, I'm going to ask her if she'd like some lunch."

"What?"

"Cora Mae, close your mouth, would you?"

Seated at a nearby table, Coot had kept his mouth shut through their entire exchange. Now, he grinned and rubbed his whiskery chin. "It appears Olivia is showin' some goodwill, Cora Mae. Might be, you could learn from her."

Cora Mae stepped closer to his table and tapped his bony shoulder. "Oh, hush up, old man."

At that, he gave a loud hoot.

On Livvie's approach, Marva put on a glossy smile. "Well, Livvie Beckman, don't you look pretty today," she cooed.

Livvie glanced down at her well-worn, practical shirtwaist of blue gingham, knowing full well that Marva's compliment was artificial. But she wouldn't let that deter her from killing the woman with kindness. "I was about to say the same of you, Marva. Do you want me to show you to a table? We have some delicious vegetable soup simmering on the stove. Or, what about a cold sandwich? Sliced turkey, chicken, roast beef—"

"I'll have to think about it." She looked past Livvie to the kitchen, where Will steadily worked. A mixture of steam and smoke rose around him as steaks and hamburgers sizzled on the griddle, and his unbroken focus indicated that he was still unaware of Marva's presence.

The clatter of forks and knives signified that folks had gone back to their lunches, but the atmosphere remained charged with curiosity. There was Nancy Alberts, leaning across the table to speak to her husband while casting a suspicious eye in Marva's direction, and Harriet Mitchell whispered something in Frieda Carter's ear in between bites of potato salad. All around the room, the patrons pretended to focus intently on their meals, but Livvie knew better. Marva Dulane fascinated the lot of them.

Outside, Reggie gave an unusually sharp bark, then pressed his nose to the screen and peered inside. Livvie glared at him and pointed a finger, which was all it took for him to move away from the door and lie down again.

"You know," said Marva, bending toward Livvie, for she was four or five inches taller in her spikes, "I have a mad crush on your cook."

"Is that right?" *Lord, give me patience and self-restraint.*

Marva nodded. "He is by far the best-looking man in town. Oops! You're probably blind to that, being a widow and all. Surely, you pine for Frank on a daily basis. By the way, I've been meaning to tell you for some time now: I was looking through a box of old photographs a month or so ago, and I came across a wonderful picture of the two of you. It was taken at a Fourth of July picnic, or some such event. There you were, sitting all close and cozy, smiling for the camera."

Livvie's mind reeled. She couldn't remember attending any community picnic with Frank, much less one where Marva had snapped their picture. They'd always been so busy in the restaurant. Could it have been a church potluck? Maybe, but—

"I think I'll take one of those bar stools," Marva said, pointing a red-painted fingernail straight ahead.

When she set off across the room, Livvie hastened along behind her. "This picture you say you have...I don't understand."

"I'll bring it to you."

"You will?"

"Of course. I have no need for it."

She had too few photos of Frank. The thought of obtaining another, especially if it had them together, excited her.

Marva slid onto a bar stool next to Quinn Baxter, and the fellow turned a wary eye on her. "Hiya, Marva."

"Hello, Quinn. Lovely day, isn't it?"

Will spun around, spatula in hand. Hot grease still dripped off of the utensil, making splotches on the linoleum. If looks could shoot daggers, Livvie was certain that Marva would be lying flat on the floor.

❦

When would that infuriating woman get it through her head that he had no interest in her? This obsession she had with him wore mightily on his nerves, and he'd about reached the point of making a proclamation to everyone within hearing range about her irrational behavior. Somehow, though, he knew that wouldn't solve a thing. She had the advantage in that she knew his history, and humiliating her in a public forum would only impel her to reveal it. Of course, he had a little inside information on her, as well, which he planned to convey to her at his first opportunity. In the meantime, she kept up a steady flow of conversation pertaining to her own interests with anyone who'd listen, no doubt believing they all hung on her every word.

Some certainly seemed to, especially Charley Arnold and Roy Scott, who'd plopped themselves down on either side of her once Quinn Baxter had paid his bill and left. Ever since Will had laid down the law with them about not smoking inside the four walls of Livvie's Kitchen, they'd dutifully complied, and he'd even struck up an unlikely friendship with them. But now, he wished they'd head back to their daytime jobs.

When they finally did, and there was a lull in food orders, Will took a damp cloth and wiped the counter under Marva's nose. She'd finished her lunch long ago and was now sipping the last of her Coca-Cola.

"What are you doing here, Marva?" he asked, keeping his voice low.

Her long eyelashes batted three times. "I came to see you, of course. Since you never visit me, you leave me no choice but to take the initiative. I told you I love a challenge." She touched his sleeve, but he jerked his arm away.

He felt the veins in his neck bulge as he held his breath and mentally counted to ten before speaking again. "Marva, you should know I've learned a thing or two about you."

She took a swig of her soda, then set the glass down and smiled. "Is that so? I'm a pretty open book, Will. Not much folks in this town don't know about me."

"That may be so, but I bet the authorities don't know about your involvement with Orville Dotson and his still." Her smile vanished like a breeze. "And, by 'authorities,' I'm not referring to Buford Morris," he added.

"I have no idea what you're talking about."

"Mmm-hmm. Then, you won't mind if I pay a visit to the BIR?"

"What's that?"

"The Bureau of Internal Revenue. They employ Prohibition agents who come down mighty hard on folks participating in underground activities."

She shook her blonde head and gave the brim of her stylish hat a nervous little tug. "Will, Will. Has it really come down to this? Threatening me?" She slid off the stool and gave him a cold, hard-eyed smile. "I don't like the direction our friendship is going."

His lips curled. "You started it." He watched a flash of apprehension move across her face and envisioned raw nerves gnawing at her confidence. Good. Maybe that would get her off his back for the time being. He could only pray it would.

After Marva stalked out, Livvie wandered over to the bar. "Did you tell her you knew about her work with Dotson?"

"Sure did, and she wasn't too happy about it."

"I hope the whole thing doesn't blow up in your face. How do we know that she won't walk straight over to the *Daily Plain Dealer* office and give them an earful?"

He shrugged. "If she does, I'll deal with it." Then, grinning, he reached across the counter to push several loose strands of hair out of her eyes. He didn't care who saw him do it. "Did Marva have anything to say to you?"

"Um, not much," she said, then gave her wrist-watch a hurried glance. "I'd better go tend to my customers. I'm taking the boys down to the river after closing time today. I told them they could wade in the shallow part."

"Am I invited?"

She gave a light laugh. "Only if you promise to bring your harmonica."

He patted his hip pocket. "I never go anywhere without it."

The river seemed to hum along with Will as he made delightful music with his ten-hole mouth harp. He moved with ease from one tune to the next, and the sound, combined with the gentle breezes coming off the Wabash River, was a regular balm for the soul.

Livvie had spread out a large quilt in the shade of a tree, and she lounged there with Will, who reclined on his side, propped up on his elbow. Alex and Nate played on the riverbank, collecting stones and almost anything else that would fit in their pockets. They'd already waded a bit, with Will close by, and she'd instructed them not to go back in the water again without supervision.

Every so often, Will took a break from playing music to talk to her. They covered a wealth of topics, from the boom in business at the restaurant to Reverend White's message last Sunday. One subject they purposely stayed clear of was Marva Dulane, and Livvie was glad. She didn't think he'd appreciate knowing that Marva had told her about the photo of Frank and her, or how excited she'd been at the thought of seeing it. That would only confirm his belief that she still clung too much to the past to have a relationship with him.

"I love your hair, you know that?" He reached up and gave her ponytail a playful tug.

The compliment caught her off guard. "I've never liked it. I think it's a dreadful color."

"You're plain goofy, lady. The color is what makes it so pretty." He cocked his head and made a little frown. "You don't have a clue how adorable you are, do you?"

"Oh, my word." She couldn't help the blush that blazed across her cheeks.

"There're these dimples"—he touched a finger to one cheek, then the other—"and this cute tooth overlapping its neighbor"—he tapped her closed upper lip—"and this sweet little chin"—he grazed a thumb over it—"and this—"

"Oh, stop it, Will." She turned her head away with a nervous giggle and checked on her boys, who now kept themselves occupied digging in the dirt with long sticks.

He surprised her by taking her hand and rubbing the back of it with his thumb. When she looked at him, his eyes had sobered into shadowy pools. He tossed his harmonica to the side, sat up, and gently cupped her chin in one hand, slowly taking in her facial features. She went as silent as a doornail when she felt his breath on her face, blending with the warm, gentle wind. If she were smart, she would duck away from him. But she wasn't, so she didn't.

"I'm strongly considering kissing you," he whispered. "So, if you'd rather I didn't, I suggest you let me know in the next few seconds."

"I…I guess I wouldn't mind…if you did," she said in a shaky voice.

His crooked grin made her heart lurch with excitement. "You don't sound too sure."

"I'm not."

He chortled low in his throat. "How about you just relax?"

"Okay." She breathed deeply. Merciful heavens, it wasn't as if he intended to sweep her off to some exotic bower in a foreign land. It was just a simple kiss.

When their lips met, however, it was anything but simple, and she truly felt transported to another place, far from here. His mouth melded to hers, as if the two were one, making her quiver at the delightful tenderness of it all. He drew back briefly, repositioned himself, and descended again, this time with soul-stirring mastery. If Frank had ever kissed her in this manner—Lord, help her—she couldn't recall it. The next thing she knew, her fingers interlocked behind his back, and his did the same, gathering her snugly to him as the kiss continued with sweet abandon.

"Eww! Nate, Mommy 'n' Will're kissin'!"

Alex's squeaky-voiced announcement jolted Livvie's senses back into their proper place, and she sat up and cleared her dry, raspy throat. "Alex!" But that was all she could think to say to her son, who stood there with his brother, both of them open-mouthed, their blue eyes wide with shock.

Will drew one leg up and rested his arm on his knee. "Does it bother you boys that we were?"

Nate turned his gaze to his older brother, the designated spokesperson in such instances. Alex merely shrugged. "Naw. We don't care."

Nate shook his head from side to side. "Nope, we don't."

"Are you gonna be our new dad?" Alex asked.

Will looked pensive. "Well, I—"

"Oh, my heavens!" Livvie exclaimed. Red-hot prickles danced across her cheeks. She dropped her gaze to her skirt and started pressing down the wrinkles.

"I guess that's the sort of thing I can't answer right off," Will said, as calmly as if someone had just asked him the day of the week. "But I will tell you this: I think the world of you boys, and, if I ever had sons, I'd want them to be exactly like you."

Alex flung his arms out in a sign of exasperation. "Then, you might as well be our dad!"

"Yeah!" said Nate. "But, first, you'd have to marry Mommy."

Mortified, Livvie jumped to her feet and looked at her watch. "Gracious, would you look at the time? It's almost four o'clock. We'd better go!"

Will picked up his harmonica, casually slipped it into his pocket, and took his time getting up, showing no trace of embarrassment at the boys' comments. He reached out and tousled their blond hair. "You two whippersnappers ready to head back?"

"We aren't whoopersnackers," Nate argued.

"Okay. Hooligans, then."

"Yeah, we're hooligans," Alex said. "What's a hooligan, anyways?"

Will chuckled, and Livvie sneaked a peek at him, finding that his eyes danced with merriment. He tilted his head at her and winked. Mercy, but he did have a way of turning her to Jell-O!

She bent to pick up the quilt, but Will beat her to it, throwing it over his arm. "Come on, hooligans," he said.

"What's a hooligan, Will?" Alex asked again.

Livvie set off down the trail, the three of them close on her tail.

"Hm, how to define a hooligan...? I guess I'd say, a boy who's too smart for his britches."

"We're smart, huh, Alex?" Nate said.

"Yeah! I like bein' a hooligan."

"Me, too."

✴

Clem could hardly contain his rage. How dare Will Taylor kiss his wife-to-be! He clutched the handle of his pistol, half tempted to draw out the weapon right then and do away with the creep. But reason dissuaded him. "Calm down, Dodd," he muttered to himself. "She'll be yers soon enough. Shootin' 'im now would throw off the whole plan."

He pulled back a thick, leafy branch to get a better view and, with his other hand, raised the binoculars to his eyes once more. Soon, the foursome disappeared into the thicket and out of view. An irksome train whistle blew, announcing the arrival of yet another locomotive.

He'd be glad to get out of this town and settled with Livvie in his little house in the country. All these trains constantly coming and going sure did wear on a person's nerves after a while.

Chapter Twenty-four

"What time I am afraid, I will trust in thee.
In God I will praise his word,
in God I have put my trust;
I will not fear what flesh can do unto me."
—Psalm 56:3–4

An odd mix of emotions stirred in Livvie's soul as she flitted about the restaurant, waiting on customers. Every so often, she caught Will's eye and noticed a special gleam of interest there, a hint of unspoken promises. On the one hand, she delighted in the sweet awareness, but, on the other, confusion lingered, as well as the sense that she was unworthy of his attention. Was he growing impatient to know how she felt about him? And had it even been fair of her to indulge those luscious kisses if she couldn't bring herself to say those three all-important words?

The restaurant wasn't extremely busy tonight. She suspected it was because folks were growing weary of the August heat and had opted to do something else to keep cool. By quarter to seven, all but a few patrons had gone home, and she sent Cora Mae home early, leaving the cleanup to Georgia and herself. In the kitchen, Will and Gus scraped down the stovetop and grill, knowing it was still possible that a few stragglers would come in and order a burger or some fried chicken. While they worked, the two kept up a lively conversation about hunting, fishing, and sports. Georgia lingered at the front of the room, water pitcher in hand, conversing with Mr. and Mrs. Wimberly. Alex and Nate had received several hand-me-down games, toys, and puzzles from Polly Atkins, a mother of four older boys, who had been kind enough to drop them off when she and her husband had come in for supper that night. To Livvie's delight, the boys had found their manners without her prompting, thanked the couple for their generosity, and then promptly hauled their treasures to the back room, from which they had not emerged in well over an hour.

At the same moment Livvie decided to check on her boys, the back door opened, and there in the shadows stood Marva Dulane, beckoning her with a bent forefinger. Livvie hesitated, but when Marva held up a photograph, she figured it was the one she'd told her about earlier, so she advanced to the door, thankful to have slipped past Will and Gus unnoticed. After those searing afternoon kisses, Will would not be happy to see her excitement at getting her hands on another picture of her dearly departed husband.

Marva had lost her sunny yellow dress and matching hat and slipped into a pale lilac getup that was similar in style to the dress she'd worn earlier, but the scooped neck was even lower, fitting for evening. She wore a single strand of beads and coordinating dangly earrings. Her golden hair had been styled with waves that molded to her oval face, and a glimmering barrette pinned a section of it above one ear. She was a striking woman, really. If only she didn't come on so strong with people, or cover up her best features with caked-on cosmetics.

As Livvie approached her, the woman backed up, still motioning for her to follow. She had no idea why Marva had gone outside, but it didn't matter much, so important was that photograph to her. Outside, not a soul was about, besides a stray cat that darted across the alley, and a horse and buggy hitched to a nearby fence post. The oppressive heat had her dabbing at her damp forehead with the back of her hand.

Out of nowhere, Reggie came bounding around the corner of the building. At first, he seemed intent on checking out the cat, but he quickly lost interest when he saw Livvie. She hadn't even known the dog was about, as Coot had not returned for supper. Deep shadows darkened the alley due to tall trees between the buildings, which made it difficult for the setting sun to peek through. "I brought you your picture," said Marva, who'd moved a good ten feet from the door. Smiling, she looked down at the photo and caressed it. "I shouldn't have told you it was of you and Frank, though. That was mean of me."

"Wh—what do you mean?"

"Well, it's actually a picture of something altogether different, but you should find it interesting, nonetheless." A cold smile pulled at the corners of her mouth and sent a strange chill down Livvie's spine. Reggie stayed at her side, but she paid him little heed.

"What are you talking about? Let me see it."

Clutching the photo tight against her chest, Marva scoffed, and the upper lip of her bright-red mouth curled. Livvie yearned to snatch the picture out of her grasp. "You do think you're something, don't you, Livvie?" the woman sneered. "Owning this big building, running your own business, making friends with everybody in town...Olivia Beckman is nobody's enemy. It must be nice to be you," she jeered. "And now, you think you're going to land the one man I have my eyes on? Well, missy"—she leaned close, and Livvie detected the smell of strong liquor on her breath—"I decided that Will Taylor would be mine the minute I first laid eyes on him." She cackled. "No more kissing down at the river, you hear?" A fierce growl came out of Reggie, and Marva glared down at him. "Shut up, you stupid dog!"

"Kissing?" Livvie shivered in panic at Marva's strange remark. "You spied on us today?"

"Me? Would I stoop that low? No, of course not." Her laughter rose to hysterical heights. "But somebody did." With a slight twist of her body, she nodded.

The next thing Livvie knew, someone grabbed her from behind, hauling her up against his flabby chest and covering her mouth and nose with an awful-smelling rag. She struggled and squirmed as his hot breath skimmed her ear. "Hello, honey," he whispered. "You're mine now. All mine."

Livvie kicked, thrashed, and tried to scream, but all for naught. She saw Reggie leap on her attacker and bite his arm until the fellow yipped, but then Marva hit the poor dog with something, and his body fell to the ground with a thud.

Lord Jesus, help me! she inwardly screamed. A powerful wave of dizziness overtook her, and her world went as dark as sin.

※

If Will had learned one thing about Gus, it was that he did nothing quietly. Now, for example, he stood over the sink, with the spigot running at full blast, and clanged the pots and pans he scrubbed. Meanwhile, his good-hearted chatter never ceased, and his intermittent bursts of laughter at his own jokes never decreased in volume. Not that Will minded having a companion in the kitchen—shoot, it reminded him of days gone by with Harry—and Gus was a definite asset to him. Still, he would have appreciated the occasional lull. He chuckled at his petty predicament, even as Gus told him all about his weekend plans.

"Tell Livvie I've finished up, would you, Will?" Georgia's voice made him turn. "I think I'll go on home, if that's okay."

He looked at her, then glanced around the empty restaurant. Alex and Nate's voices carried from the back room, where they'd sequestered themselves ever since receiving that box of used toys. "I'll tell her. Is she back there with the boys now?"

Georgia shrugged and pushed a wisp of brown hair off her brow. "She must be. I haven't seen her for a little while."

"Hm." Will felt a frown pull his brows together. He darted around the bar and hurried to the back room. When he opened the door, he saw the boys, sprawled on the floor, building some sort of structure out of wooden links.

Alex looked up first. "Hey, Will! Look!" he exclaimed. "We got this big set o' wooden logs, and me 'n' Nate's buildin' a house. Ain't it grand?"

"It is, yes. Where's your mom?"

They both shrugged.

"You want to play with us?" Nate asked.

"Not this minute, but you boys have fun." He quietly shut the door again and turned to Georgia. "Stay here a minute while I run upstairs. She might have gone to her apartment."

At her nod, he pushed open the door, but the sight of a bloody Reggie standing there on wobbly legs halted him in his tracks.

❦

Livvie was awakened by a fierce headache. Well, it might have been from the stinging pain at her wrists and ankles, which were bound, or the pressure of the rope tied in between her lips, making her gag. Or, it might have been the urgent need to relieve her bladder. Whatever the reason, as her eyes slowly opened and tried to adjust to her surroundings, a moan rose up from her chest. Her senses soon cleared enough for her to realize that she was tied to a wooden chair, incapable of moving anything but her head.

As she looked around, she struggled to sift through her jagged memory. Where was she, and how had she gotten here? Two kerosene lamps and some candles glowed in the single room, but light rays through a broken window indicated that the sun had not fully set. Did this mean that her attacker intended to return after dark? Despite the shadows, she made out a wall lined with boxes and crates, many of them holding canned goods and other food items; a mattress piled with two pillows and a couple of folded blankets; and a rickety-looking table flanked by two antique chairs.

The urge to retch came over her, but the fear of choking on her own vomit kept her from giving in. She tried to kick and thrash, but every part of her body seemed constrained. Stark, vivid terror formed a hard knot inside her chest as her mind filled with graphic images of what her fate might be. When she tried to scream, her throat, burning with sheer fright, squelched her efforts.

Lord God! Oh, Jesus, her mind cried out.

Be still, My child, for I am with you, an overwhelming presence seemed to whisper.

Alex. Nate. Oh, God, I need to get to my children!

"*Peace I leave with you, my peace I give unto you.*" Wispy fragments of Scripture drifted over her spirit like feathery clouds, tiny bits of reassurance. She breathed deep and long, reminding herself of the importance of staying calm.

Reason kicked in, and with it came broken pieces of memory. She'd been cleaning up the restaurant when Marva had stopped by with...what was it? A photo. And she'd been foolish enough to follow her outside. But why not? She'd had no reason to distrust Marva Dulane, other than the fact that they'd never been friends. The woman was plain loco, as was the man who'd attacked her. At least, she assumed it had been a man. She hadn't gotten even one glimpse of him. Who was he, and what did he want with her?

As she tried to adjust her position, she heard the rustle of paper beneath her bound hands. She looked down at her lap and saw a note pinned to her skirt. Frowning, she lifted her hands as high as she could, lowered her chin, and narrowed her eyes. When the penmanship came into focus, her stomach sank. It was the same handwriting that had appeared on the notes she'd received with the blue dress and the jar of flowers.

My darling Livvie,

I had to take back the rented horse and buggy. But don't wurry. I will be home

by dark. Sorry about the ropes and stuff.
When you lurn to trust me I'll take
them off. I love you.

C.

Oh, Lord! Tears coursed down her cheeks as she struggled to free herself. *I need to get out of here before he returns. Please, God.*

But all she got by way of an answer was a verse she'd memorized as a child: "*The* LORD *will give strength unto his people; the* LORD *will bless his people with peace.*" It came from the book of Psalms, but that was all she could recall.

Even so, she clung to that little verse with every ounce of resolve she could muster, repeating it over and over again. If she didn't, she knew she might very well lose her mind.

※

"What do you mean, you can't disturb the sheriff?" Will demanded of the deputy, who sat comfortably in his office chair with his booted feet, one crossed over the other, propped on his marred desktop. From the look of it, his most pressing business was an issue of the *Daily Plain Dealer*, unfurled across his lap, and the steaming cup of coffee in his hand.

"I told you, he ain't on duty."

Standing near Will were Gus and Livvie's brother-in-law, Howard Grant, who had met them there. Will and Gus had run to the sheriff's station, but it was Howard who looked red in the face and out of breath, as if he'd pushed his truck all the way there rather than driven it. And no wonder. Will could only imagine the anxiety he and Margie had felt since finding out about Livvie's strange and sudden disappearance. She was more like a daughter to them than a sister.

Margie had been hysterical when Will had told her the news, but then she'd quickly gained her composure and insisted that Alex and Nathan would be better off with her. Quinn Baxter had been at the restaurant when all of this had happened, and he'd offered to take the boys to the Grants' farm. Of course, they had gone kicking and screaming, hysterical themselves at the conversation they hadn't been able to help but over-hear. Will had hugged them both and promised to do everything in his power to bring their mother home safe and sound. Then, they'd wiped their swollen eyes and tried to be brave as they huddled together in the back of Quinn's Model T. "You and Mommy's all we got left, 'sides Aunt Margie and Uncle Howie," Alex had said, sounding too somber for his eight years. It had struck Will then how very much the boys had suffered over the loss of their daddy. "I know, I know," Will had said, wiping moisture from the corner of one of his own eyes. "Now, you two practice being brave soldiers, all right? And, remember: Jesus is with your mommy, wherever she is."

They'd nodded in unison. "I'm gonna practice bein' a cowboy," Nate had muttered. "'Cause they're brave, too."

With a silent nod, Will had patted the innocent child on his knee, then closed the car door and stepped back. In the front seat, Reggie had been whining and acting jittery, as if he wanted to tell them something. Too bad mutts couldn't talk. Thankfully, it seemed his only injuries were a bump on his head and a cut over one eye. Quinn planned to drop him off at Coot's place after taking the boys out to the farm.

Will blinked and gave a hard swallow. Then, he focused steady eyes on the deputy and, speaking slowly and enunciating carefully, said, "I don't care if the sheriff is on a trip to Australia." He pounded his fist on the frumpy fellow's desk to emphasize his point. "Pick up that phone and tell him there's been a kidnapping. Olivia Beckman is missing."

With lightning speed, the deputy plunked his coffee cup on the desk, splashing its contents all over the place, hauled his feet to the floor, and jumped to attention. "Well, why didn't you say so from the beginning?"

Sheriff Morris arrived about ten minutes later, his shirt buttoned incorrectly and only half tucked in, his hat sitting askew on his head. He neatened his appearance while Will brought him up-to-date on the events of the evening, though he imagined it was hard to tuck in a shirt over such a blubbery belly.

"So, let me get this straight," the sheriff said, walking to a file cabinet. He pulled open the top drawer and retrieved a folder. "She was in the restaurant, and then she wasn't? As in, poof!—she vanished into thin air? What if she simply walked out of her own accord?"

The investigation had just begun, and already his arrogance was showing. "That's what we're trying to determine, Sheriff," Will told him.

"Maybe she just left to visit someone," he said, opening the folder and sifting through some papers, as if he'd already gathered information about the case. Will prayed for staying power. He needed the sheriff's help, and this was no time for getting on the fellow's bad side. Best to cooperate and put on a patient front.

"She wouldn't just disappear like that, not when she's got two boys who rely on her," Howard put in. "She loves those boys more than her own life. She's not about to go off without at least telling someone of her intentions."

"Besides, someone thumped that poor dog on the head," said Gus, speaking for the first time.

"That, or he got in a fight with another mongrel," the sheriff argued.

"Those were no bite marks he had," Will countered.

Silence filled the next thirty seconds as the sheriff's eyes scanned a document in the folder. Will felt his patience wearing as thin as that piece of paper, and, from Howard's shifting and Gus's pacing, he could tell that they bore equal amounts of frustration.

"So, what's your plan, Sheriff?" Will finally asked. "Time's wasting."

"I'm thinkin', I'm thinkin'," he said. "Something's not addin' up."

"What do you mean?" Howard asked.

"Well, seems to me that Will or Gus or somebody else would've heard some commotion if someone had come in to snatch her away. She would have screamed or fought or put up some kind of big fuss." They all nodded, so the sheriff went on. "I'm thinkin' she walked outside of her own free will, and, to have done that, she would've had to have recognized whomever it was that wooed her out there. You with me?"

"Of course, we're with you," Will said, his own wheels spinning hard.

"Question is, who was it?"

"Exactly," Will replied. They were getting nowhere in a hurry, and he was about ready to walk down to the livery, lease himself a swift horse, and set off on his own search. Or, maybe the three of them could head out in Howard's truck and leave the sheriff and his faithful deputy to sort things out.

"Who else was in the restaurant?" Sheriff Morris asked, removing his police hat. He scratched his head, then set his hat back in place. "Maybe somebody saw somethin' and, because he recognized the person, didn't think much of it when Olivia stepped outside."

Will looked at Gus.

"There wasn't hardly anybody left, that I can recall," Gus said. "And, by the time we knew she was missing, the only people in the restaurant were Will and me and Georgia, Quinn Baxter, and, o' course, them boys, who was back in their playroom."

With a harrumph, the sheriff rubbed his whiskery jaw and went back to perusing the piece of paper he'd pulled from the folder.

"What do you keep reading there?" Will ventured to ask.

"This? Oh, it's just some report I got from the New York Police Department." He raised one eyebrow and looked at Will, his eyes wary. "They got a couple o' fellas in custody."

"Yeah?" A nagging thought pierced the back of Will's mind. "What's that got to do with anything? Olivia Beckman's been kidnapped, and you're worried about a couple of guys being held in another state?"

"New York State, Mr. Taylor. That ring a bell with you? They claim their partner's here in Wabash. Name's Clem Dodd. Apparently, he's wanted in connection with several robberies back East."

Will blinked in disbelief. A hard ball of nerves kept him from taking his next breath. *Clem Dodd never left?*

He's been hiding out in Wabash this whole time? "I know him—and he's a crazy man."

The sheriff nodded. "I figured you did. You know how? 'Cause it says right here you served time on Welfare Island. Those fellas in custody say you once ran with them and Clem Dodd."

The tension in the room ran as thick as a slab of ice. More than feeling ashamed, though, Will was angry that this development was delaying their search for Livvie.

When Gus and Howard turned penetrating gazes on him, he sucked in a gulp of air and then let it out with a whoosh. "It's true, but I'm a changed man now. The Lord did a work in my heart and life, forgave me of my past sins, and helped me to learn from my mistakes. I'm on a whole new path now."

"Don't know about that religious stuff," the sheriff said. "All I know is, you're an ex-con, and it wouldn't surprise me none if you were still hooked up with this Dodd character."

Anger made his breath burn in his throat, but he knew the importance of maintaining his cool. "That's baloney, Sheriff. I haven't seen Dodd since—"

"Since when?" he asked. "You might as well come all the way clean, Taylor."

He felt pressed into a corner. "A number of weeks ago, he showed up, along with those other fellows you mentioned, after hours at Livvie's Kitchen. They accused me of hanging on to the loot I lifted from a jewelry store some eleven years ago, but I told them I'd thrown the bag down a sewer pipe."

The sheriff nodded. "Yep. Says in this here report at least a portion of those gems were recovered a few years back when somebody found 'em in a drainage ditch."

He was relieved to hear that, but impatience to find Livvie kept him from expressing it. "Livvie overheard them talking outside her apartment that night. Hank and Rudy said they were leaving on the morning train, and, since I never heard from Clem after that, I made the foolish assumption he'd left town, as well. That's the plain truth. Now, can we get on with business?"

"That's what we're doin'," Sheriff Morris said. "I'm goin' to list off all the robberies reported to me in the past several weeks, and I want you to stop me if any of 'em ring a bell with you."

"What do you mean?" Will couldn't believe it. "There's a woman missing, Sheriff, and you want me to stand here and listen to some random list of reported robberies?"

"Bear with me, Taylor." The sheriff looked at the paper and cleared his throat. "Bill's Bait Shop reported ten dollars missin' from cash drawer, Bronson Hardware had several tools stolen, Gant's Five and Dime reported stolen cash, McCaffrey Grocery cited several crates o' canned goods and various other supplies missin' from inventory, Tom's News and Cigar Shop reported several cartons of cigarettes missin', the manager of Woolworth's documented fifty dollars taken from the cash register...hmm, let's see here...J. C. Penney reported a stolen dress, Bradley Drugstore—"

"Wait. Go back. The dress. Clem Dodd stole that dress and mailed it to Livvie. I'm sure of it."

"He's right, Sheriff," Gus spoke up. "Livvie got a blue dress in the mail. Along with a note. Tell him 'bout that note, Will. And the other one, too. And the flowers."

Will filled him in, recounting the trip Livvie and he had made to the post office to inquire about who had sent the dress, as well as how he'd come to learn that the dress had been stolen, and how Livvie had hastened to the store as soon as she could to return it.

"I wouldn't doubt he's your culprit in the majority of those thefts," Will said. "He tries to keep a low profile by sticking to petty crimes. If it's true that he's still in town, then he's the one who's been pulling off all those dirty deeds."

"Including stealin' a dress for Olivia Beckman? What would his motive have been, do you think?"

"I don't know. To get back at me, maybe. He's probably jealous that I'm working for a mighty pretty woman and that I've moved on with my life. I've no doubt he's been thinking for the past ten years about that jewelry store we robbed and just itching for my release so he could hunt me down and find out what I did with the goods. He's probably madder than a starved maggot after learning I threw them away." Will shuddered at the thought of Clem putting his grimy hands on Livvie, but he knew how demented the man could be. "He's always had a sick fascination with women."

Sheriff Morris rubbed his flabby jowls, then raked a hand through his thin, mousy brown hair. "According to this here report, the woman walked in front of a movin' train the other day. Clem Dodd's wife is dead."

"You're kidding! Well, that could have been enough to push him over the edge. I tell you, he's a crazy loon."

"You think Livvie would have stepped outside if he had beckoned to her at the back door?" the sheriff asked.

"Never," Will said. "Livvie caught him staring at her through the front window of the restaurant one night, and he scared her half to death."

Howard cleared his throat. Since their arrival at the sheriff's office, he'd said little, no doubt fretting every bit as much as Will, who couldn't help but wonder what the guy thought of him now that he knew about his prison stint. "I think we've done enough talking, Buford," Howard said. "In the meantime, my wife's little sister is missing, and I demand that you come up with some sort of plan for finding her. What's it going to be?"

The pudgy man hefted his gun belt with both hands. "All right, all right. We've got no proof whatsoever that this Dodd fellow is responsible for Livvie's sudden disappearance, but, for now, he's our best gamble, especially since he's already a wanted man, and the authorities suspect he's in these parts. I'm thinkin' we ought to start by canvassin' houses. We'll spread out and go door-to-door, askin' if anyone's seen anything suspicious. Who knows? He could be hidin' out in somebody's home, holdin' 'em at gunpoint." He looked at his deputy. "Clifford, you stay here and field calls. Someone might—"

The door blew open, and there stood Charley Arnold and Roy Scott.

"Evenin', Charley, Roy," the sheriff said. "What can I do for you?"

"We heard from Quinn Baxter Miss Livvie's missing, and we come to see what we can do to help."

They stepped inside, followed by George and Ralph McNarney, Sam Campbell, Skeeter Barnes, Dan Gillen and his two sons, and several others, until the small room was filled to capacity. Even Reverend White and a few of his parishioners crowded in.

"Well," Sheriff Morris said, scratching the back of his neck. "Looks to me like we got ourselves a posse."

Chapter Twenty-five

"Behold, the eye of the LORD is upon them
that fear him, upon them that hope
in his mercy."
—Psalm 33:18

As he shuffled along Falls Avenue, dimly lit by the moon and the glow from the windows of a few houses, Clem kept an eye to the street and stuck out his thumb whenever a car came by. Finally, an approaching vehicle slowed to a crawl. Clem moved alongside it, coming up to the open window. The driver leaned over and looked up at him. "Where you headin', mister?"

Clem put on his best smile as he kept pace with the slow-moving vehicle. He could be downright friendly when the occasion called for it. "Up the road a spell," he said. "Just past Highway Twenty-Four—Farr Pike Road, I think it's called. It's only a few miles. I could walk, but a ride would get me there a lot quicker."

The man hesitated a moment, brushing a hand over his bearded chin, and then brought the Model T to a stop. "Up as far as Kentner Creek?"

"Not sure, exactly. I'll know the corner when I see it. That's where you can drop me."

That seemed to satisfy the fellow. "All right, then. Hop on in."

"Much obliged." He climbed in, closed the door, and looked straight ahead, his nerves aflutter at the prospect of seeing Livvie. He hoped she wouldn't be too mad at him for tying her up so snugly. Of course, he'd had no choice. He couldn't take the chance of her bolting on him. She'd be scared at first—that was only normal—but her attitude would change when she learned how much he loved her. He clutched his left forearm where that blasted dog had sunk in his teeth. The spot throbbed clear to the next county, but it wasn't anything a good dose of Dotson's whiskey wouldn't cure.

The fellow put the automobile in gear and let up on the clutch while compressing the accelerator. They jostled and jerked for the next few seconds as he moved through all the gears. "Beautiful night, isn't it?" he said.

"Mighty fine," Clem answered, making sure to keep his voice steady.

"You live in the Wabash area?" the driver asked.

"What? No, I'm just...visitin' someone."

"Oh, is that right? Who is it? I might know 'em. I know lots o' people in these parts."

Clem gritted his teeth. "No, I...I doubt you would. They've been in Wabash for just a few months."

"Yeah? Well, Wabash is a fine place. Yes, indeed. You hear about lots of folks moving here, and I don't blame 'em. It's a peaceful, pleasant town. I know a family goes by the name of Carmichael who just bought the Tanner farm up the road a piece. Would it be them you're goin' to see?"

"Nope."

"Oh. Well, let's see, is it the Grodens, then? They just moved in 'bout six months ago. They hail from somewhere down in Illinois."

"Nope."

"Oh." Silence prevailed for all of fifteen seconds as they bumped along, and then, "I bet it's that nice young couple, name o' Richards," he said. "My wife just met the missus in the grocery store the other day. They got a couple o' kids, and—"

"Look, I told you, y' wouldn't know 'em," Clem spouted, glaring at the fellow. "Just leave it alone, all right?"

At that, the man nodded and clammed up. Clem was glad, but he could have thumped himself for letting his quick temper get the better of him.

A few minutes later, they were almost to the corner where he wanted to be let out. "Here's my stop," he said, and the guy pulled to the side of the road. "Sorry for yellin' at ya back there. Thanks for the ride."

"No problem at all. You sure you don't want me to drive you up to your door?"

"No! I mean, I don't mind the walk. It's just a ways. Wouldn't want to put you out any more'n I already have." With that, he scooted out of the car, closed the door, and leaned down to wave at the driver.

The man shot him a wary gaze, probably intrigued by the grotesque scar on his left cheek, and he felt a haunting fear in the back of his mind. Suppose the fellow memorized his face and reported him to the authorities? Hank and Rudy were sitting in jail, and, for all he knew, they'd given the cops a tip-off as to his whereabouts. They might be scouring Wabash this very minute in search of him. This guy could probably identify him. He reached inside his pocket and grasped the butt of his pistol.

"Well, you have a good night, now," the man said with a smile.

Clem relaxed. "I sure will." He straightened and tipped his hat. "You do the same." Then, he turned and set off up the dirt road. For a minute, the whirring engine of the Model T was the only sound he heard, save for the chirps of crickets and croaks of tree frogs. Soon, though, the old Ford moved out of earshot, and the sound of his heartbeat reverberating in his head took its place.

※

Through a broken window, Livvie saw a full moon, which cast beams of light on the floor. Outside, crickets sang a carefree song, as if all were right with the world. Something scampered past her feet. A mouse? Instant fright twisted around her heart, and a scream welled up from the depths of her being. Yet it came out muffled, a futile moan. In desperation, she tried to kick her feet, but her legs and ankles were bound so tightly that moving was impossible. The critter finally skittered to the other side of the room and out of sight, but a sense of panic still rioted within her. She now knew what the apostle Paul had meant by the exhortation to *"pray without ceasing,"* for that was exactly what she'd been doing for the past several hours while she'd sat there, waiting for her fate to unfold.

Alex and Nathan filled her thoughts, as did Will. By now, they must have realized she had gone missing and were surely looking for her. *Please, Lord, grant wisdom and discernment to everyone searching for me. Lead them straight to me, Father.* How she longed for this ordeal to be nothing more than a dream, to awaken and find herself at home, safe and sound. But the pain she felt from the ropes tied around her wrists and ankles and over her mouth confirmed the wretched reality: someone dark and sinister had put her in this awful place.

The heat was stifling, but she managed to doze, even though she jerked awake at the slightest sound. Every time she was roused from slumber, she fought down a new wave of panic and regained her mental footing with a fervent prayer before drifting off again. But then, the dread moment arrived—footsteps pounded the earth outside—and her nerves stood on end, freezing her blood like icicles, so that she couldn't breathe. Eyes anchored to the doorknob, she watched it turn, her heart thudding hard inside her chest.

A big, flabby fellow came through the door, but the dimness of the room prevented her from making out his facial features. *Oh, Lord, who is he? And what does he want with me? Please protect me, Father.*

"Wull, there you are, still lookin' as purty as a flower," he said in a croaky voice. He turned his back to her and peered outside in all directions before closing the door.

When he turned and stepped out of the shadows to advance on her, a gasp heaved past her slightly parted lips. It was him—the man with the gash across his cheek, Will's former acquaintance, Clem Dodd.

"You remember me? We hooked eyes outside your rest'rant one night, and then another time when I watched you from the alley. I been followin' you 'round town, learnin' your schedule. You're a busy li'l thing, aren't ya? I bought you that dress, in case you were wonderin', but, I got to say, it wounded me plenty to see you take it back. Didn't you like it?" He paused for several seconds and studied her, his eyes moving over her body. "I hope you read my note." She knew enough to nod. "Aw, don't look so worried. You're safe with me, long as you behave yourself. Sorry I had to knock you out back there. You got to know, I had no choice. Don't think you would've come too willingly otherwise."

"Mmmm," she moaned.

He hunkered down next to her, and the smell of his rancid breath nearly made her retch. A wily grin revealed that a tooth was missing from his top row. "That Marva lady sure had you goin', didn't she, enticin' you with that photo? Bet you're wantin' to see it, ain't ya? She shore is hateful toward you, I'll say that much. Personally, I think she's a little loony." He pointed a stubby finger at his temple and moved it in a circular motion. "You get my drift?"

Rather than respond, she merely stared into his glassy eyes. He took a deep breath and let it out in her face, giving her another urge to retch. "Anyways, Marva gave me the photo. Said I should show it to you. Wanna see it?"

She gave no indication that she did, but he pulled it from his rear pocket, anyway, and stuck it under her nose.

She strained to make out the details. When the picture came into focus, her stomach clenched in a thousand knots.

"Reco'nize it?" he asked. "Marva says it's a picture of your old house, 'fore it burned. It's funny," he went on, peering at the photo, "but I don't even know that idiot woman, and she blabbed all manner o' stuff to me. 'Course, she was drunker than a mule at the time." A deep frown quickly etched itself into his damp brow, and he pulled up his sleeve. "See this?" He stuck out his beefy arm to reveal a wide, bloody gash. "That blasted dog bit me, and it hurts to the moon. I ought to've killed 'im right then, but Marva gave 'im a good whack on the head, instead. Knocked 'im out cold.

"But, back to this here picture." He studied it again. "I bet you don't know that her daddy's the one who set your house ablaze."

What? She jerked her head back. Her dizzied senses were barely registering anything. Had she heard him correctly?

"Yeah, just what I thought." His eyes gleamed with some kind of sick satisfaction.

As she focused her thoughts, misgivings swirled in her mind. The investigators had determined that a spark from her family's wood-burning stove had started the fire that had swept through their home and burned it to the ground in minutes. To her knowledge, arson had never been considered.

When Clem reached up and fingered a lock of her hair, another scream caught in the back of her throat and stuck there like an immovable rock. She gave a sudden twist of her head to toss his hand off of her, but he held on. "Seems your daddy had eyes for Marva's mama. Did you know that?" He gave a sinister chortle. "Broke up her folks' marriage, accordin' to Marva."

She stared at him with wide, unblinking eyes.

"And Marva says she's still got notes your daddy wrote to her mama. Ain't that somethin'? I bet you'd like to read 'em."

Spasmodic trembling overtook her, and she groaned.

"I s'pose you're wantin' me to untie that rope at the back of your head, huh? Well, I guess I could, but you can't scream none, you hear? 'Cause, if you do, I'll jest be forced to put it back on—only tighter."

She gave a quick nod, and he untied the rope. After stretching her mouth several times, she started pleading. "Please, just let me go, and I won't talk to anyone about any of this. I need to go home to my boys. I know they're missing me something fierce. I promise you, I'll keep my mouth buttoned tight." Her knees took on a life of their own, bouncing up and down.

"Yeah?" He lowered his head, making three chins out of one with the simple move. "Even around Will Taylor? I'm afraid I don't believe you, honey. I saw you two kissin' down at the river. Blame near made me sick."

"I won't even tell Will. I promise."

"I know you won't, 'cause you're gonna forget all about 'im." He touched her hair again. "He ain't worth your time, sweetheart. I'm gonna help you forget 'im. Look!" He swept out his arm, indicating the room. "I done collected enough supplies to last us a good long while, you 'n' me. We're gonna be real happy together, you'll see. In a couple o' days, we'll get married—well, maybe not in the legal sense, but you know what I mean. Don't you worry, though; I'll give you a chance to get used to things first."

Beads of sweat popped out all over her body, and she squirmed in the chair. "But, I have to—to—"

"Oh!" He opened his mouth, revealing several decayed teeth she hadn't noticed before. "There's a privy out back. I'll take you." He bent down, as if preparing to free her ankles, but then stopped and cast her a wary glance. Long clumps of greasy, brown hair fell across his bloodshot eyes. "You wouldn't try any funny business, now, would you? I'd hate to have to hurt you, darlin'."

She bit her lower lip and shook her head several times.

"That's right."

Once her ankles were free, he took her by the arm and pulled her up. Her legs nearly buckled, but she caught herself. "What about my hands? I can't very well…you know…."

He chortled and dipped his face low, so that she had to endure that awful breath again. "I'll untie you at the door to the privy. You'll do your business, and then I'll tie you up again. Understand?"

She wanted to spit in his face, but she knew that the small satisfaction she'd gain would not be worth the consequences. "Yes," she managed.

Outside, she stumbled along a bumpy path lit only by the moon and Clem's low-voltage flashlight. His fingers dug so deeply into her arm, she imagined the blood flow stopping at each pressure point. In the distance, a dog barked, and crickets and tree frogs joined in a chorus of summer tunes. How she longed to break free and sprint through the tall grass. She could outrun him; she was sure of it. She could also scream, but for what purpose? There wasn't a single house in sight; her wails would be heard only by night-time creatures. As they navigated the path, she tried to take in her surroundings, but it was too dark to see much of anything.

"All right now, sweetheart," he said when they reached the outhouse. "I'll unfasten your hands, but don't even think of tryin' anything. I didn't wanna have to show you this, but, well, see what I got here?" He reached inside his pocket and pulled out a pistol.

"I see it," she muttered, determined not to show the wave of terror that coursed through her. She pulled the handle on the outhouse door, which squeaked on its hinges, stepped inside, and closed the door behind her. Inside, she felt for a lock but found none.

Silent, salty tears rolled down her cheeks and moistened her dry lips. As she stood in the musty-smelling structure, listening to crickets chirp in the distance, she begged the Lord to give her strength and courage. Somehow, she knew that if she had any hope of getting through this alive, she had to keep her wits about her.

The search party of volunteer townsfolk had set off in groups of two and three to canvass the homes of Wabash, pounding on doors and, in many cases, waking up slumbering households to ask if anyone knew something about Olivia Beckman's whereabouts or had spotted any suspicious persons in the area. So far, every response had been negative, and, as the evening slipped away, Will felt his anxiety grow tenfold. The teams had been instructed to report back to the sheriff's office every two hours to give an account of their progress, and it was at one such gathering that Quinn Baxter approached him to say that he'd taken Alex and Nathan to the home of Howard and Margie Grant.

"Good. How were they?" Will asked.

"They were pretty quiet on the way out, but when they saw their aunt, they ran into her arms, bawlin' like two lost sheep. I felt bad for the little fellas."

Will's heart swelled just envisioning it. "What about Margie? How's she taking all this?"

"She's pretty upset but puttin' on a strong front for the boys."

He glanced across the room at Howard, who was engaged in conversation with the sheriff, his shoulders sagging wearily. "She and Howard raised Livvie after her parents perished in that house fire. They're bound to be worried sick. What about Coot? How'd he react to the news?"

"He's troubled, o' course, but full of faith and confidence that we'll find her, and that God will keep her safe in the interim." Quinn scratched the top of his head. "Strangest thing, though."

"What's that?"

"That hound of his. When I dropped the boys off at their aunt and uncle's, the mutt leaped out of the car and took off, sniffin' the ground, and then ran all around the yard and out behind the house. Next thing I know, he disappears into a cornfield. Coot didn't seem too ruffled over it. Said he's more concerned about Livvie's safety, and that ol' Reggie will find his way back home soon enough. Hope he's right. The pooch did have quite the bump on his head."

That dog had been acting plumb peculiar lately, sticking close to Livvie's side as if she were his master instead of Coot, and his jumping out of the car and racing into unfamiliar territory at the Grants' confirmed that something strange was up. Were Will's earlier conjectures true? Did Reggie have a sixth sense about something?

His thoughts were interrupted when someone tapped him on the shoulder. He turned and found himself face-to-face with Silas Brown, a good friend of Gus Anderson's who had become a lunchtime regular at Livvie's Kitchen. "Hi, Silas," he said.

"Hello, Mr. Taylor. I got somethin' to tell you."

"Yeah? What is it?"

"It's probably nothin', but, then again, it could be somethin'."

Will noticed that everyone was getting ready to resume the search, and he was impatient to join them. "I'm listening," he said, shifting his weight to the other foot.

"Well, it's just that I overheard Marva Dulane and Livvie talkin' today at the restaurant." He rubbed his jaw with a callous hand. "Marva mentioned somethin' 'bout havin' some ol' photograph o' Livvie 'n' Frank. Livvie seemed pretty excited, and Marva tol' her she'd drop it off. Now, that don't mean she planned to bring it by tonight or nothin', but I just thought it was a slim possibility Marva might know somethin' about Livvie, even though I never did trust that woman. Anyway, I got to thinkin' it couldn't hurt tellin' you what I heard."

Will laid a hand on the man's shoulder. "I'm much obliged, Silas."

The man nodded and walked off.

"You ready to go out again?" Gus asked. Howard stepped up alongside him, looking antsy. The three of them had made a good team so far and were probably more determined than any other group to find Livvie. In fact, in their determination, neither Gus nor Howard had brought up the matter of his prison stint, which was a relief. The last thing Will needed was to waste his energies on coming up with an explanation. Right now, he needed to focus entirely on finding Livvie. And what he'd just heard from Amos was occupying a large part of his mind right now.

"You two go on ahead, if you don't mind. I have a hunch about something, and I'm going to look into it."

"What sort of a hunch?" Howard asked.

"I doubt it'll even hold water. I'll tell you about it later when we meet up again." He didn't want to involve Gus and Howard in something that could get messy.

Ignoring their protests, he scanned the room for Quinn Baxter, breathing a sigh of relief when he spotted him. "Quinn!" he called. The man turned at his

name, and Will waved, then looked at Gus and Howard once more. "I'll talk to you later. I need to catch up
with Quinn."

With that, he left the men standing there, blank
expressions on their faces.

Chapter Twenty-six

"For where envying and strife is,
there is confusion and every evil work."
—James 3:16

Thi his is it," Quinn said, cutting the engine of his Model T. "As you can see, it isn't much more than a shack. Marva grew up in this little house and never left it. Even brought both her husbands here to live. Neither one of 'em ever provided for her, though, just moved in and mooched off of her. She never did learn the art of stickin' with one man."

Will studied the house, lit by the car's headlights, which Quinn had left illumined.

"Sad thing about Marva," he continued, "she never had a good family life. Her daddy beat her mama on a regular basis, brutal man."

"Why didn't she take Marva and get away from him?"

"She had nowhere to turn, from what I heard, and Marva's daddy had a lot o' control. He wanted her and everyone in town to know he was in charge. He had that 'Don't nobody mess with me' kind o' mentality. So, folks mostly left him alone, includin' his missus."

Will shook his head.

"I heard there was a man who once tried to step in and help, offered to move Marva and her mama to a safe place in another state."

"Really? Who was that?"

He shrugged and turned off the headlights, so that Marva's house was lit only by a single light in a front window. "Can't say as I ever knew the name. I was a youngster with a million things on my mind when I heard that, so, I s'pose it didn't interest me much. Marva was probably seven or eight at the time."

"She must be around Livvie's age, then."

"Yeah, they went to school together, but I can't say whether they were in the same grade. Don't think they were ever what you'd call friends, either. They ran in different circles. Marva had her eye on the boys from a real young age."

Will almost felt sorry for Marva. Shoot, if nobody who had suffered abuse or neglect as a child did a thing to reverse the downward spiral of bitterness and baggage passed down from his parents, the world would be a grand mess. His own childhood had been nothing to brag about, particularly after Joella's drowning accident, after which he'd felt forever despised by his parents. But, by the grace of God, he'd pulled himself out of that ditch of despair and now even thanked God for all he'd had to endure in order to find a place of deliverance and restoration.

"Thanks for bringing me out here," he said to Quinn. "Hope you don't mind waiting. I don't know how long I'll be."

"Sure. But you should take whatever information you can and get out of there. I wouldn't be caught dead with Marva Dulane. She can ruin a man's reputation faster 'n you can spell a two-letter word. Matter of fact, why don't I go in there with you?"

"No, thanks. It would probably make her feel like we were ganging up on her. Don't think I won't motion at you if I need reinforcements, though." With a wink, he opened the door and stepped out into the suffocating humidity.

He knocked once on the door, watching through a slit in the front curtain for a sign of Marva. Seconds later, a light turned on inside, and he saw her approaching, dressed in a purple satin gown that thankfully covered her front. It looked like she had dolled herself up, as if she were expecting him—or someone, anyway. Once again, Potiphar's wife came to mind, and, in the seconds before she opened the door, Will said a silent prayer for wisdom, guidance, and strength to resist the urge to strangle her.

"Will," she cooed, taking him by the arm and pulling him inside. "I thought you might come." Before closing the door, she peered out at the driveway. "Who's in the car?"

"Quinn Baxter."

She wrinkled her nose. "Why don't you tell him to leave? I'll drive you home later."

"I'm not staying. And why did you think I might come?"

"What? Oh." She flicked her skinny wrist. "Let's just say, after all my flirtatious innuendos, I hoped you would." She touched his arm and batted her eyelashes up at him. "I knew it was only a matter of time before you realized you couldn't resist me. I can be quite convincing, don't you think?"

He looked down his nose at her. "Olivia Beckman is missing. You know anything about that?"

An unidentifiable expression flashed across her face before a frown settled there. "Missing? Oh, dear. Isn't that a shame!"

He clutched her arms above the elbows and squeezed. "Where is she?"

"How should I know?"

He tightened his grasp.

"Ouch! You're hurting me, Will. And what does it matter to you, anyway?"

"It matters plenty to me, Marva, and it should matter to you, as well. But, since you don't seem to have a heart, I'm not surprised."

If his words had rattled her, she didn't let on but merely returned a sick sort of smile.

He pursed his lips and narrowed his eyes. "Listen to me, Marva. Earlier today, somebody overheard you telling Livvie you had some sort of photo to give her." She jerked her blonde head back and stared up at him. "You told her it was a picture of her and Frank."

"Who—who told you that?"

"Doesn't matter. Fact is, you talked loud enough for someone else's ears." On a hunch, perhaps divine, and while he still had her somewhat confused, he went a step further. "You didn't bother to stay out of sight when you came back to the restaurant tonight, either." A hint of apprehension washed over her face. He was getting somewhere. "That means you were among the last people to see her before her disappearance. If anything happens to her, you'll be counted as a suspect. How do you like that?"

He felt her stiffen. "That's ridiculous. I don't know anything about any...disappearance. All I did was give her the picture."

"That right?" He decided to take his hypothesis further. "Why'd you have to lure her outside to give it to her?"

"I didn't want to cause a disturbance."

Bingo! He brought his face close to hers. "Marva, I know that you and Clem Dodd are in this together, and you need to understand that when he goes down, you're going with him."

She sniffed and tried to wrench out of his grip, but he wasn't letting go. "Who?"

He pulled her closer, pinching till she rose up on her toes. "Don't play dumb, Marva. If you met Hank Swain and Rudy Haskins, you also met Clem Dodd. They hung together like three peas in a pod—until Rudy and Hank went back to New York. It's a known fact Clem is still in town."

"All right, all right. So I've met him. He picks up his weekly supply of whiskey from Dotson. Big deal. It doesn't prove anything about Olivia."

He released her arms, and she began rubbing them as she looked at him with pouty eyes. "You're not mad at me, are you?"

He gave his head a couple of confused shakes. Was she insane? She didn't get it, not any of it. He stepped around her and walked across the room to the fireplace, above which the mantel displayed several framed photographs. It was time for a completely different approach. He picked up one of the pictures and studied it. "This you with your parents?"

"Yes. Put it back, please."

"How old were you? Six? Seven?"

She came up to him, took the picture out of his hands, and carefully set it back in its place. Since she hadn't answered his question, he leaned in to study the other pictures. All of them showed her at various ages with her father. "Where's your mother in the rest of these?"

"Mother usually declined to have her picture taken."

"Why is that?"

She frowned. "There were reasons."

"All the bruises on her face, perhaps? I heard your father beat her."

"Who told you such a thing?"

"Does it matter?"

"I suppose not." She stared at the pictures. "Mother deserved it, you know. She was naughty. Daddy even told me." Her voice had turned childlike, as if she'd retreated to some faraway place from her youth.

"Why do you say that?" he nearly whispered.

"Mother was unfaithful to Daddy with…with that man." *Like mother, like daughter*, he wanted to say. "Daddy said she was naughty for doing that. Very naughty. And, let me tell you, she and everybody else got exactly what they deserved."

Will didn't like the abrupt turn things had taken, but a new sense of urgency made him press forward. First, though, he shot another prayer heavenward. *Lord, if there's something here that will lead me to Livvie, may it be revealed.* "What do you mean, 'Everybody else got exactly what they deserved'?"

She picked up one of the photos and caressed it as one might pet a kitten. "Daddy always told me they were evil."

"Who was evil?"

On the mantel, a windup clock ticked about as loudly as a bomb about to detonate. Overhead, some kind of creature scampered across the roof. And the room was so warm that he had to wipe the dampness from his brow. He hoped these distractions would not deter her from talking.

"The Newtons, of course."

"The Newtons." A cord of confusion and dread wove itself around his chest, squeezing. He didn't want to know, and yet he did. "Who are the Newtons?"

"Olivia's parents. Who else?" In spite of the hot, dank air, shivery prickles surfaced on his skin. "Daddy had no choice, when it came right down to it."

By now, he realized that Marva had started to slip down some kind of mental precipice, a narrow, precarious, cerebral cliff she'd been navigating for some time—years, probably—trying to keep her balance as sanity and utter lunacy pulled her in both directions. And he'd helped bring her to the edge. For a moment, he wondered if he ought to move to the window and motion Quinn inside.

He decided to play along, knowing that bringing Quinn on the scene would break whatever spell she'd come under. "What was it again that he had no choice but to do?"

"Why, burn the house. It was the only way to rid it of the evil. The plan was not for Olivia to escape, of course. But, since she did, Daddy said just to let it go."

"That...seems reasonable," he pushed out while fighting down an awful wave of nausea.

She stared off into space but kept stroking the photograph. "Clem's coming along when he did worked out quite well, I think."

"How do you mean?" Without realizing it, she'd just admitted to her participation in some insidious plot against Livvie. He licked his lips and swallowed, fearful that the bile at the back of his throat might come up. *Lord God, she's insane. Give me the words to say, and show me what to do, to bring this to a head. And please, Lord, keep Livvie safe, wherever she may be.*

Marva scowled. "Things have always gone well for that girl. Even though she lost her parents, her house, and all her possessions, she just moved right in with her sister, like nothing ever happened. She got all the attention in school and always got good grades. Everybody always said, 'Poor little Livvie.' It got downright annoying. Nobody ever looked at me and said, 'Poor Marva.' Why, Mr. Emerson, my sixth-grade teacher, slapped me right across the face one time when I told him that my mother had an affair with Mr. Newton. He said I oughtn't make up awful lies like that. That made me so mad, you know?" She shook her head and looked at him with a pathetic expression.

He nodded, feigning empathy. "What happened to your mother...after the fire?"

Again, Marva's eyes took on that wild look. "Daddy locked her up back there." She pointed to a closed door across the room. "That's where she had to stay because she was so naughty. Daddy said."

"How did she—how did your parents die?"

She shrugged and turned her mouth into a quick frown. "Mother had an apoplexy about a year after the fire—at least, that's what the doctors said, but I'm not so sure. I think Daddy might have helped her along." Her matter-of-fact manner of stating this made him want to shake her. "I found an open container of rat poison in the lean-to out back two days after she died. When I asked Daddy about it, he just said he'd seen a big varmint by our garbage pile." She paused, as if still pondering the matter. "As for Daddy, a bad case of pneumonia took him about twelve years ago. Do you know, only five people showed up at his funeral? Five people! Orville Dotson, the preacher from the Episcopal church, and some other fellas I didn't even know. Isn't that appalling?"

"Appalling" aptly described all the sickening information she'd just unloaded. If she'd had alcohol on her breath, he would have sworn she was drunk, but she didn't. Plain loony was more like it.

"Let's get some fresh air, shall we?" he suggested.

She brightened like a high-wattage bulb. "Sure. You want something to drink? It is awfully hot."

"No, I was thinking more in terms of taking you for a ride with Quinn and me."

"Really?" She smiled and looked down at her gown. "I have to go put on a dress."

"Sure, go ahead."

She laid a hand on his arm, and it was all he could do to keep from brushing it away. "I just knew I'd win you over eventually, Will," she cooed. "I have this uncanny ability to attract men." She cut loose a high-pitched giggle that bordered on madness. "I told Livvie she would never have you, that I had my eye on you from the first night I saw you. Do you remember that night, Will?"

His gut twisted into a tight, painful knot. "Yes, yes, I remember it well. When and where did you tell Livvie all this?" It took every ounce of effort to make his voice sound calm and friendly.

"Tonight, out in the alley behind her restaurant, silly, before Clem hauled her off. Of course, that black mongrel wasn't the least bit happy about any of it, so I had to bash him over the head with a big rock."

"Where did Clem take her, anyway?"

She shrugged. "How should I know? He didn't tell me, and I didn't ask." Oddly, he believed her. "Anyway, you'll wait here while I go change?" Her voice still had that schoolgirl sound. Truly, she'd slipped into a world of make-believe, and all within a matter of minutes.

"Yep, I'll wait right here."

She opened a door off of the hallway and slipped inside. He could hear her humming a familiar tune, and he imagined her smiling at herself in the mirror as she touched up her makeup. "Where are you taking me?" she called out in singsong.

"Oh, Quinn and I will come up with something."

"Maybe we could go dancing. You still owe me a dance, you know."

"Uh-huh."

"Or, we could go for an ice cream cone. Daydream Chocolates opened a sundae bar. Did you know that?" She hummed some more. "Shall I wear my red heels or my white flats? Well, I suppose it depends on which dress I choose."

"I don't think it matters."

"Of course it does. Oh, won't this be fun?"

He looked down at the floor and shook his head. Her getting locked up in prison—more likely, an asylum—hadn't even occurred to her.

Chapter Twenty-seven

*"Because thou hast made the L*ORD,
*which is my refuge, even the most High,
thy habitation; there shall no evil
befall thee, neither shall any plague
come nigh thy dwelling."*
—Psalm 91:9–10

When Livvie awakened the next morning, tiny shafts of sunlight filtering through the window and the intermittent chirping of birds outside gave her reason to estimate the time to be around six. She wore a watch but couldn't read the dial because of all the rope binding her wrists together. After closing her eyes tightly several times to squeeze the sleep from them, she assessed the dimly lit room, where a lone kerosene lamp still glowed in a corner. Overall, her abductor had been mostly civil—he'd even permitted her to eat a few crackers and take several sips of water a few hours ago—but she knew one false move on her part could easily make him turn on her.

Late last night, Clem had tied her to the mattress by wrapping her wrists and ankles several times, looping the rest of the rope under the mattress, and then bringing the ends together, secured in a double knot over her chest. Escaping would have been an impossible feat, unless she'd been able to figure out a way to pick up her bed and walk! Thankfully, he'd stretched out on a blanket on the floor several feet away, where he still slept, an empty bottle lying next to him. From the sound of his loud snoring, he would not wake up anytime soon.

In the stillness, she stared at the ceiling, trying not to think about how uncomfortable she was, and prayed—prayed for her precious boys, for Margie and Howard, and for Will. *Will.* Was he looking for her even now? Somehow, she knew he had to be, along with a host of others.

The sound of a dog barking lent her comfort, for it meant that someone lived nearby. If she could just get a glimpse of the surroundings, she might be able to determine her location, even if she couldn't do a thing about it.

"Behold, the eye of the LORD *is upon them that fear him, upon them that hope in his mercy."* She recalled the psalm she'd memorized several weeks ago and thanked the Lord for bringing it to her mind again. She might not know where she was, but the Lord surely did, and He had His eye firmly fixed on her. Now, if He would just reveal her location to others!

Clem rolled over with a whiffling noise and mumbled something unintelligible. She turned her head to look at him, holding her breath for fear he'd awaken. She wanted him to sleep forever, and yet her need to use the privy almost overruled that wish. Still, a sigh of relief escaped her lungs when he settled back into a deep, silent slumber. In the meantime, she would work to loosen her wrists, which were now bloodied from the rope's abrasive rubbing.

Minutes melded into hours as daylight emerged fully, but dark clouds held the sun at bay and blanketed the room in a gloomy shade of gray-green, now that the kerosene lamp had run out of fuel. Distant rumbles of thunder spoke of impending rain, dampening Livvie's spirits the more.

On the floor, Clem had begun to shiver but did not wake up. Livvie's stomach clenched with hunger, and her parched throat longed for water, but her full bladder forbade her to dwell upon her thirst for too long. She continued to send unceasing prayers to the Lord— prayers of praise that she'd made it through the night relatively unscathed by this insane brute of a man who held her captive, prayers proclaiming her surrender to God's will for her life, prayers of confession, pleading forgiveness for the year she'd harbored bitterness and anger toward her heavenly Father, and prayers for protection over her sons and guidance for those in search of her. Interspersed with her prayers, she recited every verse of Scripture that came to mind, many of them incomplete scraps of passages she'd once known in full, thanks to her childhood Sunday school teachers.

Just when she thought Clem would sleep the day away, he stirred, opened his eyes, sat up with a start, and stared at her. Her first thought was that he looked like a wild man, with his faded brown hair sticking up in greasy clumps, his unshaven face smudged, and his colorless eyes cold and stony. Even in the dim room, she spotted a glossy sheen on his forehead—odd, since yesterday's heat had escaped out the open windows, replaced by a nippy dampness. She was thankful for the wool blanket covering her.

"Now that you're awake, I would like to use the outdoor facility," she stated.

"Is that any way to say good mornin' to your lover?" His voice held no hint of sarcasm. He rolled up his sleeve to look at the wound left by Reggie, and, though he tried to hide it, she saw him wince with pain. He'd obviously made no effort to clean the area, and she wouldn't be surprised if a raging infection had taken hold.

"Are you going to untie me? It sounds as if a storm is moving in, and I'd like to go outside before the rain comes."

"Shut up, would you?"

She clamped her lips together and heaved a loud sigh through her nostrils. As much as she still wanted to spit in Clem's face, she told herself to toe a very careful, straight line, maybe even pretend to care for him. Otherwise, she'd blow her chances, however remote, of escaping his evil clutches.

❧

That dimwit of a dog had done a real number on his arm. Not only was the bite mark red and swollen, but it felt hot to the touch and had white pus oozing from it. To top matters off, Clem's entire arm throbbed, making him feel queasy and jittery. When he stood up, a wave of dizziness took him by surprise, so he grabbed hold of a chair to regain his footing.

"Did you ever clean and bandage that dog bite?"

Livvie's voice brought him out of his fog. He wiped his sweaty brow and turned to look at her. "It ain't nothin'." No way would he let on how weak he felt or how much his arm ached. What a lousy fix. He'd brought her here to make her his bride, and now he didn't have the energy of a two-toed sloth. The predicament put a genuine damper on his mood.

"I could probably clean it for you. You'd need to go out and get some fresh water. Do you have any soap?"

He didn't know what to make of her. He'd thought she'd need more time to warm up to him. Could it be that she'd already come to appreciate her new home? He angled her a suspicious glare. "I might."

"And a bucket?"

"Maybe."

"Well, unbind me and take me out to the privy, and then, on the way back, we'll get a bucket of water, you'll dig out the soap and find some cloth, and I'll cleanse the wound."

He cut loose a dry chortle. "I ain't so dumb that I can't figure out what you're doin'. You just want those ropes off so you can run away."

"I won't run off, I promise."

"Am I s'posed to believe you?"

She lay there, looking up at him with pleading eyes. "I might be able to rustle you up some breakfast, too"—she lifted her tied hands as far as the rope would allow—"but not in this useless state. Putting some food in your stomach would probably make you feel better."

She had a point. He walked over, bent down, and proceeded to work on loosening the main knot, which kept her tied to the mattress. Before he went too far with it, though, he removed the pistol from his pocket, cocked it, and touched the muzzle to her forehead. She went as frozen as a departed duck on ice. "I'll untie the ropes for now, but, be assured, I'll use this if you try anythin' funny." Unblinking, she nodded several times and gave a hard swallow. He continued loosening the knot. "Just so we understand each other."

❧

A streak of lightning flashed in the eastern sky as they set off down the narrow path to the outhouse, Clem directly behind her, empty bucket in one hand, gun in the other. My, but it felt good to stretch her legs and move her arms. She imagined setting off across the wide expanse of fields before her, but that stupid weapon poking in her spine was a definite deterrent.

"We could certainly use some rain," she said, forcing brightness into her tone. A clap of thunder followed the lightning, which made her nerves jump, but she wouldn't let him know it. "It's been an unusually hot, dry summer, don't you think?"

Heavy, wheezy breaths were all she got in return, as if he were not accustomed to walking and talking concurrently. His overweight condition probably didn't help.

"Maybe the rain will dispel the humidity," she added. "That would be a welcome relief." While she made small talk, she took in her surroundings, making sure to move her eyes only and keep her head facing straight ahead. But they might as well have been in Australia for the unfamiliarity. Nothing about this place rang a bell.

Another streak of silver flashed across the sky, and thunder rumbled overhead, closer this time. "It's going to rain, for sure. Maybe any minute now."

"Would you shut your yapper? I ain't in the mood for conversin'."

"Well, you don't have to be such a grump about it."

At the end of the path, Clem opened the outhouse door and shoved her inside. "Make it snappy, 'fore that sky opens up."

She did her best to be quick, but she didn't think forty-five seconds had passed when he shouted, "What's takin' so long?"

"I'm coming, I'm coming," she assured him, smoothing down her tattered dress and looking around, wishing she could find a board or something else with which to clobber the no-good bum on his sorry noggin. Yet the outhouse offered no help. She opened the door and looked up at him. "Aren't you going to use the facility?"

He produced a hard, cold grin. "Don't need to. I used it whilst you were sleepin'."

"Oh."

He took her by the arm and forced her to turn. "Walk," he ordered, poking the gun into the center of her spine. "Pump's over there."

The inconsiderate oaf made her operate the pump while he held the gun to her temple, and it took every ounce of strength she could muster to get the water up the pipe. When it finally came, she couldn't help it; she bent down and drank from the clear stream.

"Fill the bucket, not your bladder," he groused.

On the trek back to the ramshackle building, something stirred in the tall grasses several yards away and startled her. She gasped with a jolt, causing some of the water to splash out of the pail.

"What'd you do that for?" he asked, pressing the pistol harder against her back.

"I thought—nothing, it was nothing." But it *was* something; she knew it, and the deep, low growl that came next confirmed her suspicions.

"Did you hear that?" he asked.

"I...."

"Open that door," he ordered, prodding her forward.

She complied, and he pushed her inside the shack, then slammed the door with a loud thud. Chancing a hurried peek out the window, she saw something black bounding through the fields, out of sight.

"What'd you see?" he demanded, pushing his way beside her to look outside.

"Nothing."

But she had seen something. A bear? A wolf, perhaps? Or...Reggie?

Chapter Twenty-eight

*"For he shall give his angels charge over
thee, to keep thee in all thy ways."*
—Psalm 91:11

As news of Livvie's disappearance spread, the town's determination to find her mounted. Folks showed up at the sheriff's station in droves, asking what they could do to help. Cora Mae kept the "Closed" sign facing out and posted a new one next to it that read: "Owner Missing. Please Join in the Search to Bring Livvie HOME." When Sheriff Morris told those who'd been up all night to go home for some much-needed rest, most of them refused, saying they wouldn't be able to sleep, anyway.

While men made up the majority of the search party, several women and older teens also showed up in the early hours to see what they could do. Some joined in the search, while others set up tables outside the sheriff's office to provide food, water, and plenty of coffee to the teams. Because kidnapping was a federal offense, two officers from the Bureau of Investigation arrived on the afternoon train to take over the investigation, but an argument arose between them and Sheriff Morris concerning jurisdiction. In the end, Judge Morehead of Wabash County ruled in favor of the BOI and ordered the sheriff to submit to them.

Once they captured Clem Dodd, the villain would face the Indiana court system first for his robberies, as well as federal district court, then return to New York for another trial and sentencing.

It didn't take long for most people to find out that Marva Dulane had landed herself in the county jail, though most of them couldn't imagine what part she had played in Livvie's disappearance. As far as Will knew, only a handful of people had a clue that Clem Dodd even existed. One of them was Orville Dotson, and, when Sheriff Morris questioned him in Will's presence, Will figured now was not the time to bring up the man's illegal operation. He'd leave that for later. Right now, finding Livvie was infinitely more important. However, Dotson claimed to have no idea where Clem Dodd might have taken her, swearing that all he'd done had been to sell the fellow his weekly supply of whiskey. With a tremble in his voice, he insisted that he'd never befriended the bum, and that he certainly would have reported him, had he known about his plan to abduct the lovely Olivia Beckman.

They left Dotson's place mostly believing him.

As for Marva, the sheriff questioned her from every angle but got nowhere. Yes, Clem had taken Livvie away, she conceded, and for good reason: he was in love with her, and what was the problem in that? No, she didn't know where he'd taken her, and, even if she did, she wouldn't tell, for honeymoons and such were private matters. "Are we done yet?" she asked after every question. "Will and Quinn are taking me dancing, and then we're going for ice cream. Buford, you can come, too, if you'd like. Is that all right with you, Will?"

Sheriff Morris and Will could only raise their eyebrows at each other. Clearly, Marva Dulane had slipped even further off her rocker.

As of eleven that morning, not one lead had come in, but Will refused to be discouraged. Search parties combed the riverbanks and outlying areas, walked for miles up and down the railroad tracks, set off in various directions through wooded patches and ravines, and knocked on the door of every house and business within the city limits.

Around eleven thirty, at the sheriff's request, Gus left with Quinn Baxter and Sam Campbell, destination North Manchester, where they were to poke around for clues. Will was getting ready to ride with Howard out to the farm to check on Margie and the boys before setting off again when Coot showed up, cane in hand. "What do you think you're doing?" Will asked him.

"I'm goin' to sit right here and pray for Livvie's safety, and I don't plan to move from this spot till she's found safe and sound," Coot announced.

"Is that so? Well, if I have my wish, you'll be out of here by early afternoon. Did Reggie come home last night?"

Coot gave a slow shake of his head. "He does this from time to time—gets hot on the trail of a rabbit or coon and refuses to give up till he's caught the thing. He can detect smells from miles away—that's the hound in 'im. Stubborn as an old mule he is, too. I'll say, 'Reggie, it's time for your vittles,' but, if he's busy sniffin' somethin' else out, ain't nothing goin' to sidetrack 'im, even food. Crazy dog."

"He got quite the head wound," Will reminded him.

"Pfff, he's been in a few spats with critters. Those don't slow 'im down none. Nope, I ain't seen the last of my dog."

By the time Will and Howard left, the sky had opened up like a colossal waterfall, making for a slow drive. Ditches and ravines overflowed their banks, and the road to the farm had turned to slimy mud, making navigation nearly impossible. At one point, the front wheel got stuck in a groove and almost made the vehicle veer into a ditch. They escaped narrowly, the old truck hissing and choking in protest. "Around here, roads flood mighty fast in a downpour like this," Howard said. He kept his eyes glued to the road and his hands holding tight to the big steering wheel, while the Folberths' wiper cranked back and forth at maximum frequency, which was hardly fast enough. Will leaned forward, as if his ability to see the road would be of some help to Howard, but he couldn't get so much as a glimpse of it, making him wonder if Howard had been driving from memory alone and not sight. He sucked in a giant whiff of air and didn't heave it back out until Howard braked to a stop at the end of the driveway.

"Good driving," he said when the motor shut off.

"Been at it for a while."

For the next minute or so, they sat in silence—well, save for the deafening rain that pelted the metal roof—each lost in his own thoughts. "I'm thinking we need to stay as positive as possible," Howard finally said.

"I am being positive," Will insisted. "I'm confident that God is watching over Livvie. We'll find her; I know we will."

"Yes, you're right. We will." Howard's voice shook.

"She's more than a sister-in-law to you, isn't she?"

He nodded and wiped his eyes. "She's like a daughter."

Will swallowed a rocklike lump. "What would you say if I told you I'm in love with her?"

Howard dropped his hands to his lap and turned his craggy, sunburned face to Will. Slowly, a tired grin lifted the corners of his mouth, and he arched an eyebrow. "Then, I'd say we both have mighty fine reasons for finding our girl."

A wave of relief raced through him, then receded just as quickly. "My time in prison—"

Howard lifted his hand. "Say no more. It's in the past, you've served your time and learned from it, and you're a fine Christian man. That's good enough for me. As for Margie, well...." He took a deep breath. "You might have to work on her a bit." With a wink, he turned and peered out his window up at the dark sky. "You ready to make a run for it?"

"Whatever you say, sir."

No sooner had they rushed inside and started stomping their sopping boots on the braided rug than Margie, Alex, and Nate rushed into the hallway. "Did you find her?" Margie asked, wringing her apron, lines of worry etched into her already wrinkled brow.

Howard stepped forward and placed a quick kiss on his wife's cheek. "Not yet, but we will."

The boys hugged their uncle but quickly ran to Will's waiting arms. "Where's Mommy, Will?" Nate said into his shoulder, letting out a little sob.

"We haven't found her yet, son. But we will."

"I ain't gonna cry." Alex's chin quivered, even as he said the words.

Will pulled them close, unable to say anything more for the aching lump in his chest.

Margie cleared her throat. "Boys, how about you go upstairs and play with your toys? I'll be there soon."

They each gave Will another hug, then trudged off, shoulders sagging. He watched them climb the stairs listlessly until they were out of sight.

"Hasn't anybody heard anything?" Margie blurted out. "Our telephone's been ringing all morning. Myra

Marshall at the switchboard claims she can't keep up. Folks want to know what I've learned and how they can help. If either of you are hungry, there's a spread of dishes on the kitchen counter from various neighbors and such. I, for one, can't stomach a single bite, but I've been force-feeding those boys. You two need your strength, as well. Best go eat something."

Will could tell her nerves had reached a high point by her fast, quivery manner of speaking.

The telephone rang, and she sighed. "I cannot talk to another person."

"I'll get it," Howard said. He walked across the room and picked up the black receiver from its cradle.

While he spoke to the caller, Margie turned to Will. "You must be exhausted. Have you eaten or slept?"

"I had a few bites at the station, Mrs. Grant. As for sleep, I haven't given it a thought. All I want to do is find Livvie."

Margie dabbed at her damp eyes with her apron. "First of all, you must call me Margie. And, second, I'm glad to see you're so determined. I truly appreciate the way the town is pulling together to find my sister." A dog barked at the back door, and she frowned. "Oh, it's that dog that jumped out of Mr. Baxter's car yesterday."

"Reggie?"

"Is that his name? He's been throwing a grand fit, running back and forth out there, and barking to beat the thunder. I set out some scraps of food and a bowl of water, even invited him in out of the storm, but he'd have no part in it. The boys know him, of course, and tried to coax him inside, but he wouldn't listen. He just stands out there and barks. I don't know why he won't go home."

Will looked through the kitchen and out the back door, where Reggie still barked. An eerie sense came over him.

"That was Sheriff Morris," Howard said, hanging up the phone. "Seems he has a couple of new leads."

"What sort of leads?" Margie asked.

"Well, I guess Rich Stinehart, the fellow who operates the livery on the west side of town, said he leased a horse and buggy for the past few days to a rather mysterious fellow with a deep scar on his left cheek. Apparently, the fellow returned the rig after dark last night, claiming not to need it anymore. Said he planned to hitch a ride to his destination."

"Clem Dodd," Will muttered, his chest constricting into a tight ball of tension. "Wonder if anyone gave him a ride."

"Someone did," Howard confirmed. "A fellow by the name of Dick Baker strolled into Morris's office a little while ago and said that he picked up a hitchhiker around ten o'clock last night. That would have been about the same time that rig got dropped off at Stinehart's place. Baker described him as big and scruffy-looking, said the fellow snapped at him when he tried to make conversation. And, when he stopped to let him out, he noticed a nasty-looking scar on his cheek."

"Did he say where he dropped him?" Will asked, his adrenaline pumping as if he'd just come across a poisonous snake.

"Yep. Corner of Farr Pike Road and Dixon."

"But, that's our corner!" Margie exclaimed, eyes popping, hands fidgeting.

"It sure is, honey. Half mile away, but it is our property. When Baker asked if he couldn't take the guy further, he said he preferred to walk, got out of the car, and started heading north on Dixon."

"Which would be behind our farm," Margie said. "The nearest house up Dixon is at least five miles. Surely, he didn't mean to walk that far."

"Are there any vacant buildings off of Dixon?" Will asked. "Maybe an abandoned barn or shack?"

"Well, the nearest one would be the old St. John the Baptist Church. It's been vacant for about eighty years, I think. It's on my property, but I've left it untouched all this time, just because, well, it's not hurting anything, and it's not on fertile soil. I haven't been back there in years. I mean, it's hardly visible from the road, unless you have a telescope or something."

Reggie gave several persistent barks in a row.

"There's that dog again," Margie groused.

"Let's go check on him," said Will. "I have a hunch about something."

"Another hunch, eh?" Howard said.

The rain had not let up; if anything, it came down faster now, in blinding torrents. Will pushed open the screen door and looked down at the drenched dog. "What's the matter, Reg?"

The dog gave another impatient howl, moved back, and danced a complete circle, then ran about ten feet away from the house, before coming back and repeating the routine.

"Well, I'll be," said Will. "He wants us to follow him."

"Sure seems that way," Howard said. He took off his hat and scratched the top of his head. "But it'll be hard finding a path to that church. And any footprints or wheel marks will be long gone. The grass is high and awful thick."

"It could be that Reggie's carved us a good path, with all his running back and forth. My guess is, he's scoped out the area. He's a pretty smart dog."

Margie joined them, and they stood there, watching Reggie's fretful movements. "I have some firearms in my cabinet," Howard said in a sober voice. "Maybe we should both take one."

Will took a deep breath. "I agree. I know Clem Dodd, and he'll have a gun on him, for sure." *Lord, grant us safety. Let us find Livvie unharmed.*

Howard put his hat back on and hastened out of the room.

"I think you should call the sheriff, ma'am—er, Margie. Tell him we're heading out to that old church on a hunch. You might also want to warn him that the road conditions are terrible. Howard had a hard time in his truck."

Margie kept wringing her apron. "Yes, our road tends to flood in weather like this. I'll be sure to let him know." She paused and bit her lip. "Do you think Livvie could be out there with that awful man, Will?"

Will didn't even want to think about it, but he needed to be realistic. "There's a strong possibility, but don't worry. God is on our side."

"You're right about that. We should pray before you leave."

Will nodded.

Howard came back, carrying a rifle in each hand. He inserted a cartridge in both weapons and handed one to Will. Then, the men set down the rifles, and the three of them joined hands and prayed, asking God for His direction and protection.

Reggie had no interest in the prayer, though, and he barked impatiently.

Howard kissed his wife on the cheek. "You should call the sheriff," he said.

"I will. We talked about that while you were getting the guns. You two be careful, and God be with you."

When they stepped out into the rain, it was like walking into the path of a fire hose. A flash of lightning streaked the sky, followed by a deafening clap of thunder.

"Lead the way, Reggie," Will called out.

The dog took off, and it was all they could do to keep him in their sights.

❋

While Livvie prepared a meager meal of cold beans, buttered bread, and canned pears, Clem sat in a dilapidated chair beside the table and kept his pistol trained on her. At least he'd agreed to leave her unshackled for the past two hours. She'd managed a hasty glance out the front window earlier. A lot of good it had done her, though, with so many trees and tall bushes surrounding the little building. Plus, the unrelenting rain had decreased visibility to almost nil.

Clem's husky breathing and his chattering teeth told her that he'd caught a raging fever from Reggie's bite, and no wonder. The infection was so serious that a red line had started traveling up his arm and was now about six inches long. "You should have a doctor tend that wound," she told him for at least the dozenth time. "I think you might have blood poisoning."

"Would you shut up 'bout my arm? I'm fine, and I don't want you sayin' another word about it, you understand? Sheesh! You're as bad as my last wife. Nag, nag, nag! I'm about to shut you up for good." Earsplitting thunder accentuated his threat.

Fear and anger coursed through her, but it seemed that her chatty charade was her best bet of escaping. "I don't see how we'll ever get acquainted if you don't allow me to talk."

"Lady, if you wanna get acquainted, there're plenty o' ways to go about it without talkin'." He gave a low, rattly chortle, but she didn't miss the weakness in his voice. If only she could get ahold of his gun somehow.

"Are you divorced, then?" she asked, ignoring his crude innuendo as she buttered the last slice of bread. From out of a box on the table, she lifted two plates and a couple of spoons. It occurred to her that she could wallop him on the head with one of the dishes, but she knew that even a cast-iron skillet was no match for a gun.

"Nope. Flo died, week or so back. Hear tell she walked in front of a train."

Livvie jerked her head up and stared at him, stunned by his cold indifference. "That's terrible."

"Not for me, it ain't," he said. "I was gonna divorce the witch, anyway. Timin' was perfect, don't you think?"

She tried to tamp down her shudder as she arranged the food on the plates. When she set one down directly under his nose, he waved the gun at her. "Pull up that chair and sit down."

She complied, and they ate their simple meal in silence.

Later, as she knelt on the floor and washed the dishes in a bucket of water, the gun trained on her back while she worked, Livvie prayed for God to intervene. Somehow, she had to get out of this mess. *Please, Lord, make that fool fall asleep so that I can yank that gun out of his grasp.*

❧

Clem monitored Livvie's every move, all of them graceful, as she washed the dishes and then dried them. She would make a perfect wife for him, and he could tell she'd already started warming up to him, the way she wanted to talk. True, she was too much of a chatterbox for his taste, but he could easily curb that in time. All it would take was a firm hand. His head had started throbbing, but he couldn't very well nod off till he got her rigged to the mattress with ropes again.

"You just 'bout done cleanin' them dishes? I'm gonna have to tie you up so's I can get some shut-eye."

She hung the towel over the back of the other chair and looked at him. "I thought I'd straighten up the place, maybe sweep the floor. Go to sleep, if you want."

"Ha! What do you take me for, a brainless idiot? I know what you're thinkin'. I close my eyes for a minute, and you're out that door."

She glanced at the window and frowned. "In this rain? I wouldn't venture out there if you paid me. Besides, I wouldn't even know which way to go. I have no idea where I am."

He examined her perfect face, admired each soft, lovely angle, and dreamed about the day when he'd feel well enough to claim her fully. "Makes no matter. I don't trust you as far as that door right there." With one hand, he rubbed his hot, sticky face, taking care to keep the gun pointed at her—not easy, he found, with his wrist wavering from fatigue. A buzzing sound filled his head. "Don't you know better than t' argue with me? Now, go sit down."

She hesitated, her eyes on his pistol, then slowly walked toward the chair.

"That's better," he said, standing and fighting off a wave of wooziness. "Sit down, nice 'n' easy." Keeping his eyes trained on her, he went to retrieve the coiled rope, snatched it up, and strode back to her. She lowered herself into the chair, but he didn't miss the defiance in her hazel eyes. "You're a stubborn one, ain't you? Gimme your hands."

She didn't budge but kept her hands clasped in her lap. He might have laughed if his head didn't feel like it was clamped in a vise and his arm wasn't burning like an inferno. "Gimme your hands, you li'l she-lion! I'm losin' my patience."

With a scowl that detracted from her pretty looks, she huffed a loud breath and raised her hands. Satisfied, he dropped the rope and grasped her hands, then lowered the gun to the floor. Next, he picked up the rope and began to wrap it around her wrists. It took every ounce of his concentration not to keel over from pain and feverish heat.

She cocked her head at him. "You know," she said softly, "this is not at all the way you ought to treat your wife-to-be." Her gentle cooing caught him off guard, and he paused in his task to look at her. Big mistake. In less time than it took to blink, she kicked him hard, knocking him to the ground, then threw off the rope and leaped to her feet. As she ran past him, he managed to snag her by the ankle, but she whirled around and booted him in the face with her other foot. Blood spattered before his eyes, and he nearly gave up the chase, but sheer rage gave him a second wave of strength. An angry growl rolled out of him as he got to his feet and snatched a fistful of her hair. Screaming and flailing, she clawed at his mouth and eyes, jabbing at his tender scar with her fingernails. He slapped her across the jaw, but she fought back with her feet again, kicking him everywhere she could as she thrashed about, so that he couldn't get a firm grip on her.

I'll kill her for this! he raged within. *I'll kill her, if I can just get my hands on my gun.*

Chapter Twenty-nine

"And be ye kind one to another,
tenderhearted, forgiving one another,
even as God for Christ's sake
hath forgiven you."
—Ephesians 4:32

When a soul-shattering scream rent the air, Will and Howard looked at each other, then quickened their pace as they followed a barking Reggie through the tall grass and thick weeds. The relentless rain soaked them to the bone as bands of lightning streaked across the sky, accompanied by earth-moving thunderclaps. Ripples of terror shot through Will as he bounded over stray rocks and fallen logs, Howard on his heels.

When the little building came into view, Howard snagged Will by the sleeve to draw him to a halt, then hauled him behind a big tree. "We've got to be smart, Will," he said, in between uneven breaths. "Busting through that door could very well send Livvie to her death. I know it's hard, but we have to approach this with caution and assess the situation. Before going through that door, you have to know what you're up against and where even to set your eyes."

Will considered Howard's words, recognizing their wisdom. "All right. You cover me. I'll sneak between

those trees, there, and see if I can get closer. Hope-
fully, I'll get a clear view through the front window."

Howard nodded solemnly. "Take it slow and easy.
I know how much you want to charge inside, but don't
do anything rash. I love that girl, too, you know."

Sucking in a huge gulp of air, Will skimmed wet
fingers down his face. "Pray for me," he said. Then, he
shot off through the rain, rifle secured in his hand.
Reggie slunk along beside him, ready, Will knew, to
pounce at the first sign of trouble. As he approached
the building, he detected noises inside—a scuffle, from
the sound of it. With his heart pounding out of control,
he ducked behind the tree closest to the structure, uttered another fervent plea to the Father for assistance,
sent Howard one last, fleeting glance, and then made
a run at the old church.

With Reggie close behind him, making a low,
snarling sound, Will crouched down and hugged the
building as he inched his way to the window. He stood
up slowly, just enough to peek through the glass pane.
Despite the filth caked on the window, he could see
Livvie and Clem, embroiled in a battle of fists and feet.
Without so much as a glance in Howard's direction,
Will shot up and raced for the door, rammed it full
force, and burst inside, Reggie by his side. Tossing his
rifle to the floor, he hauled Clem up by the arm, and
his first thought was that the man looked more slov-
enly and disgusting than ever before. Clem froze with
a dumbfounded stare, giving Will a chance to throw a
good, solid punch to his jaw. The force knocked him
onto the floor with a thud, missing Livvie by mere
inches. Gape-mouthed, she sat up and scuttled back-
wards. Reggie sprang into combat mode, lunging at
Clem's chest and pinning him down. The man cried
like a baby.

Then, Howard bolted through the door, rifle aimed, eyes wild with worry. "Livvie?" When he saw her, he lowered his rifle and breathed a shaky sigh of relief.

Will ran to her, crouched at her side, and gathered her close, kissing the top of her head, her cheeks, her chin, her wet eyelids, and then her lips, before finally setting her back from him to give her a thorough assessment. "Are you all right, sweetheart?"

With quivering chin, she gave a slow nod, staring at him as if to drink up his features with her eyes. He held out his arms, and she fell against his chest, erupting in sobs as she clung to his shirtfront. "W-what took you s-so long?"

❧

Livvie's Kitchen remained closed indefinitely while everyone recuperated from the recent events, and Livvie and her boys stayed at the farm with Margie and Howard. Will stayed sequestered in his apartment, far from eager to face the public, and sorted out what had happened, trying to figure out what it meant for his future.

News of his criminal record spread like wildfire, thanks in large part to the *Daily Plain Dealer*, which ran a front-page story about Livvie's rescue with the headline "Ex-Convict William Taylor Rescues Local Restaurateur from Certain Death." The article spared no details when it came to his identity. And, while he'd long known that the news was bound to come out eventually, he wished he could have had a chance to tell his side of the story, not that it would have changed anything. In truth, the reporter had his facts straight.

At Judge Morehead's orders, Marva Dulane remained behind bars, pending a trial for her part in the kidnapping of Olivia Beckman. If she pleaded no contest—not likely, Will figured, since she failed to recognize her guilt—the judge would proceed to sentence her to at least three and as many as eight years in prison. He expected her to be subjected to a series of psychological tests, too, and he wouldn't be surprised if the results placed her in a state hospital for the mentally unstable. For her safety, as well as others', that very well could be the best solution for the poor woman.

As for Clem Dodd, he lay in a hospital room guarded by armed officers and fought a severe case of blood poisoning. At first, the doctors had not been optimistic about treating the infection, but it seemed their methods were working, as he had begun to improve. It appeared that he would live to undergo a trial and sentencing in Wabash and also the federal district court before being whisked off to New York for further charges on several counts of robbery and a trial to follow.

Will had not seen or talked to Livvie or her boys since the night of her rescue, exactly five days ago, when he and Howard had taken her back to the farm after an interview with the sheriff. It had been a tearful reunion, with Alex and Nate squealing and crying as they rushed into her arms and later refusing to let her out of their sight. Margie had made a grand fuss over her, as well. The phone had rung almost by the minute as folks who had heard of Livvie's rescue called to express their well wishes, and then, the house had filled with newspaper reporters, BOI officers, and friends and neighbors with a casserole or dessert in hand. The atmosphere had been not unlike a three-ring circus, and the real hero, Reggie, had roamed through the rooms like he was the

King of Siam, with everyone pausing in their chatter to pat his head and say, "Good boy, Reggie."

Will regretted that he hadn't said a proper good-bye to Livvie. Sure, he had kissed her and held her close inside that ramshackle church after knocking Clem to the floor. But Sheriff Morris and the BOI had arrived on the scene minutes later, with instant chaos erupting as they showered Livvie with questions and arrested Clem Dodd and dragged him away.

He had telephoned the Grants' house twice since that night, asking to speak to Livvie. But, on both occasions, Margie had told him that Livvie was either napping or out in the barn with the boys. He'd asked after her, of course, and Margie had assured him that she was well but needed time to recover from her harrowing experience. Margie hadn't invited him for lunch or supper, which he'd taken to mean that either she or Livvie did not wish to see him. He could understand Livvie's need to recuperate, but did she also need to ignore him? Maybe the newspaper article detailing his criminal history had caused her to think twice about keeping him on at the restaurant. He wouldn't blame her if it had; he'd even told her some time ago that he'd pack his bags and move on if she wanted him to. Maybe he ought to make things easy on her and simply disappear. He could leave a note on the bar downstairs, saying that it was best for everyone that he didn't hang around. Gus was competent enough to take over until Livvie could find a replacement.

Around four o'clock on Wednesday afternoon, Will was doing what he'd put off for a long while—cleaning his apartment—when a knock sounded on the door to the second floor. He propped his broom against the wall and shuffled to his apartment door, hoping not to be greeted by a nosy reporter demanding more details about his criminal past.

In the hallway, he peeked out through the glass pane. Smiling back at him was the last person he would have expected to see: Reverend White. He quickly unlocked the door and pulled it open. "Reverend! How good to see you. What, uh, brings you here?"

The reverend gave him a teasing frown. "Surely, you've heard of the unwritten rule that a preacher may drop in on his parishioners for no particular reason."

Will laughed. "Now that you mention it, I think I have heard something similar." He shook the reverend's hand, let him inside, and led the way down the hall to his apartment. "Hope you don't mind a little dust," he said as they stepped inside. "For what it's worth, that broom over there is proof that I've at least attempted to make some headway."

Reverend White put his hand on Will's shoulder. "You're a better man than me. I don't even know where Esther stores the broom."

Will hastily cleared a chair of the newspapers stacked there. The issue on top featured a front-page article about Livvie's abduction and another about Clem Dodd, which mentioned that Will was a former friend and coconspirator. He hoped that Reverend White hadn't noticed. But, then again, what was he thinking? He'd probably read both articles. The rest of Wabash had, after all. He'd probably come here to suggest that Will find a different church to attend. And who would blame him? No congregation wanted the likes of him tainting its reputation. He prepared himself to submit to the man's wishes.

They sat down and, for the next ten minutes or so, made small talk, discussing everything from

384   SHARLENE MacLAREN

Livvie's ordeal to the weather to automobiles. Finally, Reverend White said, "As you might know, I've read all the news articles pertaining to your past."

Will braced himself. "Yeah, I figured that had something to do with your visit."

"And you'd be right. The thing is, Will"—the reverend brushed a hand over his balding head and scooted forward on the sofa, his eyes boring into Will's—"I'd like to ask a favor of you."

"Yeah, I thought you might."

"You did? Then, you will?"

"Sure. I'll start looking for a new church this Sunday. I understand that folks might look down on my attending your—"

"What's that? No, no, I'm not asking you to leave, Will. Good gracious! What I would like to ask of you is to share your testimony with the congregation. People have been telling me they'd love to hear it—how you came to know the Lord, that is. And then, if you would be so kind as to play us a tune on your harmonica—a hymn, of course—why, that would just put the icing on the cake."

Will's mouth hung open, and he could do nothing about it. Of all the things he might have expected the preacher to ask of him, speaking to the congregation was nowhere near making the list. "You want me to get up and talk in front of everybody?"

"Yes, could you do that? We'd be honored if you would."

"Really?"

The reverend studied him for a long moment. "Will, I can imagine why you're hesitant. You're rather new to the Christian way of thinking, and you find it hard to believe that your sins are fully forgiven, even harder to believe that other people have also forgiven you."

Will nodded slowly, letting the assessment sink in.

Soon, the preacher continued, his voice soft and consoling. "That's what the body of Christ does, Will. Rather, that's what it's supposed to do—embrace sinners, no matter the wrongs they've committed. If Jesus does it, then, by gum, the church had better learn to do the same.

"I don't know what you think people are saying about you, Will, but our congregation is excited to see you on Sunday, and we'd like nothing more than for you to come and talk to us about all the things God has done for you. What do you say?"

A sense of joy, tentative and new, bubbled up from deep down in his heart and spilled over. He couldn't help grinning. "I guess I could do that. In fact, I'd like to."

He had no idea what the future held for him with regard to his job or his relationship with Livvie. But he knew one thing: God had forgiven his sins and thrown them into a deep sea of forgetfulness. And if He and the people of the Wesleyan Methodist church could forgive him, then it was high time he forgave himself, as well.

❧

"Mommy, when're we gonna go back t' our own house and the rest'rant?" Nate asked Livvie, snuggling closer to her. She had been reading to him from *Winnie-the-Pooh*, a brand-new book Margie had picked up at the store last week, while Alex helped his aunt pick vegetables in the garden.

Livvie laid the book facedown beside her on the sofa and looked at Nate. "Are you getting a little homesick?"

"Yeah, and me 'n' Alex wanna see Will."

Ah, the truth comes out. "You do, do you?" *That makes three of us.* She missed him more than she'd thought possible, but returning to the restaurant would mean reliving the sequence of events that had happened there, from seeing the vile Clem Dodd for the first time to hearing Marva Dulane's enticing tale about a photo of Frank and her. Those memories would surely spark thoughts of Marva's disturbing revelation about her mother's relationship with Livvie's father and the terrifying twenty-four hours Livvie had endured in captivity.

And then, there were the letters Sheriff Morris had discovered at Marva's house and brought to the farm on Monday afternoon, letters she had yet to share with Margie. They'd been sealed in a larger envelope with her name on the outside, meaning that Marva had intended for her to have them. The sheriff had been curious about the envelope's contents, so Livvie had opened it on the spot and skimmed the letters before passing each one to him. They were the letters her father had written to Miriam Maxwell, Marva's mother. While they had been heartbreaking to read, they had confirmed what Marva had said about Livvie's father's having been in love with Marva's mother. It followed that Marva was probably right in identifying her father, Gordon Maxwell, as the person who set fire to the Newtons' house in a jealous rage.

The sound of the back door opening and banging shut, followed by the patter of feet across the kitchen floor, told her Alex had come inside.

"Hey, Nate!" He bounded into the room. "Uncle Howie says he'll take us for rides on his tractor!"

In less time than it took to blink, Nate leaped off the sofa.

"Hey, what about *Winnie-the-Pooh?*" she called after him.

"We can read more of it at bedtime!" he hollered on the run.

An hour later, the boys were still out in the fields with Howard, and Livvie found herself standing in the kitchen, peeling potatoes, while Margie scrubbed the oven. She'd been trying to do her fair share of housework; plus, she found that busying herself with various tasks kept her mind pleasantly occupied. While the sisters worked, they didn't lack for conversation.

"I think the boys are ready to go back home," Livvie said, tossing a pared potato in the colander and then reaching for another.

"What about you?" Margie asked. "Are you ready?"

"I have no choice. There are bills to pay, and I'm sure Cora Mae and the others are anxious to get back to work."

"Speaking of the others, you haven't said much about Will Taylor recently." Margie walked to the sink and rinsed out her cloth. "That man seems to care a great deal about you. Did you ever return his phone calls?"

"I tried, but, of course, he wasn't in the restaurant when I called."

Margie went back to the stove and resumed her scouring. "Does his prison record bother you?" It was the first Margie had brought up the subject, even though she'd had plenty of opportunities to do so. Livvie knew where Howard stood, for she'd overheard him talking to Margie in the kitchen on Sunday night. He'd said that he was confident Will had a contrite heart and a good, solid faith in God.

"Does it bother you?" Livvie asked.

"I asked you first."

"In that case, no. He served his time and learned from it."

"So, the two of you have talked, then. Are you in love with him, Olivia?"

Margie never had been one to beat around the bush. "I might be," she answered, tossing another potato into the strainer. "Do you think it's too soon?"

"Pfff! Heavens, no. Plenty of women your age would have remarried by now. Those boys need a father, and I could tell when Will was here that they think the sun and moon exist solely for him."

That made Livvie chuckle. "I assure you, he feels the same way about them."

"It's not a matter of time, anyway, honey. It's what your heart tells you that counts."

"And what my older sister says, too," Livvie added with a grin. "It wasn't all that long ago, you made some comment similar to, 'Olivia, he's your employee, for goodness' sake!'" She made sure to imitate Margie's indignant tone.

Margie laughed, then paused in her cleaning to look at Livvie. "I did say something like that, didn't I? Well, you know I only want what's best for you."

A few seconds of silence stretched between them before Livvie decided to dive into a whole new topic. "Margie, what was Mama and Papa's marriage like?"

Margie dropped an oven rack on the floor, and the sound echoed through the room like a clap of thunder. She bent to pick it up and slid it back inside the oven without replying.

Livvie waited, then rephrased the question. "Were they happy together?"

Her sister spun around to face her and frowned. "Olivia, what would make you ask something like that?"

"I just...I'm curious, that's all. And, well, Marva Dulane...."

Margie walked back to the sink, where she rinsed out the cloth once more, wrung it out over the sink, and then hung it on a hook to dry. This process took less than a minute, but it seemed to stretch out much longer than that. Finally, she angled her body to face Livvie again. "What about Marva?"

Livvie gave up on peeling potatoes for the time being, laid down the knife, and looked at her sister, certain she read trepidation in her eyes. "I have some letters, Margie. Letters our father wrote to Miriam Maxwell. He was trying to rescue her from her abusive husband. Did you know that our father loved a woman other than Mama?"

"Where did you hear these things? And where did you get these—these letters?"

"Marva held on to them for years. While I was tied up, Clem Dodd told me that Marva said her father had burned our house down. Do you believe that, Marg?"

With slumped shoulders, Margie stepped away from the sink and walked to the back door, where she gazed out over the fields, her back to Livvie. "Part of me always suspected that the house fire wasn't an accident."

"Did you ever tell the authorities and ask them to investigate?"

She shook her head. "I had nothing to go on but a feeling. I knew things were not good between our parents. I came upon Papa and Miriam in the bank one day. He was whispering in her ear, and she was laughing. I thought it was odd. As soon as Papa saw me, he lurched back, as if he'd just been shot. He tried to act innocent, but I could tell by the looks in their eyes that something wasn't right. It was a very uncomfortable moment.

"It seemed like every time I went to see Mama, she was crying about one thing or another. It got so that I didn't want to go over there. She never came right out and told me Papa was having an affair, but I surmised it from the way she dropped hints every now and again. Oh, I still feel so awful about it. I worried about you being neglected. Tell me about these letters, Liv."

"You can read them, if you want, though there's not much to them. They're short, mostly three or four lines, and all of them were written a few months before the fire. In every note, Papa makes a point to tell Miriam he loves her and that he will get her out of that house, that they'll go away together, just the two of them, and never return to Wabash. Gordon Maxwell must have found them and flown into a rage."

"It's quite probable."

"And then, he convinced his daughter that I somehow played a part in the evil of it all. Marva Dulane has always treated me with utmost disdain."

"Odd, isn't it, how folks can let a root of bitterness take hold and grow so out of control, they lose touch with reality. Marva's a very lost soul."

Livvie took some time to digest those words. "I think I will visit her someday," she finally stated.

Margie cast her a surprised glance. "You would do that, after she helped kidnap you?"

"If God can forgive me for the wrongs I've committed against Him, isn't it my duty to forgive others? *'Forgive us our debts, as we forgive our debtors.'"*

Margie smiled and walked across the room to enfold Livvie in her arms. "It feels like you've come full circle, honey."

"I think I have." She gently pulled away from her sister's embrace to ask, "Would you and Howard drive the boys and me to the Wesleyan Methodist church on Sunday? We can leave extra early so you won't be late for your own service."

"We'll do one better," Margie said. "Howard and I will go with you."

Livvie grinned. "And then, I want to go home. It's time I got that restaurant going again."

Chapter Thirty

"The LORD is my strength and song,
and is become my salvation."
—Psalm 118:14

Will had practiced giving his testimony in front of the mirror about a dozen times, yet he never got over feeling foolish talking to his reflection. "Lord, just give me the words to say when the time comes," he finally prayed on Saturday night. "And, if it comes out wrong, give folks an extra dose of compassion for me. Please, let there be no egg throwing in the sanctuary."

On Sunday morning, the congregants squeezed through the doors of the little white clapboard church, crowding the pews and spilling into the aisles. The deacons rushed to find extra chairs, and many gentlemen stood to make room for women and children. From his seat in the front row, where Reverend White had asked him to sit, Will gazed around in amazement. There were at least twice as many in attendance than usual, and he couldn't imagine why. Surely, they hadn't all come to hear him. Good grief! If that were the case, there would be a lot of disappointed people after the service.

"It's a fine turnout, Will," said Reverend White as he sat down beside him. "The Lord is going to use you this morning." He leaned in closer and, speaking out of the side of his mouth, added, "All I had to do was tell Mrs. Garner you were going to speak today. She works about as well as the *Daily Plain Dealer* when it comes to spreading the word about something."

Will looked at him, and they both laughed. "You don't mean to tell me all these extra folks came to hear me talk!"

"Indeed, they did. You're the sermon today, Will."

The sermon? "You mean, you're not going to—?"

"Nope. I didn't tell you for fear you'd turn me down. Don't look so worried. Let the Lord guide you and give you the words to say. There's a message inside you that folks need to hear, a message about love, forgiveness, and a changed life. Just say whatever the Lord lays on your heart to say, son. It'll flow; you'll see. By the way, did you see Mrs. Beckman and her boys back there? Looks like the Grants decided to come, too."

That did it. Will was going to lose his breakfast. He glanced around, and, sure enough, there was Livvie, sitting about seven rows back on the other side of the aisle. She wore a pretty yellow hat that complemented her floral print dress, and her strawberry blonde hair was curled so that it curved around her cheeks and fell in waves at her shoulders. She had one arm around the shoulders of each of her sons. He imagined she'd been giving them more hugs than ever in the past few days. Man, he missed seeing them— hearing the boys' squeals of laughter, watching them race through the restaurant like little roadrunners. He didn't dare let his eyes linger long, lest someone catch him gawking, but he would have given just about anything for one of Livvie's smiles about now.

He faced forward again and took in a deep breath to steady himself. Reverend White chuckled. "It's going to be a wonderful day. Got a good feeling about it, I do."

❧

During the hymns, Livvie couldn't help but sing at peak volume, no matter that she lacked any musical ability. Her inner joy had to find an outlet, and voicing her praises to God gave it wings to fly. That moment, she was especially thankful because she'd finally spotted Will—in the front row, of all places, seated next to the preacher—and because Clem Dodd was in jail, while she was here, breathing fresh air and tasting the goodness of life. If she had been given a million guesses as to what the past week would bring, it wouldn't have been enough. Margie said she'd come full circle, and she had, but it felt like more than that. It felt like she'd been given a second chance to make her life—her words, actions, and everything else— count for the kingdom.

She didn't know exactly how or why it had happened, but, sometime in the middle of the night, she'd awakened with an almost tangible sense of God's inimitable, abiding presence. He'd seemed to whisper, *Trust Me, My child. All is well. Instead of bemoaning your cruel circumstances, remember, I will never leave you in the thick of them. I never have, and I never will. Your soul is safe for eternity, and the only thing I ask is that you surrender every care into My capable hands. Seek Me first, for when you do that, every piece of your life will fall into its proper place.*

Upon hearing that peaceful, precious assurance, she had sat up, pulled the string to turn on her bedside lamp, and begun to read her Bible. She'd cried tears of joy as she'd read promise after promise, divinely directed to passages of Scripture she'd never read before and delighting in their solid truth.

As the congregation sang the final verse of "Standing on the Promises," the Holy Spirit gave her another reminder of God's grace and faithfulness, and the simple revelation made her knees buckle. Thankfully, the organ stopped playing, and Reverend White invited everyone to sit, anyway.

�֍

While the reverend stood in the pulpit and introduced him, Will was convinced that his heart would burst straight through his chest if it didn't quit the fierce hammering. Why on earth had he agreed to share his testimony? He tried to recall the speech he'd practiced but couldn't remember even one word. It was as if the light in his mind had suddenly switched off, turning his entire brain into a dark maze of confusion. To make matters worse, Reverend White's voice sounded remote and echoey. None of his words really registered, except for "Will Taylor!" at which point Will felt a hand on his shoulder, someone behind him urging him to step forward.

In a daze, he made his way to the podium. Reverend White smiled and whispered, "Speak from your heart, Will," then returned to his seat.

The place was so quiet, one could have heard a fly sneeze. *Lord, tell me what You want me to say. Prepare folks' hearts for Your message, not mine.*

"Hi, Will!" The familiar voice that cut through the silence prompted a wave of gentle laughter. Will relaxed a little.

"Hi, Nate," he replied, searching out the sweet boy and then grinning at the three people he loved most in the world. Livvie's beautiful smile gave him the courage he needed to proceed. "And good morning to the rest of you." As folks nodded and smiled, he cleared his throat and rested his hands on the sides of the pulpit to steady his slightly trembling knees. With slow, deliberate enunciation, he said, "I once was lost but now am found, was blind, but now I see."

From there, his story unfolded, beginning with his childhood—how it had started out normal and happy, with music and laughter and fun, but had wound up unusually sad. How he'd carried the guilt imposed upon him by his parents for his sister's drowning, and how that guilt had prompted him to seek love and acceptance in other places—the wrong places.

He spoke about the bad habits he'd acquired along the way, how life had held little purpose back then, how everything he'd seized hold of had left him feeling empty and wondering about the meaning of it all. He told them how he'd hooked up with a wicked bunch of friends—yes, Clem Dodd had been among them—and how he'd found himself on the wrong side of the law more than once as he searched for acceptance, for a way to belong. He shared how his beloved harmonica had brought him bits of joy in the midst of evil, and how he could now look back on those times as glimmers of God's light in his deepest, darkest days.

As he talked, Will noticed a few things. One, his knees had stopped knocking. Two, his sentences were coming out clearly. Three, folks seemed to be focusing intently on his every word; they were either sitting forward in their seats, shaking their heads in wonderment, or dabbing at damp eyes. And, four, Livvie was wearing a serene expression, a kind of half smile, which encouraged him immensely. Together, these observations impelled him to continue.

He told about the jewelry theft that ultimately landed him in prison, and how he wouldn't trade that experience, however dreadful and demeaning, for all the gold in the world, as it had led him straight to Harry Wilkinson. He explained how Harry had never given up on him, had always gone to bat for him, and had expected great things from him. He said that Harry had a way of preaching that made God sound appealing, and he described how he'd finally reached a dead end in his life and had come to realize it was God or nothing. He told them how, once he'd made the decision to follow Christ, his life hadn't gone from black to white overnight, but that the change had been a process, one that continued today. He explained how he'd learned that living a Christian life meant disciplining oneself to pray and study the Word and listen for God's voice in the day-to-day struggles. That faith didn't come easy, but it did come.

He told them about the key role forgiveness had played in his spiritual growth, how he'd needed to come to a place where he laid down the heartache of loss and handed off to the Lord the burden of guilt his parents had placed on his shoulders. He spoke of how he'd had to forgive them, even though they'd passed away, and how he'd managed to let that well of bitterness drain out of him. And then, he spoke of the wondrous sense of freedom and joy that had resulted.

In the end, he challenged folks to submit their hearts to Jesus, and then to go out, find somebody who needed to know the love of Christ, and be bold by showing it. On that note, he reached inside his pocket, pulled out his harmonica, and began to play "Amazing Grace" with eyes closed, heart uplifted.

When he finished the hymn and opened his eyes, he couldn't believe how many people had come forward and gathered at the wooden altar at the front of the church with arms uplifted in surrender to Jesus.

⚘

When the service concluded, folks just didn't seem to want to go home, overflowing as they were with praise and thanksgiving. Many people, including Howard, Coot Hermanson, the Joneses, and the Wimberlys, gathered around Will to shake his hand, give his shoulder an encouraging squeeze, or pat him on the back and thank him for his inspiring message. And they had questions galore, wanting him to expound upon one or more aspects of his fascinating testimony. Although her boys managed to squeeze through the hordes of people to get to Will, Livvie couldn't make her way through the masses, for all the people who swarmed around her, as well.

"He sure is something, Livvie," Margie whispered. "My, I had no idea."

"So wonderful to see you," said a woman Livvie recognized as the pastor's wife, grasping Livvie's hand in both of hers and pumping it up and down.

"Thank you, ma'am. It's wonderful to be here."

Margie leaned closer. "I mean, not only is he a fine Christian man, he's, um, quite amazing."

"Shh, Margie," Livvie said out of the side of her mouth.

Stepping back, Margie smiled at the preacher's wife. "Hello, Esther." Then, she came close to Livvie again. "What? I'm just saying, he's amazing. Surely, you agree."

"Now is not the time—"

"Olivia, I'm so happy to see you safe and sound. My, what an ordeal for you." This came from Hildi Sherman, a young mother of three, who gave Livvie a hasty yet warm hug.

Livvie smiled. "Thank you, Hildi. It's good to see you, too."

When Hildi moved on, Margie continued. "My opinion? You can't afford to let him get away."

"Margie, hush."

"Just look how your boys have taken to him!" She gestured at the crowd across the room.

"Livvie, Livvie! Oh, my goodness! Thank the Lord you're well." Cora Mae pressed through the masses and grabbed Livvie close. In her ear, she whispered, "Will Taylor is a wonderful man, don't you think? My, his story was so inspiring. If you don't marry that man, I'm going to sink my claws into him."

"Cora Mae!" she laughed. "You are a living stinker!"

"What?" Margie squeezed in closer. "What did you say to her, Cora Mae?"

"I said, I think—"

"I've decided to reopen the restaurant tomorrow," Livvie cut in. "Will you be ready?"

Cora Mae's eyes popped. "Ready? I was ready last week!"

"Wonderful!"

"Olivia, praise the Lord and all His creation!" Clara Gillen moved in to sweep Livvie into a monstrous hug. Margie and Cora Mae stepped off to the side, and, while she talked to Clara, Livvie saw them put their heads together.

The warm greetings, hugs, handshakes, and cheerful chatter went on for almost an hour. By 12:30, all but a few parishioners had cleared the sanctuary, and Will and Livvie finally made eye contact, albeit briefly, due to those hangers-on who were known for being the last ones out the door. While she talked with an old high school friend, Vera Warner, Livvie glanced over the woman's shoulder and saw Margie walk over to Will, shake his hand, and then stand on tiptoe to whisper something in his ear. He smiled and winked, and then she walked away.

A few minutes later, Margie and Howard whisked Alex and Nate out the door with a promise to return them to the apartment by three o'clock. Something smelled fishy, Livvie thought, but it was a good kind of fishy. Reverend White and Esther started collecting papers that had been left in the pews, and the deacons began to put away the extra chairs.

"Livvie."

She turned at the sound of Will's smooth, deep voice. "Will, you were wonderful. At last, I get to tell you."

"It wasn't me; it was the Lord."

"I know, but still...." Their eyes met and held, kindling a glow deep within her. "I'm planning to reopen the restaurant tomorrow. What do you say to that?"

"Am I still working for you?"

"What? Of course you are, you silly goon! Why would you ask such a thing?"

He dipped his chin. "Well, I don't know. I just thought, maybe, you know, with everything that's happened...."

"Will Taylor! After that inspiring talk you gave, you think I'm going to let you go?"

He tossed his head back and laughed. "May I walk you back home? I can rustle us up something to eat for lunch."

"That would be lovely. May I help you? I can cook, you know."

"Really? I never would have guessed," he said with a wink.

As they walked, their hands touched, but he didn't move to take hers. So, she did the next best thing and looped her arm through his.

He grinned down at her. "I'm glad you did that." Then, he put his hand on top of hers as they turned down Market Street, the sun warming their shoulders, a soft breeze keeping them comfortably cool as they strolled. Not once did they lack for topics of conversation. They talked about Clem Dodd's upcoming trial; Will's discussion with a BOI agent regarding Orville Dotson's whiskey still, after which the agent had promised to investigate his claim; Livvie's plan to call Joe Stewart and fill him in on the recent happenings; and Reggie's heroic role in her rescue.

When they reached the restaurant, Will took the key from his pocket and held the screen door as he turned the lock in the front door, then pushed it open. The room was stuffy, so they immediately set to opening windows and turning on ceiling fans. Livvie took off her hat and placed it on the closest table. She knew her hair must look a mess, but, somehow, it didn't matter.

They met in the kitchen, where Will scanned the refrigerator shelves while Livvie hunted through cabinets. "What are we looking for?" she asked.

"I don't know," Will answered. "What sounds good?"

"Um...." Only one thing came to mind. The dusky room grew silent, and they slowly turned to face each other. "Will, I...I need to tell you something."

"Tell me anything." He took a step closer, and she did the same.

"This morning, I awoke around two thirty with the most wondrous sense of peace. God spoke to me,

Will. He assured me of His love and faithfulness. There were areas in which I needed to seek His forgiveness, and so I did, and He forgave me."

"Livvie, that's wonderful."

"I've learned some things about my past, Will—some disturbing things about how my parents' house burned. There were some letters. Oh, dear; it's a long story. Marva Dulane's father—"

He nodded. "I already know."

Livvie gazed into his azure eyes with wonderment. "You know?"

"Marva told me. The night we were searching for you, Quinn drove me out to her house. I went there on a hunch, and my hunch proved correct. I know about her father, your father, her mother, the letters...all of it. Marva slipped clear off her rocker, Liv. She told me things she didn't even know she was saying. That's how I learned for sure that Clem had taken you. She's living in a precarious place right now, somewhere between reality and whimsy. I don't know if she'll ever come all the way back."

"I told Margie I want to visit her sometime. I need to tell her I've forgiven her."

He took her hands in his. "I think that could be arranged, provided I go with you."

Tender warmth emanated from his touch, and her love for him surged in devastating swells. But she didn't know how to tell him; she couldn't quite make the words skip from her heart to her mouth. "Margie says you're an amazing man," she said instead.

He chuckled. "Is that so?"

"She says I shouldn't let you get away."

"She said that, did she?" With his thumbs, he rubbed the backs of her hands, causing a ripple of chills to run straight up her arms. "And what do you say about that?"

"I say, my sister is extremely intuitive."

"Is that all you can say? That your sister is intuitive?" He released one of her hands and ran a finger beneath her jaw and up her chin. "Tell me what you're feeling, Olivia Beckman. I want to hear the words."

Touching his lips with her index finger, she lifted her gaze to search every inch of his magnificent face. "I love you, Will Taylor," she whispered.

The way he closed his eyes and heaved a loud sigh, the way he licked his lips and then bit down on the lower one, made her heart do a crazy, wild dance. She freed her other hand, took his face between her palms, and repeated the words.

"Livvie, I love you," he whispered back, swooping down for a kiss that started softly and tenderly but quickly grew in intensity and made her utterly breathless. When they separated, he ran all ten fingers through her hair, then rested his hands on her shoulders. "I told Howard how I feel about you. He approves."

She felt her eyebrows shoot upward. "He approves?" Her heart skipped so many beats, she thought she might swoon.

"Will you marry me, Livvie Beckman? I would consider it an honor."

She stood on tiptoe to peck his cheek. "On one condition, Will Taylor."

He kissed the curve of her neck. "Anything."

"That you take over the bookkeeping. I'm a lousy accountant."

"I think I could do that. Are you still the boss?"

"Of course. Some things will never change," she teased with a smile. He leaned down and kissed her cheek. "Serenade me, would you?" she asked before he kissed the other. "I love the way you play that harp."

He took out the instrument and played a few chords, but a scratch at the screen door put a stop to the lovely music and made them turn their gazes to the front of the restaurant. A lop-eared dog stared back at them.

"Reggie!" Livvie exclaimed. "What's he doing here?"

"Coming to check on his girl, I guess. I'm going to have to tell him to lay off. You're my girl now."

Hand in hand, they walked to the front, and Will pushed the screen door open. "Does Coot know where you are, you silly hound?" As if he owned the place, Reggie sauntered past them, turned several circles in the middle of the room, and lay down.

A breeze blew in through the window, carrying with it the scent of the Wabash, where, Livvie knew, fish jumped, ducks paddled, and soaring birds chirped, creating a lovely river song. And wild daisies along the riverbank dipped their yellow heads and thanked their Maker.

From the Author's Kitchen

My dear readers,

Who doesn't think the most wonderful aromas originate in Mom's kitchen? Memories of my precious mother, who went to be with Jesus at the age of ninety-six on January 28, 2010, flood my mind whenever I think about walking through the front door of my beloved parents' home. Often, I'd find Mom standing at the stove or kitchen counter, frilly apron tied around her waist, whipping up some concoction or another. If it wasn't bread, pie, or cake, it was a supper casserole, meat loaf, chicken, pasta, or some kind of yummy salad. For me, besides being a place of safety, warmth, and unconditional love, home meant mouthwatering smells emanating from our small, cozy kitchen.

While writing *Livvie's Song*, I simply couldn't stop thinking about my loving mother and some of her finest recipes. For that reason, I am quite certain Will Taylor used many of them while he mixed ingredients in Livvie's Kitchen—with my permission, of course!

When I finished writing the book, I couldn't kick the nagging notion that it didn't feel complete. Then, it came to me like a splash of glorious sunlight: Mom's recipes! They needed to live on through my wonderful readers! Therefore, it is with great pleasure and

406 ～ SHARLENE MACLAREN

joy that I share a handful of them with you. Remember Clara Gillen's scrumptious baked chicken? Mom's recipe. And the meat loaf? Straight from Mom's recipe box. And how about Helen Brent's pineapple pork chops? Again, from Mom's collection. I decided to let Fred of Fred's Place borrow one of my mom's recipes, too—beef stew.

May your kitchen always be a gathering place full of God's love and warmth, and, of course, delectable aromas that help create beautiful, lifelong memories.

Blessings and bon appétit!

—*Shar*

Pineapple Pork Chops

Serves as many as needed.

INGREDIENTS:
Pork chops (your favorite cut)
Salt
Worcestershire sauce
Onion, thinly sliced
Fresh or canned pineapple slices (round)
Brown sugar
Ketchup
Orange juice

1. Preheat oven to 350° F.
2. Arrange pork chops in a large baking dish coated with cooking spray. Lightly salt each chop and then sprinkle with a few drops of Worcestershire sauce. Lay a thin onion slice on each one, topped with a slice of pineapple. On top of that, put a heaping teaspoon of brown sugar and a tablespoon of ketchup. Finally, douse the pork chops with orange juice (²⁄₃ cup per pan).
3. Bake, uncovered, for approximately one hour or until tender.

Baked Chicken

Serves 6 to 8, depending on the size of the chicken breasts.

INGREDIENTS:
Chicken breasts
½ cup (1 stick) butter, melted
2 cups bread crumbs
¾ cup grated Parmesan cheese
¼ cup chopped fresh parsley
1 clove garlic, minced
1 teaspoon salt
¼ teaspoon pepper

1. Preheat oven to 350° F.
2. Mix together bread crumbs, Parmesan cheese, parsley, garlic, salt, and pepper.
3. Melt butter. Dip chicken breasts in butter, then dredge in bread crumb mixture. Place in a lightly greased baking pan and bake, uncovered, for 1½ hours or until done.

Meat Loaf

Serves 6 to 8.

<u>INGREDIENTS:</u>
1½ pounds ground beef
½ cup uncooked oatmeal
¾ cup cracker crumbs
¼ teaspoon dried thyme
¼ teaspoon parsley flakes
1 cup tomato juice
2 tablespoons ketchup
1 egg, lightly beaten
⅓ cup diced onion

1. Preheat oven to 350° F.
2. Mix all of the above ingredients and place in a greased loaf pan.
3. Bake, uncovered, for one hour.

Baked Beef Stew

Serves 6 to 8.

<u>INGREDIENTS:</u>
2 pounds beef stew meat
12 small pearl onions
1 cup chopped celery
2 cups diced potatoes
6 carrots, peeled and chopped
1 slice white bread, cubed
1 (12-ounce) can tomato sauce
1 cup water
1½ teaspoons salt
¼ teaspoon pepper

1. Preheat oven to 250° F.
2. Combine all ingredients in a large casserole dish.
3. Cover and bake for five hours.

Whole Wheat Bread

This is a very old recipe (on a brown and weathered note card), so some of the terminology may be a bit unfamiliar to us modern-day cooks. I remember Mom baking this bread. Oh, how my mouth watered for that very first warm slice!

INGREDIENTS:
8 cups whole wheat flour, sifted
1 cake compressed wheat
2 tablespoons sugar, divided
1 tablespoon salt
3¼ cups lukewarm water
2 tablespoons shortening
1 cake yeast

1. Dissolve 1 cake yeast in ¼ cup lukewarm water with 1 teaspoon sugar. Allow to stand 5 minutes, then add the balance of the sugar, water, and salt. In large bowl, knead the flour (one cup at a time), wheat, water, and yeast mixture to a stiff dough. Knead until smooth, then knead in the shortening.
2. Allow to rise until dough doubles in bulk. Knead again, place towel over dough, and let rise.
3. Grease two loaf pans. When dough has risen, split and place in loaf pans. Let rise till doubled in bulk.
4. Preheat oven to 450° F.
5. Bake at 450° F for 15 minutes, then lower oven temperature to 350° and bake for an additional 35 minutes.
6. Remove and place pans on cooling rack.
7. Allow to cool ten minutes before removing loaves from pans to cool completely on the rack.

Broccoli Casserole

Serves 6.

INGREDIENTS:
1 cup water
½ teaspoon salt
1 cup instant rice
¼ cup butter
¼ cup chopped onion
¼ cup chopped celery
1 can cream of mushroom soup
1 can cream of celery soup
1 (16-ounce) package frozen broccoli, thawed
½ cup diced American cheese

1. Preheat oven to 350° F.
2. In a medium saucepan, bring water and salt to a boil. Add rice and remove from heat. Let rest five minutes.
3. In a small skillet, sauté onion and celery until tender.
4. In large mixing bowl, combine rice, celery and onion mixture, and the remaining ingredients. Stir well and then pour into a greased 1½ quart casserole dish.
5. Bake for 1 hour.

Chocolate Mayonnaise Cake

Makes one 9 x 13-inch sheet cake.

INGREDIENTS:
3 cups all-purpose flour
1½ cups sugar
2 teaspoons baking soda
Dash of salt
6 tablespoons unsweetened cocoa powder
1½ cups mayonnaise
1½ cups lukewarm water
1½ teaspoons vanilla

1. Preheat oven to 350° F.
2. In a large bowl, whisk together the first five dry ingredients till blended, then add the mayonnaise, water, and vanilla. Beat till smooth.
3. Grease and lightly flour the bottom and sides of a 9 x 13-inch baking pan.
4. Bake for 25 minutes or until toothpick inserted in the center comes out clean.

Mama's Best-Ever Chocolate Frosting

Makes enough to frost one 9 x 13-inch sheet cake.

INGREDIENTS:
1 cup sugar
3 tablespoons cornstarch
1½ ounces bittersweet chocolate (or ¼ cup unsweetened
  cocoa powder)
Dash of salt
1 cup water
3 tablespoons butter
1 teaspoon vanilla

1. Prepare frosting while the cake bakes. In a small saucepan over medium heat, mix sugar, cornstarch, chocolate
   or cocoa, salt, and water, stirring constantly, till mixture
   bubbles and thickens.
2. Remove from heat and stir in butter and vanilla, blending thoroughly.
3. Spread over the cake while still warm.

About the Author

*B*orn and raised in west Michigan, Sharlene Mac-Laren attended Spring Arbor University. Upon graduating with an education degree, she traveled internationally for a year with a small singing ensemble, then came home and married one of her childhood friends. Together they raised two lovely daughters. Now happily retired after teaching elementary school for thirty-one years, "Shar" enjoys reading, writing, singing in the church choir and worship teams, traveling, and spending time with her husband, children, and precious grandchildren.

A Christian for over forty years and a lover of the English language, Shar has always enjoyed dabbling in writing—poetry, fiction, various essays, and freelance work for periodicals and newspapers. She remembers well the short stories she wrote in high school and watched circulate from girl to girl during government and civics classes. "Psst," someone would whisper from two rows over, always when the teacher's back was to the class, "pass me the next page."

Shar is an occasional speaker for her local MOPS (Mothers of Preschoolers) organization; is involved in KIDS' HOPE USA, a mentoring program for at-risk children; counsels young women in the Apples of Gold Program; and is active in two weekly Bible studies. She and her husband,

416 ～ SHARLENE MACLAREN

Cecil, live in Spring Lake, Michigan, with Mocha, their lazy, fat cat.

Through Every Storm was Shar's first novel to be published by Whitaker House, and in 2007, the American Christian Fiction Writers (ACFW) named it a finalist for Book of the Year. The acclaimed Little Hickman Creek series consists of *Loving Liza Jane*; *Sarah, My Beloved* (a finalist in the 2008 Inspirational Reader's Choice Contest, sponsored by the Romance Writers of America); and *Courting Emma*. Shar's last series, the popular Daughters of Jacob Kane, comprises *Hannah Grace*, *Maggie Rose*, and *Abbie Ann*. *Livvie's Song* is the first in her latest series, River of Hope.

To find out more about Shar and her writing and inspiration, you can e-mail her at smac@chartermi.net or visit her Web site at www.sharlenemaclaren.com.